FIRST
and
VITAL CANDLE

THE CANDLE INDOORS

Some candle clear burns somewhere I come by.
I muse at how its being puts blissful back
With yellowy moisture mild night's blear-all black,
Or to-fro tender trambeams trunckle at the eye.
By that window what task what fingers ply,
I plod wondering, a-wanting just for lack
Of answer the eagerer a-wanting Jessy or Jack
There   God to aggrandise, God to glorify . . . .

Come you indoors, come home; your fading fire
Mend first and vital candle in close heart's vault:
You there are master, do your own desire;
What hinders? Are you beam-blind, yet to a fault
In a neighbor deft-handed? are you that liar
And, cast by conscience out, spentsavour salt?

—Gerard Manley Hopkins

FIRST and VITAL CANDLE

by
RUDY WIEBE

McCLELLAND AND STEWART

Copyright © Rudy Wiebe, 1966

Reprinted 1979

CANADIAN CATALOGUING IN PUBLICATION DATA

Wiebe, Rudy, 1934-
   First and vital candle

ISBN 0-7710-8978-3 pa.

I. Title.

PS8545.I415FS C813'.5'4 C66-3910
PR9199.3.W54F5

The Canadian Publishers
McClelland and Stewart Limited
25 Hollinger Road, Toronto 16.

Manufactured in Canada by Webcom Limited

To my Mother and Father

Part One

1

*H*E had been walking along Portage Avenue for more than an hour, glance searching out first a store window, then a car gliding by under throttled power, looking intensely though come the evening's end and dropping into bed he would remember not one detail of the mass, couples chatting as they passed oblivious, when looking down into a restaurant below street level Abe Ross saw the girl seated alone at a table.

By that time the sidewalk under his heels had thudded his aloneness to the ends of his bones. As it had for all the evenings past he had given himself up to this walking: sometimes he could delude himself to sit in a movie house, faked by the screen or the snickers of teen-agers at a touch of bodies; or sit at a ball game; or at wider, more hopeless intervals, in a bar. But some evenings he had to retreat from arm's length and wear himself to tiredness, and then the seeming endless strength of his body ground his mind into a curse. So begin walking at that slow pace which is eventually most tiring because it knows no destination; begin and continue.

He was by, the white image of the girl drifting past his memory like any myriad of shapes passed and forgotten in who could recollect how many towns and tents and cities and farmhouses, and he stopped. He looked along the strangely empty sidewalk; turned, walked back, looked down into the window again. He could not see her face; only a white shape and the turn of a slim arm motionlessness on the rounded table.

Laughter jerked him to the street. In a moment of silence caught from the traffic three teen-age boys had emerged from somewhere to the blot of clarity under a blinking reddish neon, their faces open in bold, staring abandonment, greased hair a sheen above gleaming faces. They jostled, looked at one another and laughed louder. Their red laughter before him, half-turned from the window, rolled over him without recognizing his existence in a kind of togetherhood on this hard pavement that brayed youth into his very face. In a moment they elbowed each other into motion and were stumbling away, sometimes hitting each other openfisted, their bellows lost in the mild rumble of cars at a green light.

Abe turned abruptly, pushed open the door and walked down the stairway. He did not glance at the mirror reflecting his wide shoulders and grey temples down the stairs. The door gave to him; he went into the pale blue light at an empty table.

"Would you like the wine card, sir?" He looked up; the hostess had followed him. Above the tabletop the black dress pushed her body at him as if she were a quick-pinched tube of toothpaste.

"No," he said, "just coffee. Black." She tapped away.

On the edge of his vision like a white curve sat the girl, motionless, her white pumps relaxed at the ends of her long legs. He could not turn his head to look at her. Somewhere the restaurant seemed almost filled with chattering people; against a wall opposite a large party was finishing dessert; among its adults a boy sat waving light patterns against the wall mirror with a burning candle. A woman leaned over and the light vanished.

"Could I bring you the menu, sir?" The waitress stood with his coffee and a glass of water.

"No! Thank you." To himself his voice sounded rough and startled — one of those laughing brats would roll in and plunk himself at the table beside her — in the wake of the waitress' turn he swung his glance to the girl. Blond hair pulled smoothly back and folded in at the nape. She was looking with an almost bemused expression into her half-empty cup. The thin face and the neck revealed by the low scoop of her dress were more maturely beautiful than any woman Abe had ever seen.

His glance fell to his cup. Could he but have looked at her where he would be unseen, either by the world or by her, he could have studied her face perhaps forever. He could not find her reflection in the long mirror along the opposite wall and he could not now look at her, directly, much as he wanted to. For she might raise her head from its stillness and in some way he could not attempt to pluck apart her direct look at that moment would have devastated him. His eyes in his cup, he drank.

"Hey mister!" A boy stood there, staring with wide eyes, head barely above the table edge. Abe looked at him in bemused astonishment. "Where'd you get that beard?"

Abe grinned, envying for himself such frankness; you want so you ask. He bent forward and spoke to barely reach the adjacent table. "Okay, I'll tell, but you tell me your name first."

The boy grinned, his voice as low. "Ah, you can guess it — it's easy." He pulled a chair near and squirmed into it.

"Well, I don't know many boys' names. Johnnie —"

"Sure," the boy interrupted. "Everybody guesses right away."

"How old are you?"

"Nine. It's my birthday today. I got a new bigger bike with a sort of motor thing which isn't really a motor and a side car like cops." The small face puckered again. "Where'd ya get the beard?"

Abe saw a blond motion in the mirror and he knew it was the woman's head lifted, perhaps in momentary listening. His deep voice was low and distinct: "It just grew. If men don't shave, beards just grow."

"Yeah, but my dad shaves every day. See," gesturing behind him without turning, "why don't you?"

Suddenly Abe could have blessed the boy sitting hunched

forward with his clear, uncomplicated questions of just wanting to know — to live in such a world! — "For a long time I've been up north — you know, where the Eskimos live? And —".

"The Eskimos that live in igloos?" the boy's eyes shone in the blue light.

"Yes, in winter, when it's really cold."

"Did ya live in there with them?"

"Sometimes, when I visited them for a few days. But usually I lived in a house — a store where I traded the Eskimos supplies for furs. So I didn't bother shaving. And a beard is warm when the wind blows and the snow flies where there are no trees at all."

He comprehended the ladies at the wall table leaning back, looking towards them rather anxiously. But for Johnnie, eyes unblinking, they now did not exist. "Did ya drive a dogteam?"

Abe put his square calloused hand on the table. "Sure. That was fine sometimes, running along in sunshine; but not blizzards. And often nothing happened for a long, long time. Just in winter the cold and in the little summer the mosquitoes. How do you know about Eskimos?"

"Oh, in school we had a projec', how they build igloos and hunt seals and stuff. Did ya hunt seals?"

"No, we were too far inland. The Eskimos that live near the sea eat seal." His blunt fingers circled the water glass with its blob of ice. "But I'll tell you what happened on the sea when I first went up north, years ago, before you were born. We sailed from Montreal in a ship to go around Quebec into Hudson Bay — you know how that part of Canada looks on the map?" The boy hesitated. "Well here," Abe leaned back and pulled a short ball-point from his pocket, "remember the map," sketching on the napkin. "Here's where we are, Winnipeg — and way over here's Montreal and you sail all the way up the river — you know —"

"Oh yeah, yeah, the Saint — Saint —" in his flurry Johnnie could not find the name quite and Abe grinned at his puckered concentration.

"Right! The St. Lawrence. And you sail up and around this part north in a ship not much longer than this room," he gestured, turning around completely, seeing directly for the first time the tables and people doubly reflected in the long silver mirrors, the moving waiters and the blue-crystal mist hanging from filigreed lamps. He turned so far he was facing the woman, and he saw her as if he had forgotten her. At that instant she turned. On her gentle face lay such quiet light of beauty that he felt like a cut through him he could love her without ever knowing who she was or ever finding out. But he could not stay beyond himself and his glance was tugged down to his scribbled-over napkin, unnerved, unable to hold the look. Far away he heard the boy's voice, ". . . the ship?"

"Uh — yeah," he saw the boy's face again, mouth unconsciously open, uneven teeth glinting under heavy braces, "yes, we sailed up the coast that summer — thirteen years ago right to the month," he felt freer suddenly as if circled by intimacy — a dim livingroom and they three alone — "and there was lots of loose ice from the break-up pushed down along the Labrador coast — right along here — and caught us, tight. In a few days we got jammed so tight the ship couldn't move. The captain tried to push through but we weren't an icebreaker and he was scared the hull — you know, the front and sides of the ship, would cave in if he pushed too hard. So we waited for the current to carry the ice out, hoping it wouldn't crush us if we just did nothing. We waited for a week, waiting. And then, all of a sudden, it happened."

"Yeah!"

Abe's finger tapped the ice in the water glass. "See. When ice floats, most of it is under the water, see. There are sometimes currents deeper in the ocean than near the surface and sometimes a big piece of ice moves easier than the smaller chunks floating on top. One day as we waited we saw a great big iceberg far out in the icefield. Even far as it was, we could see it was big. Next morning it was a lot closer. It was ten times bigger than the ship and after we watched it a while we knew it was coming right for the ship and us, cutting through the ice like an icebreaker, moved probably by some funny current deep in the ocean. We watched it all day and it kept coming closer and closer. In the evening we walked to it over the ice pack — all smashed together and rough, but we could get there. The pack was piled up high in front of the iceberg, and behind was small bits of crushed ice floating in open water. It was as huge as a mountain above the water — imagine how big it must of been underneath."

Abe bobbed the small ice-cube in the glass; the boy stared at it, mouth open, saying nothing.

"By morning we knew it would hit the ship. It was almost on top of us already, moving so slow you couldn't see it at all, but every once in a while there'd be a crack and slivers of ice would fly away from in front of it, cutting through the ice. We all stood by the rail — sailors, captain, the other company men, me — I'd never been near the Arctic before — and watched it hang over us like a great big mountain. And then the captain said, 'Abandon ship.'"

"Wha-at?"

"We had to get off — off the ship. We ran below and got what we could carry and the captain got the ship's log book — where they write down everything that happens — and climbed off and ran across the ice pack, away from the ship toward the land. When we were a ways off we stopped and watched to see what would happen, what that big iceberg would do to the ship."

Abe stared down at the tablecloth, remembering that stumble over the ice, the comfort of the plane a desperate message on the radio had brought as it buzzed overhead, and the wait on the ridged ice to hear the ice grind the ship into the sea. He forgot the boy almost, and even the woman. He was unconsciously turning toward her when the boy said, "Was it s-s-sinked?"

Abe smiled, his heavy beard lifting at the corners of his mouth. "The iceberg brushed so close to the ship that ice sheered off its side on the deck. But it didn't hurt it one bit. We ran back and a sailor fell into the water trying to get back on because the ship was bobbing away from the ice pack into the open water behind the iceberg. In an hour we were out of the pack and steaming north, free from the ice, freed by the iceberg we thought would crush us."

The boy sat and studied him, arms on tabletop, chin on arms. "Gee," he said finally.

"Johnnie —" they both became aware then of a tall, gaunt man standing behind the boy, "really, you must come now. You've disturbed the gentleman enough."

"Dad!" the boy sprang to his feet, "he told me about a iceberg and being stuck in ice — a ship — and how the iceberg just came float —"

"Fine, Johnnie, fine, but we have to go now." The man smiled at Abe. "He was so insistent he ask you about your beard, and it's his birthday so we thought if he didn't bother you — thank you again for your kindness, ah — but we have to go — it's late even for a birthday." The man's half-stiff laugh at Abe's continued silence pushed his face into loose folds. "Come Johnnie." The boy was standing now before Abe.

"Mister, would you come to our place to visit and tell about the Eskimos? Huh?"

The loudness, the tall man and the thin boy standing before him, awoke Abe suddenly. He looked from the boy's demand to the man; the folds of his face had lengthened, and Abe was aware of his own cotton shirt, the other's linen suit and diamond tie pin. Beyond them at the door grouped the party, impeccable in elegant completeness — think a restaurant into a livingroom and stock it with someone's son and — "No," he said.

"Dad! You said I could have what I wanted on my birthday! Ask him!"

The tall man was fumbling in his pocket. "My name is William Briggs — here's my card. If you would have time, perhaps some evening you —"

Their glances met and Briggs stopped. The hand which had been lifting abruptly dropped, the card skidding as if forgotten to the table. "Thank you again, for being so kind. Goodnight."

Johnnie's voice rose as he was turned about, "But Dad —."

"Shush! You can't have everything you want."

The door sighed shut and the restaurant was quiet of them. White faces of people swam by like streaks outside on the sidewalk. For a little while the boy had been fine; very fine indeed. If he could have kept that fineness and held it until he could face the woman he could, well,

>William F. Briggs, Q.C.
>Barrister, Solicitor

So why hadn't he agreed with the boy: visit, tell him how Mala, his age, fought through the marsh mosquitoes hunting duck eggs and sometimes tumbled harnessed puppies over tundra rocks and stuffed his belly with raw meat when they had it — no boy on earth gives a whistle either for cotton or silk but better yet a beard and caribou leather so why? — his mind clenched fiercely. There was no need to kid himself in his thoughts; that sufficed for men dropping cards: if it fooled them.

The woman suddenly arose. She was taller than he had thought, slim, straight. He could look at her back as she stood a moment, the cashier smiling at her. Then she had slipped into a navy cape and was going out the door, her white bag in her white-gloved hand, her body's profile exquisite in grace. He sat bemused. Headquarter regulars could laugh about the stunned, darting looks of the northern men when they were dropped, after three or four Arctic years, on the streets of Winnipeg — let them try it! — At Tyrel Bay store he saw about forty different women and girls: knew each by name and laughter, how they walked in their mukluks, how they sat on the rocks below the store on the bay's edge, bouncing babies on their knees or nursing them under the wide parka-folds, or spread each others' black hair beneath their fingers, digging out lice, and cracking them in laughter between their teeth. Then in one eyeblink to be transplanted from covered friendliness to this teeming deliberately outlined nakedness as distant as revealing; though he could laugh at headquarters with the men —

But she was gone; not passing the window. He jerked to his feet, dropped a half dollar beside the upturned card and was out the door, his figure leaping at him in the mirror up the steps. On the sidewalk he hesitated. The streets and storefronts gleamed under the stark lights, but above their low revelation the jumbled heaps of buildings poked blank-square faces into the summer night. Flying in at night the reflection of the streets shone purple on the ebony of the two snakish rivers, but this slid like a wraith of a remembrance through his thought; which way had she gone? He could not see the wink of her coat anywhere, and his mind could only curse for letting her slip when he had as much as talked to her through the boy — what else was I doing? — but she had not passed the window. He began walking quickly in the opposite direction, eyes alert.

The street was almost empty; the cars ran few. The Coca-Cola sign at the end of Portage blinked 11:06: too early for the after-movie crowd, too late for most others. Surely she wouldn't go into any of the darker side streets. A taxi eased past, the driver trying to catch his eye; she might have taken one. You could walk for a week in Winnipeg and if — why was I so stupid? — he paused at the "Don't Walk," the curb balancing his feet. A scatter of people waited across the intersection. Bus-stop. The light flicked and he crossed, knowing already she was not among them. He strode through oblivious and just beyond the restaurant at the corner through the double glass of a store the edge of his glance snagged against blue.

She stood in the bay of the furniture store looking at the display. A transparent scarf added a grace note to her coiffure. His heart slowing, when he came to the far side of the store bay he turned in. "La Gallerie" a sign announced in curled black letters. "Nine piece dining room suite, now $995, regular $1595." For a few moments his usual measure of cost did not register; that even as reduced the price of the beautifully polished wood was more than most entire Eskimo families earned during a good trapping year leave alone a bad one. His mind seemed to have lost its usual money scale. A cinnamon couch on a shag-rug stretched its elegance behind a low glass table. $299.95. For a couch. The woman moved on the outer edge of his vision — *with the boy on the rug while she graces the couch and we talk in the blue light* —

An eddy of warm evening air, the last spilling of the hot

day, stirred in his beard. He turned and looked at her. For five minutes she had been facing the bedroom suite lit vaguely by a weathered brass lamp. She had not come nearer: she must know him, his beard swift identity. He could see a pale reflection of her face in the glass. If there was some polite way — god almighty six weeks out and broken to think like some stymied pimple-faced kid about a decent woman waiting for her bus home! — he wheeled from the showcase to the inner edge of the sidewalk. A black cab, motor idling, stood at the curb, the gaping street the emptier for it. He stared nowhere, the movie marque across the street flashing like bleeps in his face and after a time he understood the cabby was watching him. Grinning a little, as if all that convulsed his brain at that moment was intimately known, scrounged through, evaluated, and added to the already long long list of the cheap stuff of the human animal compiled and tabulated for years behind peering, close-set eyes. Abe moved slightly; a sign and green-steel power pole cut away the worldly-wise face. Deliberately he read: "Cross only at Cross Walks."

A bus wheeled to the curb and across the corner of his vision the woman moved quickly, following the few others boarding. He stood a moment; watched her emerge from the grouping around the ticket box and move down the white-lit aisle to a seat on the far side of the bus, and the cab moved suddenly, the wedge of the street light shading over the driver's hand as he thrust away his microphone and the lifted corner of his mouth as with a spurt the car swung into traffic. Then Abe turned. The bus doors were closing as he got there; hesitated; opened to him.

The driver pushed Abe's proffered quarter into his coin-changer, pressed some levers and dropped the change in his hand while the motor rumbled and they pulled away. Abe staggered slightly, hesitated, then said, "How much?"

An open convertible edged along half in the bus lane, its driver engrossed by the girl within his arm. The bus loomed over them a moment, driver swearing quietly; the convertible eased away oblivious. The driver thrust back his cap, noticed Abe and looked up. "How much?" Abe said again.

"Huh? Oh — fifteen."

Abe dropped it in, seeing the inevitable slow smile grow on the driver's face.

"How long were you growing that?" The man's gentle-ugly face with its frank admiration made the question not at all impertinent. Abe almost smiled.

"About four years."

"That's one beautiful bush!"

Abe braced for the stoplight. "Nothing to it, just don't cut it off." The bus stopped, its bumper exact on the crosswalk line.

"Ahh —" the driver gestured, leaning away to stare down at the cars alongside, "don't kid me. I've seen guys tryin' — looking worse than molting roosters. Shucks," his leg flexed and the diesel motors responded, "mine grows so heavy I've got to nip into the garage over lunch for a quick run over." His hand massaged his stubbly jowl. "Look at it. Four hours ago I worked it down! Man, I'd like to have one of those."

"Sure — grow it."

"Ha! Can you guess what the mayor'd say if he saw a guy with a *beard* driving a city bus? We lose a hundred thousand every year as it is! Mayor, to say nothing of the cruddy supervisor — well anyway — or my wife. I told her I could get a different job and maybe — but she swears she wouldn't come near me! So —" he gestured with both hands, dropped them to the wheel and swung for the bus-stop. "I got a lovely wife."

"Sure," Abe said, "guys with wives are heavy on trouble, I guess." He turned, paused bent as the bus sucked to a halt, then went down the aisle past an old man, a woman with a sleeping child, past her, and sat opposite the back door.

Three teen-age girls giggled aboard and tripped by to the back seat; the bus rolled, the wide street with its drapery of unnumbered tiny lights retreating on either side. They turned off Portage and with another turn the tall buildings faded to cluttered pawnshops, worn poolrooms, hotels. Men lounged about in groups, or singly, leaning against posts or doubling up in the shadow of a corner. Abe knew such streets, such faces; the years that had passed seemed very little now and the — how to pick a number? — of times he had gone down this, such a, street when for hours or maybe days he did not care, care one jot. Down this particular street perhaps twice, three times at the very most and not yet this time; he stared at the tucked blond hair three seats ahead — probably soon if this night gives evidence — a gaudy marque caught his eye and he looked instinctively across the bus to the buildings opposite. It was there, neatly white among the grimy storefronts, proclaiming "Jesus Saves" between "Big Auction Every Day. 2 pm New and Used Clothing" and "Schnitzler Good Sausages and Meats." Nothing but the paint was new. Once — that devil of a time just after the war — a sag-faced man leaned over his cot there when he could comprehend again and told him he had cried and begged forgiveness — of all the damned religious confidence tricks to try on a hangover! — he no longer believed it.

The bus braked to the sidewalk. A jagged-haired man boarded and began fumbling in his pocket as the driver waited. He pulled out a sheaf of papers with his left hand and tried to sort through them with his thumb, swaying badly as the bus stood. After a moment the driver eased the bus into motion; the man turned, dropping some papers, hunched down on the long parallel seat. Abe could see below his short right sleeve the knobbly, faintly red end of an amputation.

Presently the man found what he was looking for in the sprawl of paper on the seat. He raised himself and showed it to the driver, who nodded. The man turned splay-legged in the aisle and stuffed all the papers ponderously into his trouser pocket. He reached down for the pieces in the aisle, staggered sharply, and would have fallen but for the old man on the front seat thrusting an arm to steady him. The other pulled back and stared blearily at his helper, lips moving without a sound, then heaved himself erect and began a torturously-balanced weave down the aisle clutching his mutilation.

Abe's look darted along the bus. Even the giggles from the back seat had hushed. The passengers' attention seemed steadily beyond the windows, but a head-shift here and there betrayed their apprehension at the slow, almost nemesis-like advance. The man stared heavily at everyone he swayed by; when he arrived opposite the woman he stopped completely. Eyes blinked above his hanging jaw. Three seats away Abe tensed ready to jump — deficit or not to haul that around! — the bus jarred in a pothole, the man lurched, caught hold of a rail opposite with his single hand. For a moment he hung like flung debris, then stumbled forward into the seat behind the woman. Abe was already half on his feet but the drunk sagged lower, oblivious. And she had not shifted her glance to see what happened in the aisle; above the jagged hair her profile was mirrored against the dark.

The bus ran now as if the driver were intent to gain a cool drink and a soft bed. People left at the darting stops. Only she, the old man in the front seat and the drunk remained; the tires sang through the barely open window at his cheek; where were they riding? On and on the bright box charged, spraying its light for a moment on the great houses emerging, vanishing — how far from a blue and white store perched on tundra rocks or snowhouse under a blizzard's shriek? — he jerked his head against the thought and saw her standing, gloved hand on the buzzer cable. Her long legs carried her inevitably to the door at the front.

When he was off by the middle door she was already around the corner. The bus whined away. He stood on the corner and looked after her, the air tinged with a stray memory of her perfume, hearing only the tap of her heels lead down the dark street to the brilliant entrance of an apartment house blocking its end — what in all the wide world of loon-faced adolescence to trail her up through the corridors and into her apartment and peep on her going to bed? — his skin burning under his beard, he stood motionless. The slim figure swam away into the glassy light.

After a time he heard the insects singing in the trees. The houses loomed cavernous in sleep. Nearer, the block, set on stilts huge but oddly spindly for its bulk, rose above him in a mass of black and yellow light and iron-railinged balconies. Beyond the chairs and green plants of the lounge gleamed the night river like scattered glister. On the eighth floor a man in pyjama trousers appeared in the shadow of his balcony, looking out across the city. An airplane's take-off lights blinked over, the sound of its going a plaything to some high-flying wind. It was gone; the man went back in. Abe felt alone like a clenched fist in the gut.

He stretched suddenly in a movement that jerked taut the light jacket on his shoulders, and then he turned, walked away. He walked faster; soon he was moving in the slow lope of the dogsled trail, bent forward, arms up. His feet found a give of lawn as he turned back at the corner and he ran on its softness. A car's headlights swung onto the street, found him and slowed momentarily. But he ran oblivious, parallel to the river out of sight, his body tingling in strength, ran on over the grass the sidewalks the streets the miles between him and the heart of the lonely city.

2

IN the hallway beyond the maid opening the door a woman in evening dress moved towards them. "Oh Jim, it's so good you came! And this is your friend?"

Jim MacLaren bent over her hand. "Sherris, I said it at the auditorium and I'll say it again. You're looking simply beautiful." His smile while she laughed was as intimate as a kiss on her impeccably made-up cheek. "And this is Abram Ross, Arctic man in all his hirsute splendor. Abe, Mrs. John Kinconnell, Winnipeg's most charming hostess."

"Always the flatterer! But really, this is absolutely delightful! Really, Mr. Ross, I was completely intrigued when Jim pushed through to me," her laugh showed perfect teeth, "during the concert intermission — those corridors are so dreadfully narrow, aren't they, and everyone just *must* go out and smoke! — and said he had met a high school friend who'd been north among the Eskimos for absolutely years. I'm so happy you came!"

Abe had been smiling in suspended politeness while she ran on and her fragile hand lost itself momentarily in his grip. He said when he could, "My pleasure, ma'am," wondering what Jim had said to her that would balance the report he had received: 'Kinconnell's one of those guys had everything going for him since before his papa wasn't even dreaming of an heir to dissipate the family pile. You know, *the*

Kinconnells — grain investors, race horses, radio and television, with some railroad stock thrown in — everything where the money is. Dissipate or not, he's piled it higher. And Sherris fills all society ears with toothsome tidbits.' Jim's handsome face behind the horn-rimmed glasses had laughed at him, 'Man, you've got to come to their little ranch-house when this's over. Everybody who's anybody'll be there. Especially the singers — Sherris thinks she can get that big brute of a tenor to come, Pannelli. That'll be the stiffest feather of her social bonnet this cycle. Com'mon! Man, I haven't seen you since the war — in that London bar where the lights went out every time a rocket went over and we were in the dark most of the time and with our luck the barmaid had a face like a fossil! Imagine running into you —'

Mrs. Kinconnell was explaining, her magnificent hair whorled on top of her head like an ebony tiara, ". . . he was *so* unhappy but he *had* to catch a plane tonight. He sounded absolutely prostrate but they have only two days for full rehearsals before the Festival opens in Toronto and he just simply couldn't. He was so charming! He's even more handsome in his dressing room than when he stands there on the platform in front of the orchestra — if that's possible!" She laughed again. "Almost as handsome as you, Jim."

"Aha, Sherris," Jim's long hand touched her arm momentarily, "I know how you feel about me! And if you couldn't move him then there's not a woman in Manitoba who could!"

She laughed the girlish laugh — both of them reciting a damned script! — as other guests entered and she lifted her arm past her pointed breasts, "There are plenty of others — and especially Anton Schwafe, Orvis's new discovery for the harpsichord. Wasn't he simply marvelous? You know the way, Jim — downstairs," she turned to the newcomers.

"Com'mon. I could use a drink," Jim was striding down the wide corridor. Abe had a momentary glimpse of the living room half filled with chattering people in evening dress. "Never mind them — that's just some of the choir that's made the bottom rung. The real McCoy's downstairs."

A pretty maid with a tray of sandwiches passed them smiling. Each step downward soundless on the heavy rug Abe resigned himself more bitterly to the mistake of his coming: it was being lost in him; he could feel it drain at the spout of each laugh, each carefully-set smile. In the first thoughtless moment he had been happy — oh admit it overjoyed — to recognize a known face in the crowd pushing to get in to the Bach concert, but at that moment he had little dreamt what would happen in him listening. At that first, for him startled, encounter Jim had, in fact, said nothing of a party; only when they had stumbled together again during intermission had interest suddenly sprung. But after the opening of the 'St. John's Passion' he had not wanted to go anywhere, especially not where a school-remembered face must unearth childhood — not after twenty years living it away — rather hear out the incredible worship and return to his room and think on nothing but the evening's memory. If he had gotten through the crowd as quickly as he intended Jim would not have found him to lead him here. But he had sat immobile after the last choral, beautiful beyond imagination:

> *O Lord Thy little angel send*
> *When e'er my mortal life shall end,*
> *To bear my soul to heaven . . .*

And the approbation of the audience, which was by then a congregation, echoing the last notes:

> *Lord Jesus Christ O hear thou me*
> *Thee will I praise eternally.*

When he had at last shaded out of that brightness the thousands in the balcony around him were gone. Below the orchestra chairs were empty. He grasped then that he had felt people push past; that he had seen the conductor, soloists, choir long since being trailed out by well-wishers and a stooped man in coveralls had suspended the wide broom's push to look at him, strangely. Jim materialized in the exit and he followed numbly down the stairs and out, the cool evening hardening his conviction but his mind incapable of the effort to get away politely. As the car wheeled over

Assiniboine Bridge he had a wild impulse to leap out and dive into the water; at least no explanation would be necessary and he could float along and come to shore undisturbed but now they were inside the tindel-stone mansion with Jim ahead down the stairs where laughter and a waft of alcohol led him unerringly into a long smoke-hazy room with several dozen people lounging on leather couches and about the rug.

". . . Abe," Jim was saying, "I want you to meet Kin — over here," and he plowed into the room, scattering greetings. At its far end a smaller group of men sat; a small man with squarish features said,

"Jim. I was beginning to wonder."

"You know me, Kin. I wouldn't stay away! I was trying to find a friend here — Kin, this is Abe Ross, an Arctic manager for Frobisher Company. Abe, John Kinconnell."

Kinconnell pulled himself half-erect, his round, slightly bulging eyes friendly. "Glad to meet you, Ross. Sit down." His hand was surprisingly firm. "If there's room. Gus — drinks here."

Abe looked about at the nonchalant luxuriance. "Abe," someone nudged him and he noticed the bartender waiting.

"Oh, ah — anything — what'd you have Jim?"

"I always drink Kin's Scotch. You can't get that kind anywhere but here. Probably makes it himself in his private still." The men about laughed loudly.

"Okay — make it two." In the pause Jim finished introductions; Abe recognized only the lion-headed Anton Schwafe who had hunched over the harpsichord and the short heavy bass Denis Hugo, already red-faced, who had sung the words of Jesus.

The long room echoed with talk and laughter; after a few desultory questions the men in Kinconnell's corner seeemd to forget Abe. Jim was talking to the host who drank on without a word — give this gang fifteen minutes to get stoned and so-long — but more arrived led by Mrs. Kinconnell. "Oh Kin, Jim — you always huddle away in your men's corners to drink and tell stories not fit for ladies' ears. Come on now — break it up!"

"We're always happy to have the ladies join us!" Jim gestured to his lap, "There's lots of room!"

"Teaser," she flashed as the last of the men pushed up. "These are the Harold Grangers. They're visiting from Denver. Have you met — "

Introductions again — toothy parade that wouldn't weigh a grain against one Itooi with the laughing greasy face — and he was leaning on a chair far back when his ears caught, "Oh, and this is Abe Ross, our Arctic man. Billy and Harold Granger of Denver."

His "How do you do" was lost in the woman's exclamation: "What a simply marvelous beard!" She colored expertly. "Oh excuse me, Mr. Ross, but you look so — striking with it. Do all Arctic men grow them?"

"No," Abe had to answer, feeling his color rise, vowing with fervency of a curse as he had so often that he would strip next day and knowing as he answered he would not. "It's just to keep off mosquitoes."

"Really!" her high voice carried on as Abe and her husband nodded. "Are there so many, up north? I'm sure all the Eskimos have them then too, beards I mean."

"No. Most Eskimos, like Indians, have no facial hair."

Someone said, "Unless there's white blood in them!" and several men snickered. He pushed in before Mrs. Granger could speak.

"In the central Keewatin where I was they weren't bothered by — that, yet."

"Is that right! How dreadfully primitive it must hav —" but her voice was swallowed in the laugh that tilted them all back. She flapped her hands helplessly, blush still expert, " — you *know* what I intended — please." She turned to Abe. "And do they *still* live in what is it they call them — snow igloos — all the time —"

"Shucks, Billy," her husband muttered from the chair where he had stretched his lean length, "they have summers up there too. They haven't snow all the time, huh Ross?"

"They live in tents over half the year."

The other recent arrival, a man in air force uniform Abe distantly remembered being named Marsden, said, "What are they like? Don't they want to get out of their useless country? Don't they want to be like whites?"

"Yes," Mrs. Granger broke in, "do they still do such unique things like eating raw meat and trading wives and —" laughter interrupted her again and Granger knocked ash from his cigar.

"Trust her. Always concerned with the looseness of women anywhere in the world." He tipped back his glass to the bottom.

"Oh Harold, I'm not! They do do it, don't they, Mr. Ross?" Her bright glance caught Abe's; she was pretty when she smiled — and plump as Itooi liked his women but quiet — "And the women have nothing to say about it, do they?"

The circle of their grins ringed him; he did not like their interest. It was not humane, only sexually snoopy. He thought, remembering like a knife-thrust the warmth of the people, let's trim it down to the mechanics of staying alive. "Yes, they still exchange wives sometimes and they probably always will, because of the land they live in. They have very rigid taboos; an Eskimo man and woman closer than first cousins cannot sleep together, and their bands are all so small that very few are not related within that limit. So even if they want to — and Eskimos are interested in sex as much as — anyone —" already he was slipping aside from his intent but their laughter was hearty, as if his direct sobriety had cut away lewdness. Kinconnell, looking as if flung in his huge leather chair, was studying him without expression. Mrs. Kinconnell picked it up quickly,

"Why exchange wives because of the land?"

He should not have begun; to get out of it politely might be impossible. "Please," he said, "you shouldn't get me talking. Men who've lived in the north will bore you silly. Really, I'd —"

"Oh, but your talk is simply marvelous," Billy Granger effused — if you clack once more I'll dump courtesy and run — as into the murmur of encouragement abruptly the deep voice of Schwafe boomed,

"Yes-s. You tell us. Get us out of the claptrap."

There was a quick silence, broken too consciously by

several urging at once and a general shuffle for drinks. Mrs. Kinconnell was looking at him, nodding slightly. "Well," he laughed a little, but her smile boosted him beyond himself into the assurance he could gain sometimes talking of the people, though rarely with a large group, "in the Arctic you talk. You get stuck in a snowhouse in a blizzard for four, five days and there isn't anything to do except sleep and talk. The Eskimos fit into their world completely, they can't fight it head-on, usually. At least not with the equipment they have. The military can come in and build a base and sit in shirt-sleeves behind insulation, but they get all their stuff from the south. If you use only what the north has — like the Eskimo used to, and still do pretty much, you fit yourself in. When it blizzards you stay inside snow walls —"

"Isn't it dreadfully cold in there?" Marsden interrupted.

"No. Snow insulates better than a tent, and on the barrens there are no trees — a bit of brush here and there as high as your knee. It's small and even without heating it's usually between 35-45 degrees."

"That's not cold?" Mrs. Granger shuddered.

"But you're not dressed like —" Abe gestured, and everyone laughed, looking at the gleaming shoulders of the women. "The Eskimos wear two complete suits of caribou, the fur on the inside turned in, the fur on the outer out, and the warmth is inside the suit, not outside. If your suit gets torn you're in trouble, and you only have to get into deep trouble once in the Arctic. So the Eskimos' moral code is adapted to fit the surroundings: you just can't make mistakes and survive, and to survive each one in the family has a job. The man hunts — in the Keewatin its mostly caribou — they call them the deer — it gives them meat to eat and skins to wear; the woman makes food and clothing and keeps it fixed. A cut in a mukluk on a sharp stone —"

"What's a mukluk?" a man asked.

"A moccasin-type boot that comes up under the coat about to the thighs. A cut in that would freeze your feet in no time so you have to stop right there and sew it. If the deer don't come near the camp —" he stopped, for like a whiplash the memory cut through his mind, then he kept on doggedly, forcing exclusion, "they have to — try to — follow; you have to eat. But the camp can't always move — a child might be sick or your wife is about to birth and you're the best hunter in the camp. Everyone in camp shares the food and you have to at least try, whether you get some or not. So if you think you'll be gone, say a week, you exchange your wife with your camp partner, he stays in camp and you go out hunting with his. A hunter needs a woman on a trip because she keeps clothes in repair, scrapes the hides of the deer he gets and when he comes in after an all-day circle sweaty from running behind the dogs, he takes off his clothes and sleeps naked in the sleeping bags. His furs freeze solid; then the wife beats out the ice and kneads them so when he wakes up they're soft and he can put them on again, eat, and go hunt. It's a matter of survival. If your wife can't come, you simply get another. And when you get back to camp with the meat, everybody eats."

The circle of faces ringed him. Finally Granger said, "Then there really isn't anything much sexy about wife-trading. It's just a practical arrangement."

Abe was silent; hating his indecision and the situation which now forced him into explaining simply what was in reality as complex as one situation is inevitably different from every other, especially, in the world of the people so immensely distant — no world like Oolulik's can exist for them teetering on their spikes — but he was committed too far; he had to try again. "Well, when they exchange wives they do so in every respect. For that trip she's his wife, that's all. And — sometimes — the trade isn't made always on the basis of one woman being a better sewer than another — or that a wife is sick."

There was a general laugh and Mrs. Kinconnell said, "And this is all decided by the men. The women are just — pushed around?"

The glistening circle: it was too much to expect. Whatever he said did not sound as it should, here. He said slowly, "We started this wrong. There isn't that much exchange, and if there is, only between song-cousins — sort of blood brothers, often camp-partners. Or a courtesy to strangers. Eskimo women are quiet and — rather backward. The man is boss but when you get right down to it the women have as much to say in exchange matters as they —" and then he realized his complete faux pas and he could only try to fling it aside with a laugh, "as they do anywhere."

Kinconnell roared, and the rest echoed and then drowned his laughter; for a moment the haze seemed to vibrate down the long room and Abe realized everyone in it had been drawn about. Behind Mrs. Kinconnell a dozen people stood, now breaking into various conversation as the laughter lowered. Granger chuckled, "Ross, you know what the world's about, eh Billy?" The American's wife returned lightly, though Abe thought he heard a tinge of something more,

"You're being horrid again, Harold," and the renewed laugh hid discomfort.

"But isn't it dreadfully lonely up there in the north — all by yourself?" a rather mannish woman said.

"I had a helper," Abe replied quickly. "He lived near the store with his family. And there's lots to do, the people coming in. Actually I —" he caught himself, "You don't get as lonely as lots of people in other places. You work there because you like it; read books, and there's good music on short-wave radio."

Mrs. Kinconnell looked keenly at him as he stopped; when she spoke he was suddenly grateful for her sensitivity. "Did you hear Bach on short-wave?"

"Sometimes. But not like tonight."

"I thought it was marvelous too," she turned to a slight grey-haired man beside her. "Mr. Ross, this is Orvis Gingerton, president of the Winnipeg Musical Club. They sponsored the 'Passion' and it was magnificent. One of the finest concerts I've ever heard in Winnipeg. Don't you agree?" She turned in a general murmur of approbation. Abe smiled at Gingerton, but the little man was standing very erect and saying very precisely while seeming to look just past his glasses,

"It did work well. And the musicians — orchestra, choir, soloists —" he bowed to Hugo who sat, red-faced, almost beyond response, "and Mr. Schwafe at the continuo —" he bowed again, but the harpsichordist stared immobile from under his heavy eyebrows, "your effort was really — first class."

Granger half-shouted over the general congratulations, "That's right! Exactly! Terrific act!"

"Yes," his wife shrilled at him, "I saw you and Kin simply rushing in at intermission so you wouldn't miss the second half, too!"

"Well, we got held up on a little business at the hotel . . ."

He was out of it; expertly. He smiled his thanks to the gleaming back of Mrs. Kinconnell's head, elbowed through to the barman and gulped a quick one. The mannish-looking woman found him there but he discouraged her with a few generalities about tundra for her geography class. Feeling better then and hoarding a last drink, he started between the strident voices, to find Jim, and out . . .

"— that beautiful Italian! Have you ever seen such a beautiful thing? And singing Bach like an angel of

"— redecorated her living room and I told Harry we'd had our decor for three years and its about

"— and — this is a hummer — he got poking around in there yuh know for the — ahh — gadget with this straw and he loses it too

"— you know how high and mighty Toronto is. They just lord it over everybody so even their alleycats

"— help it, I simply have to go to Fagin in Toronto. The big robber gets every good English grad student in

"— come out wearing nothing but rubber boots and a straw hat!" laughter banged his ear as he recognized Jim's coatback. He said quickly as the other turned,

"Jim, thanks, it was nice, but I better go."

"Go? Things haven't even started! Look, there's Sherris with the sandwiches; that means the gang upstairs has been shoved — things'll start down here. Com'mon, meet some people! See that man over there — big white head? That's Forester of the biggest law firm here — com'mon, I'll introduce —"

"Sure Jim, but thanks, no more introductions. It's 12:30 and I better —"

"Alright alright — another half hour? I'll take you home. You bet. Say, you should hear Wilson here tell stories —"

"Sure Jim, thanks its okay. Half an hour." That was all

he needed to bury the evening, stories by Wilson. At least the women got nearer Bach: they oogled the tenor. Maybe that group by Kinconnell would . . .

"— work to get under ninety. Why last year my handicap was

"— you Don Juan! I bet you say that to everyone you

"— Janie is the fastest reader! Her teacher told me she'd never —"

He stopped and deliberately shut out his hearing. He'd find a corner; there had been bookshelves near Kinconnell; he looked the length of the hazy room. Drapes had been drawn back to reveal an entire wall of plate glass. The window drew him inevitably, the flood-lit lawn sloping away under the trees to the dull early-summer river. In the incredible clacking racket — a door must open out — he found himself behind the chair where Kinconnell still sat crumpled, the lean-faced Granger standing there now, almost shouting,

"— you Canadians can talk about peace, peace, peace but you're just hiding behind our hydrogen bomb payload! The Reds won't hit you first — they'll hit us! And when they sound all the alarms that never work in practice and the rockets and bombers come roarin' over, at least ours will be over there and pounding the holy h out of them too. The only reason they haven't fixed you is because *we're* too tough to tackle!"

A man said placatingly, "Well, Marsden here is in the Royal Canadian Air Force. It's not like we weren't doing —"

"No, no," Marsden's face was drawn, as though this had been going on a long time and very painfully too, "I'm with Norad and we're strictly defensive. We'll never — we couldn't — touch anything overseas. That's SAC's business."

Granger jabbed a fist, "Goddam right it's SAC's business! And SAC's strictly U.S. Even Norad has to get trained in the States — lots o' Canadians around Denver — Colorado Springs all the time. But just defense is nothing — nothing and you know it. Communism's got to be wiped right out, they're out to get us — everyone — Canadians, Americans, they don't care. We've got it too good, they'll never stop."

"But Mr. Granger," there was the faint drone of a lecturer

33

in the elderly man's voice, "the western concept of democracy is that all citizens may express their views. Some people want socialism, perhaps even a mild form of communism. If you have a free country these too must at least have the right of expression! A democracy cannot simply choke its opposition. In Canada communists are allowed to speak, but you've outlawed —"

"Are you crazy?" between fervency and alcohol Granger was obviously too far gone to be insulting but the other colored violently. "The Reds want to blow freedom sky-high! You've got to dig them out, everyone, or you undermine the whole American way of life. They don't even believe in God, so how —"

"What God?" The booming voice stopped even Granger in midstride. Behind Kinconnell's chair, Abe half turned to look at the huge harpsichordist sitting hunched forward now on the couch, only the glitter of his eyes betraying his drinking. In the instant Granger had regained his fumbled belligerence.

"What do you mean, what God? There's only one!"

"Ha — hahaha —" for a moment the barrel-chested laughter rolled down the long room and all voices fell away. Into the silence Schwafe said, lifting one gaunt finger, "That's true. Only one. One for you, one for me, one for each human being on earth. Roughly two billion of them, but for each person one."

Granger tilted forward, "Are you a heathen or something? There's only *one* God —"

"And he's yours, right? Like every North American you've got him right here!" Schwafe's fingers snapped as his glare twisted away. "I couldn't bother to spit in the eye of your god."

Abe saw Granger's wife tug at his coatsleeve but the man was beyond himself, "Christ almighty you're a Communist! That's what you are, a bloody —"

"Listen to me!" Schwafe's voice stopped him, "You're so hot on wiping out communists. How many have you — killed?"

Granger hestitated, then barked, "Enough! Every time I

send off my income-tax I'm jacking off a few more and in about one more minu —"

"No, no," Schwafe seemed calm now, "I don't mean in such an impersonal way. Not like our friend Marsden here whose men watch the dot on the screen and push a few buttons and after twelve minutes the radar reports the "kill" of a plane and ten men a thousand miles away blown into the stratosphere — not like that. I mean personally — you come up soft behind and take the man's throat in your hands, you know, like this —", he was crouched before his seat, arms up, hands high, the immense fingers that had run like water over the 'Passion' chords now splayed claws, "and you hit the windpipe first so he can't scream and you squeeze and squeeze till your fingers crack and his face is blotched purple and his eyes burst blood and he isn't kicking you anymore. How many?"

Silence echoed in the room. Abruptly someone stumbled the length of it and out the door but not even the ugly sound of sickness carrying faintly from the hall could jar their immobility. On the lawn Abe saw a rabbit as if caught in mid-spring, hypnotized at the light from the glass wall. Schwafe's voice was so low the group bent to him like summer wheat in the wind, "They had us. Trapped. All around, in that town on the river we had fought like beasts to get and whose name I don't even know now because the old devil is dead and anathema in Russia too. Two hundred thousand of us and no supplies. In summer clothing in November, in Russia. When the last few planes came in with a pick-up of rations the officers fought the men to yank out a carton and crawl in themselves. Clubbed each other with empty rifles or stabbed with pocket knives; there weren't any bayonets left. And when the plane got away without leaving even the few supplies it had while men ran after it, crying and cursing, other officers ran up and beat and yelled them into some kind of order. I stood in the shelter of the hangar. Under such madman orders as Berlin sent I had decided I was on my own. Where I liked to be. That night I crawled through the blasted buildings and the snow bare-handed to the Russian front that surrounded us and along until I found a soldier about my size."

There was a pause. Abe was still staring unconsciously out the window but the rabbit was gone. Schwafe's voice was almost inaudible, "He was watching over his trench and once in a while he'd put down his rifle and beat his gloved hands against his shoulders. He was wearing a heavy coat. The other sentry was sleeping in his five feet away."

Of them all Granger seemed the first to comprehend; his gaunt face was haggard as he said, almost quietly, "He probably was a Communist. Most Russian soldiers —"

"Gott-Im-Himmel No!" Schwafe sprang erect and for an instant it seemed the entire room would disintegrate at his voice. "No! He was a human being! Right there!" And his hands clenched before him.

The officer Marsden said, "Mr. Schwafe, we can't understand all you've been through. But we're human beings too and we have to defend our families, ourselves. Most Russians or Chinese aren't communists, true, but they do as they're told and if they attack us we have to be ready to hit back —"

Schwafe turned his head like a lion snapping at an insect, "And how many actual communists do you think your American-god-directed missiles and bombers would hit? It won't be the non-communists who know about the deepest holes and when to crawl into them. What ratio women and children per communist can you get, eh?" He threw back his head, great hands high, palms upward. "I offer you, here, two hundred laughing children blasted to bits — to get one communist — maybe!"

He stood, the light glinting on his blond mane and the blondish hair of his arms thrust from the dead white cuffs and the black sleeve of his evening suit, like an aboriginal priest praying to some unknown but fervently sought and terrifying deity that would somehow in its absolute indifference accept a sacrifice from a votary who meant not so much to it as a shrivelled obscenity.

"Mr. Schwafe — Anton —" Mrs. Kinconnell was standing before him in their circle.

Schwafe shook his head sharply. "Ma'am," his voice rang dull, thick with an accent as it had not before. "I am deeply sorry. I have never behaved so — and now the first time I am in your house." His head shook slowly. "If I could use the piano —" he looked at her, momentarily infantile.

"Why, certainly," she hesitated, "but really — do you think —"

"That's okay — fine —" he looked around at the others, vaguely. "— you may leave — I won't be —"

Someone near the piano opened it and another pulled out the chair. From where Abe stood he could see him hunch as if blind over the keys and beyond the glass the grey arrow of a cat slid across the lawn intent on its shadowy destination. Notes tumbled about for several moments like a child doodling, unaware of loud and soft, incapable of tune. Slowly, ponderously they fumbled to evenness and almost melody; suddenly the left hand stumbled over, then found a tune deep down that ran up like flight, dipped, lifted, leaped almost to the bottom, then caught up again. After a moment the treble joined in quick double triads that seemed to question the running bass. Abe's mind balked at recognition, then the bass soloist said loudly, "Anton, for h-h-heaven's sake!" and Abe recognized it from the *St. John*. His hand groped in his pocket for the program and he found the bass aria he had marked with a huge "X" as he had sat driven beyond himself in the auditorium. He heard it now, "Run, run, you souls whom care oppresses — run, run," the deep voice often ahead of the beat in its urgency, and the whispered upper voices of the chorus, "Run where? Run where?" And the answer, ever and again, "To Golgatha."

Schwafe had not lifted his head at the interruption but played on, the melody growing more powerful as the question grew more plaintive, almost pathetic. Then suddenly all ceased. Schwafe was standing, leaning on the low piano, staring at the American.

"Mr. Granger," his voice had found its Canadian tone again, "I apologize if I offended you. In any way."

Granger, slouched in the chair, lifted his glance; Abe realized that in the room only ten persons remained; he had forgotten to go. The American hoisted his glass and drained it. "Thass okay, Anton, no hard feelings."

Schwafe did not seem quite satisfied with such easy acceptance; neither did he appear certain of what he should say — like he can't remember what happened — the heavy brows bunched together: "I play every night at the 'Club 77'. That is my work now. Before the war when I was a student of the great Helmut Walcha —" he stopped. "Dance hall music — jazz — that is the only — safe — music for me now. Perhaps you like jazz? Perhaps you would care to dance? Please." With a flourish of his leonine head he sat. The same run began in the bass but it went up and up into the treble where it convoluted and trilled in bachian syncopation, clean, sharp, the rush of the piece before as nothing to its present incredible quickness. But the heavy off-beat of the bass was such as Bach had never written. It boomed like a giant viol of elemental humanity plucked at the very base where strings nub in flesh. In a moment Granger had flung aside his jacket and the tall school teacher was in his arms, their feet moving in the small space before Kinconnell's corner chair. They were pulling back the chairs; moving unconsciously in the beat Abe pulled at the couch. There were other couples already; Jim leaning over the chubby Billy. The light seemed to dim as he watched them, his foot growing alive in the rhythm, and then Sherris Kinconnell stood before him; her arms rose and they were moving together. The thunder of the beat in his ears and the clash-and-clasp shudder of their bodies were one now. Once when she hung back in his arms, only her body moving, her eyes hollows in the faded light reflected from outside and her open mouth a pink-rimmed hole, in some far off unabandoned corner of himself he shuddered at the frightful decay of what he had once thought her loveliness. He looked up. Moments before the people whirling there had been shining rich, handsome, beautiful — where have they all gone? — they blurred past battered to ugliness, gruesome, led by the thin American and his partner, faces skull-like in the darkness, their bony arms rising and falling alternately in crooked sickle-sweeps. He could feel fingers digging into his shoulder as they looped past Kinconnell still motionlessly flung in his chair and on where Schwafe crouched forward, head and shoulders heaving as if the pale piano were galloping him away, its sound now only the rush of the question and the answer long lost in the skeleton of the dance.

3

WHEN the sunlight slid off the slant of the drapes and over his face, Abe awoke. He lay motionless, pinching his eyes tight against the impossible whiteness. The texture of sheets under his skin recalled him at last, and he moved his head so the dark of the dresser, the yawning door of the closet, the glint of the mirror past the bathroom door emerged and steadied.

He twisted over and after a long blankness his eyes opened again. The spoor of his clothes: shorts; shirt; trousers; jacket: door. Shoes? Socks? Hadn't he worn a tie? And a top-coat? His mind juggled: tie socks shoes coat; socks tie coat shoes; his eyes fastened on the jacket. One empty tube of sleeve, bent, corded in the elbow like the crumpled pipe of a beast's esophagus sliced rawly through. He could not pull his glance from that hole and he seized a book on the bedtable and flung at it. The book hit the floor, splayed, slid, jerking the sleeve back to merely sleeve.

He sat up then and in the motion swung out of bed — stupid break a good book and the only suit on the floor — he fumbled at the coat, then lifted it and the book fell, covering the blue tie. Erect, book in one hand and coat in the other, he let the momentary blackness of his rising and bending tumble through his head and clear. He sat down in the armchair.

If he had held at that third glass of scotch: but last night and high-breasted Sherris Kinconnell would not be thought of; for one day at a minimum. He leaned back, eyes vacant on the whorls of the plastered ceiling. Thirty days hath September — no need to recite that stupidity — he knew without counting yesterday he had thirteen days left and today twelve, with half of it gone — June hath only thirty days — and when he came out the two months he had to make up his mind seemed like an endlessness that would, in its restful passage, illuminate all decisions. Make up his mind as always: balance carefully all factors pro and con, ponder, reach a polished, frayed-edges-trimmed decision that was sure to be right — ha! — even six weeks of avoiding one topic never decided anything. Or an eternity.

His watch said 11:22. He got up and threw the jacket on the bed and placed the book on the table. The Gideon Bible, its spine now broken. Who'd he pay for that? It was good enough still to fall asleep over.

The telephone rang as he stepped under the shower. After ten rings it stopped; he was almost dressed, his head feeling much better, when it rang again. He puzzled momentarily as it repeated and repeated its impersonal strident demand. Finally he accepted the easy way. "Yes."

"Good morning," the girl's voice was so smoothly feminine he knew immediately he had never heard it before. "Is this Mr. Abram Ross?"

"Yes."

"Mr. Kinconnell would like to speak to you. Would you hold the line a moment, please?"

"Huh? —" for a long minute only a long white gown and black hair swam in his mind and then abruptly he clenched on the figure in the armchair. "Oh, sure — fine."

The line-tone altered and he had no time to unscramble anything before a man's voice said briskly, "Morning, Ross. This is John Kinconnell. I hope you had a good night's sleep after the — I guess you'd call it 'party' — last night."

"Hello, Mr. Kinconnell." What could he want? "Thanks, I slept well. Actually, I just got up."

The other's laugh over the wire sounded warm enough. "I had them try your number at ten and a few minutes ago, but they couldn't raise you. I have to leave for an appointment so I thought I'd try just once more."

"Oh," Abe said as the other paused, "I heard it ring once but only one person in town knew the number so I thought I could call later —"

"Jeffers at Frobisher is a good friend of mine," Kinconnell said, and Abe knew they must be very good friends indeed for Horst to give up his number. "Look, I have to run. Could you come up to see me this afternoon, say for about half an hour?"

"I-I —", Abe hesitated, his eyes on the Winnipeg skyline that stretched beyond the bank of windows.

"I've got a business idea we might get interested in together. I talked to Horst and he said you still weren't sure about staying with them. He didn't actually want to admit it but I bent his arm a little. How about 2:30 this afternoon, here at my office?"

Suddenly he was intensely relieved; the afternoon had direction. "Sure — where is it?"

"Tenth floor, Kinconnell Building. I'll see you."

The instrument clicked; he went to the windows. Across the uneven city the Golden Boy with his torch and sheaf topping the Legislative Building glinted in the soft noon sun. Cars like bugs crawled the streets, and truncated blots of people at the base of buildings. Eight stories up; one could walk out the window and disappear into the world down there, stubby as they from the fall. His momentary relief fell with his thought; his head felt like a staved barrel. What did it matter anyway what one did. There must be some kind of fulfillment, if not glory, in lying squashed on pavement and people staring; the draw of the height rising in him, he could not decide, as he could not quite decide so many things, if hesitation involved anything more than cowardice; hang on, hang on for dear dull life.

He turned abruptly, picked up his coat and strode to the door. The telephone rang — at this rate I'll need a switchboard — and the voice again was strange until with a stutter he understood Jim MacLaren reminding him where they were meeting for supper. He muttered his "Sure, sure" and hung up. So the evening was anchored — lord to do what but reminisce about Selkirk! — when forced, he had walked that tightrope before — better at least than trailing a beautiful — he slammed the door on that.

Eat as slowly as he would, it was only 12:30 when he finished what he couldn't even think of as breakfast and he had to leave the restaurant because of the noon rush. Two hours to meet Kinconnell. His head felt better: walk and strip off the haze of last night. In a few moments he was in the current of Portage Avenue, its night half-mystery washed white in the June sunlight. Immediately the crowds irked him, their ceaseless noisy lurching like walruses, advertising assaulting. He walked on the street's shaded side under the five tiers of flags dangling in motionless air against the drab pile of store, seepage marks tracing the edges of its bricks. When he crossed the street, he looked back. Its innumerable windows were all blocked; the wainscotting at the very top, beneath a solitary pole hidden limp with flag, pealed in tags under the wear of the weather. He turned and went on in the flow of people, waiting at the crosswalks, striding quickly at the "Walk" as if he too were intent on somewhere. In the shade where Main bent past the end of Portage he stopped. Opposite the Grain Exchange stood the white stone sheath of the Kinconnell Building and he laughed as he looked at it, remembering his small contentment with his bank account.

The light changed and people about him surged into the street. He walked away, south in the narrow shadows of buildings. Soon he found the small oval with its ivy-green fort gate facing Union Depot. Flowers were already bright in the plots and under the tree whose shadow fell to the edge of the stone a man in blue shirt and crumpled trousers lay on the grass, his knees in the air. Abe looked at him sleeping, feet sockless in battered boots. He turned to look at the gate. A bronze plaque announced:

> NEAR THIS SITE STOOD THE FOLLOWING FORTS: FORT ROUGE UNDER LA VERENDRYE, 1738, FORT GIBRALTER UNDER THE NORTHWEST COMPANY, 1810, THEN CAME FORT GARRY

IN 1822, REPLACED BY UPPER FORT GARRY 1835 AND EXTENDED INTO THE 1850's WHEN THIS GATEWAY WAS ERECTED. DEMOLISHED IN 1882.

Five generations, four forts, glossed in fifty words on a plaque of greenish bronze. And of all the poor fools that had mixed the mud or pulled it apart, nothing. He walked through the crude archway and out on the sunside. Another plaque: ". . . 1816 Fort Gibralter destroyed . . ." He stepped back; momentarily the pile looked like a square head buried in white gravel to the chin: the brown-wood plane of face with a hole-birthmark on its forehead, two tiny eyes flanking the nose gap, gray-mortar wall sideburns defining the gigantic black maw of the entry; crowned by a grayish flagpole like a final strand of hair with a collapsed flag-ribbon twitching a little in palsy. Slowly he rubbed his beard; there was no logic to follow from that flat face, except perhaps that in its history it had swallowed many a Ross. They had been there for every company and civil war, shooting as sincerely as they said their prayers every night, but for this Ross it held — not a tinker's damn praise the lord and pass the annihilation — he walked out on the hot pavement, past a girl on a bench talking to a man with a paper-sack lunch in his hand. For a moment he tried to visualize the long-since destroyed north-south wall of the fort to where it faced the junction of the Red and Assiniboine Rivers, but the angle of the street and a warehouse with railroad yards beyond intervened so he crossed the bridge over the Assiniboine, the cars and trucks rushing barely by him. Here only two railroad tracks bisected the vee of land between the rivers, and a narrow path led down through stinging nettles, great purple-headed thistles, poplars and scrub maples. Except for the traffic roar on the bridge, he had dropped two hundred years to La Verendyre pushing through the grass and canoes manned by coureurs-de-bois bobbing on the river. The path turned and the shadow of the railroad bridge fell over him. His glance slid across the usual obscenities scrawled on the piling, and snagged: "God be merciful to me a siner." Out of some corner of himself he heard with vision-like clarity that one male voice he had long given up hope of forcing into oblivion reading from the Bible, morning and evening, and among all the thundered "thou-shalts" and "thou-shalt-nots" of damnation that forever ruled what even in this moment of past clairvoyance he knew completely without attempting to remember, there came this occasional call of recognized human break-down — a far away hesitant whisper of forgiveness? — he broke the thought and saw the mud turtle sunning on a spar beyond the shadow of the bridge. Abruptly it thrust up its skinny neck, stared, kicked to plop into the water. He walked to the end of land where the two rivers lapped against the mud.

From the apex of the land at his feet a line arched out over the width of the water marking as clearly as a chalkline the two shades of muddy Red and Assiniboine joining. Toward the bend of the united river the line faded to total blue under the rub of the wind. He sat; the merger line bent delicately across the water toward the beehive domes of St. Boniface Basilica. In the jumble of trees below it several boys fished. He lay back then, careless of his clothes and closed his eyes to the sun. The boy had been handsome and almost his own height; had he married he might have had such a son — damn it not a mouthy guide! — "Would you like to tour the Basilica?" and explain the precise cost of the new baptistry at the door and ancient gold-inlaid altarpiece and the pulpit and the replacement value of the whole cavernous mound while as incidently pointing out the station where Jesus fell for the third time. Facts at least the boy could handle; with hard irony he thought, I have saved the world from one more sum addict. Dreams were for men, not children: like the dream buried between basilica and river, under the already brownish grass beside the inevitable bronze plaque:

> TOMB OF LOUIS RIEL, PRESIDENT OF THE PROVISIONAL GOVERNMENT OF 1869-70.

Governments too preferred facts to dreams, especially if the dreamer was so foolish as to try to realize them. Ants ran over the white concrete posts that held up the square rails and looped chains of the fence; on the sunken ground within it thistles and dandelions thrust up fearlessly around the short gray shaft:

 Riel: 16 Novembre: 1885

Staring at the stone he had almost seen H-A-N-G-E-D. But there are some facts tombstones do not face — nor forty-ish men — he seemed to have dozed. He had not wished so much for himself; only to let his mind dally into deliberate unthought: the hollow blue of the sky flaked here and there by cloud and the locomotive rattling its cars on the trestle and the far drone of traffic, while near the wind stirred in the grass and the low bushes.

He looked at his watch. 2:17. He stood up, brushed his coat and trousers, and followed the path that led through longer grass over the grade toward the street. Under a willow-clump a hollow of newspapers still held a man's shape outlined among the grass. Then he was on the street, and in a moment a taxi cut through traffic for him.

The brunette receptionist smiled at him as he came out of Kinconnell's office but he hardly saw her or heard the subdued hum of the phalanx of typewriters behind her. In the hall an elevator yawned and he dropped to the lobby. People and cars flowed endlessly past. He had to find a place to think and he could not go to his empty apartment that barely gave him sleep, leave alone thought. There was only one place and he strode out and down the hot sidewalk, around corners and over side-streets to the low gothic door now in shadow under the department store. It swallowed him like a crypt, silent, and dark. He went down the left aisle not noticing the details which had intrigued him on another day: the great window in the choir where in a blaze Christ the Lord was forever ascending from the disciples lifting their hands to the circle of the godhead just below its apex, the hanging lamps and the polished gold pipes of the organ, the wood of the high dark roof where light through hidden dormers played blue and yellow and white and orange. He did not even pause to look again at the gravestone on the wall which had held him for no verbalizable reason three days before:

> SACRED TO THE MEMORY OF MAY BROWN, ETHEL WHITE, MYRTLE WHITE, AND ERNEST WHITE WHO WERE DROWNED IN THE RED RIVER APRIL 21, 1906. THE LORD GAVE AND THE LORD HATH TAKEN AWAY. BLESSED BE THE NAME OF THE LORD. THIS TABLET IS ERECTED BY A FEW FRIENDS.

He found a pew in a far corner of the transept and sat down and surrendered to remembering again. Presently his forehead tilted to the bench before him.

"Sir." Abe felt a hand on his shoulder. A bent old man stood beside him. "We're locking up, sir. It's after seven."

"Oh. Sure." He stood erect, sinews protesting. "I didn't notice it getting late."

"No sir. We're almost at the longest day of the year." The creases of the ancient face stirred in a smile. "Even long days are good for prayer."

"I guess so, sure," Abe said and went slowly by down the aisle. He stopped then involuntarily, and found himself staring again at the gravestone set eye-level in the cathedral wall. He looked back; the old man stood in the shadow of the transept, watching. "Sexton," and the soft shuffle of the old man's felt socks neared, "do you know what happened when these people drowned?"

"I've only been here thirty-nine years," he peered at the lettering, his humped shoulder at Abe's arm. "It may have been the big flood — that biggest one before this last one, a few years after the last war. Three ladies and a gentleman. It must have been very tragic, that." His rheumy eyes lifted to Abe. "Are you perhaps related, sir?"

"No — no, nothing like that. It's —", he hesitated, faced with choosing words where he vaguely felt, "— there's an odd expression for a tombstone: 'erected by a few friends.'"

"Odd, sir?"

"Well yes, as if a lot of other so-called friends didn't care to —" he shrugged, feeling a little foolish.

"I don't know, sir. Perhaps they only had a few friends."

"Sure. Probably." He turned and went towards the door. "Thank you for keeping your church open."

The old man was following. "We're happy you came, sir. There's few enough that do, except to look a little."

He was outside in the high portico and heard the bar scrape into place. For a moment there was no traffic on the street but even so momentarily he could not push himself out. He leaned against the wall, and felt the corner of the plate in his back; he looked at it.

> WHOSOEVER THOU ART THAT COMEST TO THIS CHURCH, ENTER IT NOT WITHOUT THE SPIRIT OF REVERENCE, LEAVE IT NOT WITHOUT A PRAYER FOR THOSE WHO WORSHIP HERE, FOR THOSE WHO MINISTER, AND FOR THYSELF, AND MAY GOD'S PEACE DESCEND UPON YOU AND ABIDE WITH YOU.

Strange, he had not seen it the last time he was here. Only on churches did plaques express dreams — probably "thee's" and "thou's" help — he went out.

On Portage Jim was already waiting before the restaurant. "Hello Abe. You look great!"

"Sure, bloodshot eyes and all!" Jim was grinning easily. "I can't remember much after the dancing started. Did you get me to the apartment?"

"Who else? You were walking fine, but I thought you might need a reminder about this. Good thing I called."

"How'd you get my phone number?"

"You told me yourself, very carefully, climbing out of the car. Made me write it down. You don't remember?"

"No," he said finally, "after the fourth I'm stiff, absolutely." He turned and grinned, "But they've never put me off my feet, even if I can't remember a thing. It serves you right — you wouldn't let me go when the going was good."

"Aw go on," Jim laughed, "I was further than you, only I can always remember, worse luck; com'mon," he pushed open the restaurant door. "A little wine and a pound steak will set you up."

When they had finished their ordering ceremony, which consisted largely of Jim's flirting with the plain-faced waitress, Jim leaned back, glass high. "Abe old man, this is what I like.

A friend, a drink, and good food coming up. I'd of had you to my flat but I can't cook worth a damn. Man, was I surprised to meet you at the auditorium last night. Had to look three times to make sure, behind that bush! Where've you been since the army?"

"Oh, knocking around a while, but Frobisher mostly. Actually, it's twelve years. I've been in Winnipeg about two weeks now." He added deliberately, "I haven't been up to Selkirk."

Jim said quickly, "Old home town. A guy doesn't know it, but he has fun when he's a kid," he stopped suddenly, then laughed too heartily. "At school, anyway. Remember sneaking down to the docks at noon when the fish boats were in. Or heaving guys down the spiral fire escape on their birthday — dammit," he laughed. "That time we poured down a pail of water first and threw Porky McLeish after it!"

Despite his apprehension, at the known laughing face before him the laughter rose in Abe, "And right by surly Baldwin's window, his face busting out red when he stuck it out to scare every kid on the schoolyard."

"Yeah, even Vicki Herman! Who didn't give a damn about anything. Except getting laid by the hockey team. Did —" the waitress appeared beside their table with the huge steaks. Jim said nothing until she had served them, then with a grin as his eyes followed her, "— I guess you never fell into Vicki's all-welcoming arms."

Abe said slowly, "I wasn't allowed to play inter-school sports." He looked at Jim's handsome face, and then they both roared together. "Hockey — I meant." He savored again the discovery that what of the past you could laugh at turned innocuous; he suddenly felt like saying something he had never before admitted aloud, "You know, I watched her rear waggle by more than any other girl in the class; but I wouldn't of been caught dead talking to her."

Jim's laugh struggled with amazement, "Yeah! Cats, nobody ever thought it, that's sure."

"I covered up enough, I guess. And they were too busy calling me 'Barnyard' because of my eight-ounce denims to —"

"Don't forget 'Brainy' too," Jim interjected, face slightly red.

"That I haven't," and at his expression they were laughing together, completely.

"Say!" Head bent to his salad, Jim's roguish glance topped his glass-rims as if he had found more than he expected, "Maybe my old man wouldn't have been so set on making me get to the Presbyterian Church every Sunday if he'd known the preacher's son surveyed the lay of the shanks as they swayed by so —"

Despite his beard, Abe's face betrayed him and Jim's levity caught in his teeth. "Sorry. I guess I forgot you and your fa — you weren't around Selkirk — when we were in grade twelve," he finished lamely.

"Forget it," Abe said, eyes down — a stupidity to come — and the silence grew so ponderous he heaved himself away from his anger at himself and said the first thing that fell into his consciousness, "Did Miss Milne stay — that next year?"

"You remember her too?" — no in the war just dreaming of her and that teen agony of happiness and shame in her classes facing her beauty — "No, one year was enough, too much probably. She probably went to a monastery next year, only she wasn't RC. Gad, she was nice; and liked literature. You felt she'd of taught it even if nobody paid her — you know —" he looked at Abe, almost self-conscious suddenly.

"Did you think that then?"

"Ha — not this little rat! I was worse than most, as I guess you remember. But she used to be so pains-taking — like with us reading Shakespeare — and who cared about Shakespeare? — so we'd know what was going on and *see* it on the stage. Remember she tried so hard with big Olga reading Lady Macbeth's part, and every time Olga'd read 'Out, out, damned spot,' at no matter what speed or accent it still sounded like she was bellowing at some flea-bitten black and white bitch to get out from under the table!"

In their united laughter the blight of remembrance faded to obscurity. Abe said, "There was only one girl in our class that could really act — Joan Landis, the queen of the —"

A whiff of some off-hand conversation long ago teased him.

"Say didn't somebody overseas tell me once that you were — isn't she your —" he stopped because Jim was looking at him with a blank too total for continued speech — god what Selkirk curse was uprooted now? —

Jim cut a piece of steak precisely. "Yeah, you haven't been around." His voice was blank. "Yeah, I married — I chased her long enough — all through high school, every leave. And did she like getting chased — you know, give nothing but a sort of peck now and then and dwaddle you and ten other guys around. Act —" he laughed hard and then spoke quickly, as if the words fell from a precipice, "that was all there was to her — acting — show — like a head on beer. Only she was nothing beyond the froth. She forgot herself once just long enough — or maybe it was the second lieutenant uniform — anyway, we got married three days before I shipped overseas in '41 and the kid was born long before I ever saw her again. Her letters were always so whiny but I just thought it was hard on her being alone for so long, but it wasn't that. Not much." The waitress appeared again with the menu and they said nothing while deciding on dessert. Finally Jim pointed to his choice. As the girl left with a flounce of her wine skirt Abe opened his mouth to shift directions, but Jim, immobile on the memory, was already speaking.

"I don't know why I feel like talking to you — but you've got that long quiet face behind such a biblical beard — and we knew each other for a while — before, when we were all kids before the world caught up with us — I don't know." He paused and the waitress returned with their pie. "Thank you," he said with smile that reflected in her eyes. "What did you think of her in high school — Joan?"

"I —" Abe stumbled, "I thought she was a nice girl — clever, probably lots of fun. Enough guys thought so."

Jim was studying him with direct intentness, "You never went out with girls in Selkirk did you?"

"That's right. Too many cows in the Ross barn." But he might have spared himself the bitterness of that memory for Jim was beyond mis-tracking with a joke.

"Joan would have liked to go with you."

"Sure! With shorty Barnyard!"

"I'm not kidding. She told me once, but I hooted her. I sure never would of told you, then." Jim's expression sullied. "Yeah, she was fun to be with on kids dates — in those days when you went in crowds, daringly intimate if you stood shoulder to shoulder. Small town farm kids. But man, that's no way when your sack's packed and you're boarding sub-bait for Europe, even if you're going in the Information Squad. Just batting long lashes and holding hands isn't quite enough. I guess in the excitement of '41 she rather felt so too — anyway she forgot herself and didn't I hear it when I got back after. Ooh — didn't I."

He jabbed at the cream pie and swallowed two pieces quickly. The motion reminded Abe suddenly of the way Jim would scoop a backhand at the opposing goalie, a backhand that even in grade eleven had made him the most feared defenseman on the Selkirk team. He did not try to interrupt the savage monologue that unrolled in his hearing. He ate, watching the emotions shift on the face opposite him.

"I don't know how long it was when I was back but it wasn't very long — probably already in her letters, at least she was complaining how there was nothing to do but take care of the kid and she couldn't go out and the war was taking so long — as if we were slogging up the Italian boot because we liked the scenery! So I can't remember for sure, even if it was worth it, how soon I heard her whining, 'You made me marry you! If you'd been a gentleman you'd of never taken advantage of me' — you know the kind of bosh. Well maybe you don't because you've never been married —"

Abe murmured, "That's right," but the other went on without looking up,

"You've been around and know what makes the world spin, like Granger said last night. Anyway, I had a rough time for a few years; getting a job with all the guys back was no cinch. We come to Winnipeg to get some college at night and things were pretty thin for us. They were for lots of people. But it wasn't as if we were really going anywhere together. James Jr. was growing up and her whining and living in a little hole and me just barely holding on to a photographer's job at the Press — it got down-right hellish — "

He stared into his coffee cup for a long time. "I don't know how you do these things, Abe, but there's certain things I can't do without forever. She was still pretty as anything. You know — if she'd only wanted she could of had me working like a slave for her. I was, really. She was lovely and I loved her. But whine, whine — and she'd had a hard time with James — he was wrong way being born or something and she didn't want any more children. She didn't really care much for sex, not even when she kind of forgot herself once in a while. Let me tell you, it's worse to live in a house with a nice-looking woman who goes stiff as a post whenever you touch her. Who finally works out a schedule when you can make love like — like a damn commuter time table or something, and even then just lies back and *endures* till you'd like to hurt her till she screams or throw her out of sight and never even spit at her again and even when you're thinking this when you should be past any such stupidity as thinking you know that soon enough you'll feel cheaper than scum on a drain puddle at what you done to her. You can live with that sort of thing for five years maybe, but you can't forever. It's over ten years since we've divorced."

"Divorced?"

"Yeah," and Jim seemed to understand perfectly Abe's inflection. "Divorced. You can't get one in this country without humiliation, but it gets so you're quite willing to put up with one short grinding of your nose in the public mud than a life-long grinding in your own."

"What about —" Abe hesitated, and Jim laughed slightly.

"The boy? Well, of course she was the defendant so she got custody. They live in Vancouver now. He's a freshman at UBC. I see him about once a year. There isn't much to talk about."

Their intimate table at one side of the restaurant: like the carefully preserved wooden confessionals along the nave in the Basilica. Only here there was no screen to pretend confessor anonymity, nor any penance to pronounce for absolution. Only pain, and nothing ex cathedra to offer in return but a half-hesitant smile of understanding, sympathy. And, if he admitted it, a tinge of coldness — envy? — even priests in confessionals, living as solitaries perhaps to somehow lift them above the grips of the all-too-human, could not avoid the inevitable two sides of each story. For true priests, perhaps three. But that third, as the second, was meaningless here. So what he could do was sit, as he did, saying nothing, his presence a silent shrift where no penance was asked or absolution possible until — where can you find even a restaurant priest when words themselves are what's impossible? — Jim's abrupt gaiety nicked him:

"Well Abie boy, what's doin' tonight?" In a few moments, after appropriate genuflections to waitress and cashier, they were out on the sidewalk nearly cool in the early summer evening. The tiny lights stretched down the length of Portage; over a white-marble capped building sat the exact half of a moon. They walked slowly, heels clicking together. "Lovely evening."

Abe nodded. The remembrance of the boy and the woman several evenings before slowly thrust up in his thoughts, but he had run that tyranny out of him, at least for a little. "See that?" Jim nudged him. A man and a girl in high heels were rapt at the fluffed radiance of a wedding dress in a window. "Marriage — like births and funerals — all the so-called great events of life — supported and elaborated and decked out by advertising." His tone was bitter, as if they had never interrupted their table discussion. "I'm in advertising and brother I know. Flattery — that's all that it's based on. Those kids could get yoked — that's the right word too — as easily for five bucks in front of a J. P. — that's where they'll stand anyway when they want out — but hell it's got to cost a bride at least $500 for her one-hour climb into bed!"

"You knocking your own work?"

Jim laughed hard, "Are you kidding? I'm in because it suits my style and it's good money."

Abe shrugged as they paused at a light, evasive. "Some people wouldn't work a life-time at something they thought was—" he hesitated, "wasn't really worth much."

"Don't get me wrong — advertising's worth lots. It makes people feel good. That little girl really wants to spend $200 on a dress she'll only wear once and—"

"You're going in circles! First you say advertisers push weddings to make money and then it's okay because it just takes advantage of the feelings of the bride anyway. It doesn't make sense."

"Sure it does!" The quick turn of Jim's head was still the swift assertion of the high-schooler. "They're cashing in on female weakness."

"Is it so bad women want to be beautiful?"

"Who said? The more the better is just fine. But why've you got to tie it together with marriage? That's too permanent a noose for a few hours delusion. You wouldn't believe how many men I meet who tell me, 'Boy, I wish I had your nerve and cut out of this married life.'"

"Lots of people are happily married."

"Yeah, and they should stay married. Somebody's got to raise kids. But we're civilized, aren't we? If I don't want to wash my shirts, I pay a laundry; if I don't like to cook I pay a restaurant. Why hang a washerwoman or cook around my neck? So if I want some loving, I arrange for some girl and pay her like I pay anyone else. Business, strictly. There are plenty of decent business girls in this town glad to earn a few bucks for a pleasant evening. And you won't find them sneaking around Main and Henry."

Abe was trying to decipher the grim concentration on the sharp handsome face. "You believe that?"

"Yeah I believe it! I've been married and unmarried long enough. You shouldn't have to find a dirty cathouse if you —"

"I wasn't talking about that," Abe said. "But about marriage being just one forever crawling into bed."

Jim flicked a glance at him, half-grin, half-serious. "You never been married? Yeah, well I never try to wreck dreams; and I wouldn't knock real love. There's something so great about real love that — " he could only gesture, looking awry still. "But you yourself prove that that's very hard come by. And, real love or not, need persists. If a man has enough to drink and eat his next strongest need is sex, right? So — what do you do about that?"

"Needs, sure, but is a person always just pushed around by his belly?"

"Excuse me," Abe felt a touch on his arm and they both turned. A short man with bushy white hair and a benign face smiled at their start. "I couldn't help but overhear what you were saying," he smiled, his voice as low as a rumble of thunder. "You're quite right, sir. To speak of 'wants' or 'needs' is out-dated in today's psychology. We look for values rather than purely bodily needs, because values seem to determine needs, even about such fundamental human functions as eating food. In some countries holy men, for example, do not seem to really need food for fifteen, twenty days. Their beliefs apparently affect their bodily functions. And in any case, sex is grossly, grossly overplayed. Value, the search for meaning, counts." He bowed, "Excuse me, gentlemen, the light," turned and walked across Portage. When he reached the center boulevard the light flicked red but he went on as if immune to harm and the surge of cars squealed by, his short white-topped figure lost.

"What the heck," Jim said finally, staring. "Did you hear that beautiful voice? And perfect diction. They ought to have him on the CBC."

"To read ads for toilet soap?"

Jim said seriously, "Or something like —" and then they laughed together. "Look," Jim said at last, hiccoughing slightly, "that's enough serious talk for one night. We've missed this damn light about a dozen times. Where are we going, anyhow?"

Abe said slowly, momentarily drained clean, "Why go anywhere?"

"Well, we can't just stand here on the street corner and laugh — even though we're trying." He looked at his wrist. "It's too late for a movie — I was going to call up some girls earlier but now I wouldn't dare suggest it." He laughed. "Well, how about going down to Club 77 and hear Schwafe at the piano? I could listen to that guy play until —"

"No," Abe said quickly, "Some other club if you like."

Jim began, "I just thought you might —" then stopped. They walked in silence a moment. "There's the Red Vine about three blocks over, near my car actually. It's not bad."

The head waiter showed them to a table. "The floor-show

will be on in a few minutes. Would you like the card, Mr. MacLaren?"

"Well, let's see. No, don't bother, George. A dry martini'd be fine."

"And you sir? Would you like the card, sir?"

"Just a beer."

"Any particular brand, sir?"

"It doesn't matter."

They sat silent until their drinks came. Jim said, "I'd of thought an Arctic man would be a heavy drinker when he got out where he could get it."

"Enough of them are." Abe tilted his bottle and watched the froth rise. "You saw me last night. One drink a day is plenty."

"You keep it at that when you're up north? Aren't there any whites at your store at all?"

"No, I had one of the three one-man stores left and you don't sell liquor to Eskimos. Every year I got a small drum of whiskey — one drink a day, with one extra on holidays — that's anything special. No more."

Jim looked at him and shook his head, grinning. "Rigid."

"You have to be. You don't last the dead of winter otherwise."

"Go off your rocker, eh?"

"Bushed, as we call it. Company men hardly ever, they're carefully picked and trained, but DEW line men quite a bit. They go up to make fast money, but a month is still a month long whether you earn $900 or $300." He almost grinned. "Shoot, after twelve years up there I think I'd go bushed one winter in Winnipeg!"

"In this town that's known as 'normal adjustment,'" Jim laughed. "Going back soon?"

After a hesitation Abe said, "I don't know." This question too he had dreaded, knowing it inevitable, but at least there was no common knowledge to avoid. He shrugged. "I can't seem to make up my mind this time."

"Well, you've plenty of time, eh?"

"Not much. They've been waiting — just being good to me; mostly Horst Jeffer's doing. You know him?"

"Big guy with a long face and hardly no hair?"
"That's him."
"Yeah. He shows up at the Chamber once in a while."
"He's a perfect boss — at least I can't imagine a better. I came out the second of May and I had two months but," he shrugged again.
"Got any other leads?"
"I'm still looking around." The beer-head, he noticed, had shrunk away.
"I can't believe it!" Jim exclaimed. "A Manitoba Scot who doesn't know where his next paycheck's coming from! An ex-Frobisher man should be able — say," a thought seemed to catch him and he hesitated. "This is still confidential, but maybe Kin would have something. He's moving north."
"That northern air freight? He talked to me about it today."
"He did? He must have been impressed with you last night! Maybe it was the way you danced," Jim laughed into his martini but Abe did not hear him. For a moment they sat silent under the faint red light of the nightclub. Finally Jim said, "Did he tell you anything definite?"
"Huh?" he looked up. "Oh. He said they needed a manager at Churchill — handle the work there and north. He offered me the job."
"Say," Jim whistled softly, "you really got through to him."
"He needs a man badly."
"Yeah, he does, but that wouldn't make a difference to Kin. He'd sooner wait a year than start with a weak manager. He can afford to wait. Then you're all fixed up."
"Well —"
"You mean you're hesitating? Man, on the ground floor of the biggest thing that happened to the north since Frobisher? You know the Arctic — everything's booming and transportation's the big cog. And in Churchill you're right on the edge of the barrens. You can come out any time you want, on your own planes, and virtual head of what'll be a multi-million operation, not just handing out credit to fifty Eskimos a year. You're set!"

With his finger Abe was tracing an invisible design on the beer pad. "If I want to be."

"You mean you might not?"

"I just mean I — I don't know."

Jim emptied his glass as if something in his presence was being violated. "You got anything against that kind of work?"

"No, not really —"

"Hell," Jim put down his glass, "I spend all my lousy life trying to get in the ten-thousand-a-year bracket. At forty I'm over the edge, finally. Without money in this country you've got nothing. You can't do nothing. You are nothing. And after twelve years with Frobisher I bet you're not getting half what Kin offered you to start, right? And you don't know!"

Abe could not doubt it: Jim was giving him the best advice he knew; there was nothing for it but smile. "I'm not exactly ready to give up money! But I can make enough, for myself at pretty well anything. I guess I don't know what I want. Maybe," and he stopped, for it sank through him, "maybe it's like the old man said. If I knew my values maybe I —" the totally incredible encounter, a thunder-peal on a cloudless day, crushed in him like glass the six-weeks' thought and left intact only one question: "Jim, we're forty years old. We've finished the biggest part of our life and what have we used it up for?"

"That ivory-towered coot? He wouldn't know a need if it knocked him down in the street. And then he'd have to try it out on monkeys first to find out what was going on."

Abe laughed a little — just as well it missed just as well — and hunched forward in his seat, "Ahh," he shook himself as if surfacing after a plunge, "let's get off it." He became aware of a rhythm, somewhere. "What's going on here anyway?" He lifted a huge swallow of beer as Jim grinned.

"Suits me. It wasn't me playing philosopher. This place is usually okay for fun." Looking past him, for the first time Abe was aware of the Red Vine. The table at which they sat was one of a double row set like buds on the main trunk of the narrow room that based in the immense crystal glitter of the bar to his right, led past them in a wide red-plush aisle and widened abruptly to his left, radiating into narrow spurs between tables bunched by people: suits, shoulders, dresses gleaming blue and flesh and green in the reddish light of the lanterns; and at the head, in the blaze of the spotlight, a small band with woman singer clustered around a microphone. He realized he had heard them somewhere in his inattention, but now he listened to the word droned with conveyor-belt lifelessness from the woman's yawning mouth:

> *"You made me love you,*
> *I didn't want to do it,*
> *I didn't want to do it;*
> *You made me want you*
> *And all the time —"*

"She's no Patti Page but her figure's not bad — pretty good, really — but hell," Jim's concentration deflated, "a nose! Her mother was scared by a rhinoceros! How'd they ever let that in here?"

Abe smiled; the girl stood stiff behind the microphone but her arms and hands jogging in a kind of hypnotized rhythm, her round shoulders dead white against the red backdrop like an exhausted flower. After a time she retreated to shake noisemakers while the band played dance music, flipping the tune from muted trumpet to piano to guitar to the rhythm of the brushed and beaten drum. Couples danced. The waitress brought Jim another martini, her dress and face gleaming sleek as if she had just been pulled through an oil douche, her hair still in the strained impossible erectness of the pull. Jim drank quickly, his face glistening. "I feel like dancing."

Abe roused from his blankness and grinned. "Sorry. I don't."

"Joker. Though I could take you to a dive where that wouldn't be so out of place. I was actually looking at those girls at the table there," he gestured across the room. "No escorts. We could help two of them out."

"Go ahead."

Jim stood erect, "Com'mon! You could just talk if you don't want to dance."

"Thanks. I'll finish my beer and lean back and do nothing."

Jim hesitated, began sitting down. "Dammit, I asked you out to spend the evening with you. There's always broads around —"

"Go on," Abe gestured, laughing. "Have a dance or two. You want to, and I'm old enough to sit alone! Beat it."

"Okay I'll leave. But be careful — I want you to remember the rest of the evening."

The clash of merriment was everywhere now. The laughter of women flashed bright and high through the pall of noise. The tempo of the music suddenly halted; the guitarist was at the microphone, "That was wonderful ladies and gentlemen — you just made a wonderful dance here. So," he mopped his forehead, the handkerchief white in the spotlight, "we're one big happy family — just having fun and enjoying ourselves, so let's have a sing-song — eh? If you'll pick up the song sheets, just call out your favorite and I'll try my best — hahaha — to stay with you and you just sing just as loud as you want. Okay — any favorites — number seventeen — fine — 'Shine on Harvest Moon' — good — a little early in the year, but a wonderful idea — okay, all together now — Shine on, shine —" and his voice swooped into the song, mouth mugging the microphone, the band crescendoing behind him.

The first song went poorly, but by the second and third the hand-clapping, foot-beating, and the drink-slurred voices had gotten astride the tempo. All around Abe they rocked, the melody barked out of glistening red faces, the singer at the mike swaying, smile frozen at the end of the spotlight shaft poking through the haze. Suddenly Abe knew this was too raucous, too deafening to be endured, too much inchoate and then blazingly developed ripping back and forth of all possible physical and beyond physical sensation like the revival crusade he had been at the week before, drawn by the block letters in the newspaper 'GET RIGHT WITH GOD * CHRIST IS THE ANSWER * Prayer for the needy every evening', and he had succumbed to a sudden inexplicable longing curiosity which he had not since dared define in thought and gone to the shoddy building where the strident voice of the preacher yelped above the rock-crusher tones

61

of the girl singing in a black dress and bilegreen corduroy vest with her face wiped pale of make-up and her electric guitar galloping like a fiend to the inferno; and as he now sat, beaten by clamor, wails, shouts, barks, foot-stomping, and the low-toned whispers from the adjacent tables all ran together in one grinding cacophony halleluja amen when my baby smiles at me that kind of love brings sweet harmony god is moving by his spirit can you say praise the lord rock me again like we did last summer rock me again like we did last year my religion's not old-fashioned but its ree-al gen-u-ine two and two make four like they did in rye whiskey rye whiskey you've been my baby do i just love playing footsy under the table with you but i feel strong we're beyond drink drink drink let the glass clink let every true lover say jesus jesus jesus oh my jesus put your arms around me honey huddle up and cuddle up with god's gonna have a rejoicing people you might as well get used to it on earth 'cause in heav me a kiss by wire baby my heart's on fire if you refuse if he's a bull he has to have a horn maybe he's a short ho men hallelujah the lord set us free free free so i can sing and dance and show some power for the lor did you have to leave me to this loneliness with my arms all empty of your close honey you better take your hand away from there or i can't be held responsible i feel the fire burning i feel the fire burning i got just what i take me o take me baby and make lo hallelujah praise the lor eeyyy iiiii god's got a bandwagon that's already won the victor make make make make lu-u-u-u-ve to me o jesus jesus jesus how i love you jesus safe in your arms o darling safe on your gentle breast there by your love i got just what i wanted i got just what i needed

As if dropped into a void, suddenly all was gone. After a moment Abe realized he was slumped down on the red-leather seat, head in his arms as if to shield something vital from annihilation. He sat up then, looked across the room and without a break of movement rose and went to the table where Jim was leaning back, picking up the conservation with the three girls. "Jim, I'm sorry to interrupt, but it's late and I'm going."

"Sure, Abe. Just a sec and I'll —" Jim stood up quickly.

Outside the midnight air wafted the nightclub away into fetid forgottenness. Abe breathed deeply; the moon had moved behind clouds. Jim muttered, "Glad you come. You can't imagine three more perfect duds — gad!" He yawned. "Want to do anything yet?"

"No. I'm finished tonight."

"Yeah. I work tomorrow — supposedly. Two nights like this — com'mon, the car's a block over."

The big car eased down the streets washed under light. Jim chatted, but from the silent walking Abe was already in that suspension of thought he knew well enough. Just a few minutes: he forced concentration. Jim was saying ". . . really growing. You hardly know it one year to the next."

He said, making conversation, "You come here right after the army?"

"Oh, we tried Selkirk a while, but there was nothing doing there. Let's see, I got out that September and — yeah, your mother died next February, eh?, and it was just after that we come to Winnipeg. I got on part-time at the Press."

Abe said slowly, "What?"

The streetlight glinted over Jim's glasses, his profile momentarily outlined in white. "Yeah. February '46."

"My mother died in February, 1946?"

"Why sure, I remember becau —" Jim stared at him, the car seeming motionless on the smooth pavement, "Good god, you don't mean you didn't know!"

His eyes were intent on the road. "I said I hadn't been to Selkirk."

"I thought this-s —" Jim's voice faded.

"Ever."

They rode on a moment, then Jim burst out, "But it's over thirteen — no, over — and your father —"

"Here's the block," Abe cut in sharply. "Don't bother going around the back, I'll go in from here. The side entrance has a different key and the caretaker will be in bed by now." He could stop talking then for the car halted. He looked at the other's stricken face. "It's okay Jim, you couldn't know. And thanks for the evening. I'll call you in a coupla days."

He was back in the apartment, the window opened to the

puff of the night wind. He took off his clothes, hung them in the closet, and lay down on the bed. The murmur of the night city far below, blasted sometimes by an exhaust, eddied through the window. He had always known it would come so out of nothing. But so long ago. You always think silence means — and surely it will hold off when you are already so thought-battered. But there it was. And her memory, brilliant in a few cherished flashes, drove him the more inevitably to explicate hour by hour what had tangled him in confusion those hours in the cathedral: the last months on the barrens. . . .

Part Two

4

I was in the storeroom that afternoon getting ready two sled loads of supplies when the dogs began to howl outside. From their tone a team must be approaching so I climb out, up on the drifts that cover all but the roofs of Tyrel Bay post. The short February afternoon is gray over the snow and the wind rising in a falling temperature. Paliayak and several of his people are already beside the mounds of their houses, looking west. In that direction we still hope: the fall caribou must have gone south there for only stragglers came down the usual eastern branch of migration and Paliayak's camp, which hunts east and south, just made Tyrel Bay the week before. With three of nineteen people lost to the long January hunger. Squinting against the gloom, I finally make out the dot moving where the curve of the bay would have been except for the level drifts. The figure seems barely to move; there can be only two, at most three, dogs on the sled. I shout to John on the blue roof of the store, swept bare by the wind, "Take the light sled and four dogs." In a few moments he is gone, dogs running madly. I go down into the store to brew tea and stir the beans. Beans. Eight hundred pounds of uncooked beans neatly labelled "Emergency Rations" for a land without a natural fuel supply. And the one government plane that came in just before the darkness hasn't returned to correct what may be mix-up, may be stupidity. Even after soaking six hours, it takes a rolling three-hour boil to cook a potful.

Beside the stove two of the four children staying in my room because of their frost-bite play intently with a ball of string. I watch them rolling the ball back and forth, the string running out like a track over the floor and then rolling up again. They are warm and full of food; the aroma of beans drifts through the store. The children play without a sound.

When the barking approaches, I go out. It is bitterly cold now with the wind still rising, but all the people are standing by the two houses watching the approach. In a few moments John draws up; he has picked up the driver, two dogs and little sled without bothering to unhitch anything. The dogs are barely skeletons. They lie motionless on the sled, and when the man lifts his face to us for a long moment I can see only starvation; then I recognize Keluah, Ikpuck's younger brother. We lift him from the sled and into the store. The little children look up as we come in, then run quickly to their mother who is in the group that follows.

After he has drunk three mugs of tea I ask Keluah in the language of the people, "You come from Ikpuck?" He nods. "Does his family have meat and fuel?"

His mouth moves, reluctantly, "No."

The circle of brown faces stirs but no one says a word. I ask, "Where is the camp?"

"On Dubawnt Lake, with the others."

"What others?"

"Turatuk. Vukarsee. Nakown. Lootevek." He speaks as if behind his closed eyelids he sees the grouped humps of snow houses on the long shore of the lake. It is at least ninety miles from Tyrel Bay, and there is no need to ask whether the others had food.

"Why did you all camp at the lake?"

Keluah lies on the blankets against the counter; it takes a long time for him to speak. "Some deer came last fall, but not much. We hunted, shooting stragglers and here and there a small herd. But there were not enough for caches, we always ate everything we killed. A little after the twilight came Ikpuck found a good herd at Dubawnt Lake. We killed them all, and we could again lick the blood from our hands and our bellies were full. But the others had found nothing for many days, and they camped at Dubawnt one by one when they had no food. We fished. But we have no meat since the middle of the darkness."

Incredibly, not one clear hint of this has reached the post. But there has been no movement this winter: the weather unbelievably bad and the foxes at low ebb. If the reconnaissance plane had only come after I sent John to Baker Lake in early January — but it did not and that thought is useless. Three weeks without food during the darkness. Forty-five people in six camps traded west last fall — and then I remember. "Keluah," I say quickly, "Where is the camp of Itooi?" The largest of the western camps, it contains ten people, the families of Itooi and his brother-in-law Ukwa.

The man lifts his gaunt face from the cup of broth John is giving him. "Itooi would not stay at the lake when the deer were gone. He said the few fish would give out too and we would all die in one place. He and Ukwa went south to the Front River, they said."

"Have the fish given out at Dubawnt?"

"Yes."

"Have some of the people died?"

Keluah is slowly drinking the soup, the muscles of his cheek working to control himself before his hunger. Finally he pulls back and lifts seven fingers. "I left so long ago, with the last dogs. But some had died." There is no need to say he was the strongest man left in the camp. Ninety miles in seven days, with a blizzard only two days before.

Paliayak is looking at Keluah, reading every hour of that fight in the frost-black face. I say to him carefully, "Can you make up two teams from your dogs? Are there three men who can travel?"

He nods his huge head. "We can."

"I wanted us to rest at least another day, but now we cannot. One could take four of my best dogs and the small sled to Baker Lake. If the weather holds, perhaps in three days. I could send a message to take to the Mounted Police, to fly out with food. Two could come with me, with loads for Dubawnt."

Paliayak says heavily, "It will blizzard soon — two-three hours."

"Will it be too bad to travel?"

"Perhaps." He shrugs.

I look at them all standing in a circle around Keluah who is always slumped down, his mouth hanging slack as in sleep. They are the people of this land and they know better than I what is ahead on this trail, but I do not have to ask them if they will. "The blizzard will have to take care of itself; we have no time to wait for it." A fleeting smile touches the faces of the people. Then we move quickly to complete our preparations.

Though the wind continues to rise from the north and the ground-drift whirls about our legs and over the dogs, especially in the hollows of the land, it does not snow and the sky remains clear. We have the moon and the trail at first needs no breaking. As I jog along this seems an ordinary dead-of-winter trip, where the only matters to watch for are frostbite and over-fatigue. Ordinary, if I did not have to keep sharp eye on my two companions to make sure they keep up even though my sled is too heavy for six dogs. And if, above all, I did not know that waiting for us were the people and that even an hour longer could make all the difference for some of them. That Paliayak's son Atchuk will get through to Baker Lake is as sure as anything can be; next to his father he is the best man in the band and with the light sled and fresh dogs he cannot fail. Except for the unexpected. But Itooi early taught me that the margin of safety on the barrens is so narrow that if the dangerous unexpected comes it is almost inevitably fatal; therefore it can be disregarded. Do your best and if it fails you will not likely have another chance. Atchuk: a hundred and fifty miles in about the time we make ninety. If the weather is even barely flyable the plane will be in Dubawnt within two hours from Baker Lake; arriving perhaps as quickly as we. They will fly immediately, beyond doubt; emergency sloughs bureaucracy aside, thank god. But verified emergencies are often already too late. That too is a fact of the Arctic barrens. For the whole matter depends on the plane. With no more dogs left in the camp, we cannot hope to get all the people out with our three sleds. Besides, the bigger the loads we haul in, the more dogs we need and the more food for them we need and if we are held by a blizzard even for a few days — and in this season we cannot expect to get away without one — then it is a question whether the food and fuel oil we are pulling down the trail now against the side-blast of the wind will be of any help at all to the thirty-five persons at Dubawnt, except to slightly prolong their pain. And as for Itooi's camp —

I stop thinking about it. If the people are to be saved at all it will have to be the plane; if it comes the loads we are now hauling will make a difference. What we need now is a mug-up. I whistle to the dogs.

My oil-stove is already warm under the tea-pail when Paliayak and Nukak pull up out of the darkness. We slump in the lee of my sled, faces near the meagre warmth. Presently Paliayak says, "Maybe the blizzard won't come. See, the lights." They have emerged as we went, out of the east and northern sky: a great white-frozen band tinged pink that flimmers and shifts over the endless level of the land. There are still no clouds, and now perhaps there will be none for a little. Under the lights the winter darkness softens and the land spreads blank around us to an horizonless silver. Once when we rested on the trail Itooi told me that lights were the souls of unborn children playing with their umbilical cords. Even after years between this land and sky, the lights can touch terror. I look at the other two and they smile grimly. "It is good," I say. "We will move until the weather turns."

We cannot do quite that. Eighteen hours later we are two-thirds of the way to Dubawnt and we must make a sleep-stop. The weather has held, fiercely cold but steady; for five hours I have been pulling with the dogs. Quickly we build a snow house, feed the dogs, gnaw some frozen meat washed down by tea and crawl into the robes. In ten hours we are on our way again, not rested but moving. And the weather holds, the temperature about fifty below. I pull with the dogs immediately as do the others but we are moving across the coarser grain of the land now and we make less than twenty miles in eight hours. In the last two the snow begins to sting head-on. We are almost to the lake-ice then and still perhaps ten miles from the camp, but we have to stop and risk the storm getting worse. We waste no fifteen minutes on a house but simply pull the sleds into a triangle and huddle in the robes in that shelter. Exhausted, we sleep. When I next look at my wristwatch in the darkness of the robe it is four hours later. Nearly noon. I cannot feel my left foot and I pull off mukluks and socks, massaging, until the pain comes back. Then I push half-erect. The wind shrieks but it is not yet full blizzard.

The wind shifts to the northeast after we take to the trail, which is lucky because the dogs could not have faced it for ten miles. Nor we. The lake, at least, has no eskers. There is still a trace of daylight left when we corner the last headland and see the mounds of the people's snow houses. The dogs rouse their last efforts and break into a trot at my urging. My leader even raises his head and howls, to be echoed feebly by some of the other dogs, but no answering sound comes from the camp. No figure emerges from the scattered houses even when I halloo as loudly as I can, running.

I stop at the first circle of houses and halloo again. Entrances blocked, I cannot see any tracks from one house to the next. I dig out my flashlight as Paliayak and Nukak pull up. Their faces are gaunt with exhaustion and without a sound the dogs drop in their traces. We trudge together to the nearest tunnel entrance. Paliayak pulls the block of snow aside; I bend to crawl, calling as cheerily as I can, "Someone from far has come for a visit," following the beam of my light down the long entrance.

The tunnel opens up into the house and when I get to the end I raise my head with the light. The beam flashes around the domed roof and against the worn caribou of the figure crouching almost at my face beside the entrance. My heart thuds as I struggle erect, the two behind me in the passage, "Hello! We've come from Tyrel Bay!" But the figure does not move, it is hunched forward over the stove, its hands palm-out to the heat and even as I lean forward I comprehend the house is dead cold. Paliayak's face emerges out of the entrance hole as I touch the shoulder. It topples like a stone; Turatuk, frozen rigid.

We stare at the face fallen over in the dirt against the empty oil-can, the body visible here and there through tatters of fur. No sound at all in the house, not even our breathing, and then I remember the sleeping bench along the back. Only a bumpy robe; I jerk it back and there lie Turatuk's wife and his seven year old son and baby daughter, in a row, as they slept.

Paliayak and Nukak have not moved out of the entrance. I fling the beam of light around the small house, but there is only the useless tin stove, dog skulls, bones, the empty oil drum, a few scattered pots, and the bodies. They have eaten everything — extra clothes, hides, the very dog bones are split for marrow. Someone has chewed the leather braided handle of Turatuk's dog whip. I say, "The other houses — there must be some still," and Nukak plunges out of sight with Paliayak behind him.

We go the round of the death encampment. In some houses weak voices answer when I call at the entrance and we crawl in. We empty one of the larger houses and Paliayak and Nukak help or carry the living to it, setting up stoves and melting water and heating meat while I run on, from house to house. I find several where the people, though alive, cannot answer my call so each must be searched. The darkness has long come when I have finished all the houses I can find. Of thirty-five people who should be here, we have found seventeen alive. Of the men only Ikpuck and Nakown remain; the hunters inevitably go first. I squat beside Ikpuck and in his face I cannot see the brightness of the isymatah, the leader of his people. He says, in my silence, "We sent Nayak to you in the middle of the great darkness. Then at last we sent also Keluah."

"Yes. Keluah told us. But Nayak never came."

"Ahhh," it is a sound deep in his throat.

"Ikpuck, we have searched all the houses here, three in

this group and four to the west, where you were. Are there others here? And have you heard of Itooi and Ukwa?"

Beyond Ikpuck, where Paliayak is doing woman's work, the fragrance of thawing meat fills the snowhouse with warmth and strength. Ikpuck does not move as he speaks, "One has not heard from Itooi. They were going back to camp on Front River, but one has not heard of them since the darkness."

"Yes," I say in his silence. "When the plane comes we will find them. Perhaps they have found the deer. Are there others here?"

After a moment he says, "Long ago Lootevek and his oldest son went on the hunt, but they did not come back. His wife — and his other children — are in their house beyond the others, over the little creek."

"So far away? If she is alone, why —" I stop.

Ikpuck says heavily, "She was asked to come here, several times. But she would not." As I move quickly to go Ikpuck looks up, fleetingly. "It would perhaps be well if two men went to that house."

I look at him an instant, at a loss to decipher his tone. "How many children?"

"Three."

Impossible. Outside I find Nukak unloading the last from my sled, and in a moment we are beating west along the shore. Under the overcast the wind drives like needles across the lake; it must be clear tomorrow if we are to expect the plane from Baker. One or two of the seventeen may not recover, but the rest surely will. And if Itooi's band has escaped with only one or two deaths and if Lootevek's wife and two children, or perhaps even three, remain, why out of the forty-five that had traded west at Tyrel Bay last fall twenty-seven or even twenty-eight are alive to — but I cannot face the thought at the moment: nor the fact that in ninety miles of travel we saw only two rabbits, no owls or fox tracks; nor that as far as I know only two men and three teen-age boys are left to this group of the people. I think rather of the people as they were last summer, happy, friendly, laughing together with their friends in the sunshine on the bay when the land briefly burst open with flowers. I rub the frostbite on my cheek. It seems very long again since I heard their laughter.

"There," says Nukak as the lead dog barks, then all howl in chorus. A small mound barely pokes out of a drift. We drive up, the dogs hushing. Lootevek always was a loner and his wife, a large strong woman, hardly ever smiled, but in the camps he seemed to lose some of the moroseness which fell on him when he lived near the store. I brace myself and push aside the entrance block. "Hallo! We have come from Tyrel Bay," I call, bending down into the tunnel.

And suddenly out of that black tunnel rises laughter.

The sound echoing in the narrowness is beyond measure more horrible than the silence we expect. I stop and Nukak's scramble behind me ceases. I cannot unravel thought; I can only shout, "We are coming," and lunge forward, Nukak at my heels. The house is dark but I fling the light-beam up before me and we are inside. It is as cold as the other houses, but on the sleeping bench Lootevek's wife sits erect, wearing her outside parka, her eyes glaring through matted hair, her mouth still hanging slack from the sound which greeted us. We stare at her. I move the light, but she is obviously the only person in the house.

"Where are the chil —" I begin but Nukak jogs my arm, gesturing to the floor. There are so many split bones lying about that I stumbled coming in. As I blink down at them now suddenly the woman laughs again. And in that shriek I understand.

There is no way to get her from the house but tie her in the sleeping robe and kick through the wall to the sled. We bring her to main camp and put her in a house by herself where her laughter will not terrify the rest of the people. Then, after several hours of feeding broth to those who cannot sit erect, I crawl into my sleeping bag.

Paliayak rouses me after eight hours; we go out, and clearly the blizzard that has been holding off is moving in over the lake from the north and east — the direction of Baker Lake. No plane on earth can get aloft in that. There is nothing to say, so we go back in and heat food. As we eat I explain a plan. He shakes his head, but helps load the sled. He stands looking after me as I urge the rested dogs out on the lake. Perhaps, with a light sled and rested dogs, I can cover the twenty-odd miles somewhere along which Itooi's Front River camp may be before the weight of the storm hits. And if forced to stop I can wait out the blizzard as well on the trail as in this dreadful camp. So we run.

When the blue shadow that precedes dawn comes up over the long white land breaking trail for the dogs is no easier for the wind rises inevitably, nagging loose snow, and the bank of cloud more clearly rolls higher behind me. About dawn I make out the ridges on the lakeshore between which the Front River breaks to the lake and I turn south. Once on the twisting river I cannot lose my way: I simply follow until I reach the camp. If Itooi has left the river — well, it is useless to think of that.

The diffuse sun-blob is as high as it will rise when between the van lashes of the storm I think I hear the echo of a plane. I am chewing meat as I run, not daring to stop for tea, but at that I stop and tear back my hood. There it is again! I stare around, the blood pounding in my head, searching for direction from the wind-torn sound. The dogs prick up their ears, and then I see the flash of it, between tags of drift, coming up over the esker from the south-east. I jerk the covering from the sled, clamber up a rock ridge and wave frantically. The snow swirls around me and the plane noses on obliviously west and north. Then, suddenly, it banks towards me. A red and silver Norseman; they must have radioed from Baker to Churchill and they risked a try into the storm. The plane roars over and I wave north-east towards the lake. It circles right, red light flashing. Don't be so stupid! And you know there's no place to land on the river bed or on the ridges! He passes over again, very low, so slowly the stall warning must be roaring in his ears. He dips and I see his face: Jimmy Hughes of Churchill. Swinging the tarp towards the lake, I scream at him though he cannot hear me, and he lifts up again into the wind. The wings waggle. He understands; and knows as well as I he's daring the face of the storm to try and unload, take on some of the people and get out before he's grounded.

In a few moments he will be over the camp from which I've been struggling four hours. If the storm had held off we could have searched — but there is no need for such thought, and I clamber down to the team.

Two hours later it is impossible. The blizzard has been upon us in full fury for over an hour and only because it is behind us could we still trek. In its blindness now I realize I could go within twenty feet of the camp never knowing. And I have to stop while I have enough strength to build a snowhouse. Suddenly the dogs whine behind me. I stop, look back at them and then ahead. There is nothing except the streaking snow. I get my mitt on my leader's collar. "Okay, com'mon."

We move ahead slowly, and then abruptly the snow darkens and a shape is floundering towards me. "Hallo!" I reach for the shoulder and head bent into the white wind. The figure jerks and straightens. I am staring into the sunken frost-bitten face of Oolulik, wife of Itooi.

I hold her by the shoulders then, for when she recognizes me she seems almost to crumple. After a moment I can ask, "Are you breaking trail for the others? Are they behind you?" I brush the ice from her face and she shakes her head with a shudder. "Where are they? Can we get to them before the storm is highest?"

She says through frost-broken lips, "They are in the camp by the Lake of Little Men." Somewhere beyond — perhaps five, perhaps eight miles, where the Front River runs out of the lake, where the deer cross and where for generations the people have hunted them by setting up rows of rock mounds that at a distance look like short men to channel the deer into the river for easier spearing. Three years before Itooi took me there for the fall kill; there were full meat caches that winter. I stare at his wife now, trying for a moment not to think what her being out in this storm alone means, trying not to understand the small bump on her back under the parka. She murmurs, "They are without breath in the snow houses, Itooi also. Only the baby."

For a moment we hunch there, our backs to the storm. "Come," I say finally, "we must find a drift for a snow house."

There is little time to look, and the house I build with Oolulik inside holding the blocks so that the wind will not knock them over is tiny. But it is shelter, and when I get the oil stove and the food inside from the sled there is warmth. I melt snow for water and give Oolulik the soup to drink from around thawing meat. She soaks a bit of hide in it and gives it to the baby to suck, but he seems almost beyond that. I should have remembered milk but she looks at me and murmurs, "Tomorrow one will have milk for him." I crawl out to feed the dogs; the storm is so intense now that I cannot see two feet. I check the dogs' chains, pull the sleeping robe off the sled and struggle back into the house. Oolulik is holding her child to her under the parka, bending back and forth over the little stove as if rocking in sleep. I rouse her. "The storm will be long, and we must save the oil. Here." I spread my heavy robe on the sleeping bench; she looks at it. She herself sewed it for me three winters before. "I know," I say at her look, "you could carry nothing but the child. But we must stay warm." I squat by the stove.

She lays the naked boy in the robe, then pulls off her own worn, frost-hardened clothes, spreads them out on the floor and gets into the robe. I blow out the stove and in the darkness I quickly undress and lay out my clothes to freeze. Then I crawl into the robe also. It is just large enough. I can feel the ice of her emaciated body against mine but I know that together we will soon be warm, and as she hunches closer the wind's whine over the house is already dying in my ear.

For the first three days of the storm we do little but sleep. Oolulik eats what she can and cares for the child. He is her only concern and as she grows stronger she has milk for him but he does not improve. She rocks him gently, holding him to her under the parka, and in the long hours she tells, in snatches, the story of what had happened at the camp by the Lake of Little Men. If we were not alone in the cramped snow house and her strong handsome face haggard as I have never seen it, I could almost think we were in the hunting camp as we have been so often and that at any moment my friend Itooi will crawl through the door and lift his laughing face to us and shout, "Telling old stories again? No one bothers with them now, only a few women! Ha! But just now a deer happened to run under the guns. Perhaps it will be enough for supper!" But no deer will ever again just happen to run under Itooi's unerring rifle. He lies where he has fallen over the fish hole in the ice, Ukwa's knife-wounds in his back. For Ukwa, big simply child-like man who could not hunt very well, and did not have to as long as his brother-in-law cared for him and his family, broke mentally under the long hunger. In his madness he may have believed Itooi was deceiving him in dividing the few fish on which the two families subsisted, so he — who knows — the fact was he went to Itooi jigging for fish, stabbed him, then went to his brother-in-law's house and before Oolulik knew what was happening had already stabbed the oldest girl as she lay beside her brother. Oolulik, strong in terror, succeeded in wrestling him down and tying him because he kept crawling back to the sleeping bench, insanely intent on the ten-year-old boy, Mala. Then, the baby on her back, she went out to get Itooi to do what had to be done with the madman. She found her husband face down in the ice hole. There was only one law left her: survival. She returned to her house, pulled a thong taut around Ukwa's neck, dressed Mala in what hides were left and, with the baby still on her back, leaving her dead and Ukwa's wife — her sister — and children she could not know in what condition, with time only for one desperate effort for her two sons, she began the trek for Dubawnt Lake under the threat of the storm. But Mala was too weak; in an hour he collapsed. She waited beside the boy until his panting stopped, then covered him with snow and turned again to the storm. Some hours later I found her.

We are safe now; we have food and shelter. But it is too late for the baby and on the third day he dies.

On the fourth day she gives me the body and I take it out. Finding my marker, I dig out the sled and lay the body under it where the dogs cannot reach. The blizzard howls without cease. There is no way to help Ukwa's family even if they are alive. The storm roars over me for a time, then I return into the house. Oolulik is sitting as I left her and I begin to melt snow to make tea. We have said nothing since the child died, and I cannot endure the silence. But how to break it? We have known each other since I came to Tyrel Bay and though we are about the same age, she is my mother as Itooi has been my father in the north. Now I can only make her tea.

She drinks a little. Eyes closed, she squats on the sleeping-bench, swaying slightly. I drink tea, listening to the storm, and presently I sense her singing beside me. It is not a Christian hymn such as the people love to sing when the missionary comes to Tyrel twice a year and which they sing together when they hold their daily morning prayers. It is the old song of the people that I heard only once or twice during my earliest days in the north, a song as I have long since not been able to beg from Oolulik. Like the singers of the people long ago, she is composing as she sings, and it is her own song:

> "Where have gone the deer,
> The animals on which we live?
> Who gave us meat and blood soup to drink,
> Our dogs strength to run over the snow?
> Once their strong sinews sewed our clothes,
> And their bones gave the sweet-brown marrow;
> Then our houses were warm with the fire of their fat
> And our cheeks smeared with their juices.
> Eyaya — eya.
>
> And when they would not come,
> Long ago,
> The angakok would send his soul beneath the lake
> Where lives the mighty spirit Pinga
> And there sing a charm for her that would soothe her
> And the deer would come
> In great herds that covered the land
> And the birds that follow them hide the autumn sun.
> We would hunt them at the sacred crossings
> Where the little men stand guard,
> And the angakoks would sing their songs,
> And the people would keep strictly to the taboos
> And not offend Pinga,
> And in the winter the storm would wail about the house,

The dogs roll up, their snouts under their tails,
On the ledge would lie the sleeping boy
On his back, breathing through his open mouth,
His little stomach bulging round.
Eyaya — eya."

Were it not Oolulik, the wisest woman among the western people who is singing, and were her song not so terrible in beauty, I would think her mind has given way. For though she is the daughter of a great angakok and it was whispered among the people that even as a child she had already shown some of his power, she gave her name to the missionary as a young girl and all her life she has been a fervent Christian. She told me the legends of the people only after much persuading. Itooi was the church catechist for the band, leading the services during the long months the missionary could not visit them. Like all the people, they were profoundly devotional. The two times I was with them at Baker Lake they attended church services every day six days of the week. The angakok to them had long ago been declared the power of Satanasi, the devil. And now Oolulik sings on:

"When all the people came safely from the hunt
Then we knew our amulets were strong,
And the angakok who had gained his strength
In the lonely way of the barrens
Would sing of Sila, the great spirit
That holds up the world and the people
And speaks in no words
But in the storm and snow and rain
And sometimes through unknowing children at play,
Who hear a soft gentle voice,
And the angakok knows
That peril threatens.
When all is well Sila sends no messages.
He remains solitary, silent.
And there is meat in the camp, and the drum dance
Calls the people for dance and laughter and song.

> *The women lie in the arms of the song-cousins of their*
>   *husbands;*
> *And the angakok speaks through the fire of the seance."*

She has stopped, her face tilts back toward the low roof of the house, her eyes closed. Her song in its short endlessly repeating melody has grown loud, but now it drops away:

> *"Eyaya — eya*
> *Where have gone the deer,*
> *And the people of the deer?*
> *Eyaya — eya."*

When I can bear to look at her again she is motionless on the sleeping-bench, looking at me with bright dry eyes. Suddenly she says, "When the white man came to the people with guns and oil for heating, it was almost as if we no longer needed shamans or taboo for we could hunt the deer wherever we wished, from far. Then the missionary came and told us of Jesus and we listened and soon our old beliefs seemed of little use for us to live. We have lived this way most of my life, and every year the deer have been less. And our prayers to God do not bring them back. In the old days the shaman did."

Finally I can say something. "Oolulik, you do not believe that. The shaman could not bring the deer if there were none."

"There always were deer."

"Yes, but they have been over-hunted, here, in the north, in the south."

"Because men have guns."

"Partly, but also —"

"And they no longer keep the taboo of not killing more than can be eaten. The missionaries tell us that we must believe other things, and the white men do not even believe what the white missionary says. We have seen them in Baker Lake; many never go to church, and yet they are fat and warm and never hungry. We believed and prayed, and see —" she gestures about the tiny house. "There is nothing left to believe. The deer and the people are gone."

"The people are not all gone. There are many left in the

eastern bands, and to the north, and the deer will come back in a few years. The government is beginning to make surveys and soon we will know why the deer —"

She is looking at me with a gentle smile and I cannot continue. "Abramesi," she says. "You are a good man. But you did not go with us to church. You do not believe either."

Finally I can murmur, "But you have believed for many years, long before you met me. And you still believe."

She does not look at me but stares against the wall of the house as if studying the storm that howls beyond. She says at last, "The deer are gone and the people of the deer are gone. I also wish to go away."

There is nothing to be said. Later I crawl out and feed the dogs; there is only one skimpy feeding left, but from the sound of the storm it may break tomorrow. I go in and prepare food for us. Oolulik eats little, squatting silently on the floor. She will remain that way all night, swaying back and forth, singing softly to herself. I undress, crawl into the robe, and pull it tight over my ears.

I awake to the smell of food. Oolulik is at the stove and there is no sound of wind outside. I dress quickly and crawl out. Stars sparkle in the fierce calm cold; when the sun comes up the world will blaze white. In a few moments we have eaten, loaded, and are on our way. Oolulik rides the sled with the body of the child. She leads us unerringly to the spot; we find the body of her other son and take it with us also. Travelling is fast on the wind-hard drifts. In an hour we are at the camp, and even as I clear the entrance of Ukwa's house I hear the plane coming from the north. It will spot the dog-team so I concern myself no further with it for the moment but scramble into the house. Amazingly, Ukwa's wife and two of the three children are still, if barely, alive. They know nothing; only that Ukwa has not returned. I start the stove, put on frozen meat and crawl out. The plane is landing on the ice of the lake and with a jolt I see it is the RCMP craft from Baker. A little luck now would have been too much to expect.

Corporal Blake must, of course, examine all the bodies. Oolulik has brought all hers to the sled, and after he crawls into what was her house and examines Ukwa. There is no way of concealing the way he died and I translate while the policeman questions her. Nothing can be done: she has killed the man and she must be arrested. It seems we will have to take the bodies of the two men with us for medical examination, but then it leaps in me and I curse him, long, completely. When I can control myself he says only, "Yes, it would be too much for the plane." And he permits Oolulik and me to take what is left of her family out on the windswept hill overlooking the lake. There is, of course, no way to dig a grave. We do what the Eskimos did long ago: lay them on the ground, cover them with the few wind-cleared rocks we can pry loose, and leave them to the elements and the wild animals. In the house I had found Itooi's prayer-book and now I hand it to Oolulik to read a prayer over the four graves. But she takes it from my hand and, without opening it, thrusts it under the rocks. Then, squinting against the blazing sun on the snow, we drive down the hill. Blake has helped Ukwa's family to the plane, and when we arrive the two sisters look silently at each other, one knowng, one unknowing though without hope. We climb in; four adults, two children and five muzzled dogs make an awkward load but soon we are airborne. We circle over the hill with its patch black against the snow, and head for Tyrel Bay.

Two days later when the plane comes in from Baker again to evacuate the last of the people from Dubawnt Lake, the pilot tells me that the first night Oolulik spent in jail she had hung herself. She too had gone away.

Part Three

5

*H*ORST Jeffer's long kindly face smiled at him across the cluttered desk. "I expected all week you'd call about my car to go to Selkirk. Or were you too proud and hired one?"

Abe grinned slightly, eyes on a thick folder on the desk, its cover scrawled with office notation. "No. You know economics always win." He hesitated. Facing Horst, what he had so heavily decided struck him again as abysmally second best: why not confess to him at least that when years before he filled in the small blank on the company form: Dead: he had not been lying as he then thought. But that half-truth alone would never stand and all the rest would boil — leave the past to rot the present and the future threatens smell enough — "Actually, I-I met a man from Selkirk — high school acquaintance. We had a long visit."

"Good! There must be quite a few people from up there working in town?"

"I guess." He pulled at his beard, aware again of the dilemmas friendship can provoke when it is unknowing. "It's over twenty years since I left and I've never been back," and with a motion of his hand he flipped aside all the other details that Horst as his superior knew from the data sheet: details of living uncomplicated by personality or love or hate or longing: simply lived, moved, died, worked; as good for beast as chessman as human. "Meeting Jim was pure accident, in a crowd. I hadn't seen him since overseas in the war. He introduced me to John Kinconnell."

"Is that how he got on your trail. It sounded urgent."

"Isn't it usually, with him?"

"In business, yes." There was a short silence.

"Tell me Horst, what's he like as a businessman?"

Horst's lop-sided laugh pulled his long face out of its typical moroseness to reveal his true warmth. "He's a little out of my league, really, but we've seen quite a bit of each other since he got interested in the north. He's a strange, powerful man. He may drink himself to sleep every other night but as a businessman he's at the top. He's at work by ten and the night before never shows. He's got what they call his father's 'golden touch'. Maybe that's why he drives so hard: to keep ahead of what his father built — but I can't psychologize. I know he pays well, but his men have to produce. He controls absolutely a wide range of businesses and with him the right man could go as far he wants."

"Yeah," Abe was studying the carpet. "That's just about what it looked like, in that building." He added then, knowing the other would not ask, "He made me an offer. Manager in Churchill."

Horst nodded slowly. "It figures. His mind's amazing. He once explained every major transportation problem Frobisher has had up north in the last twenty years! And also how his proposed network would kill every one of them, forever. You know the way he talks — not 'dispose of' or 'solve' — kill! never to be resurrected. Look, Abe, there's nothing I want more than to keep you, but you'd probably work well with him. And he can pay you what a company structured like Frobisher can't wangle for district managers."

"Why don't you take it?"

Horst laughed again, "I've been here too long — none of that pioneering aggression left."

"Oh sure! A guy who's just taken over a mismanaged department. Just an old organizational wizard of forty-five!"

"With twenty-seven years in the company," Horst tilted back in his chair. "To tell you the truth, if I could stand the pace, I still wouldn't want to. But it's a great chance for someone."

In the spacious office no clatter penetrated to impinge on their thoughts. Studying the half-averted face of the superior who had become the friend, Abe could not but envy the calm assurance he saw there. It appeared foundational in Horst: here plant your feet, place your fulcrum and move the world as big as you can grasp it. Yet somehow this serene, despite its strength was no less disconcerting; almost it seemed sometimes it was strong in Horst only because he would deliberately ignore some things, almost remain aloof from where most people really felt.

Horst was saying ". . . him up on it?"

Abe stood up abruptly and took a turn around the room, ending before the left wall and the picture of a Frobisher store perched like a blue and white plaything among the boulders of an Arctic coast. He knew it. He had once visited Banks Island during a mid-winter run with extra supplies but now the Eskimo had left and the buildings would be standing empty, element-battered but unrotting in the pure air. He said, facing the picture, "I don't know if I could even go to Churchill."

Horst said quietly, "Abe, there've been mass deaths among the people ever since we've got records — either starvation or sickness or something. Murder, either by Indians or themselves. I told you about pneumonia on the Coppermine the first years I was up there and three whole bands running together at the post to cough their lungs out. It's partly the white man in the north, yes, but what will you do? To pull out would be worse than —"

"Ah hell Horst," Abe flung his head about to face him, "these aren't the 'thirties. We strung the DEW line for hundreds of millions to tell Ottawa if a flock of birds is anywhere in country not a living soul crosses in five years and we can't get radios or airplanes set up to keep forty-five people alive! Hell."

A humorless snort jerked Horst a little. "I've often thought if only the Eskimos had a few communists working among them they'd all be eating out of deep-freezes and sleeping on foam-rubber before you could say 'red!' But they live communalistically already, almost; and love peace." He hesitated. "Abe, you did everything you could and practically lost yourself getting to them once you knew —"

"Oh sure. After the fact. But I knew all winter the deer were nothing in the east, and no report west. I shouldn't of let Baker get away without inspection flight west during December, or at least January. Just two recommendations — you know what happens to a 'recommendation'. And the few times the weather was flyable there were so many things that had to be done. Like nursemaiding a parliamentary committee around!"

A buzzer sounded and Horst stretched for the telephone. After a moment he said, "I'll meet him at 11:30. I'm sure you can sooth him that long. Thanks, Miss Mitchell." He turned to Abe still studying the picture. "There's nothing to be said to justify their pretty well ignoring your messages, but you know the people were working against you too. When the fall herds didn't come they should have sent to you, right? At least when the darkness set in. Then you could have sent exact information and Baker Lake would have got supplies out, one way or another. They did, right into the blizzard when the facts were known. But the people live so much for today; why look ahead when tomorrow may bring a deer? They hunt and wait until it's too late for them even to get help. It's happened before."

"Sure, sure, I know that," Abe interrupted and stepped back to face Horst across the desk, the words and thoughts and intuitions that had convulsed his mind seemingly since he could remember spilling from him, "that's one thing the white man hasn't bust out of them, yet. And who's hottest after what the people think? The churchmen. You know yourself they talk most about wanting 'the Eskimo to remain Eskimo' when they join the church, yet tear them away from some of the very things that are most Eskimo. Like this concern with the here and now; they don't care about tomorrow much as long as right now everyone can fill his belly. That's Eskimo: eat and be happy today. But churchmen don't want that. They keep hammering away that you have to get set in this life for the next, work to make sure you're prepared to meet a loving God who controls everything here and heaven and hell over there. When you believe spirits control the deer, the weather, land, snow — everything, and the weather gets bad or the deer don't come you get the shaman to try to appease the spirits. If things get better you know they're satisfied; if not, you accept that because there's nothing else to be done and you die, if it goes that far, resigned, knowing the spirits are sometimes too much for people. But now the first thing they're taught when they become Christians is that God loves them and there aren't any spirits anywhere except a few devilish ones that every faithful believer has licked before he starts. God loves and he takes care of everyone, especially those who believe in Jesus. It's plain enough he takes care of the whiteman who as far as the people can tell never runs out of food or ammunition and flies anywhere he wants at a moment's whim and even talks to someone farther away than the fastest dogteam can travel in a week. So the Eskimo tries to think like the churchmen tell him; as much as he can he ignores the old hunting taboos based on pleasing the spirits because the spirits aren't really there. Not that they weren't once — only the whiteman seems to have run them out. His religion, once part of his daily hunting and resting, is fixed up by reading in the Black Book in the morning and holding prayer meetings once in a while and especially the two times a year the churchman can make it around and remind you of all the rules and baptise the children and give communion. No song-cousins, no drum dances, no communal justice for murderers because human life is so sacred the Mounties will get you sure and send you where you'll never see your people again. Then comes the long darkness and guns are useless because there are no animals. You can't try to appease spirits because there aren't supposed to be any. You pray to Jesus because as the churchmen plainly show he takes mighty good care of them that talk about him most. But no animals come. In what state of blessedness do you end then?"

Silence gathered heavily in the room; Horst had been doodling on the desk-pad. "In the eighteen years," he said, not looking up, "I was up there it was terrible sometimes. There was no way to get medicines in fast then, or food. Only the one summer supply ship. The government hardly knew the people were there." He looked up fleetingly, pained. "But I know. It never got any worse than eighteen of forty-five people starving. You know the language of the people better than I ever did, and you know them better too, I think. How many of them really take their beliefs apart like you've just been talking — for how many —"

Abe interrupted, "Plenty," but Horst was not to be interrupted.

"You know them. You told me yourself about that spring trek where you and a group of them came on a skeleton and found from bits of clothing it was one of the men's wives lost in a storm that winter. Everyone cried like babies for half an hour but when you got into the store a few hours later they were cracking jokes again, especially the husband. How about that? Death's everywhere around them; no family ever survives intact. Do they really fight it — spiritually — like you say? Or is it just your — civilized let's say — sensitivity?"

For a long moment Abe could not comprehend the other's insistence; Horst was too kind, too thoughtful surely to force this callousness like a refusal to hear a scream at your very foot. He said at last, "You wouldn't have to ask that if you'd been four days in an igloo with her."

"All right. One. An extraordinary person by any standard. What about the ones at Dubawnt?"

Staring at Horst, he could no longer hide his bitterness. "That sounds just like Jesus Christ."

The steady look that had not left Abe's face suddenly fell. "I'm sorry. I thought maybe if we could push this — this thing to the end — but you're right. Absolutely right."

Under his feet the carpet was as gentle as forgetfulness, could he have found it. "I've tried that too — till there was nothing left to imagine, not even the craziest things. And I can't get rid of the terrible song. Or poor Turatuk over the oildrum praying for just one more drop to keep him from freezing."

"I agree with you," Horst said at last. "You shouldn't go back for a while, even to Churchill."

"So —?" Abe drew his hand across his face and faced the other, standing also. "What do I do?"

"Stay in Winnipeg. We can use you here."

"No, not this town. You work a few hours and have to kill yourself getting rid of the rest of the time."

"You've listened too much to some of the men around this office; you'll never be like that. You could take lectures in things like anthropology at the university if you'd like, go to concerts, lead a boys group maybe. Not just try for a fun life. You had such a rough time with the church up north — I still wish you'd come to our church some Sunday. I wouldn't be offended if you didn't come back; I know there are some churches that don't give what particular people feel they need," Horst stopped and grinned a little. "Anyway, you're a distinguished-looking middle-aged man. The war, the cruelty sometimes of the barrens — you've been at the ends of the world too long and there are some good things in —"

But Abe could not respond and the sourness of his mind cut like his interruption, "Okay Horst, okay. I remember what you said when I got in. And I tried it, because for a while I really wanted to. I went to every brand church there is — Lutheran, Anglican, Mennonite, Baptist, United, Roman Catholic — every Sunday morning, and sometimes Sunday night. I even went to what they call an evangelistic tabernacle — the works." He stopped, his tone betraying.

"And it's no good?"

"Yeah."

"Abe, you go once to each church and it doesn't fit. That's not a fair sampling, is it? And didn't you hear anything that seemed to hit what you need?"

He had turned and was staring at the familiar picture again, without seeing now. Need, all the time need. And in all the gibberish from precisely acted ritual to shapeless hallelujah-amen-ism, from idiotic appeals of emotion to as idiotic appeals of philosophy, from time-marking silence to banshee screams, with all the innumerable gradients of emotional and mental atrophy and massage between, far from not finding need satisfied, he had not even been able to unearth that, his very need, to recognize it. He simply knew emptiness, a vacancy with him so long now that it had acquired a kind of painful fullness, like swallowing air after a seven-day hunger. Only this was no seven days.

The manager's look was so intently sympathetic Abe said, in sudden gratitude, "Sure. That's it. I — I just don't know. They sing and preach and talk about — oh — keeping their young people and paying the church mortgage and holding up their end of some inter-church squabble — my god Horst it's like someone week after week playing with himself and thinking — ahh —" he felt abruptly shamed, of or before what he did not know. And he owed this man some honesty at least: "They're not all as bad as that — I know you're not. And I didn't go to your church. I had more than — too much of it when I was a kid. You're not that kind of Presbyterian, but where I come from you wouldn't have even been one, I think," he managed a wry grin.

"You didn't want to risk it?"

"No."

Horst flipped over a folder. "You know what you've lived with, and I can't pretend that our church is something it isn't. But churches change. And the people that go there, too. I guess I'd been going for years before I found it was changing my life. Maybe that's the best that can be said for routine church-going: you're there until a time comes when you realize what church fellowship is, what a brotherhood can be if you'll let it. When you've once stopped there's more than inertia holds you back." He smiled, and all that is possible to friendship but beyond speech was in the smile. "That's that about that for now. But what about your job? I want to keep you with Frobisher."

Abe sat on the desk edge. "You know that's been sitting in my head like a rock. Ha! Holiday — that's a good one! I can't hammer it out. You know me," he slumped into the chair. "Make a suggestion."

"That's not fair," Horst said. "There are a thousand things a man can do. Set some limits."

"Sure sure!" Abe waved his hands, "and you know them

as well as I — no city or small town, nothing in the Arctic. What has Frobisher got I can do?" Abruptly he hunched forward. "Some place that'll work me like a dog so I can lose all this trailing me and do something for somebody or something — at least forget. Yeah, something like that."

"Great!" Horst laughed. "Once you say 'give me a suggestion — any one' and the next minute you hoist so many conditions there's nothing left. Frobisher's a retail company, selling and trading — not working people to death!"

"Sure. One man northern posts and all."

"Right," Horst grinned fleetingly. "Well, let's see. You've cut out everything but the Indian stores. The Indians live pretty much around or near the store now — government payments keep them there. Would you — hmm — you get on great with languages. There's a post where you could try Ojibwa."

"Where?"

"One of the stores in northern Ontario. The way we're set up here nobody ever had time to inspect the place and a young chap in for three years has just about lost it for us. Private trader competition." Horst pressed a button, "Miss Mitchell, please bring me the file on Frozen Lake," then pushed folders aside on the map under glass on his desk. "It's out of the way, here, between two and three hours by air out of Red Lake. Ever been in that country?"

"No. I was at Brocket for five months in 'fifty. Is Ojibwa anything like Chipewyan, or Eskimo?"

"They say not. It's polysynthetic too, but no other similarity. Actually —" Horst hesitated, his fist to his chin.

"What?"

"I don't know — it would be silly to waste you on that place for a year."

"A year?"

"Yes. Things have been going so bad that the board wanted to shut it down this spring. Our man there recommended it himself. He would! And Michaels, the retiring D.M., seconded him. But I fought it mainly because the band of two hundred people is in a good location. They have lots of fur, good fishing and hunting. Before Bjornesen cut in there Frozen Lake was always near the top of Area Three stores," his hand swept the red-dot locations around the horse-shoe of Hudson and James Bay. "And there are a couple of other things. We can't just leave them to that old man — you'll see when you read the reports. So I talked them into trying it with another man for at least one more year, but I haven't found a man yet. And you —" the secretary entered at that moment with a heavy file. "Thanks. How are you doing with Wainwright?"

The girl smiled. "He seemed very annoyed, but he finally said he'd be back precisely at 11:30 and left with his back quite painfully stiff."

"It's used to that by now. Fine. That's better than any secretary's done in this place. And I'll try to be on time, so you don't have to beard him again."

The girl looked at Abe, laughed outright, and in a moment they were caught in her laughter. With a toss of her head, she was gone. "She's a fine one; makes some things around here bearable. Now, let's see —" Horst fingered through the file.

"Anyone else besides about two hundred Indians and this Bjornesen at Frozen Lake?"

"Nobody's been in for inspection for four years — I can't before next spring — and Griffin's reports aren't very thorough. But the government opened a day-school last year and they had school regularly for the first time the past winter. But the teacher they had isn't coming back and who knows if they'll get another. And there's a missionary couple living there; they have a school-age child, I think." Horst looked up. "I knew that would get a frown from you."

Abe shrugged. "What church?"

"I don't think they affiliate with any mainline church. And Griffin writes they haven't any members."

Abe said nothing. Churchmen were what they were, but the hell-fire of the ones who couldn't even work with a church but sailed out for two week stands of "saving" on their own —

that leech at Baker last summer! — he said at last, "Well, at least he probably has different ideas from the mainliners — but no members?"

Horst grinned at him. "With you that might be to his credit, eh? Anyway, I haven't had time to check and Griffin hardly mentions him. He may not be much in the picture there, one way or another, though that's hard to believe with only three whites in an Indian community."

Abe stood suddenly erect. "You need someone for a year to try and make this place go, right?"

"Yes. But you're a twelve-year man, and to take on a broken-down store —"

"Never mind that. It's for one year. You may want to close it then — or at least have good reasons for it. Let me read that file. If it looks too hopeless I might not want it anyway, even on a silver platter," the possible challenge of it flickered distantly in him and he reached across the desk, smiling.

For a moment their eyes held unwaveringly, then Horst's blinked. "Okay, read it. Miss Mitchell can give you a big envelope so you don't advertise you're going off with a file. Call me when you finish and we can take it from there — if anywhere."

"Sure." Abe turned, the blue and white Frobisher store oh so vivid in his mind. "Thanks," he juggled the file into compactness and turned.

"And please, come over some evening again. Mary and I, we've been praying for you, for your deciding."

He did not know what to answer; not doubting the sincerity of the other but unable to grasp any relevance in the manager's so oddly childish formula, as if twisting a faucet that might, or might not, spout water and whether it did or not you never doubted that the water nevertheless was there; only it might not *want* to come when you turned. He knew this was part of the other's undeniable strength, somehow; but in a thick-carpeted office it struck him as incongruously part of what the other seemed forever to ignore: the cold facts of the world — while nevertheless pulling into order a huge botched department — he could only mutter, half turned to the door, "It's just a business decision —"

"No. It's never just that, for either of us. It's your living, your life."

"Okay Horst, I —" but he could not comment. "I'll let you know," he said and went out.

6

"THAT'S Gikumikik down there — see the beach and clearing?" Abe stretched but the instrument panel cut off view. "Here," the pilot continued, "look past my nose." The plane tilted and Abe saw the blue lake like a blot in the green and the white bend of a beach flanked by greyish spots which must be cabins. "Look good," the pilot shouted above the hammer of the plane. "That's the last water but for swamps for an hour — till we're right on top of Frozen Lake."

Abe saw a wink of royal blue near the end of a point jutting into the lake and said, his mouth at the other's ear, "Out on the point, is that Frobisher?"

"Yep. Nobody but you guys bother paintin' roofs out here. Good to see that roof after the dry run from Frozen."

Abe leaned back as the plane leveled. "You haul in there — what'd you call it?"

"Gikumikik — a nice Ojibwa name. Yep, I fly in there a lot. You with Frobisher and haven't even heard of it?"

"I've never been in this district before — and I came out too fast to learn. I should have time when I get settled, maybe."

The young pilot laughed as he waggled the controls and hunched into a more comfortable position. "Maybe not, if you're gettin' Frozen on its feet. Orton Pryde, now, down there," he jerked his head at the tail of the lake that was pulling itself out of the small window leaving only the unbroken bristle of the trees below, "he's sittin' pretty. No competition, good bunch of Indians, never had any know-it-all in to mess around. He's been there seventeen years and nobody'd think of buttin' in."

"Is that what happened at Frozen?"

"Well, I —" the pilot's face suddenly reddened a little and he scowled at the instruments. "Look, I've nothin' against Art Griffin. He's okay." More loudly, "And you know more about it than me. I just fly you guys around." He shrugged, "Old Pryde's makin' money here and Sig's got the screws on Art up there — that's all. You take over and I fly you in. Okay?" He grinned at Abe belted beside him.

Abe grinned; the pilot's very insistence abruptly clenched his resolve to talk as much as he could out of him. He had already missed two hours in doodling with the thoughts that had held him since Winnipeg the afternoon before when without actually having made a deliberate decision he had found himself on the DC-3 for Red Lake simply by urging stubbornly against Horst's doubt, simply to be doing something once again — so here's your new world start your own digging and where better than the man flying everything between Red Lake and Frozen — "Sure," he said. "Okay!"

The plane hammered on as if motionless in the air; only creek-bends creeping out of sight gave a long, slow moment's impression of movement. Trying to gain a direction, Abe stared down past the wing-strut as he had for most of the flight, and the empty, tree-crammed spread of the rocky land was changing to larger swampy grass patches between the lines of the creeks and diminishing nodules of open water. He bent forward and pulled the maps back on his lap. After a moment he turned to the pilot — dammit his name? — and gestured, "Dave, if you don't like rock and swamp, why don't you swing wide over the Innes River and Gotmar Lakes system — this way," his hand traced a curved route to the blue patch that represented Frozen Lake in the top right corner of the map.

"Holy cow!" Dave's thin young face hunched together in laughter. "Mid-Ontario Airlines sayin' 'Go ahead, Dave boy, you don't like to fly over swamp no more'n anybody else so fly around the long way. Who cares about takin' three-quarters of an hour more gas!' That's good! I can just hear old Pettibone saying it, after last week."

"Something happen?"

Dave looked at him swiftly, as if doubting his sudden interest. "Oh, just a thing that happens flyin' long enough. Nothin' terrible, except it's me. I got into this trouble with a kid out here a while ago," he gestured vaguely north, "and it blew up a little so I haven't much lee-way, especially with Boney." He fumbled in his shirt-pocket for the cigarette pack and proffered it. Abe shook his head,

"Thanks. But he keeps you on."

"I'm just his best pilot, is all." There was no grin; it was a simple statement of fact. Smoke plumed in the drafty cabin as he continued, "Just one o' those things. Boney got the government contract to fly all these new nylon fish-nets to the fish-camps. They was piled up to the ceilin' in the Super-Cub — they don't weigh nothin' and there was about twenty camps I had to get to. At Donaldson Lake — way south and west of here, about 45 minutes out of Red Lake — I give them their five nets and taxi out. It's nice and calm — terrific flyin', like today, and I gun her and hell if a little twister doesn't come out of nothin' and catch the right wing and flip me slick as jujitsu right over in the water, pontoons up."

"Flip you?"

"Yep! Just before I had enough speed to get through. Clear over. Just like that."

"What happened?"

"Well you don't sink right away — you plow ahead and the plane floats for a minute, but you have to get out fast, the cabin's under water and leakin' — hell, it hardly makes the water hesitate. But them fish-net bundles flopped all over me and me upside-down and arms and legs all fouled up in this slippery nylon and I couldn't get my hand on the latch and when I got it unhooked the water just poured in worse. I had to kick out the windshield. I wouldn't of made it but I got out my knife here and cut outa that nylon line. See," Dave thrust back his shirt-sleeves; a tangle of half-healed scars, some still deeply scab-crusted, criss-crossed his forearms, "that's line cuts, and busting the windshield." His laugh bounced in the tiny cabin, above the engine roar. "You should see my chest. Like a goddam war! But that hole was big enough for my head. Get your face cut up and the girls won't look at you."

— a worthy thought sinking in an unplumbed lake snarled in fish-net — no bush pilot Abe had ever known thought reasonably, first. He laughed and pushed on, "You got out I guess, and the Indians picked you up. Have you got the plane up yet?"

"Yeah, them Indians! Standin' on shore and seein' everything right under their runny noses. And not one o' the buggers got in a canoe! I dog-paddled every inch."

"What?" Abe stared at Dave's scowling profile.

"They saw it, that's why. A twister's evil to them — bad. When it hit I was supposed to die; after I got out of the water they helped me, sure — bandaged me, fed me till a plane come over, but they wouldn't touch me in the lake. One of them, a friend of mine, he told me. You get in dutch with the spirits yourself if you help people they're after. Right now any Indian that's heard of it won't fly with me, not if he's dyin'." He faced Abe and smiled. "Old Boney doesn't even test them. I just fly Frobisher men now!"

"You don't believe it?"

"What?"

"That a spirit's after you?"

"Huh!" Dave jerked his head so sharply that the black curl on his forehead snapped like a wire spring. "Think that stuff and you don't fly outa Red Lake. You hit for Hamilton and stand on concrete all day and screw a nut."

"But not you."

"Do I look like it?" Dave joggled several controls, peered sharply at the altimeter, then settled back again, "Some start thinkin' about stuff and first thing you know they forget something. Zingo — when you find them it's always a 'mechanical failure'. But talk to an old timer Indian who'll talk, somebody you know well enough, and he'll say, 'His guardian spirit was too weak; it couldn't save him from the evil.' That's for the Indians."

"No church has been in here, eh, to work that out of them?"

"Oh they're all in some church book, but alone they do like they've always done — see spirits, and talk about them. And sometimes you'd just about —" he stopped and ground the last of his cigarette under his heel; the floor was littered. Abe waited, and suddenly the other's jaw-muscles tightened as if he had crushed something between his teeth. "Call it luck or reflexes or guardian spirit, I get out of it, quick. Like maybe some nut who fuels you up not turning the tank caps tight and the wind blows them off and siphons out all your gas." Dave jerked a glance above him to the fuel indicators. "Connected tanks — if you forget to check it's maybe bad luck, or bad flyin'."

Abe looked again at the ground far below. There had been no flash of lakes for the last twenty minutes, and even the rocky outcroppings and the stubble of trees had faded now to the low scrub and twisty creeks of marsh and swamp. Nowhere, to the very edge of the horizon, was there relief from the stare of the dull-green flat lying in gigantic hostile emptiness below them. He had flown often in the Keewatin but there had always been lakes. He said slowly, just above the steady drum of the motor, "And if they show empty over this?"

Dave stared out. "They never have."

"And if they did?"

"I'd hit for the nearest water — maybe ten-fifteen minutes over that ridge northwest."

"And if there wasn't ten minutes left?"

"I'd get at the best swamp I could spot that might give us some slide. Okay?"

"Sure! You fly and I'll ask questions."

For a time they flew in silence, a silence accepted now, and easy. Abe studied the maps on his knee, memorizing the sketched lie of the terrain; but his glance was pulled to the land below that spread away into nothing with its almost featureless green under the high summer sun. Only the squirms of the thin rivers hinted lines of perspective; when they had flown out of Red Lake the clash of the blue lakes with the green trees and white rapids made the land graspable and less foreign; even the glacial drift of the summer barrens pointed towards pattern. But this was sheer cosmic unthought.

Dave jogged his elbow, pointing, "See, the black dot in that swamp — the water flashin' through the grass — over there, just off the strut — a moose." Abe peered until the dot of animal was lost in the vanishing green.

"Good hunting here?"

"Great. The Indians pretty well live off them. When the season is open for us they feed on the brush in burned-over patches, like that ridge there. That'll be good huntin' come November."

Abe said, "How come Bjornesen moved into Frozen Lake a couple of years ago?"

The pilot said nothing for several moments, checking gauges as if completely absorbed. Abe had decided his abrupt tactic was the worst he might have tried when the other turned, "There's no point pumpin' me. I don't know enough to bother —"

Abe said quickly, "I don't want to *pump* you —"

"Okayokay — whatever you call it. Unless you talk Indian you won't — do you talk it?"

"No."

"Yeah. And it's such slurred together junk — though Josh Bishop at Frozen speaks it real well. Yeah, he could tell you some things. He's been there for three-four years, but he doesn't talk about other people much. "He's —" he hesitated, then gestured emptily, "— I don't know."

"What's the matter with him?" Abe pushed the last word slightly. In Griffin's reports the missionary seemed of no significance whatever.

The other twisted and glared at him, "There's nothin' the matter with *him!* He's just a decent quiet kinda guy. Him and his wife pretty well live with the Indians, in their own house but there's Indians runnin' through it all the time and stayin' to eat. Any other preachers you see up here keep them out like flies."

"They feed them, you say?" Abe could not grasp that.

"Aw, once in a while there's one stops for lunch, but they don't *give* the Indians nothin'. He's workin' with them — like the saw-mill we flew in last year, piece by piece; Josh and the Indians paid for it together, and they saw wood for house partitions. Now they wanna get the government to maybe pay them to build a school outa the lumber they saw. Josh got the winter school started, and I bet he'll swing it too."

"That sounds good," Abe murmured. There hadn't been a thing in Griffin's reports about a mill; how in an isolated settlement something that momentous could be avoided Abe could not comprehend.

"Yep, it gives the Indians somethin' to do. That's just it about Frozen. There's three white men: one a preacher who doesn't preach, one old nut of a trapper tradin' the hide off Frobisher, one young guy that lets his wife run him like a dog. And the Indians runnin' 'em all against each other for what they're worth, maybe. I dunno. And in the bush three hundred miles from god knows where." He laughed, and then his eyes tightened in concentration, "Hey — see that there? That's it."

Abe followed his glance. There was nothing below them but the land, indistinguishable from all that they had traversed for what under the unwavering drone of the motor seemed an endlessness. Look as he would, the land had no face, its very creek-traces a nonentity under his eyes; he was too accustomed to the grey and white lines of the barrens to decipher this greenness; he would have to wait for his sight. He looked at Dave, who pointed, "Just off the prop," and then he saw on the edge of blur two blue dips in the circular horizon, like thumb hollows in the green sand of the world that had filled with sky. Even as he saw this he was seeing more as Dave continued, "See the green changin' just ahead — that's trees and rocks again. The swamps lie pretty high and run into Frozen Lake, and that's pretty high too for lakes around here, and the Frozen River drops fast into the Brink — north, not on that map — the next one."

Abe shuffled rapidly, "Oh, sure. The Brink River drains into Hudson Bay, huh?"

"Yep. Over two hundred crooked miles."

He could see the texture of the green below changing. You could not tell where it began or ended but imperceptibly, if you looked with concentration, the weak green of the swamps disappeared into the virile green of trees and mosses and the creeks slid together until light gleamed at their bulges. He lost himself completely in this metamorphosis, never having dreamed that trees sprouting from humped rock could be so alive in contrast to endless swamp; only when he distinguished what looked strangely like streaks of grey lichens, as he remembered they looked from aloft, on the bare gashes of the rocks did he feel the sensation in his ears and, glancing at the altimeter, found they had slid down over a thousand feet. He looked to the horizon but his glance did not go so far: in the green before them lay Frozen Lake. He could seem to see most of it, shaped as he had expected from the map: a boomerang roughly pointing away, its ends nearer them, disappearing into a tangle of creeks and marsh, and at the point of its outer bend, which they were charging directly now, between two ridges of rock and trees that stuck out into the lake like prongs, the wide blue streak of Frozen River leading out to the north through a sprawl of waterways fading over the horizon. In the bright sun tufted islands gleamed on the lake blue as ice. Abe swallowed quickly, and he could not have said if it was because of the pressure in his ears or the inhuman beauty of the lake as they fell towards it.

Dave shouted above the braking whine of the motor, "Wind's wrong. I'll swing around. See the clearings on the river? That's it."

As they banked away Abe could not see anything except the ridges directly below but in a moment the expanse of the lake turned and righted open before them, ripples wrinkling its surface. As they touched, touched again, splashed, settled and finally leveled, he remembered their conversation and said, "How come this Bjornesen's got ahead so fast in three years?"

"I told you," Dave flicked controls, then leaned back as they taxied ponderously around the ridge guarding the entrance and turned into the river, "Sig's a trapper. He trapped around here down towards Gotmar Lakes, all over the place. He'd get as much as any band put together, any winter. He's been here all his life, knows Ojibwas and furs. He knows every-thin' they want or are scared of — just how to make 'em come across. Not that it's always too nice, but Art can't do much. For him it's a nine-six job. And his wife — well —" he flapped his hand against the controls. "Any man with a rooster woman is finished in Indian country. Too bad you ain't seein' her. She was a sight, after an hour's dry run! She sat right there two weeks ago goin' out to Fort William. A slick lookin' bitch, but yawk, yawk, yawk — she'd need her ticker fixed every night for a month before she'd be good for anythin'."

Abe grinned — and wouldn't you have liked to — and he pulled back to what he had to know. "Does the band still get as much fur out as they used to?"

Dave shook his head as if to unsettle the clinging image of Mrs. Griffin. "More, I'd think. There's more of them and Sig isn't trappin' between 'em. But Sig gets it. I guess you know that. If it wasn't for the government pensions, family allowances still goin' to Frobisher like always and them· havin' to take them out in supplies there —" he shrugged.

Hate such common knowledge of company incompetence as he would, there was no way to make denial. He opened his mouth for another question but Dave said, "That's her — Frozen Lake. All there is," and up the cleared slope of the right bank Abe saw the two white, blue roofed buildings with the familiar red-crossed blue flag limp on the pole between them. A dock stuck out from the rocks supporting a huddle of figures, with others running down the slope and among the trees at the shore-edge. Several canoes further up the channel were crossing to the dock also. "Where —" Abe began, but Dave was already answering.

"That's Sig's store across the river, by that clump of trees. The Indians mostly live on that side too, in summer mostly behind us on the ridge we just passed but some still up ahead there —" then Abe heard nothing for a moment as he saw the shabby log buildings greyed from the weather in the clearing, and the wharf below heaped high with barrels. It hardly looked like competition, but the barrels hinted. Dave gestured over his shoulder, "They're all coming," and Abe saw the canoes emerging now from the left bank as the plane burbled towards the dock. Dave cut the motor. They drifted in sideways and the man who first caught the wing tip, a thin young man in a heavy quilt jacket, Abe knew must be Arthur Griffin.

He could hear the taut voice before he got the door unlatched, and as he swung down on the float it hardened into comprehension ". . . watch it — hold it off so it doesn't bump the float — hold on there, dammit James!" as the pontoon jarred the floating platform and the plane shivered. "— bust the damn thing, and there'll be hell to pay. Now, get the ropes on."

Abe stepped to the floating dock between the two Indians holding the plane, and with a spring he was on the solid wharf beside the thin man who stopped talking and stared at him, pale eyes intent. "Hello," he said, "Arthur Griffin?"

"Yeah. You from Frobisher headquarters?"

"Yes. I'm Abe Ross, and I've got a letter here from Horst Jeffers —"

"Sonofagun it's about time! Put her there, man, I've waited a long time for somebody!" His hand in Abe's was as tense as a wire, "Every day waitin' for that damn plane. I've got everythin' stacked and ready to go — just throw a coupla things in the bag. Hey, George," he wheeled to an Indian still holding the wing steady, "get this stuff up to the store and bring my stuff down comin' back. Take the pile behind the counter — and keep these —" he swung his arm to the group of men standing, listening, "keep 'em away from behind the counter. I'll be up — Dave, good to see you, man! You got some mail?"

"Hello Art, just a few things," the pilot grinned as he tossed up the small green bag. "I'm sure there's a letter."

"Aw go on, you bum, if I wasn't countin' on you to get me outa — but sonofagun, you're here to take over — uh, what'd you say your name was —"

Abe, staring almost incredulously, said quickly, "Abe. Abe Ross, but here's a letter for you from Horst Jeffers. It seems to me —" he stopped for the other seized the letter and ripped it open. Abe could not tell whether the sense of unreality arose from the slight dizziness of the motor-silence after three hours of rumble or the solidity of the dock under his feet or the flurry of the man before him in contrast to the soft moccasin pad of the silent men accepting baggage and supplies from Dave and piling it on the dock, with no other sound but the thud of freight, the lapping water, and the small chuckle of women sitting alongside in canoes, watching and whispering as they watched.

Art dropped the hand that held the letter, "I guess you know what's in here, eh Ross?" As Abe nodded, he continued, "It's a bit rough on you, I know, but you know as well as me I'm three weeks overdue right now, waitin' for replacement. Three weeks past my contract, and I stayed just so there'd be somebody here, but I ain't goin' for Jeffers' line. I'm packed and goin'. Right now, on this plane."

Abe finally managed, "But — but you've got to give me some idea of how you've handled things, introduce me to these people, so I know where I'm at —"

Art jerked in a laugh, "You've read my reports? Well then you know what I know. Com'mon while I throw the rest of my stuff into some bags — I'll clue you in on what I can. I know it's tough for you — you don't speak Ojibwa do you? Yeah, neither do I. George Kinosay, the handyman, is okay. He does interpretin'." He hesitated, and a sardonic glint showed in his pale eyes. "It probably wouldn't do you any good me hangin' around another week."

Half an hour later Abe was more than willing to agree with this abrupt candor. Following Art up the path to the cool, dim store and beyond into the living quarters, up to the bedroom hot under the peaked roof, listening as he tossed the last items of clothing out of wall cupboards and from the tousled bed into several dummy sacks, explaining over again the few points he had made in his reports: Sig Bjornesen, trapping in the country forty years, speaking Ojibwa like any Indian and thinking like them, living with an Indian woman all the time, and above all threatening to cut off their yeast unless they brought good furs to him: even if you paid higher prices, how could you fight competition like that? By the time they were in the aluminum canoe crossing to Bjornesen's dock where the orange Cessna now stood, Dave filling the few spaces Art's duffle left with the other trader's empty drums,

Abe was already counting it blessing that Art's frenetic activity was ending so clean. As the motor roared under George's touch, the canoe spanking the wavelets of the blue water, Art, sitting by the last of his bags leaned forward to Abe,

"You know Jeffers probably lots better than me, and I'm only reportin' to Winnipeg before I get out — my wife's got things set for me in Fort William — but I'm tellin' him again and maybe you can talk him into it, that if we're gonna beat Sig — and two companies can't stay, there ain't enough people — we'll have to sell yeast too. That's the biggest hold he's got. Sonofagun, despite the prices I offered last fall he'da got every fur in the country, even George's father and two brothers, if I hadn't told George that he could kiss his job good-bye and set on the trapline if his family didn't stick with Frobisher. You bet George managed, all right!"

Abe said quickly, unable to cover a tag of distaste in his tone, "It's against Frobisher policy to sell yeast."

"Yeah! They don't make as much money on it as on whiskey!"

"Have we *ever* sold whiskey here?"

"Maybe not, and that high and mighty attitude is okay when you've got no competition and can keep the Indians sober; but they want their homebrew here now, and boy they get it. If Jeffers doesn't get on the ball and quietly make an exception here, there's no point in you comin' here a year. Hell, in a year —" he gestured emptily, as if a man could barely get out of the plane in a year, but at that moment the canoe swung in toward Bjornesen's crowded dock. Clearly everyone who had been at Frobisher had followed the plane and all the children who had found no canoe-space to cross over in the first place had joined them. Art swore under his breath, "Everybody not in fish camps is out — damn them — to see me go. The sonofaguns. Yeah — and the big grey-headed brute is Bjornesen."

Their canoe pushed between the rank of the others without scraping, caught its length by a dozen brown hands, and Abe scrambled out. The dock was solid; it would have been under water from the weight had it floated. He was barely erect when the huge white man he had glimpsed towering above the crowd came plowing between the unblinking Indians with hand out-stretched, "And this must be our new Frobisher man! I'm Sigurd Bjornesen and I'm glad to see you." His voice grumbled deep, his hand-clasp like a vise; Abe smiled but before he could say a word Art thrust between them.

"Yeah, Sig, this is Abe Ross, the next Frobisher man. And he'll be here when you leave, too!"

"Well, you know me Art," the big man laughed like the earth shaking; any child could comprehend the power the giant Icelander would have over the Indians at the expense of the other. "Trade is trade and let the better man take it! Hahaha," he laughed again, and the Indians who crowded about laughed too, jostling each other back a few paces on the narrow dock as the trader flung his arm over his head. "Frobisher Abe Ross with the great black beard has a strong fist. I haven't felt one as solid for a while. Listen, you all —" and he wheeled to face the people as they stood on the dock, up the slope of its walk to the rocks, and scattered about on the grass and leaning against boulders or barrels, his voice probing to the children chasing each other from behind trees or peeking past their mothers' skirts. The old trader's voice rose in high unintelligible language, and Abe understood he was being introduced. He looked at the people, trying to see and remember an individual, but they were only blurs in their mostly tattered clothes; here and there a clean skirt or a pair of half-ironed trousers stood out from the rest, but their faces he could not individualize, only note a gap-toothed mouth and a long scabbed nose and all the heavy hacked away hair and high cheeks burned black by the summer sun. When Bjornesen seemed to reach climax with something about Frobisher and then said "Abram Ross," Abe smiled at them, but there was no sound from the people facing him. Only their frank stare and, here and there, a smile which, when he caught the glance, slipped aside unembarrassed yet intractable — say something quick! — and he put his hand on Bjornesen's arm.

"Please tell them from me personally," he said loudly and slowly, "that I am happy to come to Frozen Lake and that I want to be their friend and that as soon as they can, whenever they can, I want them to come to Frobisher for a visit and a pot of tea."

Bjornesen's smile widened as Abe spoke. "Of course I'll tell them that!" and his language shifted. But Art jerked Abe's sleeve, hissing as the old man spoke,

"The first thing to remember with that old buzzard is — *never* use him to translate! He never says exactly what you said, just twists it so it comes out stupid. Doggoneit, you shoulda got George if you wanted to talk to them — hey —" he wheeled to the Indian still sitting in the canoe, "is he sayin' what Mr. Ross said? Huh? Why's he talkin' so long?"

The handman's head was bent, his right hand rubbing a torn spot on his left moccasin. "Yes. He's saying it."

Art turned to Abe, words running together swiftly, "Best thing is: don't trust nobody. George can't think things up fast like that old buzzard, but he'll never tell on him either. Best is never say a thing — just do. They understand good when their gut's empty."

Abe said harshly, "What about the preacher? Can he translate?"

"Josh?" the other was staring across the crowd, almost unmindful of the question. "Yeah." Art turned, his eyes still bright with anger, "he'll translate right enough, but he —"

"Hey," Abe interrupted, mind catching, "where does he buy his supplies?"

"Josh? Staples he gets from me."

"And he doesn't go along with homebrewing, surely —"

"Ha — that's the nuts of it! He talks against it and doesn't trade with Bjornesen — he used to half and half till he brought the yeast in — it's not much because his friends outside send a lot — but he doesn't *do* a —" Art's voice was lost in laughter and shouting as Bjornesen turned.

"Hear that?" the trader said, grinning, "they like your idea of tea. They'll be coming over for the next week — and longer than that if you let 'em!"

Abe looked at them laughing, the ring of Art's tone jarring in him, and he laughed with them all, lifting his hand, "Good! Good! You come," he shouted above the noise, and as he did so he saw a slight man appear among the press at the top of the sloping dock and the crowd part as he came down. Bjornesen pushed forward to intercept the smaller man, ducking under the wing and sticking out his arm.

"Preacher, you've got to meet our new Frobisher man — just arrived. Com'mon over here —" his huge hand cupped the other's shoulder, who smiled up with what seemed to Abe a completely innocent good-nature. His voice was quiet:

"Sig, he'll be here longer than Dave and Lena just rushed to finish these letters —" his eyes found Abe and he seemed to forget completely the envelopes in his hand. "How do you do? I'm Joshua Bishop — usually called Josh —"

"Around here he's the preacher!" boomed Bjornesen behind him. "Preacher, meet Mr. Abram Ross, Frobisher Company."

"I've heard about you, Mr. Bishop —" he hesitated over the familiarity as they shook hands, their glances level with each other, and Abe, poised as he was for resignation to the inevitable ooze of charm was not prepared for the serene friendliness that met him in the middle-aged face.

"Well, this is nice. Art will have to bring you around when he shows you the settlement. Can I tell Lena you'll both come for supper, say tomorrow? Or tonight, if it suits better."

Bjornesen said loudly, "Oh, that ain't fast enough. Art's out as soon as Dave can get this plane aloft. No stayin' around here for him," and his grin hardened just slightly at the corners as he looked around at Art standing on the strut-step adjusting baggage in the aircraft.

"Oh," Bishop said.

Abe cut in quickly, "He's long overdue here," and Bjornesen's grin tightened. "It was all arranged by the manager — Art has another job waiting in Fort William." And then Bjornesen turned away and Abe could have kicked himself for letting a glance lever him into cheap cover-up. That old Icelander was no buzzard; he would obviously feed on nothing he had not hawked himself.

". . . too bad," Joshua Bishop was saying, "In that case you'll be cooking for yourself right away. How about coming over to our place for evening meals until you get settled and have time to cook? We'd like to have you."

Abe gestured quickly, "That's very kind of you but I'll

113

probably be eating on the run for a few days. I've had a long holiday and a few days without full-course meals won't hurt this at all," he slapped his stomach. "I'll take you up soon, don't worry."

"Fine."

Dave was shouting, "Josh, you got those letters?" and Bishop turned, still smiling.

The final hustle of loading the plane — get identified with nobody just stay independent the store being over the channel helps — but as Abe watched Bjornesen knock a few boys' hats over their eyes and shout at a group of women that squatted on the shore, swaying their babies' cradleboards in the sun, he knew quickly that the channel was not wide enough, and too many of them lived on this side, near Bjornesen. There were women and children, but not many men; he remembered suddenly and pushed to the plane where Art was stowing his last bag.

"Art, you said some of them are out at fishing camps? Many of the men?"

Art's face bobbed around, red from exertion. "Nah. Most of the men of these women here are out fightin' fire — though Dave says the fire was licked last week. Probably drinkin' up what they got. There's some family camps out — the families that don't want to live just on destitute rations. Stupid thing is if they don't we don't get their trade. Bjornesen and MOA've got their fishin' tied up tight — MOA flies the fish out with Bjornesen as agent. So I always told them, when they'd listen, they should forget about fishin' — just hard work and the government would keep them alive anyways." Abe's face hardened and he added quickly, "Oh, I don't like the line myself, but it helped business — but —" he shrugged. "Anyway, they don't listen."

Abe cut down hard on his revulsion. "How many fish camps out of this band?"

"About five or six. Maybe seven."

"Where are they?"

"How should I know? They're no Frobisher business. What —"

"I'm going to fly around and see them," Abe wheeled, leaving the other with mouth agape. He found Dave, got what information he needed, then hunkered down with his notebook on his knee, writing:

Frozen Lake, July 7

Dear Horst: Arrived here at 11:10 this morning. Seven household groups are in fish camps; they stay pretty well all summer. I should visit them right now when they're away from S.B.: the best way to get to know the more active people here. I need your okay to rent a plane for a day or two — maximum not more than $250. Can you get this back to me immediately?

Abe.

He read it over, then added, "P.S. Art will explain details," tore out the page and folded it. He had no envelope; he looked up towards the plane but his eye caught on the tall grey-haired trader standing alone, staring across at the Frobisher buildings, and there was no laughter on his face. So intent was the look that, though his lined, heavy face was only half-turned from Abe, he did not shift his glance when Abe moved. For a moment Abe studied the old man unnoticed, and had he not seen it he would not have believed it possible for a human face to express so clear and clean a hatred. With a jolt he knew he had been thrown — I threw myself sure as the devil — into a no-holds-barred tussle, and even with the jolt he felt the spurt of excitement. This was what he needed; not mumbling thoughts flinging about like boneless arms; here it was, seize the known, and fight. At the thought he moved towards the plane and Bjornesen's eyes flicked to him, and in the very motion they blinked back into their original ice-blue blandness. Abe grinned and passed to the pilot on the near pontoon.

"Dave," he said, "it was good flying with you. Will I see you again?"

"You couldn't get away if you tried! I come in every week with the mail and sometimes I fly fish too."

"Good enough. I may need a plane soon for a few days; I'd like to get you, if possible."

"Yeah, that's for Boney to say," he grinned. "I'd like that. Good luck." He looked along the wharf, "Well, I guess we got everythin', eh Sig?"

The trader at Abe's shoulder boomed out. "All I can get in. But then this is Art's trip." He bent to look at the open door where Art was already belted in. "Make sure our friend gets out safe to the little wife. He's wanted to leave so long."

Art jerked his head forward and glared at the old man peering under the wing. "You're doggone right. And you can put all your Frozen Lake right up your —"

"Art," Abe pushed in loudly, blanketing the other's obscenity in the silence of the listening people, "there's something I want you to do for me." As Dave, grinning almost to open laughter, gripped the prop and swung across under the motor to the off pontoon, Abe stepped down to the near one and leaned in. Art's eyes were red-rimmed, his mouth still open in snarl. "Hell man," Abe said in fierce undertone, "don't leave a bigger mess than you have to." The other glared at him but said nothing, his words seemingly caught somewhere deep in frustration. Abe thrust the folded note into his hands as the pilot clambered in. "Here, give this to Horst. Read it. You'll know what to explain about it. Okay?"

"Yeah," sullenness settled over Art's face.

"Good enough. And good luck to you in Fort William. So long Dave — see you soon."

"You bet!" The pilot bent forward, "Okay men, push it!" Abe sprang to the dock. The men at wing and tail heaved and the plane bobbed away as the motor whirred and caught. Abe turned and walked the length of the dock to George Kinosay now standing by the Frobisher canoe, his black eyes almost carelessly following the wash of the plane.

"Let's go." Abe said. "Here, okay if I take this end?" he gestured toward the motor.

"Huh?" George's eyes shifted to him, a mild surprise waking in them.

Abe laughed, "Just see if I can still run a kicker."

George shrugged. They got in, George pushed them away with the paddle and at Abe's yank the motor barked. As they wheeled in a tight circle from the crowded dock the plane, far out on the water, bellowed into the silent noon and slashed across the channel mouth into the open waters of the lake. Before they had crossed it was a tiny orange dot in the sunwashed sky.

7

THOUGH the spruce of the distant shore smudged in the afternoon heat, in the canoe on the water a thick wool shirt was precisely comfortable. Abe sat in the bow, maps neglected on his knees; if he stretched out his hand the prow-spurt sprayed chill to his skin. He sat, watching, feeling the prow split the wavelets moving endlessly towards him. The motion on the long plain of Sandhole Lake seemed no motion at all, only an unwavering coming towards them caught in neither time nor place, the motor's unwavering whine shaping no sound but a great stillness that suspended him and canoebow above the relentless incoming ripples. The very spray was so regimented, so regular, in its falling and 'splut' drumming gentle as rain through the metal into his bones that, far from distracting him out of vacancy, it sketched against the vacancy a frill of white and spasmodically-flung rainbow color. He could almost feel some Elysian hand stroke down the thickness of his beard to brush his lips when a piece of wood bobbed across his vision and the suspension flicked away as quickly and all his senses told him they were driving as fast as a fifteen horse-power motor could propel them toward an island's long finger. And when they turned it they would see the Crane family fish camp across the last neck of water.

He pushed back his hat, held his hand to the spray, and ran it over his forehead. He looked back. George Kinosay sat bent as usual, left hand on the motor tiller and right propped on his right knee. Behind him the white wake belled blue across the lake. Abe grinned; a smile flickered across George's bony features.

Abe looked ahead again, content. In three weeks there had been little time to even guess what Griffin must have done or undone in three years to make a competent man who had risen to lance corporal in the Canadian Army in France so sullenly and uninitiatively useless unless directly ordered. The Tyrel Bay pattern of discussion and working together seemingly would not catch until he needed advice on the best possible way to get to all the fish camps on one day's plane rental. After several days of hesitancy, of looking away over the lake and shrugging vaguely George's idea had materialized out of mumbles, hints. And excellent too. On the first day they flew to the three camps on lakes unconnected by waterways, the third being the Kinosay camp of George's father and two brothers. There the plane left them, and they visited three other camps on the lakes off the Brink River system using a canoe they rented from old Kinosay and a motor brought in the plane. After a week they were before the last camp; and finally, too, the suggestion of a smile.

Tree by tree the far shore pulled out from behind the island as they approached the point. He studied the maps a last time: the Crane camp on the mainland a mile from the island; five miles further the Brink River emptying north-east, meandering broadly without narrow water; but then upstream against the Frozen River the twenty last miles to Frobisher, three long, five shorter portages around falls and half-mile rapids — god this trip should last a month to work the lard out of the brain! — Sandhole Lake opened on the edge of his vision; white tents dabbed between spruce and lighter poplar on the far shore. The motor had announced them for miles and figures were running together over the grey rocks, shading their eyes against the lowering sun, shirts and dresses and sweaters flamingo brilliant against the dark spruce and rocks like running fireworks tangled against a blotchy strip of evening. The usual things must be said most certainly here for from what he could gather, if the band had a single leader it was Kekekose, patriarch of the Crane family and the only remaining conjuror among the Frozen Lake Ojibwa.

The laughter and shouting reached over the water, fell to silence as they approached. The adults stood motionless; only the children dodged quick-footed over the round rocks. An old man made a gesture and a young man in red shirt and blue denims stepped down and caught the canoe before Abe could ease its speed with extended paddle. The move caught him by surprise; they had stood in such sober-faced ranks for so long he had expected to ground and scramble out without their hand and the smooth hoisting of the canoe onto the first rocks lost the Ojibwa word for thanks in his teeth as he looked into the pupilessly black eyes studying him. He said in English, "Thank you," and the lad's lips drew back in a grin and said,

"You're welcome,"

with such flawless accent that Abe knew immediately this must be Alex, Kekekose' youngest son, who had been out to Sioux Portage residential school three years and had suddenly returned, refusing to go back. Propriety overruled continuing in English however, so he smiled facing them all. "Bonjour!"

As the men answered, "Bonjour" in the usual high run-together nasal, Abe could without introduction recognize Kekekose with his long hair and heavy forehead over fierce black eyes, and the other old man who was his brother. Looking only at the six men, he gathered together the Ojibwa he had memorized and told them he was the new Frobisher trader at Frozen Lake, Abe Ross, visiting the people in the fish-camps and that he was happy to meet the Cranes. He could see laughter well silently in them as he fumbled the to him largely meaningless sounds and before he said the last he laughed aloud himself, easing their politeness, and the men and the women behind them and the frowsy-headed children peeking at him goggle-eyed, having all stared, breath-held and intent, on efforts which no white Frobisher trader had ever deigned, burst into laughter and talk. He turned to George on the rocks beside him, "Say, I don't know much Ojibwa yet, but wait and see in another two or three months!"

He could recognize some sounds but George spoke fast

and high-pitched, mouth open and large teeth clenched tight, running all as it were into one gigantic word, and Abe felt, as he had despairingly when first learning Eskimo, that his ear would never be able to pry apart the distinctions of the language. But he kept his smile, waiting for response.

It was old Kekekose who answered, voice thin and vivid. His face was folded in seams but it retained a near roundness which pulled to him a kind of youthful intensity; the people laughed and Alex translated, "He says that you are welcome and that he is sure you will learn Ojibwa better than English."

Only the men deserved the courtesy of introductions and under general laughter these were quickly made. Before George could name the last and youngest man, Abe smiled, hand reaching out, "You're Alex Crane, right?" and in proud embarrassment Alex could say nothing, only grin. According to George the lad was only eighteen, but physically he was as big as his two older brothers who had wives and families; beyond a doubt if Alex had not been out to school so long he would already be married. Abe, studying the lean handsome face, feeling the hard handclasp, understood why the gossip of his abrupt, for the unmarried girls heady, return still echoed at Frozen. And in the camps.

They pitched their tent near the others under the trees where moss lay soft in the hollows between blades of rocks. As Abe cut spruce boughs for bedding, followed and watched everywhere by toddlers and tattered little girls and lanky boys — so many more than in Eskimo camps — Alex came to invite them to the evening meal their arrival had interrupted. The day before William, Kekekose' oldest son, had shot a bear and the men squatted in the eating area between the tents beside the tripod over a smoking-fire eating the last of the meat, alternating with chunks of fresh bannock flavored with blueberries and sugar. The bear was stringy but Abe found it a fine change after fish and duck. Washed down with tea it was a good meal and he smiled his thanks as Kekekose' wife, the largest fattest woman he had seen in the entire band, a size that spoke well for her husband's (or sons') food-supplying ability, offered him the last of the hacked-up carcass skewered on its smoking-pole. "Good makwa," he said as he stripped a piece and she leaned back, her great stomach protruding over him, and laughed uproariously to the echo of others in the quiet evening. "Better, pukwaysegun," he held up the bannock she had evidently baked and she looked about her to all the gallery of women and girls — glory to hoist them intact to that basement parade-ground and give Sherris Kinconnell and her playtexed friends one solid whiff of primitive! — and laughed even louder.

After the meal he passed around his last tin of tobacco; the men stuffed their pipes and smoked. Black-flies going with the sinking sun, rich pipe smoke lingering about their nostrils: this was the good life. Even Henry Crane, Kekekose' younger brother, who nevertheless looked almost twice as old as the conjuror, seemingly had lost his moroseness. He squatted across the circle from Abe, breathing deeply, soaking in the smoke, allowing barely a twist to escape into the air.

The tin was passed a second time; it was empty when it returned to Abe. Immediately Albert, Kekekose' second son, went to his tent and brought his tobacco; there was little left but there was also no way to refuse politely and whatever joy he had in smoking lived in such a circle: on the second pipe puff little, inhale nothing, and wave the pipe freely in talk. There would be none until he spoke; he asked Alex to translate.

He did not try to follow words, as at the other six camps; rather he watched the men's faces. Tree-shadows fell like beams across their circle. Old Henry stared into the glowing bowl of his pipe; his only son Joseph, much older than Kekekose' married sons, peeled a poplar stick; William and Albert watched Alex intently, William's hooked nose livid in the low blaze of the sun. Only Kekekose sat in direct shadow where Abe could see nothing of his face. In any case he knew he was too shallow with them; in three weeks he could not yet tell what they might be thinking. He looked at Alex beside him; translating had only slightly blunted the look of amazement: that Frobisher would now accept every item of fur at an honest price, trying to out-bid no one; that the checks for family allowances or old age pension need no longer be taken in supplies at Frobisher but could, if they wished, be cashed to buy things wherever they wanted; that the government would continue to provide destitute rations only through Frobisher but if they wanted they could change that too by talking to the Indian agent; and finally that any trapline owner or young man who had not trapped on his own before but wanted to begin and had trapping territory would receive as large a grubstake as the average of his last three years trapping for his father, with supply prices held steady throughout the winter.

But Alex had been out three years; his reaction meant little and from the others there was no point waiting. There had been no response at the other camps — if George at least would mutter one word if this was stupidity! — but into the silence that had fallen to even the rowdy children the voice of the conjuror suddenly brought a snort of laughter from his two older sons: Abe looked at Alex, who grinned. "He says, 'Bjornesen will be really good friends with you for this.'"

Abe blinked. "What word did he use for Bjornesen?"

Alex hesitated, looking quickly across Abe to George, but he was looking down, motionless. After a moment Alex said, "Wagoss — fox." It was the first time the other trader had been mentioned on the trip and he had not heard that name before, not even from Bishop. Clearly it was the trader's Indian name, but no hint of expression now betrayed Kekekose' real meaning. And there was no more talk.

Abe stood up, knocking out his pipe. "I have something for the children," he said loudly in slow English so the older ones would understand. "Everyone twelve and under come with me." Before he had taken five steps towards his tent the children had bunched about him. "Say," he turned, the more curious middle-sized ones nearest him, the youngest with some taller girls hanging back, "we'll need cups to drink. Will you bring some cups?" Two older girls, with a giggle, turned and ran back to the smoking frame. "Come," he waved and went on, the children pushing close and he tousled a head. "I don't know your names, so you'll have to tell me. What's your name, fella?" The boy, perhaps ten years old, his hair bristling from his long-nosed face as if it had been hacked with a dull axe, said on the bare corner of audibility, "Simon."

"Hello Simon. Can you introduce me to — are they all your brothers and sisters?" Laughter, more seen than heard, a suppression of incomprehensible merriment at a white man's ignorance, rippled over them. Abe's glance caught a little girl's eye and she ducked away, her giggle smothered behind her hands. "Nah," said Simon, "cousins, too."

When they reached the tent the girls with several tin cups had caught up and Abe had heard the by now usual roster of children's names: Fred, Samuel, Eli, Henry, Albert, Margaret, Amy, Agnes, Emily, Lucy. The littlest ones, whom the taller girls heaved about on bent backs or prodded along now and then with their bare feet, apparently did not deserve identification. After a pause at the tent for the water bucket and a brief hike to the spring nearby to get it filled, they were hanging about him like a flurry of opossums, clutching his trousers where they could, elbowing to touch him. They rolled down the path to the lake in one laughing shouting body, dropping here and there a squalling straggler no sooner marooned than hushing and flinging forward into the thick of them shouting down the tilt of the rocks to the lake, Abe holding the bucket aloft to keep at least some water in it and feeling like flotsam on the crest of a riptide. Then they were down by the canoe, swirling around and Abe halted, shouting, "Okay, okay! Now quiet. Quiet! Before I do anything you all sit down, in rows like in school — right here on the rocks. All along here. I'll do it where you can all see. Simon," he shook off the hacked-haired boy leeched to his right elbow, "tell them — right — everyone sit down." With shouting and shoving and knocking about a body here and a head there they were finally seated, though squirming still, on the rocks and Abe begun unbuckling his pack.

"Now, I need a stick. Can I use yours — Fred, is it?" and the boy quickly stuck out the white-peeled poplar he had been waving even during the flow down to the canoe. Abe leaned back and swished the stick in the lake. "Sure. That's fine. Now, I'll open these little envelopes and I'll — watch —" he leaned the bucket forward so that all could see, even the craning necks in the back crescent of half-moon about him, and one after another he poured out the fruit powders.

The children sighed like wind in rushes as the deep color flamed through the water. "Now, plenty of sugar — there — and we stir it with Fred's nice stick." They bent forward, unblinking eyes pulled inward by the whirling funnel and he stirred well, drawing out the moment. "All right," he said at last, "Now, where are the cups?" and two girls and a boy jammed their long arms between the clustered heads, cups poised to plunge. "No, no, hold it! I'll use my cup to fill yours, and the littlest get turns first. Isn't that the way you do in school? Eh?"

"Yah," said the boy. "I'll hold for my kid brother. There's him."

"Sure, Eli. Now, everybody sit down on the rocks again. Just sit — right. There's plenty."

With only three cups it took some time; Fred sucked his stick while waiting his turn and a few heads bumped when others demanded a share, but the simple ecstasy of the flavored drink dried every tear. When the bucket was drained, Abe passed out the last of his candy and sat watching them, drawing out their talk. By then there was little they would not have done for him and so many charged into Ojibwa and English at once that understanding was impossible. He let talk who would, several at a time, sometimes quieting them for a moment with a question, sometimes merely watching them show-off pushing ram-like on the rocks. But most of all they wanted to sit near and look at him, running their thin hands, often scab-covered from neglected sores, over the black hair on his arms. Only an occasional hand reached up to his beard, though the way it mesmerized their glance told its magic for them. He had known this at every camp, and not for the children only, but they alone were frank enough to betray themselves. Simon brushed his hand gently down Abe's beard; Abe grinned into his friendly face.

"It's sof'," the boy said in his pale voice, and the little girl who had ducked away in laughter, now sitting on Abe's lap, reached up again as if the whisper were enough for another reassuring brush.

Simon said suddenly, "You fly jet?"

Abe remembered a day several weeks before, "You mean like

the Air Force planes that fly over Frozen Lake sometimes — with a white streak over the sky?"

"Yah! Today — one," Simon swung his arm in an arc, northward. All the children were staring at Abe again, incredulously.

"Those are planes for one person only — just the pilot. I can't fly like that. But I've flown in big, big jets, that're as long as from here to the tents and hold more people than this camp." He gestured, and their eyes followed his spreading arms as if they were wings to snatch him into the sky. "They hold as many people almost as live at Frozen Lake."

"Over hunred?"

"Sure, over a hundred. You could fly in one from here to — in — less than an hour to —" he stopped, searching for meaning.

"United 'Tate," Eli said quickly from the low shadow of the canoe.

"Sure, that's right, to the United States in less than an hour. Very very fast."

The sun had long fallen behind the island; several smaller children tilted in sleep against their sisters, yet even when they stirred and awakened the older ones would not leave. Finally they all shuffled up to Abe's tent together; when he waved they left him, without a word. Simon looked back just before they vanished in the black under the trees. Abe bent into the tent where George was already asleep.

He lay motionless on his blankets, struggling with wordless thoughtless shapes like bee-swarms droning through his mind. His hands came up to his forehead; he roused to stickiness. With a groan he hunched around and dug out towel, soap, and wash-basin and scrambled out again. A spot of firelight flickered from among the tents; perhaps the sheet of rock-supported tin that served as a stove was still warm. He poured water into the basin from the bucket he had brought from the lake and walked towards the fire.

Among the farther trees a baby cried, then hushed. They would be up at dawn to empty the nets and clean and ice the fish so when the sun sank they dropped the sides of their tents and rolled in their bedding. The camp was the cleanest of any he had seen; even the floors of the tents were covered with clean spruce boughs and the smells were only of crushed needles and green tamarack smoke drifting over the gutted tullibee on the smokerack. It was a good camp, facing the island and the vanished sun.

And there were white coals in the stone circle. He placed the basin on the hot tin and hunkered down, looking between the tree-trunks at the washed strip of the lake, the bulk of prickly island, and the final flush of the heated-lead sky. After a moment he realized, startled, that two small figures were hunched beside the stones across from him. He flicked on his flashlight, down into the basin, and at the edge of illumination he saw the faces of two girls. With a scramble of memory he remembered the younger and he said softly, "Hello Lucy. I didn't see you there. Who's your — friend?" There was only a smothered giggle. "Your sister?"

"Yah."

"I haven't met her. What's your name, Miss Crane?" The girls giggled loudly this time and in the darkness Abe knew he had seen her standing with the women about the tents while the men ate — not likely to miss the best-looking girl since Winnipeg — he could think of no reasonable excuse to switch on the light again. "What's your name?" he repeated finally.

"Violet." Her voice was full and womanly. She must be at least fifteen; and not married, looking like that. Probably that was why she was waiting here; she would not wait alone, and the younger girl would leave when the boy came. But they were so closely related in the camp, who — he could not leaf that complexity apart and then he laughed to himself for concocting a romance because two girls sat by a fire late at night. He stuck his finger in the water; it was warming and he would not have much chance left, so he tried. But they would not talk; they giggled or made no sound, neither did they make a move to leave. He could think of nothing to do finally but get up. "Well girls, water's warm for washing. Have a good sleep." He picked up his basin and turned back towards his tent. Their soft laughter followed him, but whether it was affectation or the strangeness of him heating water to wash he could not tell.

Even after a thorough wash he could not sleep. He lay in his blankets hearing George snore beside him and a stir in the spruce fingering the tent-flaps. If he could get to Kekekose he would trade not only with the two best-producing families in the band, the Kinosays and the Cranes, but also the public weight of the old conjuror, whatever it amounted to — it must be plenty — would work for him in the band. But there would be no way of deciding where Kekekose stood, not during this trip, as there was no way of deciding about any of the other fish camp people. The purpose of this trip was merely to become acquainted; just a start at wrecking Griffin's overpaying for sub-standard furs and cheap little blackmails would be success enough. Patience was needed, now as much as always, and there was no way of rushing them — once they sense that they'll never budge — but now this sleepless spell tangled him in an at-the-moment bind as it did sometimes, and there was no sleep. So think somewhere else, if possible. The song his mother used to hum as she came towards the barn with the milkpails shining like fire from the setting — no! — Bjornesen still pretending laughing openness when occasionally met, though that once he had surprised him on the docks cursing honestly enough. Surprised himself too. The Bishops. In two weeks at Frobisher he had almost succeeded in avoiding them; it was just barely possible without rudeness because they lived across the channel. The man seemed devilishly clever at walking the thread between casual friendliness and pushing himself — maybe it was just plain decency? — and he was certainly no preaching leech, for all Bjornesen's loudmouthed "Preacher, preacher!" More mill-wright and gardener, if anything, keeping whatever men were around Frozen sawing logs at the mill and youngsters in group-shifts pulling a cultivator in the one potato-patch across the lake huge enough for the whole settlement. There wasn't any Sunday service, leave alone a church; there was no preaching at all. No wonder no mainline church would — ahh get tangled in that again —

He shook his head clear and stared open-eyed into the

darkness. Shreds of light, from the cloud-hidden moon perhaps, fingered along the white slope of the tent: the wings of a night-hawk whistled overhead; from the lake a loon laughed in maniac. On the water marks of the tent roof he could see as if physically caught aloft the bent shore where the camp stood bulging out black into the night-pale water. It was a fine camp-site and the people cleaner than most. Though the girls giggled at warm water for an evening wash. At that the laugh of the girl, and the deep sound of the one word she had said, 'Violet', nicked him, and, slowly like the pulse of his blood the thought of her spread through his body — there'd be something to root out sleeplessness! — he dug into his remembrance, trying to find and see her precisely among the women in the background while the men ate bear and bannock but it helped little; he could only remember the black shoulder-length hair outlining oval face with glinting black eyes in the penumbra of yellow light beyond the sheet-stove. Indian girls were often strikingly beautiful before teen-age childbearing crumpled them. The very imprecision of his knowledge blossomed his conviction of her beauty and thrust his desire deeper — of all the sacred stupidities! — his peculiar density enraged him again, as it had times before. He should have understood: Lucy had been the contact. Violet had simply been using her to get talked to, and he, lost in whatever it was he could not recall, had tried to get them to talk about camp and whether they were waiting for school — dense wasn't the word! — his mind rode on uncontrolled for some time until his body overruled and he threw back the hot blanket. A touch of air through the open tent slid across his naked body like a caress.

Cursing, he jerked erect. The luminous dial showed 11:05. Thirty-five miles tomorrow: fifteen clear sailing and then eight portages hoisted up twenty miles of Frozen River. A streak of moonlight glinted a path over the lake and with a lunge he got up, fumbled for towel and shirt, tucked them under his arm, slipped on his boots and walked down over the rocks to the lake. Nothing stirred. The air brushed cool over the alert sensitivity of his nakedness. He dropped towel, shirt and boots in his canoe and stepped into the water. It was warm against the night but the rocks hurt and after three gingerly steps he slid forward in a shallow dive, surfaced, shook back his hair and began to stroke a slow steady crawl toward the island. As in the flow of water his muscles loosened their bunching he swam faster and faster; the last hundred yards where the shadow of the island blotted up the moonlight from the surface he was sprinting for the little pier where the plane docked to pick up the fish. He stretched an arm and clung to a piling, chest heaving, not touching the rocks below, the air only against his face. Gradually out of the darkness of the spruce the blacker hulk of the icehouse and the shack where the pickerel and whitefish lay packed in ice emerged. His arm circling the ooze-barked piling, for a long time he hung limp as a slit fish, held in the water's limbo of no force and insensate equilibrium; foetus buoyed in fluid, warding off all sensation, every nerve-cluster over-satiated, over-fed. At long last his consciousness reasserted itself and he pushed away, loafing back slowly, soundlessly. When he dog-paddled he could see only the mass of the mainland, but when he kicked easily on his back, the broken path of the moonlight led without end over the lake.

So well did the moon draw him that when he reached shore and touched the canoe he found it wasn't his. He had been pulled to the left among the camp canoes. He paddled past their sterns, feet avoiding the shallow rocks, and when he got beyond the last of them fish-stinky in the night he saw his canoe's shape against the lightness of the shallow inlet fifty yards away. He squatted a moment, only eyes and nose above water, staring at the incredible black and light before him. The lake shone as the southern sky and from low in the water the black bulk of rocks and trees towered overwhelmingly above him, their top line slanting straight away, their bottom curving into the inlet and then back on itself to meet somewhere beyond in the indiscernible, distant light. At precisely the inward turn of that bend the slight curve of his canoe blunted by the hump of its motor poised black and tiny. Looking, a kind of mystic immensity grew to a tearing apart within him and fell away into the waterway that wrapped him to the bay and the ice-flecked ocean far east and north. On a ball under the turning stars he knew himself a speck and with that he knew all, simply staring for perhaps an hour perhaps half a minute. And when the two figures materialized against the inlet and bent over the canoe he did not comprehend what less he was seeing; what he had seen and what he had gradually lost feeling for held him beyond particular caring as he began to paddle forward; he was not even annoyed at interruption for he knew without conscious thought such an experience could not be held to be interrupted. He did not even remember that he had no clothes on to step out and challenge whoever it was had come to pry in the canoe. In a limbo, unattached, he simply paddled silently, the splash of his progress less than the waterlap upon the rocks, the two figures so intent on unbuckling his supply pack that they had no alertness for the lakeside in any case and when he thrust his head up beside the canoe at their very feet he said, "What do you want?" They leaped back and apart, tensed for flight like animals, yet not fleeing quite.

At their very motion he recognized them as they must have recognized the black hairy oval of his head in the silver water. "Alex — Violet? Huh?" He would not have thought alarm would fade so quickly from their moon-lit faces. Alex said, peering,
"That you, Mr. Ross?"
"Yes."
"Gee," the boy's breath eased out, and he laughed slightly, nervously, "you sure come from nowhere."
"I guess." Annoyance stirred him. He looked past Alex's burly shape to the girl who stepped forward a little, and even in the dimness he could understand that his earlier imaginings had barely done her justice. And that was why he had originally come out; but hardly now. "Well, how about it?" There was an edge of anger in his tone which the boy caught, to judge from his start. But they remained silent.

"Hand me the towel — there, in the front." Alex hesitated, then came nearer. Abe sat up, dried his head and torso, then stood erect wrapping the towel around his waist. He teetered a moment on the slippery rocks, pulled on his shirt and sat down in the canoe. He plucked a cloth out of the sprawled open pack and slowly dried his feet, not looking at the two. "You're the first in all the camps that tried this," he tossed the empty sack back on the clutter. "Anyway, there's nothing left worth taking. I guess you found that out. Or would have soon enough." He pulled on his boots and stood up, tucking the towel tight. "Eh?"

It was obvious the boy was trying to look devil-may-care but not even the half-light could hide his growing apprehension. Finally he said, voice a little heavier with accent, "We were just — you know — see what it was. Not take nothin'. Honest."

Abe looked to the girl. They had not run away and the curve of the girl's full lips — by god her eyes gleam — he said, "She dared you, huh?" Alex stared but said nothing, "Sure," Abe probed, suddenly awake to their humanity, "and what are you running around in the middle of the night for with your sister?"

"Sister! She's not my sister!" Alex spluttered even as the girl laughed her low, immensely womanish laugh.

"I guess not," Abe's voice was clipped with double meaning. "Who's your father, Violet?"

"It's —" Alex began and Abe cut him off,

"She can talk. Who's your father?"

"Joseph Crane," her voice was low as her laugh, and still hung on the edge of it as if being thought Alex's sister at this moment carried innumerable varieties of infinite amusement. Abe was thinking, If she's Joseph's daughter, then she's Alex's second cousin — ha who wouldn't know what to chase after that in the dark — he looked at Violet, then Alex, and abruptly he laughed. Immediately they echoed him. The sound bounded back from the trees and over the lake and they hushed.

Abe put his hand on the towel and the girl's laugh belled again. "I'm not really dressed comfortably to entertain you, but I think," he bent to the pack, "maybe there's a pocket here you missed. Sure —" his fingers found it and dug out the last two bars of chocolate. "I was keeping these for the portages on Frozen River tomorrow, but —" he stretched his hands to them, "Go head. You don't get to Frobisher very often."

In defiance Alex might have spoken but before laughter and generosity he was dumb — this is luck sure! — "Here, take it. My legs are cold and I'm sleepy." Alex took one and Abe extended the other to Violet. "Alex, maybe you could repack that like you found it?" Abe was looking at the girl and her teeth flashed in her smile. "Be careful with him, girlie. Don't get him into too much trouble." He walked up the hill, knowing their eyes followed him; he was asleep almost before he flipped the blanket over.

In the morning they ate their own salt pork fried and the fresh bannock Kekekose' wife had left for them. Though the sunlight hardly brightened the island across the channel, only an old woman and the smallest children were in camp. They loaded the canoe and crossed to the island where the night's catch was being gutted and packed. Even in the early morning shade the air was aswarm with flies but everyone came down to the dock to say goodbye. Abe tried to draw Kekekose into conversation but the old man found it convenient, it seemed to Abe, to hear very little that morning, even when Alex translated. The women all had small sacks of smoked fish to send relatives at Frozen Lake; though they had refused these at earlier camps, since they should reach Frozen Lake before nightfall Abe agreed here. While stowing the last of the sacks he noticed Joseph Crane talking rapidly to George; the night seemed to have cured his silence. George was coming down the pier, Joseph waving his arms behind him, but the interpreter looked as noncommital as ever.

"Joseph, he wants you to take his girl back."

"What?"

"To Frozen Lake, his girl. That one," and he pointed behind the older Indian and Abe saw Violet. In the flurry of morning he had not allowed himself a thought of her. She stood carelessly behind her father, wearing the pale-blue sweater and cotton print dress he remembered from the night before, her expression completely blank as if they were talking about something in which she had no sliver of interest. Everyone stood, listening.

"Why?" Abe said slowly.

Joseph clutched George's arm and broke into a stream

of Ojibwa that rolled on and on swelling with anger as the listening children began to snicker, first a few, trying to hold back, and then all, until Henry Crane, the girl's grandfather, shouted one word above Joseph's harangue and silence fell again.

George bent forward and said as an excited boy tripped and fell with a great splash into the water, "She and Alex are running around too much, at night."

"Well, why don't they get married then? They're old enough," Abe said as quietly.

"Old, yah, but they — it's maybe not so good if they do —" he shrugged, not trying to explain. "Joseph says now they're just — you know —" he shrugged again, not yet quite sure of what words to use and not knowing how to talk around them, "— you know — around. So, he asks if you take her to her aunt in Frozen."

Abe looked to the family; the youngsters snickered but the adults showed no amusement whatever — Alex disappeared why don't they marry? — his eye caught Violet's an instant and the gleam he saw jabbed him. Perhaps it wasn't Alex or the family that created the problem; in Indian society that would be a very odd turn indeed. He turned to Joseph,

"Sure, Joseph, sure. The girl can come. We take her."

An immense relief brightened the Indian's gloomy face. While the girl and her mother went with George to get her few clothes, Abe talked with the others, Simon and Eli beyond pride in translating. There was talking everywhere but their curt answers kept his questions at the usual distance and he could not risk their probable annoyance by asking the two boys to translate what they said among themselves — a few months and they won't hide so easy! — then the canoe was back and, with Abe in front, George at the motor, and Violet sitting in the middle on top of the main pack, now neatly buckled, they roared away toward the southeast corner of the lake where the Brink River twisted east to Hudson Bay. The Crane family stood on both shores, watching, waving, the children sprinting over the rocks after them at break-neck speed. But the girl in the canoe sat erect, motionless, her eyes on her hands folded in her lap.

8

THE orange September sun bulged over the western spruce across Frozen Lake when Abe climbed up the path of the point where the Indians lived in summer and found men already busy. The children who had swarmed when his canoe touched tugged at him, but he walked on, careful not to stumble against any. At his greeting the men quietly responded, and he watched their hatchets slit the bark off the long poles. He asked, in his slow Ojibwa, "Where is Kekekose?"

Joe Loon, a tall man sharpening the end of a stripped birchpole, bunched the scar on his face when he laughed: "No need for him yet! We can at least build the shaking-tent." The others laughed quickly at Abe's expense; especially, he noticed, a huddle of men somewhat apart whom he could not recognize and who were merely watching also. He grinned; his efforts to learn the language held for them any depth of repeatable laughter and he was content that it should be so.

The children had scattered. Moving without the discussion that usually accompanied even the smallest common effort, one by one six men pounded their poles, alternately birch and spruce, into the ground until they stood rigid in a circle about four feet across. The men stood about then, speaking in swift Ojibwa Abe could not follow, looking away at the flaming sun or testing the give of a pole. Occasionally a loud guffaw from the men merely watching barked at them,

135

and once a brutal looking man with a smashed nose yelled a word Abe did not know but whose tone half-sounded challenge. At that one of the workers, James Sturgeon, jerked about, but Loon spoke sharply, "They are coming," and Abe saw Albert and Alex Crane walking up from the houses. They brought thin willow poles and tied them at three levels horizontally inside the circle, making hoops that bulged the structure like a barrel. Then James got up on the rock from which they had pounded in the tall poles and, with other men bending them, tied the pole-tops together. Albert handed up some caribou toe bones and these were hung inside the top of the cone. In the meantime several other men had brought up stiff sheets of untanned moosehide and they tied these over the framework. Finally there was nothing to be seen but the hide-covered beehive about seven feet high with six pole-ends angling out at the top.

The usual small joking was gone now as the men stood about, their job done, waiting; even the broken-nosed Indian — where has he been until now to escape notice? — and his group waited silent. Abe got up and moved nearer. The green hides stank slightly in the motionless air. He said to Alex in English, "How strong is it?" The boy grunted, half-turned away. Since returning to Frozen Lake from the fish-camp Abe had seen him so rarely that the only explanation was that he was being avoided; perhaps he should have refused Violet the canoe-ride — Alex was saying,

"Try and see."

Abe looked at James Sturgeon but no expression of understanding registered on his face. So he stepped forward, thrust his arm through the entrance flap below the bottom hoop and heaved at one of the poles. Strong as he was, it took a full-body jerk to rattle the bones dangling at the top. He turned to the men with a grin, about to exclaim at the rigidity, when Albert flared into quick Ojibwa whose tone was clear enough. Alex translated quickly, "He says you shouldn't touch it; not till the conjuror's done."

In the silence only tensing jaw muscles betrayed the younger man; all the others were looking at Abe grimly. His eyes found Albert and he said carefully in Ojibwa: "I'm sorry. I don't know."

Albert shrugged and muttered something unintelligible but across the circle Joe Loon dropped a few quick words that opened laughter in the whole group. Abe thought he caught the words "white man" and laughed apologetically, not pretending amusement their quick perception would have discredited in any case. Patching words together he faced Joe, "Good joking now," he pointed to himself, "but soon, I know too much Ojibwa." At least that is what he thought he said; the ready laughter seemed at least partly with him and he knew he could leave as he could not with them sneering. He pushed past Alex — cheap little trick! — between the crowd beginning to gather, and walked up the slope toward the log shack where Harry Sturgeon lay on what Josh Bishop insisted was a death-bed.

Picking his way between rocks, he did not think of the dying man or the mystery of his illness, or even of the conjuring Kekekose was about to attempt to dig out its cause. The others might write off his mistake as ignorance — did I break a vital sequence or something? — but Alex showed his hand too plainly to ignore. When the Cranes paddled in from fish-camp and came en masse to collect the summer months' family allowances, Alex's initial sullenness gradually lifted to what then seemed warm-hearted laughter as all the men lounged on the store-porch steps and the children chased each other up and down the tree-hedged path to the dock, faces streaked with the first candy in a month. Yet Alex had not once come across the channel in two weeks. It must be Violet.

He was almost at the doorless opening of the Sturgeon cabin and he did not quite know why he had come. Inside the bustle of people about the mattress in the corner where the sick man lay seemed more stifling than the night before; if either of the Bishops were there, as they were inevitably, they could tell him what little there was. He suddenly did not wish to face the to him silent women and the sick man's gasps for air. He turned; the sun was gone like a blaze dying in a sprawl of livid coals and the evening lay black behind the cabins and rocks and under the spruce along the lake rim. To the left of the blunt point the channel of the river and before him and away to the south-west half of the lake's boomerang bend the water held the pale remembrance of the sun's dying and the moon's red-faced birth humping up in the east. On the slope below figures eddied about the white point of the conjuring lodge in the clearing between scattered cabins and thrust up on the last, farthest, bulge of the land before it dropped away into the lake stood the big cabin where the dance, the prelude to conjuring tonight, had boomed out for two evenings past, its roof faintly orange in the light. All the Indians of Frozen Lake had danced to Kekekose's water-drum, men alone and women alone, the thin line of the single-file swelling against the low walls of the house. He had stood with those not dancing at the frameless window watching — the dance wasn't white imitation yet — an occasional young man signal to the drummer and the rhythm shift to the howe-anay or gift-giving dance. The other dancers would stop and the man would go to another (usually his cousin, George explained) and, chanting the howe-anay song, offer a small gift. That person in turn, sometimes in embarrassment for the dancers and watchers always laughed, would follow the singer back into the dance circle and the original rhythm would continue, the sound of thumping feet and smell of bodies pounding the house tight with heavy sensation. What little Abe could see, George looking over his shoulder and explaining when he asked, it appeared that Alex and Violet never glanced at each other. Several girls gave presents of hair-clips, small combs to Violet and she danced slowly behind them, everyone staring at her, her long red dress a foil for her olive face and gleaming hair but Alex, when he danced, did not recognize that she existed. And she had never raised her eyes, even to her girl partners.

A hand touched Abe's sleeve; it was Lena Bishop. "I saw you hesitate out here," she said, her usually brisk voice gaunt with fatigue, "so I'll break into your evening-dream." It was like her, despite her alternate watching with Josh beside the desperately ill man for days, to greet him with a gentle pleasantry. He smiled.

"How's Sturgeon?"

"No better. Perhaps a little worse." She moved abruptly off the main path and sat heavily on a stone, as if the long hours weighed in the clean air. "It's so crowded but there aren't any windows so he at least gets a little fresh air. The relatives are so afraid he's dying and everyone wants to look for a last time."

"Really that bad?"

She nodded. "If only James and Mary — and the rest would let the plane take him back once more to Red Lake —"

Eyes on the cone of the lodge, Abe said, in an effort to cut the heaviness, "Well, the doctors only had two tries at him. Maybe Kekekose can —"

"Don't talk about him like that!" At her tone he jerked towards her in amazement. The last sun high etched her motherly features.

"Why," he stuttered, "you don't think he can do something — in that — thing?" he gestured. "You and Josh, of all people —"

"We've been here over three years, and we've heard enough never to underestimate them — ever."

"Have you seen him conjure?" Abe tried to fumble some comprehension into his thinking. For several weeks he had been working at Ojibwa grammar with Josh; to understand words they often talked long about Indian concepts but now as he wracked his brain to drag up some sliver of what Josh had said about their conjuring beliefs he could not recall a thing. They had talked about it so little there could be only one explanation: Josh avoided it altogether.

Lena was saying, "No. We always thought we never could go there. It's too — devilish, somehow. Josh wanted to go, sometimes, but I always persuaded him to do so would be — a kind of recognizing devilishness." She hesitated, sensing his opposition. "Abe," she burst out suddenly, "when those drums beat on full-moon nights — it's really worse than their brewing, almost. With brew they're — it's terrible and they go almost crazy — but they get over the drunk, but the druming, and the lodge — they — I know you think I'm silly."

He was staring at her. In the heaping up of that evening

he would never have time quite to analyse how her words now shattered him; for what little he had known of her and Josh, he could never have even distantly imagined that she would shudder before such a fear. He said, hardly knowing what, "Why, I thought you believed in a god —"

"Abe, I believe in God. He alone has kept us here. But that man can do things, in that lodge."

"What? Besides maybe curing people who think they're sick?"

Down the slope before them beyond the cluster of people a great fire flared up against the gathered darkness. Lena's face was in shadow. "You don't think Harry Sturgeon is sick, do you."

"Oh sure, he's sick. I can tell a man as sick as he is. But why can't the doctors in Red Lake find it out? He's never sick there; why's he sick a day after he's back? He probably thinks somebody's got it in for him here, eh? If a man thinks he's dying long enough he'll die, I can believe that all right. George almost said as much today. Who's put the pressure on him — Kekekose? What good'll it do him scaring Harry to death? He's got nothing but a big family —"

"No, it's not him. And the medicines we give don't help a thing; I've tried everything."

"Sure, I know. Well, if it isn't the old boy, who is it? How many magic men are there in this little place?"

Abe laughed despite himself, the warmth of his insistence lifting him over his disappointment in her but her face as it turned to the last light snuffed even that momentary easiness.

"Bjornesen," she said quietly.

"Bjornesen!"

"Hasn't Josh told you about Harry and Kekekose and Bjornesen?"

"No."

"He intended to, really, last time, but you got telling your Arctic stories and then time passes so fast. But you would have learned of them soon enough. Harry and Kekekose are the only Indians who have protested against Bjornesen. A few others might want to but are afraid and the rest are pretty well under his thumb —"

"Why those two?"

"Kekekose knows what's happening to the band, especially with drink. Harry respects him and he's worried about the men getting so drunk they don't care much what they do. Last spring it got just frightful and Harry told Bjornesen he was going to the RCMP. You know Art Griffin swore out a warrant two years ago and the police came and couldn't find anything. Bjornesen just laughed at them. But Harry could have shown them the stills —" she stopped.

"And?" Abe asked at last.

"In front of all the Indians at his store he cursed Harry. Just terrified him. And about a month later Harry got sick. Like he is now. He couldn't go fishing this summer, his family just on rations —"

"But Bjornesen's white! He doesn't know anything about —" Abe stopped, his knowledge of native susceptibility to threat cutting his assertion. "Sure, sure, so Harry was scared. But, good heavens, Lena, a thousand white men a day swear at Indians!"

"He cursed. He used all the Ojibwa curse formulas; he knows them maybe even better than Kekekose, Josh says, because they say he has never cursed anyone. And I don't know how it can choke that poor man like it does, how should I? You've seen him, and he's dying, and all our prayers," her words fell away. Her face was turned from him towards the final shimmer of lake to the west and Abe stood inert — incredible superstition! — when a voice said behind them,

"Lena?"

They turned; a slight figure materialized on the path. Lena said, "Yes Josh," and in a moment he was beside them.

"Oh, good evening," he said to Abe. "I came to get Lena and the two girls wanted a walk too," he gestured as two shapes emerged behind him. "It's a bit dark for introductions. Abe, you've met our daughter Anne; and Miss Howell, too?"

"Good evening," Abe said, "Sure, we said 'hello' at least, when Miss Howell came in."

Her clear voice said, "Don't you think, Mr. Ross, that at a second meeting we could be less formal? I'm Sally."

141

He could not see her. When he had first heard from Josh that the new teacher would be a woman he had toyed with an occasional thought of getting to know a woman concerned enough about teaching to spend her efforts on Indian children, but when she clambered down to the pontoon and was helped to the dock his abrupt disappointment had forced him to admit his subconscious at least was still dominated by the spume of Winnipeg girls in tight skirts and piled-up hair and that somehow his sometimes dull imagination should have prepared him for the sturdy, low heel oxfords, the neat bun of indiscriminate sandy hair, and all the maidenly primness between. They had not seen each other since; though she lived with the Bishop's, she was never there when he went for language discussions, the light in the old government warehouse now roughly converted to classroom still burning when his canoe took him back across the channel. When, in a pause of other thinking, his mind slipped to the thought of her probably struggling to get these wild children disciplined to the regimen of school, he had felt a kind of sadness that, of all the world of teachers, Frozen Lake — admit it in thought at least! — should be granted the mercy of such severe schoolteacherishness as her tight-lipped face betrayed at first meeting. Not even Anne Bishop's thirteen-year-old rapture at returning home from a long holiday outside could offset — stupid to expect anything else! — but in the darkness she sounded abruptly different. "Oh sure," he said, "I'm Abe," but he had no time to puzzle that for the second time that night his considered estimate of a woman had bent before facts for Anne was saying breathlessly,

"Daddy, I'm sure they're ready to start. Couldn't I stay — just once — and watch? I'd just stay with Violet, among the women. Honest, Kekekose wouldn't know. Please!"

"Anne, we talked this over long ago," Josh's voice was its gentle self but the girl did not insist against it. "We just came to get Mama."

"Josh," Lena said quickly, "I have to tell Mary again about the medicine. It's little enough —"

"Okay. And remind them I'll come as soon as its over — when they're finished down there."

Lena turned to go, then hesitated close to Abe. She started to say something, stopped, then hastily, "Whatever you think now, Abe, when you stay a few more months you'll not doubt what Bjornesen can do. Not anything." She turned. "Come Anne. Help me carry the empty pans."

The two figures moved up the slope towards the cabin where a small aura of lamplight now outlined a shifting crowd of people. "She give you some background on Harry's sickness?" Josh asked.

Abe could have laughed at this matter-of-factness: as if they were doctors discussing a case in a sterilized operating room. He said, "I don't get it; I thought you were a practical man and now I find out you think that old Icelander's thrown some kind of spell on Sturgeon because he had the guts to speak against him? And he's dying of it?"

Josh sniffed humorlessly. "Well, isn't that a reasonable conclusion? The doctors never find anything wrong with him; he's always well when he's away, but he's no sooner back than he's sick again. And Bjornesen cursed him last spring. I heard him myself, all the way from where I was digging in our garden."

"But he'd of got sick without that — curse."

"How do you know? He was never sick before and such an odd sickness, like muscle spasms." Josh's voice carried the sometimes brutal logic that is the more difficult to accept for its soft-spokenness; Abe, abruptly angered that in the twentieth century educated people had to talk of this superstitious voodooism, said harshly,

"If he's got this — this power of whatever it is, why does he just try it on scared Indians — why not on Art Griffin, or you — in a certain way you've tried more than poor Sturgeon to stop homebrewing. Why just Sturgeon?"

"Why should he try anything on Griffin when he had him running already? And how do you know what protection I have?"

"Protection?"

"Yes. Protection against evil."

In the now total darkness Abe could see nothing of the other except his outline. The cabin was strangely quiet but from below voices drifted on the still air; a second huge fire had been lit and shadows moved, contorted there. For a moment it seemed to Abe that on a night like this with the red moon pushing up on the horizon one would be able to believe a great deal that daylight would prove ludicrous — he jerked his head,

"Oh for god's sake, Josh! Of all things, I didn't think you were superstitious. No wonder you won't go to see Kekekose conjure."

Josh laughed softly and then turned to the teacher, who, Abe recalled with a start, had been standing silently by. "Sally, I guess this will explain to you as well. This isn't the best place to talk about it, the moon coming up and all, but you can hardly get acquainted with some facts comfortably. I don't go to see Kekekose conjure because I don't think he can get his spirits to do things. I know he can. But I don't want to have anything to do with them, if I can help it. Or with whatever it is Bjornesen has in his control either. Certain things are better just let alone."

— hell if you've got all this protection no doubt from the fine angels sent by dear Jesus why don't you set them on the bastard's devils and help that poor slob up there choking to death and Frobisher and maybe even whatever it is you're still trying to do here after three years of nothing — the teacher's presence kept Abe silent, and after a raging moment he was content it had. Finally he could say, almost calmly,

"If you believe in what Kekekose can do why didn't you get him going long ago?"

"I'm not sure he can do that; neither is Kekekose. The Indians believe that some men have the help of stronger spirits than others, but once it comes to a direct contest between them, who knows where it will end? Whole families have been wiped out."

Abe said, with no effort to hide the disgust in his tone, "Sure. The Eskimos sometimes told such stories too and I always believed them — especially when it turned out they died of murder or starvation or sometimes syphilis picked up at TB hospitals. But for an educated man to —" he stopped, staring down the slope. "I guess I better go down and see what's going on. I wouldn't want to miss being convinced."

"You shouldn't fight so hard," Josh said, "It takes an educated man to be less human than a heathen."

"Less human!"

"Yes. Thinking he can logically explain everything that happens." There was a short silence before Josh continued, "Look, I don't have to tell you you can be convinced of things without logic. Why dance and conjure only on full-moons? You can't explain that scientifically, but look at that moon and you'll get a feeling why they do. And if you want evidence, what more do you need than that man up there dying?"

Abe shrugged and started for the path. "Sure, Josh, sure. I'll just go and see — say, what kind of things can conjurors do, besides heal people?"

From the tone of his voice, Josh was smiling. "I just know what they've told me; they mostly detect evil in the band, or report about how far-away family members are getting along, if they're well —"

If old Kekokose could tell him at that moment how they were in that house at the end of the wagon-road twisting between scrub-oak and poplar and the willows around the creek from Selkirk — from where did that thought form itself? — he interrupted, "Is that all?"

"No. They fight windigos if one threatens the camp, and James Sturgeon told me Kekekose once brought back a lost child —"

"He did, eh? I've got an idea of maybe putting him through a little test. Want to come along, Miss — uh — Sally?"

The moon was higher and he could see the outline of her small face and the hollows of her eyes. "I'm not sure. I — I think I'd rather follow Josh's method." Even in his anger Abe could tell there was no fear in her low voice. "I don't have to be convinced of his power any more than Josh."

Her very calmness irked him. "Sure," he said, "I guess that to believe such stuff is — comfortable anyway." He caught himself then. "Ah shucks, I — look, I don't mean to sound so superior. I really didn't mean it that way."

"I'll *believe* that too!" Josh chuckled. "Go ahead — test him if you want. But the old man won't try it unless it's something you really need. Ojibwa conjurors don't do things for 'show.'"

"Oh, it's something I need all right," and at the word he remembered that other old man who had fallen into his life on a Winnipeg street and he laughed, but without humor.

Josh said, "Sally, we better go. They're about ready down there —" They were on the path, the moonlight just bright enough to see. Josh said, and with his words probed Abe so deeply in the very spot of particular sensitivity that he could not have despised the other had he wanted to, "Abe, I wouldn't want you to have the wrong impression of my belief in God. I believe that the Indian conjurors and even Bjornesen control some spirits, and that through them they can do things that are to us inexplicable. Prayer does inexplicable things for Christians too, but it's nothing like Kekekose persuading his spirits to take pity on him and helping him. We've all — Lena, Anne, Sally, I — prayed for Harry's recovery, and God could heal him. And he will do it, if it suits his good purpose. And not before. But he's not a God to be manipulated by conjuring. Or bellowing curses."

"Then why pray?"

"Who knows. Probably it helps us more than it tells him — that we care, at least." A woman's laugh suddenly loafed so easily, so happily, on the night air, cutting through all the emotion that was snarling them that Abe could not grasp it was the teacher until she said,

"Josh, that's deliberately ambiguous!"

Josh laughed then too, but his voice was almost sad. "Prayer isn't explainable in fifteen words or less, like toilet soap. Little that matters is."

"There come Lena and Anne," Sally said. She turned quickly to Abe, "Are you really going to ask Kekekose to do something?"

"Sure. Why?"

"I was thinking — perhaps you shouldn't. You might have to start believing something you wouldn't like."

Abe guffawed, "Shucks, if I'm just ignorant now then I'd better learn, whether I like it or not."

"Oh. There are people who'd rather not know, if it wrecks their system."

"And I've got a real one to wreck," the twist of self-sarcasm betrayed him and he added quickly, "Good night," and picked his way down the path.

The edge of disappointment widened in him: going to their home once a week for two crammed months, seeing them help build better houses for the band and grow vegetables, their daily belief seemed to hold vital meaning for them; and they talked about it without heavy-handed clichés, they laughed at their ignorance at what in their religion was inexplicable, even while believing it true. But whatever the churchmen in the Arctic were, they weren't superstitious — that loudmouth an evil-eye of all things! — he stubbed against a rock; it invariably happened in the dark with moccasins. Fingering his toes, he laughed. That inept front of bellowing overfriendliness would stub up too, with a narrower running room. Just as he had thought, few Indians took their government checks across the channel; the very privilege of holding money in their hand, deciding, even though there was no choice in either store as to what they could buy, kept them more happily at Frobisher. And in a week trap-line outfitting would show who had hold over whom. Bjornesen's curse was nothing but homebrew; Kekekose was too smart not to have some scheme for wrecking that spoken curse stupidity tonight and that would leave only the yeast problem for Frobisher. He stumbled again — a foot! — and he realized the spin of his thoughts had carried him down the slope and he was among the outer stragglers of those grouped about the lodge, fiery-green in the firelight. He had not time to think further for the stare of people awoke him to the immediate. Most of the men were seated to the right of the lodge, the women bunched on the other side. If Kekekose was already inside how could he work the — George — he moved around the edge of the crowd, looking. There were more people than had come to the dances, and they looked at him curiously, their voices dying as he approached. He was almost beyond the men; he hesitated, looking at the women and a leap of flame showed Alex momentarily, half-hidden by a clump of brush beside the nearest house. He picked his way past the squatting women, his moccasins silent on the rough ground.

"Alex!"

The boy's face glinted in a spurt of firelight, expressionless. "Hi."

"I thought I'd find you or George — to translate — is he in yet?"

"No. It's not shaking."

"Where is he? I want to ask him something."

"He's over there, in our house," pointing.

"Would he mind if I watched?" The boy shrugged. "Could I ask you a favor? Come along, and ask him for me?" Alex said nothing, his handsome face set without expression. But suddenly, as if almost against his will, he moved around the edge of the women in the direction he had indicated. Children, bright-eyed but amazingly quiet, played here and there or paused momentarily to fumble at their mothers and nurse noisily, ignored. Then a door slurred open somewhere. Alex stopped. "He's coming."

The distant firelight hunched the darkness behind the cabin squat as a toad out of which a shapeless form shaped itself. It was wrapped in a blanket, and then Abe could distinguish the bare head and long hair held in place by a wide headband. The old man's face seemed more wrinkled than at the fish-camp; he walked as if he saw nothing and Abe moved a step.

"Kekekose — could I — watch —" he gestured, uncertain. The other stopped and stared at him and Abe realized he had spoken in English. He wheeled to Alex but the conjuror was speaking and Alex said, without inflection,

"He says you can look. Also, it's okay if you want to laugh sometimes." Abe bent forward to the old man's face, not quite believing his ears, and the wide smile with which Kekekose confronted him nudged him over the brink of daring.

"Alex, please ask him if he would — uh — find something for me, when he's in the tent?"

Without hesitation Alex continued the mechanical translation. The old man had not shifted his look and immediately said a single word which Abe understood: "It's a revolver; I lost it below the fast water on the Half-mile Rapids when we came back from the fish camps." Alex translated. Kekekose stood mute, glance across the darkness at the moon over the tree-line of the point that now probed where the fire-light did not reach — the old fraud! — finally Abe said, "Huh?"

Alex looked at him, eyebrows slightly raised. "He won't answer with words. Offer him a present. If he accepts it, he will."

And he had nothing — to flounder now and no time to cross the channel! — his thoughts caught; he pulled out his notebook, wrote "Credit Kekekose: 3 tins tobacco" and signed his name. "Here," he tore out the page and pushed it into Alex's hand. The boy shifted it in front of Kekekose and translated, his long finger pointing out the words. Suddenly the old man's hand emerged, closed over the paper and vanished under the blanket again. Then he walked on towards the lodge.

Abe stood staring after him. Least of all had he expected this silent, almost confident, acceptance. Alex snorted a little. "He likes to smoke!"

"We looked for that gun for half an hour — Violet too — and there wasn't a trace —" Abe stopped. There was no time to explain for something seemed to have happened to the boy, as if awaking.

"We have to find a place."

Kekekose stood before the lodge flap speaking to the men seated there when Alex, with Abe behind him, pushed through to the front of the circle, Joe Loon, after a quick glance, lurched aside and made room. Kekekose had turned, as in thought, facing the lodge. Presently he raised his head and spoke, and all the people greeted his words with a long laugh. Alex said, at Abe's look, "He says the men built a strong tent and he's getting old and maybe can't shake it."

"Why laugh?"

"What's the difference how old he is? He doesn't shake it."

Alex was watching his father, trickery and cynicism gone from his tone; quietness that had fallen over the people. Kekekose was walking slowly about the tent, arms still folded under the blanket, a point trailing in the dust behind his naked heels. At the second circle he knelt down, lifted the flap, and vanished.

There was only silence. Not even a child stirred. The giant moon was well up and its reddish light fingered out the tent flap and the folds of the moose-hide. Then, like a whisper of dead leaves in a far forest, the bones sounded. Sitting four feet from the lodge, Abe looked straight up; through cloud-streaks the point of a star showed, was wiped away by the gaunt-crossed poles of the peak, then reappeared as the bones hanging there aloft sounded again. For an immeasurable time the blink of the star was ex-ed out again, and again, by the swaying of the poles until a vagueness like a suspension slurred in whispers, and the poles themselves groaned against so violently that the bones banged on the poles, the hides slurred in whispers, and the poles themselves groaned against each other. The top of the lodge was moving in a three-foot arc and Abe, kinked from staring up, remembering the heft of the lodge in his grip, could only think numbly that no old man would ever maintain that. However it kept on and on until he had to look away to the Indians around him, finding himself, as they, swaying in rhythm — something has to break — as quickly as it began, the violence died away and again the gentle chatter of the bones could be heard. Abe shook himself; he had not realized he was so tense. He felt a touch, looked up and saw Albert Crane offering a tobacco can.

"Take it," Alex said beside him. "All the men smoke."

Abe clamped a pinch, "Why?"

"Smoke offering to the pawagan, the spirit helping my father."

"Was that why the tent shook so hard?"

"Yah. The pawagan coming then."

The boy was stuffing his pipe, eyes resolutely away. Abe said, "I haven't a pipe."

"Chew."

There was no way out; he craned around. Grey twists of smoke wreathed up from the crowd of squatting men. The big man with the broken nose was directly behind him, obviously content with the tobacco at any rate. The women in their group were offered nothing. He was going to ask when he noticed Albert crouching near the flap, his head to the very ground. "What's he doing?"

"Albert's my father's skabewis, helper. He's listening to him."

"What's he saying?"

"I don't know."

"Have you helped your father in — this —"

"No." Alex shifted.

"Why?"

In the dim light Abe could see the muscle along the other's jaw tense and he thought he had pushed too far, but abruptly he said, as if spitting, "I never had no dream."

Whatever that meant; Abe had no time to edge further for a low rumble seemed to rise out of the very ground at their feet and a sigh stirred the men around him. Alex whispered, "The pawagan is singing," and as the tent swayed a little more strongly, the deep sound opened, powerful, cleanly rhythmic like a Russian bass singing held by immeasurable steppes to resonate his song. As the sound, accented by the swaying lodge, rolled through the drifting smoke of the pipes, Abe could not imagine how the conjuror could make that sound with his old voice. There seemed no point in asking Alex how it was done; obviously enough, despite a high school education and three years out, the lodge moving had pulled the boy back into the being of the Ojibwa people. And there had been protest, almost like longing, in that, 'I never had no dream.' Or so it had seemed in the throb of the emotion that had built up so quickly, even unconsciously in himself. The trouble was looking up; he should not have watched that crossed apex against the star; it was hypnotizing — cats out-face night clubs and gospel campaigns and get piled up at this amateur show! — the deep singing was ended and the Indians seemed to awake out of their silence; several loud voices called to Kekekose. Abe leaned over to Alex, "What's 'mininak'? What —?"

Alex was almost laughing with some of the men, "Snapping Turtle, Mininak, whose spirit makes — that's him," and an odd falsetto voice, like a record spun too quickly, quavered from the lodge. Immediately the crowd was convulsed in laughter;

some yelled, "Annen!" and the voice replied high and thin to convulse them again. Alex was laughing completely, and Abe insisted above the noise, "What's he saying?"

"He always makes joking — with everyone — listen — he says he's scared of the man with the wide shoulders and black beard," and a wave of laughter and pushing forward to look at Abe proved without words how clever — and ridiculous — such an admission from the great Snapping Turtle was. Albert, still crouching by the lodge flap, yelled suddenly and he too was greeted by a roar from the people and a high squeek from the tent. The people were looking at Abe, laughing so hard they almost lost their balance as they squatted; even Alex could not translate for a moment. Finally he managed: "Albert says to Mininak it's okay. You're strong but don't hurt. Shoulders are wide because Frobisher's very heavy."

Whatever he had expected at a conjuring, it was hardly wit; for an instant the glimpse into what seemed the real Indian thinking about him was a relief that washed him clean and the laugh that started in his chest roared with those about him.

The jokes and laughter continued, the conjuror in the lodge asking, the voice of Mininak answering. Even to the Indians the latter was not always intelligible, wavering sometimes like a fading radio, and a great cry would go up "What? What?" and the conjuror's ordinary voice would speak from the lodge. The lodge was never without motion, moving sometimes violently, sometimes gently. Try as he would, Abe could not discern the effort of the shaking in the accent of the conjuror's voice. He nudged Alex, "Just one spirit in there now?"

The boy, laughing openmouthed at a sally Abe had not understood, said, "Oh, many. From stars, moon, animals — listen — when Great Turtle stops you hear other voices — careful — there —"

Momentarily it seemed he could hear wavering whispers. Concentrating, he could not quite align them with the rustle of hide or the poles groaning; it did sound curiously like voices. He said, "Can you see them? Inside?"

Alex' face lost its amusement, as if he suddenly remembered

himself. "I've never been inside," he said glumly. "When Albert was —" he stopped. Abe could not decipher his expression; the moon was now high and south-east but the firelight had fallen. Finally: "Kekekose says they're just small and sit on the hoops. They bring the winds shaking the lodge. When the hoops break from shaking, they go away."

A woman had approached from the women's side and spoke to Albert. The assistant bent at the lodge-flap, spoke, and then nodded. The other sounds, both inside the tent and the joking among the people had died away so that the loud call of the woman, raising her gaunt head against the sky, could be heard. Abe thought he heard the word Gikumikik, but it was spoken in such sing-song he could not be sure. There was a momentary silence and then the reeling voice of the Turtle. Abe leaned over, "What's that?"

"Martha," Alex gestured with his head, "asked the Turtle to tell her how her mother is in Gikumikik. She heard from the plane she had cut her leg." The Turtle's voice ceased, and Kekekose inside the lodge spoke. Alex translated, "He says her mother is no longer sick." Martha stood as if waiting, then called, "She is well?" and again Kekekose obviously repeating the same answer. The woman started to speak, but Albert said something almost fiercely and she turned, her body deformed by labor and childbirth, and vanished as a man moved to take her place.

If he had not deliberately refused, Abe knew the ceremony he was seeing would have been completely convincing. People rose to ask questions. There were sometimes bumps, songs, indecipherable noises from the lodge; the spirit answers were translated by Kekekose in his normal voice, but sometimes the unintelligible spirit mumbling changed a questioner's expression, Alex explained, because the spirit's voice sometimes sounded like the person about whom they asked — to hear his voice after all these years of not even admitting that — Abe jerked his mind away, enraged; twice in one evening was twice too much. Clearly this was faked: the answers were ambiguous, like Martha's, and could never be verified immediately. And the evening was moving on; there had yet been no mention of his request, leave alone the main reason

153

for the session. But let them believe, as they obviously all did; after the stage was well set maybe Kekekose could pull something that would get Sturgeon out from under Bjornesen; that would leave Frobisher so much the better. And then the thought struck him. He needed Kekekose; the old man could not be humiliated here — where the devil were my brains to mention that confounded gun! — he was staring up at the high moon, clouds driving greyish red over it, as he cursed his stupidity, and then he felt Alex nudge him. The high voice of the Great Turtle was coming from the lodge and Albert beckoning to him. Alex hissed, "Ask what you want."

Abe looked from brother to brother and the confusion on his face must have been too plain; Joe Loon beside him snickered in the sudden silence. Comprehending, he stood up, scrounging for something easy, something possible and in his motion he found himself facing the people, men before him and women to his right and out of sight behind the lodge, looking at him, accepting what they expected to happen, their high-cheeked, black-hair straggled faces numberless in the reddish shadows. It was the first time he had seen them all together and suddenly he forgot his dilemma in his great longing to shout to them all as they sat, so willing in belief, 'Get rid of that bastard Bjornesen and Frobisher will take care of you! It cared for your parents and grandparents and it won't let you down. You won't have to fight every old boozer that comes along with —' but even in passion his mind would not form the ending because he did not believe what he would have had to say to explain himself to these people that stared at him, man and woman and child, waiting to hear his request from the pawagan of Kekekose.

He glared down at Alex, squatting unconcerned at his feet, and said fiercely in English, "Dammit, let's cut this game! I can't believe this stuff and I don't want to embarrass your father here. Call it quits."

The boy was grinning, totally smart-aleck. "What don't you believe?"

Abe hunkered down, exasperated. "He can't bring the gun back! Tell Albert to pass it off somehow, I don't want to mess up the show he —"

"What does believing matter? You ask." Alex laughed aloud, a spray of firelight glinting in his eye. "If the spirits can't find it they'll say so."

Albert hissed behind him, and Abe straightened abruptly. "All right. Sure. Translate like it should be said."

Still grinning slightly, the boy pushed erect, and Abe, his hand to his beard, said aloud, "I lost a revolver, Colt .38 in the Frozen River when coming back from the fish-camps. I had it for many years, and would like very much to have it back." He said a few of the words in Ojibwa, such as he knew, and he could hear the rustle of understanding before Alex quickly, in a long almost sing-song tone elaborated the request. The bones were chattering when the boy's voice faded, and out of the lodge came a short sound. Albert bent down, then straightened.

"Where?" Abe understood without Alex.

"In the deep pool below the Half-mile Rapids, almost under the right bank of the river," and as he said it, he could see the gigantic imperceptible turning eddy of the pool just before the portage where they had come around the bend, motor sound lost under the long white water's roar and saw the rabbits staring at them ears cocked on the starting logs of the portage. He signaled to George to cut the motor, picked up the revolver and sighted carefully for a head shot to give them rabbit stew for supper, and as he fired twice, on the instant without aiming again as he had drilled during and regularly after the war, George, fascinated as he had been twice before on the trip by such shooting, forgot the drift of the unpropelled canoe and it clanged against a protruding rock. All would have been well, for Violet amidships instinctively countered by clutching the rock, fighting the canoe's yaw but he, sensing they could spill all, including themselves, lunged for an overhanging branch and the revolver plopped down and out of sight. After three years in the army and twelve in the Arctic, and some scattered between. He dived till he was exhausted, a rope around his waist for George to pull him out of the current, and he had not once touched the bottom. All for two headless rabbits that weren't enough for a meal, not with Violet along. And they had to camp out that night as they had no light for the portages.

In the silence after Alex' final words Abe recalled himself. There was a stirring among the people. He looked at the lodge; for the first time since the conjuror had entered it was motionless. Almost as if gathering itself for effort. Suddenly, out of the very immobility the bones that hung at the peak in the opening where the spirits were to enter sounded harshly and Abe felt a brush of air over his face. He started, but the night air was quite still, as it had always been. The bones fell silent and a kind of nothingness spread over the people, immobile around him in the dimness. Somewhere a mother shushed a child, and then there was furtive scrambling behind the lodge. It was so still all could hear the child making water on the fall-dropped leaves under low bushes. Another quick flurry; all sound died.

It was too much. He moved excessively, staring deliberately at the men as motionless as buddhas before him, then squatted beside Alex and whispered, "Why the devil can't he cut it short?" and as he spoke some men stirred beyond. Alex said, his voice without a trace of cynicism, "It's over ten miles to the rapids," when Albert jogged Abe with his foot. The lodge was beginning to move; suddenly a tremendous violence drove over it like a shudder and the very hide seemed to stretch before his eyes. Above the groan of the lodge and the sounding bones came the gibberish of the pawagan, rising and falling to the zenith and depth of audibility and the people began to clutch each other and shout in unison with the fiendish sounds that tore from the lodge and in a moment a veritable deluge of screaming ripped Abe's ears. He clutched his head, eyes unblinking at the seething movement of the people squatted about him, and twisted to Alex, "What the dev —" when as abruptly as it began, the lodge ceased its swaying and the sounds burbled and were gone. The wail of the spirit faded quite and then the voice of Kekekose naturally, unwinded, said a single word. The flap twitched. Albert thrust in his hand, turned and dropped something at Abe's feet.

He could not distinguish it on the dark ground. It seemed

shaped like a revolver, but whatever it was it was obviously a fake that somewhere during the long evening Albert had by some sleight of hand smuggled to the old rascal. As it was, it was more than he could have expected from these two; they were obviously no amateurs. He had asked the spirits and now he could play the game by the rules and accept as genuine. He was suddenly aware of all eyes upon him. He reached out his hand.

The instant he touched it he knew it was his gun. He did not believe his senses even when he jerked the rust-splotched revolver up an inch from his face, the water dripping onto his legs, and saw the worn groove in the walnut stock which the conjuror, no matter how clever he was, could not have known about because he had never seen. He joggled the rusty cylinder and the two spent shells dropped out. The Indians were pushing close, elbowing him in their effort to see, and he finally had the presence of mind to say as he had planned all along, "Yes, it is my gun — yes —" nodding his head and having no resource within himself to even marvel at their calm acceptance; he could not trust his eyes or the known fit of the gun in his hand or the faint mustiness — my god the deep smell of the river! — much less shape in his mind what had actually happened to him.

And as he was trying to arrange at least his posture and facial expression into normalcy, as if being handed a rusty revolver two months lost in a bottomless eddy ten miles away was after all little more than passing three pounds of flour over a counter, the sudden movement of people recalled him that this was but a thoughtlessly arranged prelude. There was pressure around him to move; he followed the flow for into their space before the lodge-flap four men were coming bent to a weight between them. When they lowered it and stepped back, Harry Sturgeon from the cabin on the hill was squatting there, swaying weakly in his worn clothing. James Sturgeon, his brother bundled a blanket around him and seated himself directly behind, supporting him; as the light flared suddenly from some wood thrown on the fires, the sweated face of the sick man seemed to leap out of the darkness, its eyes staring, mouth gaping for air. At the torture obvious there and the desperate attempt to remain erect Abe forgot himself and tugged at Alex, "Why pull him out? That'll kill him sure!"

The boy's voice hissed answer, "He has to be here — to answer." The lodge was already swaying violently and the calm and wit of the earlier questionings were quite gone now. Over the chatter of bones, groaning hides, and mutter of spirits came the great noises of the pawagan, followed quickly by the voice of Kekekose, shouting now to be heard above the lodge sounds and the sighings of the people swaying in what appeared to be mutual prayer. The sick man gasped a few words in reply, jaw muscles bunching, and back and forth crawled the torturous conversation, Kekekose straining to grasp the spirit's meaning, the dying man clawing for breath. Sitting almost against the man, Abe could not endure it. "God almighty, what are they trying to do?"

Alex bent to him, mouth working but eyes hypnotized on the sick man. "He has to explain everything. Harry says Bjornesen cursed him — when he said he'd tell the police so that he couldn't sell yeast for homebrew — cursed him to die of thirst. Now he can't hardly drink — or breathe. And last night when he slept Bjornesen stole his soul and it went down the Ghost Road but he fought all night to get back before his body woke this morning —"

"What's the Ghost Road?"

"To the Land of the Dead —"

"But Kekekose knows that, at least the first part. Why this —"

The boy was stuttering in his intensity, "It — it — has to be said — before the people — Harry maybe has done wrong, and must say it. Everything, to see what is wrong. Then the spirits fight with Bjornesen's — hey —"

The bones were knocking wood now and the violence of the tent's shaking was more terrible than his troubled memory could recall of that evening. The sick man had spent himself in answering; he lay fallen against his brother, head slack, only the heaving of his muscular chest where the blanket slid back showed him still alive. But he had said all or confessed all that seemed necessary for the lodge rocked on now without Kekekose's voice ever interrupting the deafening song of the pawagan; the moosehide bulged with the winds that raged inside. Abe saw and heard it, still holding the .38 in his hand, but he no longer could believe his senses and he knew of nothing else to believe; the gun dropped between his crossed legs as he hunched forward, clenching his eyes tight and his fists balled over his ears against the roaring of the ledge and the groaning, swaying, crying people.

Then, as if on the very edge of the clustered people, a dog howled. Reaction flamed everywhere, as if all had been tensed for something, not knowing what, but when it came it burst instantaneously in them all; Albert, bunched swaying beside the two Sturgeons, leaped up screaming, waving his arms and Alex shrieked in English, "Get that dog! the goddam dog!" The dog kept on howling, not the free rolling of its voice, but tight and pinched as if in terror, which suddenly cut off and a curse and thump of kick rang through the abruptly silent air.

Through the sound of the dog kiyikking away into the underbrush an incredible bellow of laughter broke where the Indians were already scrambling aside and out of the darkness strode the gigantic Icelander, his white head thrown back, teeth gleaming, whipping a double-bitted axe in circles around his head that scattered the people like straw. He rammed his way through to the huddle of men before the tent and stopped, his long arm like the axe of judgment thrust at the dying man's contorted face and his laughter shifted into roars of Ojibwa and English, "Thought you could stop Sigurd Bjornesen you —" and a rip of intersnarled English and Ojibwa oaths, "Kekekose — the howl of one dirty dog and his spirits —" he flung out his arms, the axe thudded broadside on the moosehide that now hung limp and motionless on the poles. "You're finished, Harry —" he leaned forward, screamed more Ojibwa. James and Albert cowered back, only the dying man's chest heaved up where he now lay flat on the ground. "See!" Bjornesen's hand like a talon ripped a hide away and the axe swung down and through the hoops and he swung again one-handed at the tied crossing on top and with a whirr the poles sprang apart, sprawling the hides to expose Kekekose cowering, head down, among the debris when Abe finally found legs and feet and swung the giant around with a grip on his shoulder and a yell,

"Bjornesen!"

The old Icelander wheeled, towering above him, and the madness on his face contorted to laughter. "Hahahahah, our new friend from Frobisher." For a moment they were roaring together, maniacally, then Abe was shouting into amazing quiet,

"You're killing that man and his family and you'll tear these people apart —"

The other's laugh cut him off, "Don't tell me you believe in this spirit bullshit, Ross! And you even carry a gun!"

Abe looked down at his hand where the revolver he had unthinkingly clutched squared with the other's stomach; he thrust it into his jacket. "I don't need a gun to talk to you! Terrify these people to suck the blood out of them! It won't work! I'll —"

"You'll stop me? You'll have to do it yourself then. He," swinging the heavy broad axe like a pointer towards the conjuror who was crawling out of the ruins of the lodge, "isn't going to help, much. Not like with the gun."

Bjornesen wheeled away as if Abe had ceased to exist. He glared once at Harry Sturgeon, prostrate with one arm crumpled under him, and strode away. The sobs of women broke from a far huddle and the trader stopped, bellowed one word in Ojibwa and his laughter ground their crying into silence as he strode away through the cowering people.

It was beyond midnight when Abe pulled his canoe high on the sand in the tiny Frobisher cove and, flashlight in hand, picked his way up the trail. Josh had come immediately; he must have been on his porch, listening, sounds carrying easily the half mile from the point, and understanding instantly when the dog-howl and Bjornesen's laugh echoed through the night. There had been little enough to do after they carried Harry up to his bed again, except wait. The children were gone, asleep somewhere, but the people sat where they had between the fires before the ruined lodge, silent as if lost. He showed them the gun and told the story in detail, and they listened, passing the gun from one to the next. But no one, not even the noisy broken-nosed man, whose name he learned was Amos Quequeish, had anything to say. When the wail of women arose from the house on the slope Abe rose with them and left. The familiar Frobisher bulk before him, exactly the same in a hundred lonely spots all over the north, the sound carrying over the water and on into the forest — maybe insulated walls shut it out — he reached for the door latch and the last piece of the full-moon September night fell into his consciousness.

"Mr. Ross."

He froze. After a moment he flicked on the torch and the the girl arose in its yellow light from the edge of the porch where she sat and came towards him. It seemed almost logical at that moment for the evening not to end — perhaps never end just slide into tomorrow with this kind of imperceptible fluidity that will strip away any odd resources still left and leave nothing but a jangle of bones sounding to some will-o-the-wisp that comes when that Icelander laughs — so he could say almost naturally, "Oh, Violet. Waiting for me — long?"

Her laugh was husky in her throat, "I was there," she shrugged towards the point, "until Bjornesen left."

"Oh." The cool sound of her voice recalled him to the world; the roll-warped boards of the porch under his feet suddenly held meaning again. He swung the light around, past her, asking, "You come alone?" knowing that from around the corner of the building Lucy's low titter would come, as it did. "Come out here, Lucy." But she did not; he shifted the light. "Tell her."

At Violet's word Lucy appeared, but refused to come on the porch. Abe turned, waiting.

"Did you want something?" he asked finally.

"Oh, I thought you are maybe tired. I could make tea."

Abe brought the flashlight up to her. There could be no question; this girl had been shaped in mind and body to comfort tormented man. Staring at her, her eyes unblinking and wide in the cruel light, he wanted as much as he would have wanted salvation if he could have conceived such a thing existed to fall asleep with his head between her high breasts and his hands and body cleaned, dead of the touch of her, to fall away so into nothing as he had oh so rarely ever in his life in those rare times when he had thrown away his mind for a quick, soft love. But whatever he was now was in too big a tangle to solidify it with this girl — good god she's all I need to finish me but good — and he said, deliberately proffering his misunderstanding of what she was saying to avoid even a hint of rejection, "That's really nice. I didn't think anyone would do that for me. But it's so late. I stayed over there until —" he gestured to the channel where the sound of keening rose and fell, "— he died just a few minutes ago. Your mother will be wondering, won't she? Let me take you back —" he turned but she said, and the slight tightness told him she was, if not suspicious, at least beginning to doubt,

"We didn't swim."

And he returned as quickly still balancing on the hair between thoughtful misunderstanding and insult, "Sure. Why don't you come over some other time and make tea for me? But it's so late now —"

And using a gentleness that each moment hovered on the brink of a curse he led them down to their canoe almost hidden by the naked willows beyond the dock and finally could pull his door shut behind him. Then he dropped the rusty .38 on the table and stared at it. More than a month would pass before he remembered that the first thought he had when that woman's voice spoke in the darkness was that it belonged to Sally Howell.

9

*H*E remembered the last week of October when they tried for moose south and west of Frozen Lake, where out of the great marshes in the heights of land the first large streams formed, bunching here and there below the joints of ridges to nameless lakes. The lakes hung on the edge of freeze-up and Dave, never certain now whether the glare of ice would not greet him at Frozen, took Abe with him south. In half an hour they spotted Josh in one canoe and James Sturgeon leading in the other; they had started two days before. Josh waved one paddle, which meant one moose downed, and Dave then roared on up the watercourse, circling, and searching for the brown blot that would betray a moose feeding among the now stripped poplar and birch striplings of the burn-over. Back and forth; they were banking, a long glide sliding them toward a little lake when down between ribs across the land sifted with the first snows Abe saw and shouted, "There!"

Dave took the plane lower, throttling down, and they slid over the huge bull so low that in the focusing glasses Abe could see the roots of the young poplar dangling from the jaw and great shovel head shake irresolutely as if annoyed by some gigantic insect it could not quite place.

"That'll do, fine," Abe grinned, "and even headed toward the lake!"

"He stopped when we come over — see," Dave lifted sharply

and they could look back up the vee; "He won't follow, that's for damn sure."

"Sure, but it's only about a mile. Josh and James will help get him out if I get him."

"It's your back-ache," Dave was already slanting for the lake, a giant leaf veined by the open water of creek currents between great splotches of green shore-ice. The open stretch was enough for landing; behind the ridge which now hid the moose they inched into a creek spilling over rocks. Abe clambered to the pontoon and paddled them in sideways. Dave handed out the pack, supplies, and gun case, waved, and, with a push from Abe, idled out into the open water. In a moment he had roared away; he would drop a tobacco tin with directions to the others.

Alone, Abe hesitated. The creek was impossible for a canoe. The snarl of the burn-over — perhaps wait? — and already restive from the plane, the moose would certainly wander. He piled the supplies high, conspicuously foreign against the gnarled spruce along the stream edge and the fresh snow, picked up the rifle, checked his vest for ammunition and knife and matches, and headed up the ridge. At least a mile up the vee, perhaps more now, the bull fed; and the breeze was exactly wrong. He would have to keep on this side the ridge, get above, and come back into the wind. That way perhaps he could be moved a little nearer the lake — he laughed: better yet ride the beast to Frozen and shoot it at Frobisher!

He felt so good he laughed aloud, then knelt by the stream to drink. He shrugged the clothes comfortable on his shoulders and, gun in hand, hiked up the valley. It was torturous; he did not dare stay close to the barer ridge-crest that curved hugely northward for fear a play of wind would betray him, so despite the high leaden overcast he was quickly asweat from slipping on deadfall. Once a spur broke under him as he balanced for a step and he crashed down with an echo that leaped to the overcast itself and sent a swirl of snow-buntings across the creek madly down the valley. He sat down to rest then, rubbing through his knee-boots the ankle against which the limb had sprung. But neither the pain that diluted quickly nor the possibility of losing the moose could squelch his happiness.

The air hung in immense soundless calm of waiting, waiting for winter. The lump of half-sweet chocolate melted in his mouth and he was wiped clean of every possible memory of the past frustrating month at the store. Except for rabbit prints he had seen no animal signs, but presently a mouse whisked along a grey side of tree-skeleton and stopped, its nose quivering as its pin-prick eyes surveyed the mountain suddenly fallen beside its home. With a twitch it was gone; Abe left a wedge of sandwich near its hole.

Over an hour: he should try for the top now and see if he was beyond the moose. But time could play tricks and he did not quite dare. He should have set himself a guide while in the air. Another fifteen minutes; he angled up the slope. Perhaps the animal had moved closer to the lake, hopefully. To pack a thousand pounds or more meat through tangle like this would take all the energy the meat could give. At least there would be three of them.

When he reached the crest he knew from the distant pattern of the lake that he was well beyond where they had seen the moose. He focused his binoculars, sweeping, and then suddenly the brown-black shape leaped into them. On the opposite ridge, nearer the lake feeding with abrupt great heaves of head. In this valley through a small growth of poplars and fluffs of spruce thrust out of the snow between the spines of the fired trees as if the fire had run faster and flayed the soil less. If the wind held and he did not stumble, it could do. Anyway, there were not many things that brute would be wary of.

So he began the stalk of his first moose, across the valley and up the opposite ridge above the level with the bull because shooting up would mean squinting against the noon angle of the sun, stuck now like a smeared knob upon the overcast. And, if the moose was not knocked down with the first shot, hopefully he might blunder down the ridge, towards the lake. All the better for packing to the canoes. Treading the snow-filmed rocks Abe chuckled to himself: Itooi would have loved stalking such a mountain of meat. He would have worked his way close for the one shot, precisely placed, that felled it crashing. To his memory: one shot.

And in shaping his memorial he waited too long. He worked the ridge to within a hundred and fifty yards, intent on a flank shot. The animal fed leisurely, tearing up young trees, staring calmly down the fold of the land, jaws grinding. Suddenly the gigantic head shifted. Abe froze. Then he too heard the snarl of canoe motors barely drifting up from the distant river that emptied the lake. The moose moved, and immediately the flank possibility was gone. Abe dropped behind a rock; only the rump thrust up on the slope below. Any instant now — break his leg and make sure he doesn't move far fast — that was hardly worthy of Itooi, of that giant, the great shovel horns lifting now like bone banners frayed against the far slope. The scope jerked the bull up into Abe's eye and he shifted his elbow to the rock, waiting, and suddenly the great head turned sideways, listening, and in the scope Abe followed him, shifting the barrel like a long invisible caress along that immense neck for the lethal shot to collapse him in one exploding instant, and fired.

His eye at the scope saw the hide jerk exactly where he had aimed — that's it you great lovely brute — he lifted his head. But there was no collapse. For an instant the huge head remained in profile high now above the spine of the far ridge and then the bull wheeled as some freak of wind carried to him and with a snort or bellow or scream charged up the slope towards Abe. He stared, incredulous, unconsciously rising to his knees, and the sight of his red cap lifted the bellow louder above the snapping trees and crashing hoofs. Abe began to fire, once and again, but there was nothing left visible now except the monstrous low-swinging head blundering nearer with its great armour of bone and Abe heard one bullet splat there and whine away to nothing, and then another as he levered the rifle, firing instinctively now for the scope was useless and still the charge with brush and deadfall cracking like his shots and the gigantic nostrils flaring in flung bloody spume until, with the innate knowledge of the hunter when he has only two shots left, Abe leaped up and aside as the madness crashed at him, unseeing in the long savage gash of head and as the bent-spade horns swung by he fired again, the gun nozzle seeking like instinct the left ribs behind the still-driving, thudding foreleg. With a jerk he sprang the last cartridge into the chamber and swung about, but the great ruined head had ploughed into the slope, horns catching and held by a final limb of deadfall. He stepped forward, finger crooked but there was not so much as a quiver from the beast at his feet. One last charge; to the finish. Abe clicked the gun to safety. Suddenly he had to sit down.

When Josh and James came up two hours later, guided by the smoke of a green-poplar fire, Abe had his first moose skinned and ready to quarter. Josh looked at the bullet slashes across the head's bone-ridge and laughed a little uneasily. "You try to get him from the front?" and Abe explained what had happened. Josh said, after a thoughtful silence, "They don't usually charge. Two years ago at Deer Lake an Indian got his leg crushed by a charging moose. He was trying to knock one over with a twenty-two —"

Abe looked at James studying the moose-head impassively. "Would he try for a bull with such a pop-gun?"

The Indian shrugged when Josh translated, then said, "If you surprise him on the trail — it's fresh meat."

Ridge-top going was easier and by nightfall, with two trips each, they had packed the moose out, even to the gigantic horns. They brought the canoes and Abe's supplies around, breaking ice to get to the shore, and made camp. The brief fall day darkened and the frost pricked through their clothes as they sat on logs near the fire, drinking the last of scalding tea. The flames ate the logs in ragged sheets.

Josh pushed up, stretched, went to the lean-to to scrabble in his pack. When he came back, at Abe's look he gestured with a thick book he was carrying towards James, lying on one elbow, smoking. He said slowly in Ojibwa, "James and I read every night from this. Okay?" Abe grinned. "Understand?"

"Sure, understand. You teach, three months." James laughed, and Abe answered it, "You don't think so?"

James nodded, still grinning, then offered out of his usual silence, "Three months, you know more than Art Griffin in three years."

"Sure, sure," Abe laughed, hastily steering from associations the former trader would arouse, "you read, I listen."

Josh said, "As I told you, they've used the Cree Bible for the Ojibwa for about a hundred years, but it's no good because most of them don't know Cree that well. And only the older people can read Cree syllabics. The Wycliffe translators are working on Ojibwa now — so I use this mostly as reference and translate it myself." He turned the worn book open to the firelight, "We were going to finish the last part of the story of the prodigal son, where the father goes out to talk to the oldest son who won't come to welcome the prodigal." He leaned forward and began to speak slowly in Ojibwa.

Abe concentrated, understanding here and there but missing gaps; he could not remember anything about an older brother to the prodigal son. James laughed abruptly, then spoke incomprehensibly. The guide's dark face flushed in the firelight; there was obvious interest in his voice and the laughter that half-covered his seriousness. Abe wondered if the man, one of the more industrious of the band, wanted to become a Christian — whatever sort of Christianity Josh has that until school started apparently made no more distinction between days of the week than the Indians themselves and simply works at helping them live a little cleaner and meets now and then in one house or another with the children that will listen to stories never pushing itself or even speaking in such a absolute-godly way if he did have a church instead of not one identifiable convert to whatever it is he's preaching without ever a sermon perhaps it'd be possible to identify a little by going to a service and getting on the right side in case the Indians ever — he shook his head in anger. That was as cheap as trying to out-conjure them. He looked up; Josh was praying aloud, eyes closed. James lay on his elbow, the the firelight outlining his shape against the darkness, his hands holding the smoldering pipe.

Josh got up, put the book away. He returned and, with a cloth and a handful of snow, began wiping out the tin cups and dishes. Abe said, "That's a good way."

"It's handy."

With a long pole Abe rearranged the pattern of a brand. "I didn't get some of that."

Josh looked up, grinning. "If you knew the story it would have helped."

Abe smiled at the banter in his tone; the quiet of trees and lake wove their companionship around the firelight. "Well, I *do* know the first part — I didn't know there was something about a brother in it."

"Most people don't know. But the story is as much about the second as the first, maybe even more. He's the one that stays home and works like a dog and when his brother has spent everything he envies him one calf though he owns a thousand others." Josh picked up another plate. "You hear these parables when you were a boy?"

"Yeah. My — when I was a kid things were pretty religious." Abe hesitated, then said abruptly, "Actually, it was more than that. Religion come out of everybody's ears, mine too. I don't remember much of it."

Josh said nothing.

"What do you do, you just take their word for god — you used 'manido' when you prayed — the sort of god that they conjure with, and talk about him, or what?"

"Did you hear them use the word 'kische manido' that night?"

"I can't remember. Alex talked a lot about the four winds in the tent and of Kekekose's pawagan."

"That's it. They believe there are many spirits, and the Great Spirit, the kische manido, is so great and sovereign he would never have anything to do with ordinary people. He's above that, but the lesser spirits sometimes help them through the conjuror. These sort of commit themselves to a boy during his puberty dreams — they have pity on him when he is sent away by himself and sometimes put in a tree, or by himself on an island for days, and sleeping there, having dreams."

"Do all boys dream like that when they become men?"

"They used to try more for it. Most of them still try, but some never have it. If they don't, they believe that they will be weak and someone with a strong spirit can harm them."

"Maybe that's what Alex meant when I asked him if he ever

169

helped his father, like Albert, and he sort of blurted out he'd 'never had a dream.'"

James had gone to cut more wood and his nearby axe thudded on the motionless air. Josh said after a moment, "Perhaps — but they're very secretive about it, and he's more mixed up than just that. But — to get back where we started, what I've been trying to do is show them that the kische manido is not so careless about them, that the idea of greatness they have is right but that he has come to man through Jesus Christ and that we can know a great deal about him."

"You leave as much of their idea in and just give it a Christian twist?"

"You start where they believe, yes. Saint Paul did, when he talked to Greek senators in Athens."

"And what do you say about all the other spirits they talk about?"

Josh hunkered down and began flipping butt-ends of burned log into the fire; the birds had long gone and there was only silence over the lake. "You mean like the ones that got your gun back?"

Abe stared into the fire. "Sure," he said at last.

"Well, if you doubt it's yours —"

"Hell no!" Abe jerked to his feet, went to the lean-to, unzipped the pocket of his pack and returned, tossing the gun into Josh's lap. "I can't doubt something I hold in my hand, not even when it gets there rusty and stinking of the river more than forty feet down where it's lain two months."

Josh twirled the empty chamber. "So?"

"So?" Abe flung his hands wide, "so how do you explain this to them from your Christian idea — that apparently there are spirits they can get to do actual work, physical work, on earth right now, and not just take them to heaven some day?"

Josh was smiling in the half-whimsical way Abe recognized as a kind of sorrow with himself. "You ask that way and you can't be answered. Knowing about Jesus can, for one thing, mean a good bit more than just an escape hatch past hell; it means living life on earth first of all. But I guess I've got a rather simple approach to such things, and I can't pretend it will satisfy you — but I think that God is over all, and that whatever happens for good is of him, whether it happens through people or animals or what, always keeping in mind that what to me seems at the moment good may not necessarily be so. Nor what I think is bad. About a lot of things, even those I think are good or bad, I have to say I don't know — I don't know enough of how things will work out, ultimately. Even about natural things — those neither good or bad, apparently, I don't know why they happen. Why, for instance, did that bull charge you?"

Abe shook his head violently, "No! That doesn't fit the pattern we're talking about. Maybe he had a bad time rutting — he looked battered enough — and he was still mad about not having enough and when he saw my hat and smelled me it hit him. But he was an animal, with muscles, he wasn't a invisible spirit carting visible horns around to gore me."

"Okay, maybe that bull didn't have a good time lately, but you could as easily argue the other way that it should have made him despondent, discouraged, and when this new thing showed up he'd run."

"Ahhh, go on Josh —"

"No, I won't go on." Josh laughed and leaned back to the log, "You're talking about that moose as if he were human, and therefore may be, and probably are, quite wrong about him. But who ever said that everything in the world can be seen, felt, smelled, or heard? It seems to me you've got as definite proof there's more than any person I've ever met." The oily blue steel flashed in the firelight as he tossed it in the air. "And if we can't even tell about animals or humans, who we can see, whether their actions are good or bad sometimes, how should we be able to tell about things we can't see? I don't know whether the spirits Kekekosè says he uses are bad or good. I know that the Indians tell me in the past they did mostly useful things — like making people well or protecting them from the windigo — and if this is mere suggestion, so what? They're still well, aren't they? If it helps them to live in the bush —"

"Then why wreck it by coming here and telling them they don't really need all they've had, that they need Jesus, about who they've never heard, or care?"

"You can see that as well as I," the other's voice was intense now, almost cracking in the frosty air. "When white men come they tear old ideas apart and in the end leave the Indians nothing — because they simply don't believe what the Indians do and when every day they live out their care-nothing, faith in the old beliefs is lost. After what Bjornesen did in September, how much faith do you think they have in Kekekose, and through him in all their old code? The one good thing that still holds some scrap of belief is that this gun was brought back. That proves to them there's a little in the old way yet. But if it hadn't been for this —" he shrugged and stared into the fire.

They had seen each other every week, lately almost every day, and never had they spoken of beliefs; perhaps because Josh was not one to pry, or he to push; but this sounded too near his own struggles in the Arctic to be trusted when voiced by another. He said slowly, "You're bothered about them still believing in magic."

"No! About them being human beings with some concept of belief, something that's everlastingly important to them! If they just throw themselves down the whiteman's care-nothing road because he has things and things and things they'll simply drown like animals in homebrew and disease and swill. Abe, there is sometimes more point in talking of Jesus Christ to a heathen who believes in a kische manido than to someone like Alex who tries to be an Indian with the Indians and a whiteman with the whites and alone he can't stand himself, or Bjornesen who has no god but what he can lay his hands on. Or even —"

He hesitated as James appeared at the edge of illumination, arms heaped high with logs. The logs fell with a crash; after a few words to Josh the guide moved away and bent into the lean-to.

"Say it," Abe said finally.

"I will." Josh's voice was low, "Or even you, Abe, a kind moral decent man but you haven't dared believe in anything except maybe yourself. That seems possible for some; I think maybe Bjornesen was like that once, long ago, but he got to care less and less about anyone or anything — if you think at all you get discouraged with yourself and slowly it all turns sour. Now he tortures these poor people with their fears, for his own gain. Or more likely, amusement. He's old and no one to leave anything to."

"He has a wife," Abe said irrelevantly.

"He lives with a woman, yes. He's never had a child." The fire spit a spark upon Abe's boot and he watched it die there, studying without emotion the black stain slowly expand on the leather until the bright center hissed out; he brushed the ember carefully away, leaving the mark, irretrievably. Josh was saying, "Most people can't hack a way out for themselves, they couldn't stand the pressure if they had to; if you take away one thing they grab another. Like Alex; he's pulled every-which-way now." Abe wanted to push in another question here but the previous remark levered him around and left no peace.

"And you think I'll end up like Bjornesen."

The thin face lifted to him, smiling and gentle. "No. I can't possibly. You're too human despite your logic, and you do some warm, illogical things. Maybe you're one of those who can doubt everything, especially everything spiritual, and cut your way through yourself. But no Ojibwa that's had his pawagan taken from him can do that. He'll end wrecked. And you — you're kind and thoughtful — a good man and I thank God every day for that. But human decency and goodness, beautiful as it is to man, the biblical prophets tell us isn't worth much in God's eyes; in fact it's worth nothing. And in the long run it proves so to man too, because it's never enough. There's just never enough of human goodness. We need God's grace for all the rest."

They said nothing for a long time while the fire sputtered down to coals. At last Abe said, "It'll be a long day tomorrow, to try and get in. You said the moose you got was cached on the main stream?"

"Uh-huh. Won't take too long to pick it up. But by the feel of it we'll be breaking not just shore ice."

"A little sooner and we could have flown in and out." Abe pushed to his feet and Josh said,

"Here's the gun," the butt warm from his hand. "If you don't mind, I'd like to pray."

"Sure, go ahead," Abe hunkered down, staring into the last white coals. Josh's quiet voice came as the pines shivered in a wind,

"O God, the Father of heaven, have mercy on us miserable sinners. O God the Son, Redeemer of the world, have mercy on us miserable sinners. O God the Holy Spirit, living in us, have mercy on us miserable sinners. O Lord, save your people and bless your message. Give peace in our time, O Lord because there is no other that may fight for us, but you only. Make clean our hearts, and by your agony and bloody sweat; by your cross and passion; by your precious death and burial; by your glorious resurrection; by the coming of the Holy Spirit; by your grace, good Lord: deliver us. Amen."

Abe said, scraping the coals into a heap, "I didn't know you were of that church."

"I'm not, now. But I grew up in it, and the prayers are — common." Josh chuckled. "Recognize them?"

"Sure. Even in Eskimo they sound — like they sound — different."

He went to the bivouac under the spruce, pulled off his boots and outer clothing and rolled into his caribou sleeping-robe. As he stretched his legs and spread his feet sideways in its width he did not hear Josh settle down between him and the sleeping guide; like a stab of the cold from the robes' recesses through his socks and knit underwear he was remembering the feel of Oolulik when they had bunched together such ages — only a few months? — before in the snowhouse; a kind of recognition growing, welling as if it would choke him, and he knew he would not sleep. He lay motionless, eyes open to the darkness that crept over the glow from the fire on the canvas of the lean-to like cold hesitant on tiptoe. He had been told, had heard, before but he had not actually recognized it though at times he used it for his own purposes in argument: Oolulik in the snowhouse keening for her husband and children, Sally Howell on the night of the conjuring and the gun's return and Harry Sturgeon's death, and he knew with bell-like clarity that when the girl's voice had spoken to him out of the darkness at Frobisher he had wanted it to be Sally's voice and he had heard it as such because she had seen what he refused, and had refused so much the more adamantly this past month when he had walled out all but trading and making sure every one of the few Indians that came to him for trapping grubstake was more than completely satisfied, and drilling Ojibwa an evening a week with Josh and all day every day with George until the handyman was surly with exhaustion; avoiding even trying to talk Alex out of going to work for Bjornesen not only because he knew it wouldn't help anything speaking about it but far more if he didn't talk to the boy somehow that concern could be pushed off into a vacancy where it could be ignored until it leaped out of its own potency; avoiding Violet's covert looks with bare politeness; tonight by the fire hearing Josh carry to its ultimate personal conclusion what he himself had sometimes ventured to begin in thought but never dared probe: all gathered to a point now like an imperceptible ooze of oil whose bulb grows and grows until it drops splat and its too great wetness forces recognition at last. Now the exhaustion of his body could not snatch him into sleep. He must wake. The cold crept round his head and then the men beside him breathed gently in sleep as he remembered those two times...

Part Four

10

*L*AST October nights also, walking through the globes of light under the street-lamps from the university library down the side-streets to the men's dorm and the Trick-or-Treat! cries of children spread on the bone-dry air; the air three years later sodden like the squitchy Dutch field under our clods of boots that sank into the earth rotten as apples even in the shallow bivouac when we piled the weight of our rifles and shells and grenades in the corner and stretched one of our groundsheets over a ridge-pole we stumbled upon in the hay-field. Reggie looked up under the green eyeshade he affected when I came in and slid my books on the desk; he didn't say anything until I stretched out on the hummocked bed, arm over eyes against the staring bulb, but I knew his big rather bulgy eyes with delicate patterns of blood-vessels in the lower corners must have stayed on me and he said, "Laboring, every night, till they lock up the book-morgue. And just a freshman yet." After a moment he continued, "You've got me working too — can't withstand the insult of your industry. My head even almost aches. You shouldn't drive so hard." And, after another stretch of silence, "Hey, before that big bastard down the hall Hayes gets there and scums it all, let's go down and have a hot shower." "Huh!" Ken, oddly for him, didn't so much as stir an eyelash or flex a finger to unbuckle the pack under his head to unroll the coat and cover himself. Usually after every night-watch he cleaned his rifle and then his fingernails before he stretched out, if the hole was long enough. He had been the executive secretary of some Baptist organization before the war and when we first met he was the kind of person who even if he wasn't nominated secretary kept private minutes so when the official minutes were read at the next meeting he would inevitably have errors and omissions to voice. The infantry had dunked a lot of Baptist out of him. His seat on half the other ground sheet, his knees in the air, he swore softly. "This is the *third* hole I've dug today and there's damn near time for a fourth. If the shelling starts the lieutenant'll be foot-happy again. Stir, my butt." I hunched forward, head past the sheet above and the glow from the barn burning just past a straggle of orchard trees sleek and black from the rain lightened the gloom along the ridged sheet where the rain now did not patter. The shelling had stopped, as if the Germans were tired too. I said, "No. We're set for tonight. They're way past our position over there. I haven't been warm — or clean — for days. Come on. Old Jeff and I used to go down last year for a shower just about every night together, just sit on the bench and the water woosh over us. Com'mon! You'll sleep clean and warm like a bug." He was standing already with his long pale hair shading one side of his face and I heartily wished old Jeff's father had come through for one more year at least and thereby saved me from this faintly amused glance and soft insistence that even expected roommates to go up for meals together. But this shower was new. The zoology complexities crawled in my head, mocking as on the glossy pages all evening; they left no spine. I just said, "Sure. Let's go," as I knew from the beginning I would. "Who wouldn't rather be clean and limply warm than fall asleep in the first damn-near dry hole in one entire week's sloggin'," and Ken jerked his helmet forward on his head and lurched out after me into the resiny smell from the fire — a giant bonfire exactly right for wiener roast where young people might discreetly hold hands ha! — and we picked a path between the holes of the rest of the company, away from the German side of the fire to form no silhouette and as we passed Hayes' room we could hear his bull-moose voice booming through the angled transom, ". . . an animal and he doesn't need a god any more than a dog sniffing after a bitch in heat does and any more can he prove that there is one other than the jerk of his own guts and the . . ." his voice fading to unintelligibility though still roaring down the hall as Reggie tapped back the door of the stair-well and slopped down in his slippers with me behind him, a towel over my shoulder. The shower room opened off the basement corridor, its atmosphere struggling between week-old captured and held sweat and the tang of cleanser. Reggie tossed his towel and shampoo and soap and other towel on the bench and sat down and untied his shoes and before taking them off took off his shirt and undershirt and dropped them in a heap on the floor beside his shoes. I stood hesitant for a long moment, the stupidity of giving in so easily to coming mixing poorly with red-faced apprehension at seeing his long flabby body emerge completely; not yet quite able to forget it and take off my clothes and duck under one of the three shower-spouts and Reggie looked up at me, tossing his hair back from his right eye. "Well, get your finger out and com'mon! Over here," and we inched around the fire to where a small jumble of sticks once used to prop the hay for drying burned like a private catering service behind an unsmashed corner of the barn blocking out the Germans. We hunkered down, holding our hands to the flames, the warmth beating back from the wall smelling of cows and barely musty clover. "This is it, this is the place! Snug — I'm shuckin' my boots and pants and dry 'em —" and in a minute, chuckling now, I was holding my pants to the fire but the incredible warmth recaptured Ken in his complete and improbable thoroughness and before he even loosened his boots he pulled some poles from the fire and stuck their still-burning ends at angles between the cobblestones of the barnfloor and began arranging a rack for the clothes. After I held my pants a while abruptly I tossed them on the bench beside Reggie, stripped off my shirt and shorts and stepped under the shower. Reggie was already under the middle one, his lank neck thrusting his head out beside the faucet, grinning at me turning from him as I twisted taps and the water and finally the heavy suds of the soap running down my chest and back and thighs and buttocks hid me a little from his laugh. When I and young Adam hoed potatoes on the long field leading down towards Lake Winnipeg we would unbutton our shirts sometimes and have them flapping about us in the summer heat but never did we dare to take them off, even where we could not be seen from the house as on the field because once he told us, once, and despite the years and my hardened resolve it was still enough to balk my unconsciousness, that animals had to die for God to make clothes for Adam and Eve when they brought sin, heinous and terrible, into the world and that the sin of man was in his body and that no Ross would expose himself, ever, for any reason. And now I stood hearing the other laugh, laughing myself at the fine silt caught in the wrinkles of our tough hide that had oozed through our clotted clothes when we dived in the mud from the mortars. "Hey, you old coot you," I said to Ken, for he was all a year older than I, "put 'em up," and tapped him on the shoulder and he spun away in mock ferocity and we leaped about the clothes-rack we had piled together, round and round while wisps of steam twisted, the firelight flashing close against our gun-oily skin, at each circle the cool soft Holland air brushing us over once with gooseflesh. "All right," Ken said suddenly and with a lurch he stopped to pull his usual reserve around him, "we're like heathen." "Sure, that's us, beautiful heathen," I hissed back, not loudly for the night air carried and I spun him around again and we sparred, our shadows on the broken corner-wall crouching and weaving and clashing when we tapped each other. We thought of our buddies stooped miserable in their holes, clothes clammy on their bodies, and we laughed at our so simply daring release. We had been careful for weeks but now the fire wiped away such narrowness, such caution for our hard-used hides. We did not hear the first sounds of the barrage; the first mortars fell on the far edge of the orchard and we only heard them when they exploded. We stopped, unbreathing, and had plenty of time to get back for it was only light though moving toward us relaxed in the shower, the water falling like a curtain in front of my knees as I sat on the shower bench and Reggie settled a few feet farther looking sideways the length of me and laughing his even-toothed and slightly popeyed laugh shifted his eyes, oddly not breathing now, and the booming voice of Hayes exploded in the shower anteroom, "We are we are we are we are we are the engineers, we can we can we can we can demolish forty beers." He droned through part of the verse and hit on "and we don't give a damn for any old cuss that don't give a damn for us oh glory —" and then he cut off sound at the very entrance of the shower. "Com'mon," Reggie swore under the sssh of the water, face pinkly purple, "let's scram —" and we ran naked, leaving our clothes, crouching close to the earth, the trenches of our company so close we could see their shadows ahead of us through the barrage pattern exploding nearer and nearer and suddenly our timing slipped a cog and Reggie stepped through the shower entrance and jarred Hayes in the chest with his shoulder coming in. Hayes swore, "I coulda guessed you'd be in here you —" and then he caught up for I stood glistening wetly for an instant before I slipped by them both and snatched my towel. The two stood motionless, almost in the exact position of encounter. Then Reggie was looking at Hayes and Hayes at me. Then Hayes twisted away slightly, his eyes hard, "That some freakish pairing of house committee stubs should have put you two together, of all people." Reggie jerked out of his inertness, "The shower's empty, Hayes, it's all yours," he gestured and I suddenly understood that whenever he mentioned the engineer the thin edge I had heard in his voice was hate. Whatever was between them, I was merely the bone to whet their bare-fanged assault. I turned my back, rubbing hard to wipe away the shame that pushed to my skin at their stare, at their implacable, inexplicable violence towards each other, running twisted as between explosions I heard the falling near-whisper of the shell and I dived down, buried myself, my hands over my head and when I dropped them I was facing the full length mirror and I saw myself, entirely, as I had never realized myself, the wide solid shape of me and beyond, below my arrested arm still holding the towel at my ear, the long image of Hayes' broad white chest and the black sprawl of hair on his arms and belly and down the inside of his thighs and finally his tanned face handsome in a sardonic grin, "See yourself, Ross. Even a frosh straight from a Saskatchewan farm is a beautiful naked animal. Know it. That's what you are, a highly specialized and adapted animal." And I sensed the last props of what I hated because of that one man in my childhood and had slashed to rid myself and which had held despite the assault of all my previous oh-so-hard-headed-and-discerning thought give way like an explosion so near that its sound shattered to gentleness and the hiss of shrapnel as I clung to the marred old earth. The barrage was short; over before I had time to think more. Reggie jerked his slightly paunchy body across the other image in the mirror and I was gone and running, feeling the spring in my legs as I dived for the hole and sitting up, happy in the momentary silence after the barrage, poked my head out to catch Ken in his dive when I heard his soft, almost considerate tone, "Lord, lord, o lord I've been hit," and I jerked erect, yelling, "Ken! Ken! I'm coming, hang on to your own stupid ideas and don't stuff them down others' throats that are better without them," and Reggie was twitching into his bathrobe almost without drying himself as Hayes tossed back his head and laughed that the sound echoed about the lined shower room like an earth-spawned roar, and I followed Reggie out, the sound stalking us through the swing of the doublehinged door, my mind and eyes held by the sight of the white body lying like an off-white flower on the sodden Dutch earth as a flare exploded over the far corner of the orchard showing the black sprawl of blood down his thighs and where his legs must be. Our company was counterfiring, heavily; under that cover I got him under the arms and we got him back to the hospital corps and later I was told they amputated what was left of his legs. I was lying down then. The firing had ceased. I tried to feel not having any legs but I could recognize only that I myself was, the immunity that I had feared or rejoiced to have stamped on me immutably easily wiped away by stray shrapnel blasting near me and probably intended mostly for someone else. Waking, on watch, eyes and ears open to the sounds of the night and humans breathing in sleep near me, I could feel none of the relief that should have come with recognition, with my bodily escape. Perhaps the emptiness that I felt was only the earnest of the coming long years where at worst I would be a bone to quarrel over, at worst nothing more or beyond but only myself.

Part Five

11

THE mid-morning sunlight lay on the kitchen table between them in six rectangles tilted to parallelograms and paled by the film of ice that had filtered it. Josh's words had been entirely in keeping with what Art had muttered that first day on the dock and Abe's five months' experience of him at Frozen Lake, yet all these experiences too had unconsciously angled him toward the conviction that Josh could perhaps bend a little, for his sake, when he at last asked.

"Sure," he said after a long swallow of tea. "I guess I understand, but isn't it about time you see he's blocking you at least as much as he's blocking me?"

Josh's finger fanned out a spray of sugar on the oilcloth. "Bjornesen worked on the Indian agent for three years to make Griffin let them get their government payments in cash, and all the answer he got was it would take too much explaining in Ottawa. Now you come along and play right into his hand. Why?"

"I guess maybe I didn't know what I know now." Abe laughed without humor. "I'd hardly heard of Harry Sturgeon, leave alone why he was sick. And it worked, the first couple of checks. Hardly any of them went over — dammit I hate this 'great-white-father' stupidity! They're people, and it's their money." But that argument now made no sense, even to his own ear, for if the evening of the conjuring had proven to the Indians that Kekekose's spirits were powerful enough to help Abe, they nevertheless collapsed before Bjornesen; the gun was far worse than useless.

Josh was insisting, "But it isn't working now so call it off. The Indian agent doesn't know."

"He's never been around; I don't know if he knows."

"I know him; he wouldn't care, one way or another." They were both silent for a moment. "Eh?"

"Cats! What do you think I am?" The very articulation of what had nagged him for weeks prodded his anger. "If a trader can't keep word with his people he can as well — there's enough cheap handling here."

"Exactly. You did the right, the moral thing, last July. They're grown people. The money belongs to them and they have a right to decide. And if —"

"Sure, sure," for early morning, weariness felt too raw on Abe's tone, "you didn't have to explain." He had been so confident his argument would hold; the government order for lumber to build a new school *was* a major industry and *must* be seen differently than their earlier private lumbering efforts — squelched by consistency! — "But I doubt you'll last any longer than this store."

Josh smiled. "Lena and I've thanked God many times for the man you are: honest, frank. You can't imagine how much it's helped." Josh had never spoken of their problems with Griffin, and Abe knew he would not now. "But my work here depends no more on Frobisher than Bjornesen. You can't say how fast he'd tangle himself up if he didn't have you to blame when things go wrong, if he had to supply everything himself."

"He'd bleed them to death and take off without a look back."

"Maybe. I know. I could have pressured them against him long ago, but I know another thing at least as certain as that: there's no point in my even being here unless I can keep my hands clean of making the people have to do what they're not —"

Abe flipped his hands open on the table. "Yeah. Yeah. We've talked about that before. Purity. Theory's fine but you're in a dirty world and to get somewhere you have to move some sometimes."

"You move dirt but you don't get dirty. That's Christ's way."

Abe looked at him; it was too early for this but the thought would not hold longer. "Josh, the winter's here. Keep your ideals, sure, but good heavens man isn't it time you forget about clearing the next patch of good potato soil and *do* something to stop that brewing? You can't just talk —"

"No logs bought, no school building unless they stay clear of Bjornesen's yeast?"

"Yes."

Josh was staring at him without seeing him. "No. There'll be a time for outward doing — there always is — but it won't be that."

"Ha!" Abe got up with a snort as the subdued murmur from beyond the wall broke into placeable sounds with the door in the elongated kitchen-living room opening, George entered from the store.

"Joe Loon and Henry in from trapline," he said in Ojibwa. Abe reached for the kettle. "Good. Real good. Any furs?" George shrugged. "Have they been to Bjornesen yet?"

"I don't know. I don't think so."

"It doesn't matter. Ask them both if they'll come in for tea." He sensed Josh get up and he turned, embarrassed. "W-would you stay? My Ojibwa's not that good, and George has to stay up front —"

Josh laughed — my god he's a good man! — "That at least I can *do!*"

A man wearing a dirty wool jacket and ski cap entered; that the cold had touched him was obvious from the white edges of the scar ridged across his cheek-bone, but his surprise shifted to grin at Abe's outstretched hand,

"Bonjour Joe. Bonjour Henry," to the boy who followed, looking little short of amazed. "You know Mr. Bishop."

Joe's smile widened, "Bonjour, yes we know —" and the word left Abe in ignorance. He looked at Josh, laughing with the newcomers.

"Bonjour. He just called me the Good News Man — that's their name for me."

"I can't know everything," Abe said in Ojibwa, and though he'd used that carefully memorized line times without number, their laughter in the warm room again proved its success. "Sit down — there. Tea and rolls. Talk slow," he was ramming split wood into the stove, "I understand. Come far now — morning?"

Joe's hard hand sticking from a frayed cuff dumped two heaping spoons of sugar into his cup. "Got in last night, sleep in the old house again." He guffawed, watching his son handle the sugar spoon, then nudged him, "He's alone now," and guffawed again.

Abe smiled and sat down. "Family fine?"

"Family okay," Joe pushed on the one English word everyone knew. "Children go to school and learn English and the wife stays in a warm house and rocks baby while I and Henry tramp snow. Family okay!"

"Old days better, huh?"

"Yah. Wife and children came along and we lived in the trap-shack and worked together. Now only his wife," Joe gestured at his son staring below the table in embarrassment, "along; mine stays here for school — family allowance."

"Good money. Five children, almost thirty-five dollars a month."

"Yah. Lots of good money. More than trapping," the trapper snorted and almost spilled the tea mug he was lifting to his mouth. Abe reached for the kettle and refilled.

"Not a trapper like you," he said, but Joe was too delighted to stop ringing the changes as he gestured at his son.

"He's got a boy — three months. Makes more with him too than trapping," and they all laughed so that the dishes rattled. Finally Joe said, "We stay away too long, leave too much to laugh."

Josh turned the conversation easily, avoiding any mention of furs, "Good hunting now?"

"Yah, real good. We got back in the evening yesterday because we found a deer near the trail. He —" Joe jerked his thumb towards the lad beside him looking down again, in pride now, "saw the tracks and we ran down a nice buck."

"Run? Too fast, huh?" Abe asked.

Joe shook his head, delighted at showing up Abe's poor knowledge of deer. "He starts with big jumps in the snow." Suiting action to words, his horn-hard fingers bounded in imitation across the table, "but then he has to rest; we come on snowshoes. When he sees us, he jumps again," the fingers bounded, "but not so far this time. And we walk fast, a little to one side so he circles, each jump shorter until he's tired. Then we get close and shoot him. And he was only a little way from the sled — from here to across the river."

"Good," Abe said. "Come home, fresh meat. Loons good hunters!" The men's beaming faces were masked by their upended cups. "How's little boy, Henry?" he asked the teen-age father.

"Okay."

"Don't see your women much," Abe hesitated, struggling for words, and then afraid this slid too close to problems to fit hospitality he stood up quickly. "More tea? Lots here," and he refilled their cups. Would Joe show his furs? With the trap-line laid out and catching — they wouldn't come in without some — and his good dogs, Joe could stay at Frozen two or three days a week while Henry and the younger son John worked things at trap-shack; and in Frozen he'd get thirsty. But he had taken some supplies at Frobisher — if he just starts it! —

"... big spruce, like this?" Josh was arching two hands to show a ten-inch diameter.

"Bigger, east of camp. Plenty," Joe nodded.

"Good. The government wants to build a new school, like we talked with the Indian agent last summer. I got a letter on the last plane before freeze-up," Josh patted his shirt-pocket. "We need lumber for the mill — 2,000 logs to cut this winter. You want to cut a boom of 200 logs and float them in the spring — like we did for making rooms in your house?"

Joe was grinning, "Good pay this time?"

"Yes sir! Good pay, government pay," and they all laughed at that one, inexhaustible, supply.

"Yah," Joe said. "We could cut that near the river; not much work to float them. Big ones, like last time?"

"Right. I'll give you a stick how big."

Henry cleared his throat, looking askance at his father, and as Josh looked at him he said quietly, "My wife's at the camp. I won't come in much," he hesitated, and Josh smiled.

"I know. But we have a paper only for 2000 logs and we have to share with as many as — ahh —" Josh laughed, clapping the young man on the shoulder, "we'll need more anyway. You cut fifty more. You're starting a family, not like your father with lots of help," and their laughter together around the table and empty cups and plate in the warm smell-thickened room was so open and uninhibited that it seemed to Abe Joe would surely start.

There were more people than usual present when they came out of quarters behind the wooden counter that walled off three sides of the store. Abe did not like the counter, so carefully keeping merchandise at more than arm's length from the buyers, but until things went better here — if ever — the old way would have to do. He lifted up the counter-lid and Joe and Henry and Josh pushed past him into the crowd. The chatter died away a little, then focused in laughter as Joe's three-year-old son ran from his mother to Joe shouting, "Eat something, eat something!" Laughing, Abe leaned over the counter to the boy hopping in excitement, "Eat good, Levi! Good deer!" he gestured at Joe, and everyone roared as they always did when the 'hairy boss' made jokes in Ojibwa. Little Levi, almost stupefied at the results of his cry, hid his face against his father's overalls.

The store resumed its hum and shuffle. Men leaned back again on the benches along the counter; women rocked their cradle-boarded babies; Josh chatted a little, shook off five or six toddlers and left with a wave. Abe was inside the right aisle, clearing boxes near the fur bins. The ice was too thin to trap beaver but Joe might have mink; he would surely have more than the squirrel and red fox caught around Frozen; all of which Bjornesen had so far. If the mink were good, grading high just to draw — damn that was Griffin's first and last mistake — a high voice penetrated the noise. He shifted; George stood mute before Mary Sturgeon talking as no Indian woman talked to a man. He caught George's eye and nodded, already moving, wishing momentarily Josh had not gone. The widow Sturgeon spied him and, pushing the baby flat on its cradle-board through the small pile of groceries before her so that George had to lunge to save a four-pound paper bag of flour from bursting on the floor, she talked on, loud and fast. Abe waggled his hands, "Slowly, slowly!" Noise died away behind her.

He got the gist of her complaint without the usual concentration that was necessary to follow even known accents because he knew. In her excitement her kerchief had slipped off her braided hair and her face, already seamed though she could be no more than thirty-five, and body crushed shapeless by child-bearing and malnutrition: the usual ignored-or-simply-used Indian woman. But her talk showed her change; the dreadful death of her husband in his prime had left her seven children under fourteen, the oldest boy ten, yet alone she abruptly revealed resources no Indian woman would dream of while she had a husband. Refusing advice, she sold Harry's trapping equipment, outboard motor, and best canoe to anyone who would buy them. The money bought children's winter caps and jackets. The day after these arrived by plane the entire family put out in the broken-ribbed freight canoe left them, though ice already skimmed the water along shore, across the river to the Frobisher wharf and down and even more slowly past Bjornesen's and then back again to their shanty, the three oldest girls and one boy paddling and the mother with the three smaller children erect in their finery amidships. Harry had been buried in his best clothes, including new moccasins and blankets bought for the price his best gun would bring; he had been a good provider and she would not let him trudge shoddy the road to the Land of Souls. She had accepted the arrangement for her widow's pension as logically as she would have shot at a moose that stepped into her trail, and though, in the bureaucratic way of governments, no check had yet come, she had found out from Sally Howell how much she would have coming and had used every cent in food debt. Though she had never before had anything to say about what was acquired even with the family allowance check which came in her name, every second day now she was at the store, never bringing a list like the men but deciding as she pointed at the shelves. Invariably some other women followed over the ice to see her make up her sack, babies in cradle-boards on their backs, pre-school youngsters tumbling along or clinging to the sleigh pulled by a single gaunt dog. The men sitting on the benches near the stove did not move; simply watched her as she stood at the counter, one hand holding the cradleboard with its black-eyed baby upright, the other pointing. There had been widows at Frozen Lake before but never one like Harry Sturgeon's.

"Okay, Mary, okay. Here," Abe held high the account book and began in Ojibwa: "Today November 20," he pointed to the company calendar beside the window, then back to the book. "This month debt $110.00 — only $30.00 left, so many days. Teacher says every child — all children need rubbers, dresses, and pants — jackets good, but no rubbers, pants. You buy only food —"

Mary was nodding rapidly and burst in, "Yes, yes, yes — George said that already. But we have to eat — six big children and a baby and —"

"Sure, sure," Abe soothed. "You eat, not hungry. But no candy, no stew."

She seized the one arguable point, "We need meat. Good canned stew —"

"Too much money — don't buy meat — eat moose James Sturgeon shoot. He says you don't take some moose."

Her eyes shifted uneasily. There had never been any question that she could out-argue the 'hairy boss'; to insist twice was a triumph. The delicacy now was helping her without shame before the listening people. She said slowly, "Stew good meat."

"Sure," Abe smiled as he pushed the supplies on the counter toward her sack again, hands and face talking more than his voice, "You buy good food. Good meat, but cost 60¢ can — two cans one meal not much — seven people — cold day," he pointed to the frost-thickened window and shivered violently. The silence broke as even the children laughed. "Moose good, fat — costs nothing — James bring. You buy good food: flour," and he slid the items toward her sack, "sugar, lard, tea, rice, milk — and rubbers. Lots of snow now —" he leaned forward to the tiny girl hiding her runny nose in Mary's skirts, "eh little Mary, want new rubbers?" and at her look and slowly forming smile Abe caught her under the arms and set her on the countertop, bright jacket and dirty skirt and double cotton stockings where holes coincided at the heels of half-splayed runners. "Sure, you need them," he patted the tousled head and turned to George, saying in English, "She should have rubbers for each child, and herself too, and maybe she could pick them out." George nodded, impassive as he said to Mary still standing, irresolute, "Rubbers are over here," and followed Abe already walking around toward the fur bins.

The crisis was past; Mary was almost through, the boxes of the rubbers sticking in angles against the inside of her sack, when Joe lifted his trap-pack to the counter. The people fell silent; even the children, candy smeared, were quiet and though Joe would have scorned to show off in front of women and children, the attention of the men on the benches, through with their morning smoke, was another matter. Abe bent to get a note pad; when he looked up the slim skins of three mink shading from medium brown to what seemed almost pitch black stretched across the counter. Arctic trading had been largely a matter of white and pale-blue foxes; this rich color touched deeper and he murmured, "Aha, nice one!" and picked up the darkest, over two feet long, and took it to the window, rubbing his thumb into the luxuriant underfur. In the sunlight from the snow it was black, with imperceptible shadings in black-brown under the throat. He turned to Joe, grinning, but the trapper was busy pulling out squirrel and weasel so he began jotting down prices as he examined each fur. Feeling the fur between his fingers, the half-dry crinkle of underside smelling faintly of dried, scraped-away animal fat and the tang of spruce fires in the shack stove above which it had dried, he had a blinding sensation of his Eskimo friends helping him make up fur bales in the warehouse at Tyrel Bay: the smell of furs and the give of the half-tanned richness in a solid bale and Itooi laughing to expose all his worn-down teeth, wondering how he could make up his mind so quickly about a fur and never be wrong. He shook his head sharply; thoughts could ruin him before them all at this first opportunity — Joe Loon will be a great one to get — he knew mink for the Eskimos trapping south Keewatin sometimes brought some in, and weasels were everywhere, but he took his time about the squirrels though they were the least valuable of all, sorting each into quality groupings. At last he looked up and smiled at Joe. "Good fur. And good price from plane last time before ice — three weeks. Good money here."

Several of the other men had bunched close now; some fingered the furs, the underside to note the quality of work. Suddenly a small grimy hand appeared at the counter-edge and a squirrel-skin twitched away. Joe did not so much as move; his wife caught the light boy flashing between legs and lifted him up. In absolute silence the boy laid the skin back on the counter. Abe flipped it to the right pile. Joe's eye met his then and he got out his note-book. "November fur best fur. Good grade."

Slowly, shaping the words as he had drilled with George, he went from pile to pile, writing individual sums as he said totals, "One weasel 60¢, four weasels $3.00, three weasels $3.00, four squirrels 70¢, two squirrels 50¢, six squirrels $2.40. One fox $1.50, one mink $10.00; one mink, $14.00, and one mink," he held the prime one a moment, "$25.00" he dropped it and added quickly, "All, $60.70," he turned the paper in front of the trapper. Only the grunt of agreement needed and slide the furs into their bins. But Joe hesitated and he remembered with a jolt that for the first time in his trading days he was not the only trader. Joe did not have to take the price; he probably had more debt with Bjornesen than here — whatever else that old dog can give! — the past months of irritation started to stir like gall in Abe when the trapper reached into his pack and pulled out another fur.

It was so black that even the prime mink paled a little and Abe knew before he unrolled its three-foot length, almost five times the width of the mink, that Joe had trapped a fisher. A murmur of wonder ran through the watchers, and one of the men grunted something Abe could not understand. He felt the fur, thick and incredibly soft, and in the very size of the pelt could imagine the huge black streak of it through the spruce branches and down on an unsuspecting rabbit. It was a male and so not the most valuable, but it was still worth as much as the two best mink. He looked up but Joe had a story and was already in full oratorical Ojibwa:

"Two years ago he started his round in our trapping area. Every year he stole from my traps. I put the nicest, smelliest fish in my traps on his hunting round but he did not step in them. He was smart and he needed lots to eat so sometimes he ate animals still living in my traps or . . ." — trade's sure with James Sturgeon and Albert Crane and the two Sturgeons which makes eight trappers in three families and with Joe that's the four best trapping families at Frozen Lake — ". . . he wanted that fish but he did not like it there around his tree by the devil water," Joe's hands were talking now, riveting eyes and ears. "He'd go forward, stretch a paw, draw back. There was no whiff of me there, but he . . ." — pension trade of Mary Sturgeon and occasional rations for the others but still twenty-six trapping Cranes and Kinosays and Mackenzies and McKays and Loons and Quequeishes and Sturgeons so much tighter in that old bastard's grip —" . . . no fear in him. I would never have caught him by trap alone for when I stood and looked he put his head down and began chewing at the leg. He did not look at me again, not even to hiss, or when I shot him where it wouldn't show on the fur. See," he pointed and the men crowded nearer to look. The left front leg was mangled.

A Mackenzie said slowly, "Ochoyk had great spirit," and the others nodded.

Abe grinned at Joe. "Good trapping — good story. One fisher," he lifted it up for the children and the women behind to see, "$45.00."

Joe stood in thought. The door scraped and someone breathing hard pushed in among the crowd. Joe said, "Henry," and the young man emerged through. Abe moved Joe's furs slightly aside and the same procedure began. Though he had as long a trap line as his father, Henry was less skillful and so had less furs, but the grade was good and he had one fine otter to bring up his total. Finally Abe checked his notebook. "Henry $56.40, Joe $105.70."

Everyone waited for Joe; Abe did not look at Henry who, though he was married and had a son, would not decide independent of his father. That was exactly the trouble, he thought bitterly, watching Joe's unmoving profile against the noon-bright window: when the young men thought like Indians they did as their fathers; and when they wanted to think like white men, like Alex, they —

Joe said, "Come," and began to push his furs together. Abe put down his notebook and passed the fur; the trapper rolled it neatly and repacked it. Abe slipped his fingers over the fisher a moment. Perhaps forty-seven — bah! — he gave it to Joe, face as expressionless as he could keep it. "Another one before spring maybe?"

Joe looked at him inscrutably and said, as if understanding only one part of his meaning, "No other fisher in our area now. Maybe one will move in with this one gone."

Abe said, smiling a little, "Good," and turned to Henry. He had already packed his furs but was looking at Abe with a curious expression under his heavy brows — trying to make up his mind where he's never thought he had one to make up? — Joe buttoning his wool shirt, turning, and Henry followed his father out. Mary Sturgeon and her small following were already outside, and the cold with the warmthless sunlight rammed in at the door.

The store was quiet; Abe cleared away the last boxes, and re-aligned, rather needlessly, some hardware items on the wall shelves. "You could go eat," he said to George, bent over an account book.

George straightened, then looped his jacket off the nail. "$118.40 debt," he said as he walked the length of the store and out.

After a while Abe opened the counter too and went out on the porch. Another day, two at most, and the ice could be thick enough for a plane. It would be good to find out whether late October fur prices still held or whether — he grinned wryly. His eyes found the black line of figures straggling over the ice to Bjornesen; Joe and Henry with their dogteam were moving up the opposite bank. They had seen him work. One hundred eighteen dollars and forty cents debt. Loon would take his fisher over there and with Josh's tacit blessing — he could do something! — get murderously drunk and get his face smashed again and — he stopped thinking. There would be no one now, perhaps all afternoon; he had better eat.

After the blinding snow the store was black as tar. He felt his way to the heater, lifted the lid, poked wood among the coals. He dropped it just as a voice said in Ojibwa,

"You trade well, quickly."

The light was focusing and he saw Kekekose sitting behind the stove. He had no idea when the old man had come in; he had not been there during Mary's tirade, that was certain. He never came near where she was; he heard the Indians speak of this sometimes, but without laughter. Abe said in his ponderous Ojibwa, "Ah, Kekekose, can't see, sun," he eased down on the bench. "You say?"

Kekekose repeated his words. Since summer the conjuror's years had seemingly collapsed on him, shrivelling him, hunching him over. He had not gone on trap-line this year; besides their own, William and Albert were working it between them.

The old man was looking at him wistfully. "Yes," Abe said. "I trade furs, many years."

"We heard, with the Eskimos. But it is good to see a man buy furs like in the old days, not always looking in a book, waiting for a plane; to change prices."

Abe smiled. "When the plane comes, tomorrow maybe, I change."

"But now you don't look in the little book. You look at the fur. No change. Like in the old days with McKay. He was a good trader — best trader we had, maybe." The old eyes looked up at Abe, almost a twinkle lost in their dark corners. Abe nodded his head; he had had time to read the history of Frobisher at Frozen Lake: seventy years established and the middle thirty-six until eleven years ago Peter McKay, half Ojibwa, half Scot, as trader. The conjuror was speaking in the silent store. "Every summer we went out with the fur brigade — all summer to take out the furs, in the big freight canoes, thirteen days out to the great water, the — how you say?"

"Hudson Bay."

"Yah, 'Hudson Bay', then load and back twenty-five days and sixty-three portages to Frozen, with supplies: flour, tobacco, tea, shells. No candy; no yeast. McKay traded sometimes a long, long day, then closed the store and hunted, ran his trapline. Everybody lived as one, and the white man stayed where he belonged, far from here. We had lots of meat, enough trapping to buy bullets and tea and tobacco."

Abe relaxed from the concentration of trying to understand. The old man had not spoken so freely to him before; as if dreaming after a utopia. Perhaps that was what it had been for him: those years when white men no more than touched his people with the basics that eased life but did not contort it. Abe said, "Your father, conjuror too?"

The other shook his head, greasy braids looped up and tugging inside his jacket.

"Chief?"

"Ojibwa people never have chief until the government said it, with the treaty, and they voted one."

"How you — a conjuror?"

Abruptly the old man laughed, silently, entirely to himself, long straight nose profiled, bent to the growing warmth of the stove. "Any Ojibwa boy — any one, son of a good trapper or poor — can have the dream. It comes when becoming a man, when the spirits take pity. Who knows why, or how?" He shrugged a little, as if he had puzzled over this ten thousand times and it still remained as simply inexplicable as if it suddenly sprang new-born in his thought, unimagined before.

"Didn't you, before — dream?"

"Before the big dream? No. Never dreamed before. After, yes, and I learned about herbs and the ways of animals from others of the midewiwin, the medicine society, but not before the dream. The spirit comes first, where it wants."

Abe juggled some sounds in his mind, but there was too much complexity here for him, both to think through and certainly to comprehend in question. He gestured, "Still?"

The old man peered at him. "Still?"

"Yes — boys dream — like you —"

"Boys learn to count now, read, talk English. They do not want it, any more."

Abe said, trying for nonchalance, "Alex want?"

The old man was silent for a long time, hands folded motionless in his lap. "Once. But it did not come and he would not wait and the trader, before Griffin — Nelson — and the agent took him to the school —"

"Did you want him to go?"

Shoulders moved lightly. "He did not have a dream."

After a silence Abe said, "He came back."

"Yah."

He had ventured so far that to hesitate now would be foolish; the worst that could happen would be once again nothing. He shifted words around, "He works — Bjornesen — lives." The old man was silent. "Bjornesen," Abe fumbled, "how — where — the power —"

Kekekose faced him smiling faintly. "Bjornesen is a weak man," he said.

"Weak?" For a moment he did not trust his knowledge of the word, and he said it in his own accent, exactly as Josh and George had drilled him, "Weak?"

Kekekose sat with the same smile on his face, a smile that left his eyes undisturbed in their immense blackness, "Yah. Weak."

"Well!" Abe threw up his hands. "Who's strong?"

"You. I."

Abe did not even say anything, staring at this as if careless reversal.

"You trade better than he, though he was a trapper all his life. You have a big company, here for years and years; lots of money, work with the government. He cannot conjure, have the spirits talk of relatives, or bring your gun back."

"Sure," Abe said in English, laughing without humor. "But he kills Harry Sturgeon, and —" he gestured towards the counter over the empty fur-bin, then started heavily in Ojibwa but the other nodded understanding. Abe said, "Who gets over — weak one?"

"He is weak because he has only one strength. But it is enough for our many."

Abe said again, the language straightening a little, "So, this bad 'weak' man, who," he pondered the word and chose, "who — breaks him?"

The old man stared vacantly, the known smell of the small store gathering the warmth of the heater around the Indian in his aura of sweat and dirt and long-worn clothing, his rubbers scuffling on the plank floor, almost as if hesitating to say something not because he did not know what to say but because he would not be believed. At last he said, in his faintly oratorical tone, "Maybe Josh, maybe the teacher."

"The —" and Abe stuttered on the name he had heard used that morning — nothing but irony or spleen for no grownup believes enough of what they've named to listen except maybe James Sturgeon who like the children wants a story before going to bed! — Kekekose supplied the word for him,

"Yes, the Good News Man."

Except for the diplomacy of keeping a straight face he would have laughed aloud. He did laugh later, alone, as he leaned on the counter, the account book in front of him barely visible in the fading afternoon light. He had been heaping snow higher around the building when Joe Loon drove up with his dogs and watched him silent after greeting as he worked. Finally the trapper said, "Where's George?" and Abe waved the shovel at the storage building where George checked stock. The other did not move, and then Abe realized that the question had not arisen from any wanting to see George but rather an oblique attempt to find out why he was doing what the, according to the structure of things, handyman should have done. He straightened up then to the trapper looking across the bay of the lake before the store.

"Good exercise," Abe said in English, flexing his muscles, and the other grinned, almost understanding. "Come in," Abe said in Ojibwa and they crunched into the store. From his jacket-front the trapper pulled the fisher. He said, not as if it would really work but simply to follow some pattern in this highly unpatterned move, "Bjornesen says $48.00," and Abe said without expression, "Forty-five" and the trapper tossed the fur to the counter and said, "Three pounds of tobacco and two number four traps." When the yelping of dogs faded Abe was laughing over the counter, hands in the silky fur — soft like a fine woman's breasts — laughing aloud at himself.

So when the knock came on the living-quarter door that night he was relaxing, flat sloppy relaxed on his back on the moose hide on the floor almost asleep to the turned wide-open radio across the room booming and snarling in Thursday night concert. He could not even tell how often he had heard it when he at last comprehended and sat up, listening, then hitched over and turned the radio down and listened and it came again, gentle on the rock-frozen wood, and he thought, Violet — well once or twice extra never hurt any young Indian un-maiden! — he went to the door so content and dazed in his smug contentment that the only other thing he knew was no thought at all but merely a kind of suspended conviction that you can't forever keep a beautiful girl from making tea for you especially if she hasn't insisted for a while and he pulled open the inner door as the outer squawked on the snow circle under it and in the yellow umbrella of light stood Sally Howell.

"Well," he said when he could find his voice. "Come in."

"Thank you." She stepped in and flipped aside the long scarf that wrapped her head. "I thought for a while you didn't hear me." She looked to the radio and smiled, "I knew you were home."

"Well, let me take your coat," he shook himself mentally. "I guess I always turn it on as loud as it goes. The best sound that way. Anyway, I was almost asleep, I think. Drugged maybe."

She bent to the radio, hands pressed together in front of her. "My, a lovely sound. Is that Winnipeg?"

"Uh-huh — CBC station. It's good."

"It must be a good radio. Mine sounds simply hopeless."

"First rule of survival north of the road-end: get a good radio. Or better yet, a record player. At least there's no static. Since, thanks to Mrs. G., there's electricity here, I've ordered one. With everything of Bach that's recorded."

"Bach?" She was still studying the radio and he watched her.

"Yes. Don't you like him?"

"Not really. It sounds very childish, but to me he just seems to go on and on. What are they playing? Not Bach —"

"I don't know," he laughed, draping her coat over a chair beside the table, "but I'm sure it's not him. I was dozing when the announcer spoke and I just generally listen to sounds — I'm not really a intelligent listener —"

She looked around at him and he felt, knew with a start that woke him completely, that he was over-talking, blurting out so loose-mouthedly that if she had not looked at him with what he realized at that moment were dark blue eyes he probably would have confessed his sins and asked for forgiveness — stupidity! — an uncanny voice, so easy, gentle it pared you down to essentials seemingly without your pain or its effort. He scrounged his mind together and gestured to the chair, "I'm sorry I don't have a couch, or decent chair. Freight canoes and airplanes can't pack them very well. I usually sit here," he squatted on the moosehide.

"Didn't 'Mrs G.' have a couch?" She sat in the chair, white rolled socks on her feet, legs crossed at the ankles under the dress rather too long to be stylish. He grinned at her emphasis.

"I think so — probably. But I never saw it."

"Lena told me a little about how fast he left when you came."

After a moment he realized she was not going to say any more. She was looking about, openly curious. He said then, "Besides the gas power system, thank go — goodness for that — about all that's left of her is that pseudo — I don't know what — New Orleans society I guess — wall-paper. They had a sort of wall there, but I pulled it down one evening when I —" he caught himself again but she was looking soberly at the strip on the ceiling where the wall had divided living-room and kitchen, "when I felt especially destructive and didn't like that horse-and-coach stuff all around."

"It's a nice large room."

"You never can tell when I'll have ten trappers in at once and the kitchen be too small for tea."

"Don't be ironic. It doesn't suit you," her voice died, startled. "Oh, I'm sorry — I — it's talking to children so much I forget to —" she was half-confused now, half-laughing.

"To cover up," he completed. They laughed and in their frankness the air seemed changed. He stood up, "I have a good bottle of Scotch in the cellar — I don't suppose —?"

"I wouldn't know any more how to drink that!"

"Then you'll have to settle for tea, like a trapper." He did not quite dare push the hint she left, but he would remember. He got the kettle from the stove and put it on the heater. "I'll make it a bit stronger than they like."

"They really use the tea-leaves, don't they. I had tea at Mrs. Sturgeon's last week and I thought she'd forgotten to put some in."

Abe prodding the fire. "Say, we worked around her today. Your note yesterday was good; gave me an out to stop her getting all that candy and canned meat without embarrassing her too much."

They spoke of the Indian children as the water warmed, the tea brewed; of their interest to learn and yet almost insurmountable hesitancy to speak English in school and virtually never out of it; of their fishing in the channel after school for supper; of several older boys away on trap-lines for weeks and who if reported would lose their family allowance: parents caught between needing help on trap-lines and government money. "But even if it is hard to feed them," Sally said, "I think they love their children more than most whites I met teaching."

"Sure," Abe grinned, "if never spanking them is a sign."

"Oh, it isn't that. They don't spank but they do punish."

"How?" he asked, knowing.

"By social pressure, by laughing at them, by —" she was studying him intently, her eyes so wide in her slender white face that for a moment in some recess of himself he was amazed he had ever found it in his mind to label her 'prim'. She stopped as if she knew his thought, and with the ease in which they spoke he almost believed she did.

"Sure," he said, facing her directly. "Do you have trouble with them in school?"

"Not really. Oh, the boys want to show off enough, but then we all laugh at them, or with them if it's really clever. Behaving isn't their problem."

"It was that way with the Eskimos too; they seemed to be able to do anything they want as children and they grow up better behaved than any white you'll meet. And the only punishment, for almost anything, is group pressure. I guess there aren't more law-abiding people in all Canada than the Eskimo — or the Ojibwa. In over seventy years that Frobisher's been here they've had exactly two arrests."

"I know — but they still fight on drinking nights —" her voice fell away. She sat with her ankles crossed, which seemed womanly in her.

"Yeah. Before Bjornesen came here with his yeast there was never any need for arrests. You've seen that Quequeish, haven't you?"

"Big Amos, with the broken nose?"

"Uh-huh. You could hardly miss him or his mouth. He cut Joe Loon in a brawl last winter and got six months in Kenora — more a warning than —"

Her voice flared at him, jerking his head up, "But you know, it's only made him worse! What does jail mean to them anyway? If the way they discipline themselves is to use group agreement to get the rebel in line, what's the point of police coming in from outside and making arrests? They all have to want to stop drinking and fighting and then —"

He interrupted, "That's exactly what Josh said when I tried to get him to refuse the log-contract till they stop. Look, you don't seem to understand how vicious homebrew is: it's not just giving up tea for a while! We'll just have to use some outside pressure — maybe even a little dirty pressure — until they see the light and get enough pride back to get up a community feeling against —"

"Pride about what?"

He said, instinctively, before he quite knew it, "Pride in themselves."

"No." Her tone was gentle as always but the ring of

assertion edged it with iron as it had once earlier that evening, "Pride in self is too vicious."

"Vicious?"

"Yes. Pride, the original sin — of Satan anyway who infected man with it. And that's what makes Bjornesen move — pride."

"No, no, that's not pride like I meant it. That's ruthless selfishness, not human dignity —"

"Oh but Abe," she faced him, knees drawn up and feet squarely on the floor, "that's exactly it. What happens when a person has pride in himself but that he denigrates others? Pretty soon there isn't anything too good for him and too awful for them. That's not dignity, that's pride."

"Sure, so I used the wrong word. I never did — by the way, you majored in English, huh?" She nodded, a small laugh tugging at the corners of her lips but her intent too concentrated to allow it, "Alright, teacher, my word-choice was poor! I meant that the Frozen Lake Ojibwa have to have a little outside pressure to get their human dignity back. Okay?"

"No."

"What do you mean, 'no'?"

"Just that. No."

"You can't just say it." He studied her face, and she was completely in earnest. "Okay. Universalize the principle. I was overseas during the war; I grew up on Manitoba, Saskatchewan, farms; I've lived with all kinds of people in all kinds of places. They all have human dignity, in some form or another. And you can appeal to them, using it. Surely the Ojibwa with their past —"

"What does 'human dignity' mean when you say it that way?"

He puzzled a moment, feeling suddenly he must probe this out again because her clear eyes were on his face so unwaveringly, and then he tossed that aside with a jerk of his head and said what he had known since the violent discoveries of university, war, Arctic, and which he sometimes had to relive, "An understanding of themselves as physical human beings, with mental powers for rational thought."

Her eyes did not shift from his face; they did not blink so that for a moment he had a startling sensation of seeing unfathomably deep into her. "That's all? Just themselves? The recognition of self as an entity. Psych jargon: personhood. The most heinous sins a person could commit then would be matricide and cannibalism, either separately or together, right?"

"Yes." In honesty he had to add, "And I've known persons who did both. But only under the extremest necessity — war — torture, starvation —"

"That's just the trouble," she spoke almost fiercely now, leaning down towards him from her chair, "with Bjornesen too. Necessity. To have, to stay alive."

"Yes." He had been battered with that last summer in Winnipeg and he recognized now, as he should have earlier, and had in some recess of his mind, that there was no ultimate basis for his 'human dignity' argument; that it was wiped away by the rip-tide of necessity and necessity was itself then the only direction-giving value — god that's too terrible! — he felt the emptiness grow he had known last summer and under the bivouac, even sitting here while the last brown circle of their tea stood between them cold in the cups.

"Do you know Violet Crane?" Sally asked.

"Huh," Abe jerked out of his thoughts, "Oh, sure. She comes in here sometimes."

"Recently?"

Abe thought a moment, angered he had instinctively explained. "Two-three weeks maybe."

"All the fellows are after her. You can't blame them. She's a beautiful girl. Girls like that don't show up every generation. Maybe every hundred years even —"

"Oh, come on —" Abe began and she laughed, serious nevertheless,

"No, I mean it — not just body but mind too. Once in October she stayed late after school — wiping up dust, as if by accident. We talked about all sorts of things. And several times since. Her comprehension is phenomenal. And she's really in a corner about Alex."

She paused, as if choosing her words; he was happy her eyes were on the floor, but when he spoke his voice was too loud still, "I don't know what she's told you but she fooled around so much with him in summer fish camp her father sent her home. With George and me. I don't see why Joseph just doesn't make them live together and be done with it."

"Don't you know? They're too closely related to get married."

"What? Her grandfather's Alex's uncle; that makes them — oh, at closest, second cousins."

"Alex doesn't care; he's thinking like a white man, or at least trying. But Violet is Ojibwa and they have incest taboos about persons related only through their fathers — you know, patrikin. At least that's what Josh and I can work out. If somewhere their relation was made by a woman it would be all right, but it's all men. Joseph and Alex, sons of brothers, are also classified brothers. Alex isn't trying to marry his second cousin but, according to their beliefs, his brother's daughter — his niece."

Abe said at last, "How does that fit your argument, that it's not human dignity?"

"Don't you see? The taboo comes from outside the family, a value system that has nothing to do with their normal wishes as people. Actually, it goes directly against them: wanting to have a son-in-law who can provide well, a strong healthy daughter-in-law."

She was silent and he puzzled; she seemed to be reading her tea-cup before her on the floor. Finally he said, "I still don't see what's that got to do with Joe or Amos getting drunk every week or two."

"They'll keep on getting drunk — doing what they want as people — until something so great, so beyond themselves overwhelms them that they no longer want homebrew."

"Okay. And that overwhelming — thing — is?"

"God's mercy."

"Mercy!"

"Yes. The knowledge that God Almighty has a heart; compassion for their misery."

He sat, not looking at her now. There was nothing in what she said that convinced him of anything; it seemed, merely, ridiculous. She must have sensed this for she said suddenly,

"Have you been past Brink Island?"

"The island where the Frozen and Brink Rivers join? Yes. George and I passed there last summer. With Violet."

"The Bishops have a cabin on it, where they go sometimes when they can to be alone. Their house is so full of people, always."

He did not know why she said this. At last he said, "I didn't know that. You can't see it from the water; the island's too high, I guess."

"We're going there over Christmas."

"We?"

She did not note his amazement. "Josh and Lena and Anne and I."

He straightened his thoughts. "Aren't you going home for the holidays?"

"No. Things are coming to a head — Josh feels this winter something will break and we're going there for some days of prayer."

He tried to keep his voice neutral, "Can't you pray here?"

"Yes, of course, we do — and desperately too — but we think we should get away where we'll just be alone to pray for Frozen Lake. Abe," she was facing him, her gentle voice holding him rapt, "I know you feel that same way about my not using the government allowances like you wanted Josh to use the log-contract. We can't do things that way; we have to try what we believe in. Please believe us."

He could not have denied her that had he wanted to; and he gave her his word, because he did want to, because at the blaze of her conviction he seemed abruptly such a vacancy, because he did want to.

She looked at her wristwatch. "Goodness!" she was on her feet and he stood also. She was almost tall enough to look level into his eyes; they smiled, just self-conscious enough to sense they understood one another better than either could have expected after so short acquaintance. "Actually, I had some very practical things to ask you."

"If they're practical they should be easy, I'd say."

She laughed with him. "Oh they are. Number one, can you get some proof of Kekekose's age — trading records — anything from long enough ago that it seems reasonable he's sixty-five and can apply for pension?"

"Has he come about that?"

"Yes. He looks old enough."

"He didn't last summer. He's aged like you can't imagine."

"So Josh says too, after Harry's death."

"And me getting my gun." She looked at him steadily. "I remember what you said that night."

She nodded, knowing also. "What do you do — with it," and he understood her exactly.

"Nothing. I just leave it among all the other inexplicable things."

"Why must you have to explain everything?"

"Why —" it hung in the air between them like an aboriginal longing, fused of the dust and sweat and gore and bone and muscle of innumerable generations in the very stuff of them both.

She said finally, "Will you look?"

"I'll try. I may have to write Winnipeg."

"Whatever you can do. Number two, would you come to the school on a Thursday afternoon and tell us about some cities that you've visited — London, Paris? No," she lifted her hand against his expression, "you really haven't much choice; after all, all the men who've been out are helping. Alex about life in Sioux Portage; Dave Oakes about his plane next time he comes in; Josh about a small town near Toronto. Have you been to Ottawa?"

"I'm not saying a word."

"Then you have — wonderful!" She clapped her hands, face lit with happiness — whom did I imagine clambering out of Dave's Cessna last August? — "I've been talking about our government and have some pictures, but if you've been there — and London — you will come."

"Yes," he said laughing, "I *will* come."

"Good. I'll send you a note with Small George again." She slid into her coat before he thought.

It struck him then, "Say, let me walk you over the ice — just a sec —" he got his parka. She said nothing; as he pulled open the door she grinned up over her shoulder and he felt something jolt in him.

There was no moon and the ray of his flashlight led them down the path as they walked side by side. "I thought you'd ask," she said.

"Ask?" in the off-balance of his thoughts at her grin he could not dare think what she meant.

"What Bjornesen is going to tell the children."

"Bjornesen!" in his throat it cut strangely like a curse. "You're not having that — him talk to innocent kids!"

Her voice sounded roguish and he could only recall her at the door; he had seen her so rarely — damn me anyway — he had no idea whatever what she usually looked like. "Did you know that Mr. Sigurd F. Bjornesen was born on Hecla Island, Lake Winnipeg, Manitoba, and that he visited his father's ancestral home in Iceland for three years when he was twenty-one? He is going to tell us about Iceland." She was laughing aloud at his silent angered protest. "After all, whether you admit it or not, he has seen more than just the inside of certain houses off Winnipeg's lower Main Street."

Their footsteps sounded on the snow packed on the channel ice. When he could at last control his multi-leveled astonishment he said, "You're the teacher," and at his tone he sensed her turn to him, quickly.

"Don't misunderstand me. He's an evil man — I don't think we know yet how terrible he — if Violet —" she stopped. "I've no right to talk of that. But he is a man, and we have to show him honestly why we think he's wrong."

"And you do that by letting him talk to those poor kids? They hear enough about him already."

"In one way, but maybe not in another. No one's just bad."

They were near the middle of the channel and the wide night sky above gave almost a sensation of light, though it was overcast and no stars showed. On the far shore a few kerosene lights blinked in the winter cabins of the Indians, and in the mass of the trees to the left brightness fell through the window of the trader's house upon yellow snow. In a few minutes they were walking up the slope to the Bishop's house, the black dog Ringo baying as they approached.

"Thank you for coming over," he said on the porch, her hand on the latch.

She was smiling again, he knew, though he could not see her face. "You're such a recluse, I just had to brazen my way in." Her laugh covered his exclamation. "Why don't you join us for Sunday dinner? Josh has talked about it all fall, but — surely you don't work *all* Sunday too."

"You can't really tell," he said lightly. "Okay, some Sunday soon, when it suits you all."

"We'll expect you. Goodnight," and she vanished — when will I sort and classify this evening? — as he trudged back up the path to Frobisher's he heard George at the woodpile piling logs on his arm to settle the store heater for the night. They took turns every week and this week was Abe's, but the handyman must have noticed he had a visitor. It was rare enough.

He swung his light around and lit the path for the other. "Thanks," he said. After dark they spoke English. Hemmed inside the store, the light seemed stronger. He continued as George worked at the heater. "Saw a light in Bjornesen's furloft above the store when I was coming back. Any idea what he'd be doing up there this time of night?"

"The fur loft?" George's high voice was hesitant.

"Yeah. He couldn't have much fur there yet. And he wasn't looking at Joe's fisher!"

George coughed a short laugh. "No. And he won't talk about that very much either. But Joe'll get it for that."

"You think so? How?"

When George answered it took Abe a moment to comprehend: "I don't know who'd be up there — this time of night." The Indian was already moving toward the door. "Goodnight." The doors closed quietly behind him.

So strange was his abrupt going that Abe was in his livingroom again, alive now to the radio's murmur of the late news, before he remembered that he had asked what George thought Bjornesen was doing in the loft and that the response had hedged on another question altogether.

215

12

THROUGH the streaks of overcast a sharded saucer of moon showed now and then the rippled snow of the lake-surface, but he needed little light to guide him. He had searched out the intricacies of the lake-shore one early winter afternoon and now often in a half-lit evening moved over one of the trails he had more or less organized in his mind, body beating rhythmically to the thrust of his legs, cushioned on the give of the skis riding the wind patterns, his face hardened against the cold, nostrils flaring at the flame of frost in his nose. After the bruit of the day in the store, a quick supper and he would pull the skis from their rack and schuss down to the lake, body bent into the cold pincers of the flung air, the movement and the cold driving out columns of figures and the never-ending plans of trade that did not quite come. The Indians had never seen skis on anything but airplanes before; they had watched in amazement when he first strapped them on but now his movements were accepted like the long flushed movements of the northern lights, to be looked at when noticed, but uncontrolled and unpredictable. Let them think what they would; on these flights — is there nothing else to call it? — he almost forgot them at last and moved in the world of relaxation and freedom, free from much thought save the stride of his legs and the tension of shoulders and arms against poles. Across the channel, around the longer point where the Indians' summer hovels stood empty, and down the long western rim of the lake to circle south and then come in straight for the channel again, eleven miles around. Or down the slope to the bay facing the store, east under the bluff of the cemetery and its tiny grave-cabins and after that nothing but spruce and gaunt poplar and birch motionless in the darkness, sometimes cracking in the iron cold like pistols firing, around the eastern arm of the lake, six miles and almost two hours of skiing that bunched muscles like coiled steel in his legs. And, along the southern shore again, now almost opposite the channel of the river notched in the spruce-bristle of the northern shore, standing motionless, chest heaving gently, he could hear a dog of the settlement howling like distant agony drifting by him to desolation. From the mass of the land behind him a wolf answered, so near it seemed the animal breathed at his neck and he looked around, skin stirring on his back as from the stroke of a long cold finger. Only the land, rocks and trees snow-heaped, impersonal and gigantically cold, loomed like an immense fist thrust into the darkness, shaping a darkness all its own.

He moved suddenly, no longer feeling the quiet. The evening was well down and out of the west the overcast of night roiled, advancing over the sky. On the open lake he could still sense his way; as he neared the channel the point humped out of the land. Beyond store and school in the village the same dog was howling, echoed occasionally now by others. It was too early; he should have gone around the entire six miles. He turned right angle to the channel and pushed toward center of the west wing. After perhaps a mile he stopped and sat on the back of his skis.

The wind-glazed surface of the snow hard under him, he sat listening. There was nothing to hear. No dog or wolf now; not even the bare scrabble of wind in the eddies of snow-ridges. His ears pricked; he pulled up his hood again and bent his face to his mittens, rubbing the frost-stiff skin. Before his clenched eyes the off-balance boomerang shape of the lake emerged, with the blue of its summer body etched around by a dead-yellow line, complete as he had seen it aloft to the shorter east wing, round little bay before the store, the short ridge, the river channel, the Indian point, and the longer west wing, with the blackness of the land squatting like a beast about the very edge of its outlined brightness. He opened his eyes but the shape persisted long against the overcast piling higher where he faced. He found the poles then and stood up, purposeful. In a moment he was gliding north, directly toward the one huge star still visible but not looking at it; conscious only of the gathering rhythm of his body against cold and darkness. When he looked up at last he had gone too far; he was behind the point and he swung east.

He had found his western-loop trail and was already moving well in its familiarity around the inner bend of the point when he stopped for a breather. He could just make out the roof lines of the summer cabins against what was left of evening lightness. He would have to use the torch anyway before he got home round the point so he could as well go where he hadn't before. When he moved again he was sliding towards the point to cross over its narrow neck to the river.

Even with the torch he had hardly thought finding a place to mount would be so difficult. There seemed to be only steep heaped rocks, and when he finally found a small inlet, despite skis he sank knee-deep in the buoyed-up snow among the hidden reeds of the shore and had to heave himself out onto the gentle slope by sheer strength. In two strides the slope tilted so sharply he had to herringbone; when he topped the rise at last to the flat behind the cabins he was breathing harder than he had in many an evening. With a thrust of his arms he slid over a drift into a cabin's shelter, only its roof and window-hole above the snow, and leaned sideways against the weathered logs.

He was looking over a space he would never quite forget. Alex had emerged that night from the low bush near this cabin; in front of him under perhaps three or four feet of snow was the spot where the lodge had stood surrounded by the people, and he needed no light to remember the ground hard under him squatting, the sound of the bones, the shape swaying against the autumn stars. Without stirring a muscle he could suddenly feel the hard bulk of the revolver in his parka-pocket and with a jerk he stood up, rest lost. The roof-ridge was so low in the snow he could see over it to the last faint lightness in the east. After a moment he switched on his torch. Its light probed out the scattered moss-and-mud chinking and the wide cracks between the boards, still faintly bright from the summer saw-mill, that covered the window-hole. He pushed forward, jerked one board and then another aside, kicked off his skis and, balancing on the sill-log, swung feet-first into the cabin.

He had expected nothing so he was not disappointed. The narrow beam of his light showed only the grey logs, a few boards as shelves above a half-hanging table built against a corner wall, its pole-leg knocked awry, the door where a drift of snow through a broken plank was sprayed over the floor, and a window, sashless as the other, roughly boarded. A shell. Only in the sharp cold the lingering Indian smell, pungent and, when you sorted it out, abruptly grossly impolite, as if it oozed into the very logs and earth, irradicable, animal. Human animal, he thought pushing back his hood and sitting in the angle of the wall and packed dirt floor where all the filth would be sterilized by cold and even the forsaken lice hibernating in a hidden crevice. Only the unwashed human body covered with rags or hides not of its own growing smelled really fetid, as if rotting while it moved — ugh! — he flicked on the light and its beam snubbed on a tiny grey box. With a ski-pole he hooked it within handreach. A hole had been punched in one end and a rag of string tied to it; from its markings it had been dragged here and there, everywhere across the dirt floor; he recognized the box even before he looked at the last side and read 'Peter Pan Shoes for feet light as a fairy'. He looked at the box a long time, the slim flexed form of the eternal boy in the yellow beam of light, the dirty string hanging over his glove-thumb.

That was all they had ever wanted, and they spoke of it again and again when you could understand them a little: pimadaziwin. When he had asked George what it meant he laughed his rare laugh, more frequent now, but still rare, and shrugged his shoulders. "The good life" was all he would admit. Josh helped more: a life with enough food for the family, unmolested by evil spirits or men that hated you, above all a life free from sickness. Pimadaziwin, the Good Life: Kekekose, Mary Sturgeon, George, Joseph Crane, their families, even Alex and Amos Quequeish and Joe Loon, no, those three already wanted not merely freedom from the disease that was to them evil, a penalty for some bad conduct or social transgression or the sign of witchcraft against them, but the life made possible by the power of the whiteman, the ability to earn money which meant they could drink themselves stupid. Drink; that alone rarely satisfied long. Amos — that night here he already scoffed — and Alex, pushed by frustration or love or whatever it was it could be called, he would know by heart what a residential school definition of 'marrying for love' was. His ancestors had gotten on very well indeed for their entire buried history without finding the whiteman's idea of love at all necessary either for marriage or continued existence. And Violet shaped for love-making in any race — with traders and preachers and conjurors will she ever recognize pimadaziwin even if she finds it? — perhaps the little child that had tugged the box over the foot-packed earth too had been dreaming about flying away where he would be forever child, an Indian child with sure knowledge of pimadaziwin — no — the children, if anyone, were becoming the most distinctly, most forcedly non-Indian. Sally couldn't allow them to speak one word of Ojibwa in school, though she would have liked to — we only picnicked that once under the trees in the pasture drinking lemon-water where the crocuses thrust up and little Adam's excitement had to bla-blab when he got back from Presbytery and she never dared again — Sally couldn't let them speak Ojibwa not only because it was government regulation but because otherwise they would never learn to speak proper English — so wash your face and read about Dick and Jane whoever they are and open doors for silly girls and no wonder Peter Pan is left behind when even for a child it's impossible —

His mind seemed to be getting away from him and he laughed to unsettle himself. He laughed again, louder, the sound echoing in the tight little room, and as he heard it he also heard the distant sound for which he had been unconsciously waiting. He got up then, shook himself, and clambered out of the window onto the snow. The air was so immensely cold that with his hood off he could hear the drumming though almost a mile up the channel. As he wriggled into the ski-harness and moved on he remembered Alex emerging here the night of the conjuring — perhaps this is Violet's summer home and sure the change that's come over her since that night is Sally's — his mind lurched and he found himself on the land trail towards the settlement, and stopped. It did not really matter; he had not even seen the other trader from a distance in over a month. He strode to dull rhythm of the drums ahead, the black spruce on either side defining the trail. He did not quite need the torch.

The trail had not been used since the last snow; quickly he grew hot from fighting the softer snow in the turns: after the lake the trees bent here stifling. He had sensed in the plane, and now again, the oppression, almost threat, of the land and the friendly open of the water — silly — he paused for a breather and his light-beam picked out the bunching of a squirrel house among the trees. That was it: slow down the flow of life, curl up, drop half the year down the hole of unconsciousness.

One window showed light when he emerged into Bjornesen's clearing. A drawn curtain; Bjornesen apparently taught his squaws some minor aspects of whiteman privacy. With a kind of shock Abe realized that he had not spoken to the Icelander since the first day at Frozen Lake, and never alone. Looking at the yellow patch on the snow he understood suddenly that his thinking about him had made the old man so real, so rigid in his stereotype perhaps, that talking to him had never seemed necessary. What he heard via the Indians was enough — the dirty bastard — the channel between them, they could not meet accidentally. The mail plane came to each first on alternate weeks; social occasions: Abe was not likely to get an invitation to the drunks, and neither of them were exactly welcome at the drummings. As for the Sunday services Josh held mostly for children in whatever Indian house would have him — the drumming is too loud — Kekekose's house would be literally stuffed with people and staring in at the open windows, the wizened conjuror bending over his water drum and praying or pleading or whatever it was he did to arouse his helping spirits to help him solve his own wife's illness, the woman who had laughed with Abe at summer fish-camp about his pronunciation of "Makwa," her enormous belly and breasts shaking above him as she proffered the hacked hambone, her very laugh whorling up a visceral vitality that could seemingly defy any disease germ leave alone malignant spirit. But for two weeks she had been held immobile by a strange intensifying paralysis. She, and Kekekose with her, was adamant against a plane trip out; the surly doctor who finally flew in left no diagnosis with useless medicine: 'She has to have tests, at the hospital!' — move her with what small army? — so she lay an inert, heaving mountain and for the third successive night the drum was beating. If Kekekose could discover her secret sin she would confess and become well; so Josh said they believed. They believed also that the evil done by parents could be called home in the bodies of their children but apparently not the other way around, as Abe had half-jokingly suggested. Or, if some foreign object had been projected by witchcraft into her body Kekekose need but discover it and remove it by sucking to break the spell. Who at Frozen Lake would attempt against the wife of Kekekose? Every child knew the answer: somewhere behind that lighted window, warmed by wood carried in by a woman whom no one at Frozen Lake had ever seen before a chartered MOA plane came in one day from some northern point and there she had been, who did not even speak an Indian language anyone here understood and who had no name save 'Bjornesen's woman' and would never have until the day, who knew when, she would leave alone as the succession of women before her and after a time Bjornesen would come back with another who would only serve to pile up the evidence, already blocked up ponderously enough to be beyond doubt, that it was not their fault Bjornesen had no son. Against this gigantic sapless fraud Josh — and Sally — said, 'Abe, I can't help you in trying to break any human being.' They could have done it, together. But to pray — even a week of nothing but praying and praying coming up! — was holding up fingerdabs of decency against a flood. And the drums now every December night were little more than the rhythmic accompaniment of their going, all their going.

He understood sharply he was cold. It pricked through the padding of his boots and he was moving, keeping clear of the light around the darker hulk of the store and warehouse, down the well-traveled trail towards the Indian settlement. The drums drew him; he might have gone across to Frobisher much faster by sliding down the slope and striking directly across the channel.

He was not a hundred yards into the blackness of the bush, striding without light for as long as he had the foot-prints and sleigh-runner-tracks hard under the skis there was no need to see anything, when he saw the light prick far ahead of him, immediately lost behind some bend and as immediately alive again. He stopped, listening, and when he heard he cursed. They were noisy; a group obviously coming towards him — stupidity to be seen here! — no matter what, his tracks betrayed him, and even the shack window left gaping. Their sounds came nearer. He unsnapped the skis and turned, committed already by a kind of instinctive reaction, flicking his light on the trail behind him where his body would block it if they looked ahead. He gathered the skis under his right arm and backed down the trail towards the approaching sounds, keeping the light on the trail but staring at the edge of illumination against the spruce and low brush. He backed as far as he dared; it was not really far enough but he had no time for better; thrust the light into his pocket and, holding his free arm before his face in the impenetrable darkness ran a few steps forward and leaped, as high and as far as he could, to the left. He could have jumped better with the skis on his feet but he could not risk it into the brush, and it was as well he had his arm up for he cleared what must have been the first low bush he had to get over but the spruce beyond were nearer than he thought and he landed full length on lower branches, slid, and thudded into the snow. He hunched around and got his feet under him, panting, not sure why he had put himself into a position where, should they notice his tracks and swing their light barely off the trail they would inevitably see him, and if they got beyond their inevitable laughter at his only possible explanation, the oddity of his jumping would make him look sillier still. But he had no time to think logically; they might miss him completely. He hunched down under a spruce branch as the light came around the nearest bend.

They approached noisily, more than he had expected; perhaps six or seven, speaking so fast that he could grasp only snatches. He bent lower, mind rigidly intent that they had to pass him, spruce needles jabbing at his face. When they were almost opposite him, the usual smoke-greased lantern plotting out a dingy spot on the snow, someone at the rear yelled the first words Abe clearly understood,

"Amos, stop!"

The light paused and Amos Quequeish's guttural voice barked, "Somomabeetch, what now?" The broken-nosed Indian swore in English partly because it was impossible to swear in Ojibwa, which had no words for it, but largely because it gave him status.

Someone further back yelled, "Joe has to lift his leg to a bush" and all laughed. Men only. Amos bellowed,

"He should wait till there's something to lift at," and they laughed again.

Another said in the silence that fell after, the drum insistent, "Old Kekekose is working hard. He wants to get back to it too," but the usual obscene variation brought only a guffaw from Amos. A voice spoke in different assertion,

"Don't laugh at him. He still tries the old ways —"

"What are you coming for?" The light wheeled sharply. "Go back and wait if you want."

There was a momentary silence, then, "He did many good things before and —"

"Somomabeetch, so maybe he did when nobody knew better but Wagoss has finished him and his spirits are finished and he can drum every night and not even find out what's with his wife," and Amos ended with a long fizzling curse, English sounds strangled in Ojibwa. So that's what Amos was: A toady — just right for a graduate of a six months' pen course

224

— they were still standing although Joe Loon's voice had come from the rear,

"Hey, let's go," for another voice said,

"Amos, would you go to Bjornesen if you got sick?"

Amos cursed again but a new voice charged in, "— I wouldn't get sick. Who get's sick like that but —" Abe recognized William McKay, who had spent over two years in a tuberculosis sanatorium, a disease not considered evil or retributive. The voice fell silent to the mutter of men. William said lamely, "I'd fly out to a hospital. Get moving, Amos. It's not going to wait all evening." They were moving again, the lantern low against Amos's denims shaping shadows as they moved past. Eight Abe counted, all grown men. He had only recognized two voices, and Joe in the rear, and they were well past him, going to whatever Bjornesen had drawn them away from the drumming with, and he was already gathering himself to flounder out to the trail when a sudden,

"Hey!" from Amos jarred him. They had stopped and light reflected faintly against the spruce, though the men cut off his vision. Amos said,

"Sliding-board tracks." There was a murmur as the group bunched, then Amos's voice again, "What's he done over here?"

Finally Joe's voice, "They just here now?" The light came back along the trail, moving between men, then Amos said nearer,

"Don't know. I just saw them now, but with all you walking I can't tell."

Someone muttered, "He's probably just going nowhere, like always around the lake."

Amos swore heavily, "He does nothing for nothing, that one."

"Maybe he's going to school," William said and across the tail of their snicker another responded,

"There's too many children there now," and their laughter roared into the darkness.

Joe carried above it, "Not too many for Alex!" but then Amos bellowed and they silenced.

"What do you mean, Alex?"

"When we passed the school, he said he'd come soon."

"Somomabeetch, I thought he was here. That girl will get him over his head. I tell him and tell him, one hole is like any other —" and he swore the same indecipherable formula with more virulence.

Joe said, "Alex can take care of himself," and then his voice fell to a murmur. All Abe could see was the light drawing into their huddle; arms gestured. Then the light flared as Amos' arm wheeled high in a circle and he had a glimpse of the man's crook-nosed face, not lean and hard as most of the Indians but slack as if fist-beaten. The whole group was moving away, bunched and silent except for a muttered expletive and crunch of feet.

They were beyond sight and hearing at last. A sifting of snow brushed his face; the tracks would be covered soon but now he did not care — they know blast my stupidity — he thrust himself ahead. Knowing their gossip he should have expected what he had heard about himself and he should also have known they would draw Sally into it — damn their obscene minds! — for the first time he thought that perhaps someone else could do this job better: someone married, or at least willing to pick up some — if last September that night invitation — he snorted at himself in disgust, not without a perverse tinge of longing nevertheless, that in scrabbling to out-maneuver Bjornesen he should be pushed to such thoughts and, embroiled in this, he slid past the mill clearing with its saw-dust pile a snow-ghostly mound above black slabs of a recent sawing, into the trees again and out in the school clearing where gas-light fell in naked whiteness to the snow. So silent was his movement and so enmeshed his thoughts, he noticed nothing until he was directly upon a shape contorting with low gasps on the snow and he stopped with a violent twist, even as his light flicked on and he said, "Bonjour!"

The shadow split and the light found their faces. They were not now, as they had been last summer by the lake, faces startled while at happiness, though on the surface of it they should have been more alarmed when they were caught in a probable act of stealing than here at the far edge of a clearing on a bitter-cold night where there was nothing clearly obvious to steal. But if on Alex's face flared fear and rage too clarion to misread even in the feeble torchlight, on Violet's terror was already fading to relief, her eyes staring huge in her blanched face as if she did not see light, only sensed another presence of no matter who as long as it was someone, and then she flung up her arms to hide her face, her breath coming in gasps again. Abe dropped the light-beam to the snow and said, after a long minute, "Probably Miss Howell wants you to practice," he gestured towards the windows where children flitted. With a jerk Violet swung away, stumbling towards the school as if still hiding her face in her arms.

Abe plopped his skis around, going. Alex still stood where he had sprung in his surprise; he had not even straightened up fully. Abe said, "I hardly expected this of you."

Alex found his voice, "You —" and stopped, not quite daring to curse though the beginning word itself sounded expletive. "Mind your goddam business."

"I do. I almost run into you before I saw you." Abe fought to keep his voice down. "But if I'd of known I'd of come on purpose."

The lad said nothing and Abe went on, despite a faint but certain knowledge he should stop, "Didn't they tell you, whoever those 'experts' were you had in the dorm at Sioux Portage, that it's most fun when the girl wants to too?" Alex just stood there, rigid, not quite erect and Abe pushed past, but he could not leave it; some devil nicked him and he said, "How's your mother?" Goaded beyond measure, Alex cursed then, swiftly in well-practiced scummy fluency, and Abe turned. With a small push he slid down the low slope, the slime of sound trailing, and around behind the school. When he looked back he saw Alex's outline vanishing beyond the heavy spruce in the opposite direction to the insistent beat of the drum still thudding out of the darkness — damn that boy damn that girl with her staring beautiful face damn it all for blundering around on this side the channel and taking my own thrice-stupid frustrations out on that crazy chagrined kid — the only thing worse than being refused by a woman was to have that refusal known; despite all of Alex's white-man pretensions that certainly remained Indian in him. And twice he had fumbled between them. In summer Violet wanted to "have fun": getting tackled on the way back from the outhouse or wherever it was she was coming from or going to at twenty below on a dark winter must be a little beyond fun even from an Indian girl's definition.

The snow fell against his hot face, and as he became aware of it he heard also the song which he could not tell how long had already been playing on the back of his consciousness. He thrust himself back to the edge of illumination. The school had been hastily fashioned from an old government warehouse and the light from its three irregularly-sized windows was streaked now by falling snow. He could partially see them lined in rows at the head of the room; their voices in the unison of one clear line reached out to him through the glass and one slightly-raised window that puffed warm air against the cold:

> *"Twas in the moon of winter-time*
> *When all the birds had fled,*
> *That mighty Gitchi-manitou*
> *Sent angel choirs instead;*
> *Before their lights the stars drew dim*
> *And wondering hunters heard the hymn"*

and then he recognized the melody they had been drilling, over and over,

> *"Jesus your king is born*
> *Jesus is born*
> *In excelsius gloria."*

She had said they would need several evenings of nothing but practice to get the choir numbers into complete unison for the pre-Christmas program, and there she was, tall, not slim like a girl but with a woman's fulness, leading them, some of whom he recognized as Simon and Eli and Margaret and Henry Crane and some small and older Sturgeons and Small George Kinosay and in the back row Lucy Crane and Anne Bishop mouths wide in song on either side of Violet, now singing also in seemingly complete forgetful happiness, only her face still slightly pale; leading them all in a song she had sung alone in her light voice that Sunday afternoon when he had at last braved himself to go to the Bishops' for supper and they sat about after on the hooked rug floor, Anne laughing in early teen coltishness from one to the other while the heater beat back the cold of the heavy day, explaining how it was Canada's first Christmas carol written by the Catholic Brebeuf for his Huron converts over three hundred years ago, and only eight years before he himself had been burned alive by the Iroquois; and at this moment, as all this slashed through his mind to raise a wale he knew he would bear forever, to ache whenever again this combination of darkness and light through falling snow with the prick of cold in flaring nostrils caught him, he was watching her conduct, her movements like a grace to the children's ringing voices — children's voices defy even Bach —

> *"Within a lodge of broken bark*
> *The tender Babe was found.*
> *A ragged robe of rabbit-skin*
> *Enwrapp'd his beauty round;*
> *But as the hunter braves drew nigh,*
> *The angel song rang loud and high.*
>
> *"The earliest moon of winter-time*
> *Is not so round and fair*
> *As was the ring of glory on*
> *The helpless Infant there.*
> *The chiefs from far before him knelt*
> *With gifts of fox and beaver-pelt.*
>
> *"O children of the forest free,*
> *O sons of Manitou;*
> *The Holy Child of earth and heaven*
> *Is born today for you.*
> *Come kneel before the radiant Boy*
> *Who brings you beauty, peace and joy."*

And again, their voice all one like a great clear bell, its swinging the swing of her arms:

> *"Jesus your King is born*
> *Jesus is born*
> *In excelsius gloria."*

Suddenly, before he comprehended anything further, they were all tumbling for their coats, voices rollicking in confusion. Sally was talking to some, then others, lost occasionally in the flurry of bodies. They would be out in an instant. Instinctively he plopped himself around and with a push slid down the slope to the river's edge, his light picking out the terrain as he moved. On the frozen river he used the torch; after looking so long into the brightness of the school his eyes could not seemingly adjust to the heavy overcast despite the open channel. He strode back to Frobisher, his tiny light flashing on the crystal surface of the river, his mind lost in the refrain; not feeling the corner of the tiny box bent double in his parka pocket; not hearing the drum still beating in the settlement, more urgently now than all that evening.

13

THOUGH Air Force jets had been laying vapor trails across the sky for several years and during the last summer and fall even occasional helicopters trundled past in the northeast, no craft had ever come directly over Frozen Lake. So on the dull day in late January when the long bluish machine came beating out of the overcast and eased down at almost the exact middle of the channel between Frobisher and Bjornesen, though Abe was surprised, the Indians were astounded. A few moments later Abe experienced the same sensation when, hurrying out to greet the two men gesturing futilely at the first people to run over the ice, he discovered he knew the officer of the craft. As they shook hands, not bothering to remove gloves in the cold, he remembered only too vividly the night after the concert at Kinconnells when the hulking harpsichordist Schwafe had beaten their collective conscience to its knees; it was clear from the look on John Marsden's face that he too remembered. Abe said, "Captain, welcome to Frozen Lake. But I sure didn't know you were around here."

"I wasn't last spring, but you know — military transfers. I knew you were here — that's one reason we came."

"Yeah. That's why you set down right here in the middle," and they laughed together, looking at the huge military helicopter and past its bubble nose toward Bjornesen's store where the Icelander was already approaching, surrounded by a covey of followers. From every direction over the ice everyone else that could move was coming too, from the mill and the houses; only the children could not; for the moment they had to be content staring from the school windows.

That noon at the Bishop livingroom table Abe said, putting down his fork and looking across to Lena seated at last and eating, "Well, I'm really proud of this dinner!"

Marsden lifted his head, grinning, " 'Proud' is hardly the word. All you did for it was eat it."

"Sure. But I thought you knew; no matter how good a cook Lena is, this would have been impossible if I hadn't shot the moose!"

"Ha!" Josh snorted. "As if we didn't have enough of our own frozen in the meat-house!"

Abe lowered his face despondently, "Okay, Josh, okay, you ruined the perfect cue for him to ask about the moose and me to tell the story. But that's okay."

They were all laughing by then and Marsden gestured obediently, "How did you get that moose?" the innocence of his tone sparking them again. The back door scraped open in their laughter and Anne tumbled into the room. She slid behind the table, her coat spreading behind her on the floor,

"They're so funny, your men, Mr. Marsden! The radio man, Mr. Clemens, draws cartoons all over his radio pad and never has any space if he has to take a message —" they were all laughing again at Marsden's too-heavily despondent nod but Anne ran on, reaching for her fork, "— and the pilot said I wasn't supposed to look because they weren't pictures for a nice girl to see, but they were just deer and beavers building dams and animals and he couldn't draw any more anyway because he was eating the blueberry pie and the pilot grabbed one of the drawings I liked and got a big drip of blueberries all down his — oh, I forgot, I wasn't supposed to —" she stared at Marsden, her hand to her mouth, and began as if she had said nothing at all until that moment, "They really liked the pie, Mama. They said to say thanks."

Marsden recovered from his laughter, "That's fine, Anne. I don't remember what you said. The pilot, Ken Lewis, has a daughter just about your age and he hasn't seen her for three months."

"Where does she live?" Anne asked.

"North Bay — the whole family lives there. We've been on assignment up here for a while, and we didn't get back for Christmas."

Lena said, "All the more reason I wish I could have lured them in when you didn't know it so they could eat in comfort."

"It's comfort enough not to have to eat Air Force chow for a meal. They have to stay by the radio."

"I wish we had one," Abe said.

"Doesn't Frobisher have them in most places?"

"They're working on it, but they haven't got to Frozen yet. Probably not for quite a while."

Sally stood up, "If you'll excuse me, it's one-fifteen and I have to talk to your crew about the details of the children touring the helicopter. Thank you again, captain; they restrained themselves so well when you arrived." She walked away and for an instant Abe allowed his eyes to follow her; she turned at the door, looking at Marsden. "You won't change your mind about staying half an hour longer and talking to them? They get so few visitors."

"After this," Marsden smiled gesturing at the table, "I really couldn't refuse anyone at Frozen. And I could stay an extra half-hour but as I said I'm just a so-called 'defense expert' — all I really know much about is — you know, the military." He was looking quizzically at her, her light hair pulled back straight on the sides of her narrow face and coiled at the nape of her neck. "Do you think the theory of Canadian military defense would make sense to them?"

"No," she said. "They have trouble enough learning about the countries of the world right now leave alone learning which they should hate."

"Now just a — minute," Marsden stumbled over a word.

She stood motionless. "Yes?"

"I was talking about defense, not hate —"

"But," she interrupted and Abe too stared at her in amazement, "those children are very straightforward. It would make no sense to them at all preparing to shoot down someone

233

who might come over to kill you, and not hate them. Anyone you plan to kill before he kills you you just naturally hate. Right?"

"You don't talk about it like that. If the possibility of aggression exists a government has to make plans to deter it, that's all."

"Yes, but these children are simple. Even the oldest hasn't had much western history to — condition — them. They can't imagine anyone making plans to kill and doing so without any particular emotion. For them, to kill one must —" she stopped then, not quite turning but reaching for her coat hanging around the doorway in the kitchen, and distress was vivid on her face. "Oh — excuse me — please — it was rude to — I shouldn't have brought the matter up."

But Marsden would not yet let go. "Are they really so uninformed about wars? Surely some of the men here — fathers or brothers — were in the last one — overseas even."

"A few yes — but most of those aren't here anymore. George was, wasn't he?" Abe nodded, not quite trusting his speech and Sally continued, "They were in the infantry and bayonet practice would hardly change their simple, direct ideas, do you think?" There was not a trace of sarcasm in her tone; just a kind of sadness that made anger impossible.

"All right," Marsden threw up his hand and laughed a little in discomfort. "I'm not saying the need for modern defense can be explained simply. Or even that it's something 'nice'."

"I agree." Sally smiled faintly, "That's why I can't understand a kind person like you in it." She turned. "Anne — only four minutes left," and she was gone.

The girl gulped the last of her pie, "Oh, I can't be late!" and in the rush of her going the men could shuffle aside their discomfort a little and ease back with their coffee. Josh said as the back door slammed behind his daughter, not as if he were attempting an excuse but simply providing information, "Her brother was in the Dieppe raid. And stayed there."

Marsden said heavily, "Between wars civilians can afford to be pacifists; when Hitler marches into Poland, or the rockets and bombers come over the Pole, they change their minds.

But that's a bit late for a government to start thinking defense."

Josh answered as if the officer had not thrust at him. "She's only been here since last September, but she has the direct psychology of the Indian right, I think. The Ojibwa as a tribe have an excellent record: few fights, little violence —"

"That's hardly what Bjornesen told me just a little while ago," Marsden said.

"What'd he admit?"

"Admit? He just told me, when I asked what kind of people this band was — if they were industrious, anxious to work, steady — the sort of questions I intend to ask you yet — that they seem to be getting worse all the time. So he said. Fight more, work less, and happy to get handouts from the government. And I know the RCMP were in here just after Christmas and almost made a couple of arrests, only nobody would testify who fought who. Right?"

Josh was looking at him almost grimly, and Abe wondered how he would explain, if at all, the drunken brawls that were embroiling Frozen Lake. But Josh did not even try. He said, "I said, 'admit' because Bjornesen is responsible for most of the trouble and he knows it, Oh, nothing that anyone will be able to convict him on; no one will ever inform against him because the Indians, and they alone have the facts, are, for one thing, afraid of him and for another actually want what he's doing, even though when you talk to them soberly most know it will ruin them and has to an extent already. But this illustrates what I began saying about the Ojibwa in the past, and still here now. Like every one, they have their bad types — like one man here whose getting sent to jail last year only made him a little smarter and a little worse than he was, but direct open violence is rare among them. If it happens like in that near arrest, it's when they're drunk. But the police simply can't arrive when the brawl is going on — they came around on a routine check after Christmas — and afterwards no one tells for fear of that person when he's free again. Whiteman's law doesn't work here because little that's outward, provable — like what Amos did to Joe last winter — is ever done when they're sober. So in the past

Frozen Lake has a good record: only two arrests, in over eighty years of government records."

"Frozen Lake is then completely law-abiding and there is no need for our law," Marsden's lip twisted slightly.

"I didn't say that, at all. I said that of the kind of open violence which police can punish there never was much before Bjornesen sold yeast and helped them brew themselves stupid-drunk. But, there were killings; yes. Because these people hate, very strongly, all the more strongly because no one has much more property than he can easily carry about. The group was and is so small it's impossible to steal anything, either axe or wife, without everyone knowing it. Gossip and insult: those are the checks, but there's no way to repay that except in kind. So people hate. Sometimes for years and years. Until by a trick or magic or sickness, buying a conjuror to use a more powerful spirit than the other person has, in some sly, hidden, way that other person gets sick and dies. There's no provable crime; no RCMP detective could ever prove a thing. But everyone in the village knows why that person is dead. Hate. And they know who's done the hating."

Marsden asked, grinning, "Anyone die lately?"

"Yes. Last September. And right now the conjuror's wife is almost completely paralysed."

Marsden started. "Didn't you get them out to a doctor?"

"We flew the man last fall out twice — he was fine every time he came back, but as soon as he got back he became sick again. Dr. Warner in Red Lake didn't have an idea what was wrong with him. And Mrs. Crane, he was out to see her again just two weeks ago. He doesn't know; he leaves medicine, but it doesn't seem to help. And she refuses to go to Red Lake."

"Can't you make her go?"

Josh grinned a little, humorlessly, "Want to fly in a troop of your men? We'll need them to hold back her relatives."

Marsden stared first at Josh, then at Abe who was not even trying to think; only listen. "Josh, what the hell is going on here? Do you know who's doing it?"

"On the man last fall, we're all pretty well sure."

"Well good god man, get the police and arrest him! You can't have this kind of vendetta —"

"I talked it over with the corporal when they were in. Arrest him for what? Threatening — swearing at an Indian? Breaking up a conjuring session? Abe would witness to that, but he'd be the only one. Everyone else who saw it was an Indian. You might convict on that, but at most it would be a fine for making a nuisance of himself."

"Well with the kind of money they make around here anyone would have to take a fine in jail time —"

"The man isn't an Indian."

A slow kind of incredulity dawned on the officer's face. "You mean that laughing old Icelander I was havin' a whiskey with?"

Josh said nothing, and Marsden stared at Abe. Abe said, "Sure. No," he shook his head sharply, "I don't know — nobody knows — how should we — how he does it, but it's being done. And he's the one." Marsden was looking at Abe as if he had declared himself insane; in chagrin he could only add, "Look, John, it sounds stupid but this isn't Winnipeg. The fact is Harry Sturgeon did die of no medically discernible reason after Bjornesen cursed him, and at his dying the old — bum — took credit for it. I saw it — I don't know how."

"Okay. Leave that. Now couldn't the other Indians break him — not trade? He has to earn his money off them."

Abe said, "A few want to break him, but they're afraid. Sturgeon died after just talking against him. Kekekose tried to help Sturgeon by conjuring and now, however it happened, his wife's paralysed. That's pretty strong coincidence. And he's tied the weaker ones up, one way or another — mostly homebrew —"

Marsden was looking steadily at them; Abe's scalp prickled and the color rose under his beard. He looked at the frost gleaming on the window, hearing the thump of dishes in the kitchen. Marsden said "Okay. If he's got the Indians buffaloed, what's the matter with you two?"

Josh said nothing. The silence spread like a bottomless quag of weakness; Abe could not endure it. "John, I've been here seven months and tried to bust his trade every way I know, but he got too big a start, too good a hold. When I started here I thought I'd be right about it and let them take their family allowances in trade or cash. So right now I'm getting in a few more furs than Griffin — not much but some — and at better prices, but my total is down. Alone, I'm stumped. He can hang on for years, a lot longer than Frobisher will ever think is worth it."

Marsden was concentrating, his eyes intent on something working profoundly in his head. "I've seen all the Indian Department figures. You've got a government contract for 2,000 logs to be cut into lumber; a dozen people here live on nothing but pensions and widows' allowances. One way or another, over a third of the band's income comes from the government. Who advises the Indian agent?"

"Josh did until the permanent teacher came," Abe said slowly. "They do it together."

Marsden's voice hit like a hammer, "This band has to come to you for this third and they can't survive without it. Bjornesen couldn't hold them. You could break him before spring."

Josh still said nothing; he was staring at the table-cloth, face set in sadness, the hands too large and heavily veined for his slight body folded on the table before him. Abe said finally, "Josh and — they won't do it."

Marsden stared, mouth working. Abruptly he scrabbled in his pocket and produced a short pipe and stuck it empty between his teeth. "All right Josh," he said. "It's a little dirty — blackmail them out of their money, and you a minister. But they'd know it's for their own good. The thinking ones want Bjornesen just as much as you, eh?"

"A few."

Marsden jerked out his pipe. "Always what choice have you got? If what you're saying is true, it's your moral obligation, before any more get hurt."

Josh lifted his face to them both facing him. "I have the choice to do the Christian thing. Not to fight evil with evil."

Marsden snorted. "That's a goddam fine point to quibble about after what's supposed to be going on here — drunkenness, fighting, paralysis — deaths even."

"I happen to believe what the Bible says, 'Be not overcome

by evil but overcome evil with good.' Just a minute," Josh raised his hand over Marsden's protest, "Let's get at this thing from where we started — or where Sally left us, anyway. You're a decent man. From what little I know of you I'd say you're a good father, give the neighbor boys rides to the little leagues — maybe even coach a team. None of your neighbors in North Bay would say, 'There's a mean, vicious man.' But you spend the biggest part of your life, all your employed waking hours, working how to kill people more efficiently. Why?"

Marsden said heavily, "I don't see what the Air Force has to do with your problem we're talking about, but keep one thing straight. I don't exactly see my job as a study in efficient killing —"

"No, I'm sure you don't. But in the last analysis, when the bomber comes over and you see it on your screen and order the interceptor rocket fired, your only interest is the 'kill', right?"

"That's my job: to stop that plane from getting through to people like you —"

Josh went on imperviously, "And you gun for the kill whether it's a rocket or ten men in a bomber — makes no difference."

"I don't think about men at all. I'd probably go crazy if I did — families, all that stuff. I don't think of that; all my job is, right now, stop that bomber from getting through to you."

"Why?"

"Why? Because you want to live is why, and you pay the government taxes to pay me to protect you."

"But you admit you don't like the idea of blowing up fathers and husbands. Why do you do it, of all the jobs in the world?"

Marsden was looking at Josh sourly. He turned a little, "Abe, you were in the last war. Infantry. And when the time came, you killed your man. Why were you in?"

Abe guffawed humorlessly. "Right now you wouldn't want to hear my original reason. But I know what I understood of why I was there, slogging through those French and Dutch fields. Somebody has to do this, dirty or not."

"Yeh." Marsden sat looking hard at Josh, pipe clenched in his teeth, his tone as clenched and hard, "Because somebody's got to do the dirty work."

Josh said, "Why?"

"Why what?"

"Why does someone always have to do the dirty work?"

"So idealist Christians can stay idealist and not get their heads blown off!"

Josh was studying his hands folded on the table. "No. No Christian worth the name would want you to bloody your hands to save his head. Never." There was a moment's silence. "You say that, given the evil in the world someone has to fight it on its own terms — get his hands mucky trying to clean up the muck. But that's not a good analogy. Everyone can justify any shady actions this way. But the point is: why don't we, who at least think about it, refuse this dirty work? Refuse aggression, which only frightens an equal counter-aggression in our enemy of the moment? Why not refuse to do the dirty work of meeting force with force; rather meet force with what we now think of as weakness — love? Why not believe that God means what he says, that evil can only be overcome with good?"

"I go to church too," Marsden said, "but our preacher doesn't waste time talking like that."

Josh said softly, "Most don't. That's why I don't preach in the Anglican church. Christian belief for too many people is simply one facet of belief in the state: Christian and state demands are equally binding. That I do not believe."

"Oh, it's all right for you, an individual, to talk, but how could a nation-wide church say that, even if there was something to it? Evil men would march in and take over. Then what?"

"Perhaps they would march in. And some good men would be killed. And more would die or be tortured because they would refuse to obey orders. But many men die in fighting also, and at least the former are spiritually more prepared for death than those who die in the hate and violence of combat;

I don't have to tell you the state of mind needed to kill a man. However we may think about Christian emphasis on love, it's a universal value. Everyone agrees, for example, that you can't raise a child hating him, knocking him around, giving him nothing of what love can give. You'll raise a monster, not a child. Read about any primitive society: love is essential for growth — because, I believe, it is part of the very stuff of our creation. We all see it for children, but we don't for grown-ups because grown-ups can so much more easily return evil for trust, hate for love, whatever selfish reasons they may have. But Jesus Christ said that the only way to overcome enemies is to *love their hate, their ambition, to death*. Because when you love your enemies you've got their consciences working for you and —"

"Okay, Josh, hold on," Marsden's cynicism was like a razor. "What kind of conscience did Hitler have? Who would have stopped him if it wasn't the allied armies?"

"Hitler couldn't conquer the world by himself. He had to use thousands and millions of soldiers and weapons manufacturers and communications experts and sweet mothers at home writing encouraging letters to their sons. Were they all without conscience? When did the Allies ever appeal to the conscience of the German people? By hammering the Treaty of Versailles down their throats? That was retribution, and they were asking for someone like Hitler to rally the people. They were much wiser after the last war, sending in food, using the Marshall Plan to help rebuild bombed areas. But I wonder how much of that was compassion and how much was because, facing the Communists, they couldn't afford to have the Germans hate them. The point is we *know* how to act if we want people not to hate us. I disagree with you completely when you say Hitler would have overrun the world if the major nations of the world had refused to fight him and appealed to the German conscience. Evil men could never dominate the world without the help of men who deaden their consciences with 'Somebody has to do the dirty work' or 'I just carry out orders.' If the people of the western world who call themselves Christians actually acted out what Christ said, would dare to love rather than submit to hating, refuse to act out hateful commands, the machinery of evil would break down for lack of people to keep it running. Or get plugged up by Christians getting in the way by simply refusing. But so-called Christians don't dare to do it. They've too long worshipped the pagan idea of aggression as the only way to freedom and peace. They mouth the word 'love', and smear it on their movies and on their posters, but don't dare use it when it matters most."

"All right," Marsden pushed his chair back and stuck his long legs in front of him, "grant that for the minute. But most people in the world aren't Christians. The Chinese for example. God help us when they get the H-bomb!"

"You don't have to be Christian to know love, to have a conscience, do you? If I needed some outside proof that Christ was right when he put his whole emphasis on love I'd get it from that very fact: and humanity, in whatever form you find it, recognizes love is essential. It's Christ, the originator of our faith, who gives us the power to live it out to its fullest extent, to the extent seemingly necessary by our very creation, but you can't say non-Christian Chinese are without love or conscience. They are some of the finest, most profoundly sensitive people in the world. It was a Chinese philosopher, not a Christian, who said, 'Love conquers want of love as water conquers fire.' Men's deeds of love today are like taking a cupful of water and pouring it on a house that is burning. When the fire burns on, people say, "See; water does not put out fire. We've just fooled around with cups of love; it doesn't work and we throw a bomb. That'll show them!' How do you expect it to work?"

Josh was sitting now hunched forward in his chair, almost as if kneeling beside the dining-room table scattered with the marks and crumbs of their meal. Finally Abe said, "Sure, Josh, we were over some of this last week for a bit. It's logic-tight if you believe all your presuppositions. But if you look at the world right now —"

"All right," Josh wheeled suddenly on them both, pale blue eyes as if afire, "Look at the world! What have you got? Two huge blocs threatening each other with bombs that, if either of them are ever crazy enough to use, would almost certainly end all human life. Even if some survived, it would be in a way that hasn't been since civilization began — all of it concerned with the barest necessities of survival and protection and scrounging together uncontaminated food. Never in man's history has such a crime against creation itself been thought of, leave alone been possible. When the destruction of the first A-bomb on Hiroshima got known, every thinking person was horrified beyond words; but every week, year, we talk about it and it's not quite so bad, until now we can calmly speak of 80 million killed and 100 megaton bombs — a year by year build-up where people are deadened to every human consideration: there is no other way. So today we can calmly say what was too horrible to even think a year ago: we'll blow up every person in the world if we can't have things our way. Two camps bluffing each other to keep hands off. But for a bluff to work both sides have to believe the other will actually dare all if its bluff is called. So okay, it works for the two camps. But the bomb is there and as years go by, other, unnoticed, nations work and work and finally get the bomb too. How long can you carry on a bluff if half a dozen hands hold the ace that can finish everything? What if some nation gets the bomb and is run by a madman like Hitler who doesn't care whether creation survives or not? You can't bluff him. So the world is blown to smithereens. Why? Because the so-called sensible nations to begin with still carried on this game of dare even after aggression was no longer possible if man was to survive. Given the horror of the hydrogen bomb and modern bombers and rockets to carry it, war, open violence, hate, is a luxury no nation on earth can even afford to think about. War has to be forever forgotten as a way to settle differences, even limited wars, because no country will deliberately *not* use its strongest weapon when facing defeat. General MacArthur was maybe the most brilliant Allied general of the last war and in Korea he wanted to use the A-bomb on the Communists. Why? Because it was the most sensible military thing to do, and —"

"And how many fine Christians didn't scream when Truman fired him, eh?" Marsden charged in.

"That's exactly the point! Given war, you have to win using

your biggest guns. That's the hydrogen bomb now, and knowledge of it cannot be destroyed. Even if all the bombs were dismantled, if war should come how long do you think it would be before the nations being defeated would have made new ones? The only solution: *no more wars.* That can happen only when people stop hating. That's possible only when love overwhelms hate. There is nothing else.

"And who will begin this hard campaign of love? The followers of Jesus Christ: that's where it must start. With the Christians who have begun most of the wars in mankind's history and who've been most effective in perfecting ways of killing; the bravest and most dedicated, and deadly, soldiers. Despite supposedly believing man is made in God's image, as the individual being worth more than anything on earth. And this killing has brought us into the final corner — stop now, or smash all God's creation forever."

After a silence Josh continued, again in his sad calm, "Like you say, John, it's probably an impossible ideal to expect any nation ever to stop taking the dirty-shady way to achieve what it hopes will be good results. But can't the individual, at least, where he lives, try? That's why I'm so happy for Abe here. He hasn't forced us out of what we think is right. Sally — Lena — I — we have to act on what we know as right, and not allow ourselves to be levered into what we believe is less than that. Three, four years isn't —" he seemed to catch himself. "And even if we still can't see the end results of our action yet. To me that's what it means to trust God's guidance."

Marsden said slowly, "This — whole machinery of belief you've outlined — it's not common to most people, even those who consider themselves Christians. Like me. I believe that God helps those who help themselves."

Josh smiled a little sadly, "But when you read what Jesus says about 'My Father in Heaven', how can you sum up God's immense concern for man with such — such a cliché? And if most people don't believe it, so what? I do. At least I can try and live it here."

"But does it work?"

"How will I know if I never dare try?"

Abe said, at last, "And if you find out for sure it doesn't?"

Josh shook his head heavily, "Pure conjecture. I'm still in it and neither you nor I can see the end."

Marsden shook his head, sticking out his wrist to look at his watch. He stood up, swaying a little as if the action were too abrupt. "Time I explained something to my men — if you'll excuse me." He stood looking at Josh. "I know, people have to live as they see right. But I still —" he stopped, turning his head but not going.

"But you still trust guns," Josh completed softly, then suddenly his face suffused and he banged his fist on the table, "When will you professionals use your heads? Where have guns brought you? In the last war 25 million soldiers and 24 million civilians killed in Europe alone! And that's peanuts — absolute peanuts — when we get into the next war. Guns! And you're supposed to be the ones thinking logically!"

Marsden tilted forward, fists on the table as if Josh's passion had at last released him from restraint, "Okay preacher! And what else will the goddam Commies listen to?"

"So you do hate them!"

"Okay have it your way! I hate them! Who doesn't when he really thinks about what they're trying to do to the people they're grinding out of sight, to us if they had the chance? Only a blind stupid fool would think —"

"That's it." Josh's tone was so quiet that its very calmness slit Marsden's speech the way no shouting would have, his face now only sad, "You have to be a fool to think that loving your enemy will change him. You're right, too, it wouldn't really work for any except a few. They wouldn't dare risk it, even if the other hasn't worked a thousand times in every generation. So we try to do it here, not in Washington or Ottawa."

Marsden looked down, a little shamefaced. He said after a moment, "What are you *doing* here, anyway?"

"The ordinary job of a Christian — showing people that the life of following Jesus Christ is one of concern and care for others, not self."

Marsden's words echoed the months of Abe's thoughts, "But

man, if you've got this Christ-like concern, do what you can and help them break out of this bind!"

"By organizing a 'Ban Homebrew' committee? Holding public meetings on the nights they drink?"

"God man, you control the allowances! And you're supposed to be a preacher! Build a church; teach them if they don't understand why you have to do it for their own good."

"All right," Josh was looking at Abe. "That's what you keep poking at me. No government money unless they stop brewing, and get them together and make them listen. We break Bjornesen and win them to the church — and to Frobisher." He was staring at them, the muscles of his jaw clenching. "It would probably work. All Frobisher Christians: money ahead if they did. Listen," he raised his hand at their common exclamation, "Sally and I have to advise the Indian agent because we're the only non-business whites in here and the government apparently never listens to advice from non-whites; it's a big club neither she nor I will ever wield for force. For practical purposes that club does not exist and by now the Indians know it. What we are *doing* now is *showing* them what a Christ-follower lives like — at least we're trying. It's a hard way to live, and nobody ever levered anybody into it. And when, if ever, they understand that to follow Christ is the only way, they'll come. And Bjornesen will be finished and he'll be the first to know it. And maybe Frobisher will be finished too."

Abe could not help himself; "No wonder you haven't a single convert after almost four —" he stuttered, seeing Josh through his own emotion. "I'm sorry. That was below the belt."

"No it's not. You've never said it but you can't help thinking it. You're right. By making it easy we could have had them like the original churchmen who came in one summer and had everyone on baptism roles in a week; and with one visit a year they could make sure every baby got a Christian name. But that's not Christianity; that's just social conformity and making sure you get on the right side of the all-powerful whiteman. If that's what we have to do to found a Christian brothers' fellowship here, we'll never found one!"

They stood for a moment in silence, no glance meeting. Through the top of the window melted free from frost Abe could see the path straight between the trees to the far end where the shadow of the school blocked further sight. A troop of children stampeded around the corner and down the path. "Look, Josh," Marsden said, "I came to ask you about some things — not argue mission tactics or pacifism or whatever you call it." He grinned, waving his arms, "No, don't explain any more. What you say of Bjornesen, I better get your angle on this band too. And I want to talk to you Abe —"

Abe fumbled back into the workaday world, "I'm long overdue — George has to go home and eat. Come over when you're finished. And," his mind caught now on an earlier thought buried under others, "if you want to give the kids something to remember, why not take them up — as many as can go. Five minutes a ride would be enough."

Marsden laughed. "Maybe that's an idea to placate Miss Howell!"

"It would," Josh smiled. "And much as they like talk, they'd like you better than if you spoke two hours. Most of them have never been in a plane, or seen Frozen from the air."

Marsden was buttoning his tunic, pipe gone now. "Good. I'll go tell them — hey, that gang is already out here." He went to the kitchen door and reached around for his greatcoat. "I'll be right back." He stood in the doorway, tall and handsome in military bearing. "Not too many people annoy me so thought-provokingly as you, Josh. When I come back in about two minutes, please, no beliefs. Just facts. I'll figure out the beliefs necessary!"

"Yes, sir!" Josh snapped a slightly-off-target salute; Marsden laughed and was gone. Abe glanced out the window; the children with Sally behind them were already clustered at the helicopter.

"Josh, you're a bum," he said softly, "Every time we meet you spin your spider web a little tighter."

Josh grinned, but his tone was sober, "I just say what I believe and am trying to live."

"Sure" — as if that isn't enough — "it's getting worse at

Bjornesen on drinking nights, eh? What are they doing there besides the usual — drink, fight? He's got the lights on in his loft — just drinking?"

Josh shook his head. "I've been trying to find out, but no one who gets in there will tell. I've never known them to be able to keep a secret, but somehow this is drastic enough to keep a lot of people quiet. I don't know — there may be women involved —"

Abe began, "Do you think —" and stopped.

The other's head was bent. "Abe, I can talk to Marsden as if — it were pretty straightforward, but you know how rough this is, hearing them fighting, Mrs. Crane sick — we're right in the middle of it — between the settlement and him —"

"That one last week —" he stopped.

"It was terrible. I don't know how long — we thought so certainly after that week at Brink Island and we came home and the police —" for a moment it seemed to Abe emotion would break from him. But it did not; when their eyes met the missionary's were dry as fire. "We prayed for years that a Frobisher man with — conscience, like you — would come here. You can't imagine how Sally — who we tried so hard to get the first year, but couldn't — and your coming have helped us. It will work. I know it, as I believe in God. So, please, don't give it up."

"You know Frobisher," Abe said heavily. "The way it's going, we'll be out by summer. Even if Horst Jeffers comes up and you — we can convince him, he's still got to convince the Directors. And they mostly look at accounts. Five years heavy loss, and another trader —" he shrugged his shoulders, not looking at the other. "There's not much I can do now, by myself — and the police are no good — you can't arrest half the husbands in the camp — but I'm telling you, Josh, if I can get something on that devil I'll use it for every inch it's got. I won't involve you, but I'll bust him with pleasure any way I can."

"Abe, everyone knows we — we get on. They might believe — if it was really rough, that I was pushing you."

"That can't be helped. I haven't interfered with you, though

I can't see how you've gone anywhere" — that's too hard but I'm clean of it at last! — "vice versa is only fair."

Josh stood by his desk, head drooping, saying nothing. Abe became aware of Lena; she must have come in from the kitchen where she could not help but have heard all said in the past half hour. "Of course Abe," she said, "As long as we trust each other."

Marsden's footsteps thumped on the porch and Abe zipped up his jacket. "Right," he said, smiling for their sake. "Never say die!" He pulled open the door just as Marsden opened the outer one.

"All set, and you wouldn't know those kids! Great idea, Abe."

"I have them all the time, only there's never anybody around to make them work. See you."

"Yeah, we have to leave in an hour — we'll hop over."

He was outside where the rotors beat in the air and the older children not on the first ride were leaping and somersaulting as demented before the plastic nose that lifted straight into the air. Sally turned, saw him, and came quickly to him through the snow. "Oh Abe, you had a marvelous idea! I didn't dare ask him, after — and I was kicking myself all the way to school —"

Shaking free of the room he laughed with her, her face shining in the cold, "That's more than once we've thought alike. You know I'd do anything for you!" The usual polite nonchalance gained a flick of tone not quite in keeping with their laughter and her response, already shaping on her lips as he began the formula, hesitated just for that fraction which made them both suddenly, almost agonizingly, aware of possibility beyond convention, but then she tossed her carefreeness back to him with an equally light,

"Careful! You can't tell when you may really mean that." He stood a moment, her slim legs in their tall boots striding through the snow to her charges, and then he walked quickly down the path that led toward the school. If she didn't work herself to exhaustion every day and night trying to teach them in one year what many of them should have learned in four or five perhaps they two together could listen to more Bach — if she just comes over without waiting for me to unravel whatever it is damns me to hesitation when I see her! — like the preceding weekend when she had knocked during the second movement of *The Well-tempered Clavier.*

"That's Bach, right?" she laughed as he took her coat.

"I haven't any other records, yet."

"And you can hear for yourself why I can't like him. Just on and on and on —"

"Oh, but the variations, the movement of the lines — just *listen.*"

She did a moment, but clearly unconvinced. "How can anyone play that?"

"That happens to be the late Helmut Walcha, Europe's greatest recent harpsichordist."

"Name-dropping?"

"Not as much as I could! I met a student of his once, at a party in Winnipeg last summer."

"I never meet people who know famous people. But that —" she fluttered her fingers.

Overjoyed at even a skeptic sharing his pleasure — and that skeptic she — he quickly admitted, "A harpsichord isn't a fair start. An oratorio or cantata, here." She shuffled quickly and then paused, her expression growing earnest.

"That's a good title. It's meant just for us at Frozen Lake."

He looked and started. "The title's misleading. It's really a funeral cantata."

"'God's Time is the Best Time'. That's so hard to believe, sometimes. The drinking has been worse than ever and at Christmas on Brink Island we believed so —" her head lifted and she forced a smile. "Mr. Ross, the only Bach I pick and you refuse to play it!"

"Excuse me!"

Now, the snow crunching under his boots, he beat the rhythm of the opening flutes and cello against his legs, the tune floating on the crest of the remembered sight of her listening, bending forward to the repetitions:

> *God's own time is the best,*
> > *is ever best of all.*
> *In him live we,*
> > *move, and have our being.*
> *And in him we die at his good time;*
> *When he wills.*

Her expression changed, softened as the tenors sang; at the basses'

> *Set in order thy house*

she was almost smiling, and when the sopranos at last broke through the lower voices' repeated

> *It is the old decree,*
> > *man, thou art mortal*

with

> *Yea, come Lord Jesus, come,*

her eyes already held the flash that culminated in the chorus:

> *The holy blessed trinity*
> *Whose power through us gives victory*
> *Through Jesus Christ. Amen.*

After he had played it the second time he could not deny his original intimation: despite her oft-repeated ignorance of Bach, she had heard more in the cantata than he. And what that more was —

Eyes down in his thought, at the edge of the clearing he almost stumbled into Violet and Lucy coming from the school. "Oh —" he gathered himself. "You better hurry and not miss the ride. They're giving everybody a helicopter ride."

Lucy's eyes gleamed suddenly. "We thought they go already —" she said, but Violet did not respond. She just looked at him, her black eyes almost lifeless. Abe looked up into the overcast.

"Look, they're bringing back the first ride. Lucy, run and see if you can get on the next — Violet —" the older girl was moving also, the younger already running down the path, "just a minute." She stopped but did not lift her glance. He had spoken to her only twice, fleetingly, since the encounter here on the dark schoolyard. "Is it — does — he bother you?"

Her face lifted to his as beautiful as last summer, perhaps more, because her beauty was of the quality which adversity could only refine, never destroy. She said, "Nothing yet."

"But he still threatens you?"

"I don't talk to him now. But when he sees me, he looks, you know —"

Abe jerked his eyes from her — the damned rutty dog with just the worst of boarding school training to stoke his Indian pride needs the vinegar whaled out of him that he'd understand — a few forgotten hints jogged in his mind and he tried again, "Violet, I want to help, for sure, but you have to tell me what you know. Is what Alex is trying to do — does it have something to do with the drinking — what they do in the loft —" and then the flush sprang to her cheek despite the biting cold. "You know. Tell me. I'll straighten it out — just trust me." Her black eyes found his and something wheeled over in him and he was cursing within himself like one long unending slur of damnation pouring at the impossible waste of this kindness and warmth and perception and beauty in this impossible sink-hole with its impossible bullheaded gut-driven — everyone and me too! — clots. He could send her out, educate her, help her to brighten some corner of the world with herself. What did he have to do with his money? It could be the one joy of his life, his one positive stroke, and even as the curse tailed off he knew, as he had always known without ever breathing it to her or to Sally, who had told him of this girl's strange perceptive ability in understanding people, which once he had heard he had known he had been aware of all the time without ever articulating, though he had acted intuitively on it when he first met her in the dark with Alex and had known she could ruin the boy or they ruin each other, that the whole idea was preposterous because she would never do it. She was an Indian woman. So when she looked unflinchingly at him now with her unreadable eyes, he could only curse in helplessness and plead, already knowing her negation before she shook her head.

"Sure," he said at last, "sure. For whatever reason you won't — can't — tell me. Sure. But just one thing. Listen, and I mean this. I want you to do this. Promise."

She looked at him, wordless. He simply had to trust her though she still denied him the same, "Listen." His great hand clenched on her shoulder; thin against the cloth through the coat he could feel its smooth roundness, but she did not flinch before his glare. "Listen. If you ever get into any trouble — any kind at all, and you know you're beat — any trouble, understand?" her head nodded a little, eyes steadily impenetrable, "anything at all you come, or send Lucy if you can't, you come to me. Tell her to come to me. First. Don't go to Mr. Bishop or Miss Howell. Come over the channel to me. If it's at night, throw a stone against the window — you know the window where I sleep. Anything, understand?"

Her lips moved against her white teeth. "Yes, Mr. Ross."

14

PONDEROUS time plodded on. In anticipation it hung motionless in retrospect by the middle of April a generation at least seemed past with not so much as daily or weekly pattern to structure remembrance. Violet had not said a word; probably she never would. Probably the entire settlement would simply rot-gut itself out of existence with old Bjornesen. Then Josh would have his answer, though even such an answer would never alter his conviction, of that Abe was by now convinced.

Something had to crack; if some drunk would only get killed the police could come — that sadistic old bastard in his benign omnipotence regulates them so precisely now there's never a fissure all bound up and sealed and delivered — when the men sat morosely about the store as they still did when a trapper came in, there was hardly any talk, never a slight allusion to the light burning in drink nights in what should have been Bjornesen's furloft where even at the tail of the season there could not be much fur. There was less fur not because of less animals but neglected traplines. Abe would hardly have known this by comparing his records; his take was up from Griffin's because, of his eight trappers, only William, Kekekose's older son, had fallen into the rot-gut. Albert held out, trapping for the entire huge family, his face one set of fierce silence when he came to trade.

Kekekose's drum beat faintly, at long intervals, his wife immobile on her slab bed shrinking into unrecognizability. A — mess; Abe could not find words for an adequate curse. He had done nothing of what he had confidently expected to do. He could speak Ojibwa understandably and knew most of the band by first name, but nothing basic had changed since the fall. In spring Horst would come in and they would close the store; not even the best of spring rat-catches could turn it. There was hardly enough work to keep him occupied during the working day, leave alone at night. And when he was exhausted from juggling the sounds that were now at last becoming intelligible and he simply could not turn once more to the music played and replayed until the movements ran amuck in his head day after day until he burst out weighing two pounds of flour into a paper sack, "It is the old decree, man —" and the pupil-less eyes beyond the counter gagged him: if he went to bed too early he woke long before daylight and all the problems he might conceivably face and all his own tangled longings and shame took on such aspect he could never recapture sleep but had to start the day with blackness already in him so he never ventured upstairs to his bare room before midnight when most of the lights across the channel would long since be doused; when they weren't it was a sure sign of carousal, perhaps fight, and whatever else the men, and the women who wanted drink as badly as the men, found to do in the loft week after week.

That was just the trouble: he did not know.

The children were clearly warned; they stayed near their homes and even the stray information he discovered from Little George, like about the women drinking, was clipped and the boy now rarely came near the store. He did not want to push George himself; of all the Indians in one way he was the poorest possible assistant for he resolutely, almost with dedication, refused to gossip; nothing would come of prying there except to make him regain that complete, sullen uselessness. Though beyond doubt the Indian was concerned about the drinking. Sometimes a worried, "William (or Henry or Amos or Joe or some other) got cut last night" would open up Abe's question "Oh. Was it bad?" and the arm's length stolidness would fall and the now habitual slight, noncommital shrug would end it, save for a few words, "He'll get over it." Only sometimes, a flick of derision at the enslaved men who could not extricate themselves, he would add, "Anyways, before the next batch." That was part of the devilishness: it seemed he never would grapple with it unless it somehow outdid itself. Bjornesen gave them yeast and sugar for one good brew at a time and then they had to wait until he gave them another. Simple, fool-proof; no one once caught broke the circle. And enough, especially women, would want to get into it. For one evening a week, or two, the drunks at least were lost to the darkness of the dead of winter and the cold-leaking cabins and the stench and the howling of misfed, too frequently candy-silenced children. What work-ground woman would not want to reach the nirvana of alcohol even if the sickness after was longer than the escape.

He sat almost every night as he sat now on the moose hide draped over an easy-chair frame he had made, mind exhausted from logical, retentive thought in struggling with Ojibwa vocabulary, hearing in some far-away area of himself the music from the static-snarled radio, alone and defenseless. Sometimes he still skied on the lake but too often, though in a way he wanted nothing more, he knew he might meet her as he had that night when the impossibly dark snow-clogged February was dragging itself along and the stars and open skies had only been scratchily visible for over forty days. He was sitting in the lee of a rock when he heard a slow scrape on ice and a light bobbed around the shore. He waited, mystified, and suddenly the light toppled over to the snow, the scrape stopped, and then clearly he heard her voice, "Glory! Glory!" and he was up, scrabbling over the snowed lake in the darkness, his torch flaring in his hand as he approached her and she stared up in alarm which changed even as he said, twisting to a halt,

"Sally! Are you hurt?" Then her face collapsed in laughter.

"Abe!" between laughs, "What a fright, you charging out of the dark to find me humiliated!" and he,

"Humiliated — shoot, are you hurt?"

She wasn't. She had fallen to her knees, already tender from earlier falls in daring to venture beyond the ice cleared for the children's skating and hockey on the channel, but the wind had been strong lately and she had felt so — cooped she calls it — and with a torch dangling about her neck she had thought surely she could skate out over the lake though now she knew better. He helped her up, lithe and hotly breathing from her exercise. He had not seen her in over two weeks, since Marsden had fluttered away. As he held her hand and arm, strong and hard under the clothing, he suddenly wondered why they stood so much in their own way. That they did he did not bother to doubt, as he once had, and he had fumbled on into such poor understanding of himself that he had long ago stopped thinking he was sure of anything she might think about him. What did he understand of her, really? She had listened — once and she came on her own — to his music; whatever it was she heard, it sounded only faintly, if at all, in his ears. Understand of a woman he had seen through the blindless window on his way home late from the Bishops sprawled asleep in exhaustion half-over her teacher's table, arms helpless in sleep and face hidden by papers against the merciless light; a woman who believed in God's mercy and spent hours praying for it to show itself, somewhere, soon. These things he could not probe, so he stuck to what he knew, albeit in confusion, sometimes thinking of her as a self-sacrificing teacher who spent more strength than she really had drilling children who, though almost worshipping her, had not the slightest encouragement in their homes where light was impossible most of the evening and where never a corner was available for a pinch of private study. Sometimes he thought of her kindness and gentleness towards them and everyone else she met, her unflagging efforts to think only good of people until their actual nature forced her against her will to think otherwise; sometimes her concern over what was happening to Violet, inscrutable and little understood, but obviously driving the girl into some kind of morass — damn her if she'd only give me an excuse just the smallest! — he thought of all these lovely, proper things about Sally, but lately he remembered more and more the slight angle of her nose set in the delicate oval of her face against the hood-fur and the cringle of her skin at the corners of her eyes when she laughed in the yellow glare of his torch and the tension of her arm, alive under his hand, the warmth she exuded into the cold as if clothes were inconsequential to her in the winter cold and that she wore them only for the custom, decorum, for the benefit of other people, but certainly not to keep herself alive and warm. All his life he had known himself powerfully affected by women, more so probably than most men because he had never found one he could forget himself with more than for a few suspended and later to be derided and deliberately forgotten moments; drink had certain advantages, he knew, but to allow himself to fall its victim, whether because of his clarity of remembrance of inevitable nausea or the shame of his acting a buffoon, a spectacle even in unconsciousness, or the ineradicable stamp of his childhood upon him — come Saturday and the kitchen hot with the baking bread she would be humming still roamin' in the gloamin' wae my lassie by my side — which he had long despaired of erasing completely in the further undisciplinable corners of his soul, he now no longer bothered to consider. Black as it had been, he had not been drunk once all winter; even in private it was for him no contemplatable escape. Only at the stupidity of a party — Sherris Kinconnell with her mockingly-generous breasts — or by fiercely willed deliberate effort could he achieve that detached distance of drunkenness; otherwise he was too aware of himself to speak unaffected once womanliness had consciously driven through to him.

But Sally — ahh what's to be thought about her that I haven't in wildest craziest blasts of thoughts get drunk and forget it a day a month take Violet and live with her away from Alex's clutches and live with her and have some forgetting set a trap and trick Bjornesen into something criminal and Violet — Sally persisted. Committing him to an honor he could no more bend than explain; his long resigned bachelorhood far from being the unthinking contentment it had been in the Arctic, now offering him nothing but this irrational apprehension of meeting and talking to the one person he wanted to see, whom he could have met almost as easily as not.

He stirred, looked at his wristwatch, and stood up. He was too old, too set in his idiosyncratic ways. He walked to the coat-rack, slipped into his parka and pulled open the door to the dark store. With her convictions. He did not flick on the light; no need to waste charge in the batteries: Griffin's one positive achievement at Frozen Lake Post; rather, that of his wife's implacable nag.

He found the heater-lid handle and the red glare of the embers warmed him as he thrust it aside; he piled in the logs he had carried up after work and in a moment was on the swept porch outside, looking at the darkness. In the south, at Red Lake, the faint fan of spring air must be but here only winter. Not that her convictions fit any particular pattern, and certainly not what he knew of conventional dedicated Christianity. He could still hear her laugh one evening at Josh's when in passing she had mentioned riding down Grand Canyon on mule-back while doing a summer's community service work among migrant workers, "Goodness, Abe, why shouldn't I ride down Grand Canyon. There it's far more beautiful," and he could do little but look away, afraid his thoughts would show too clearly even through his beard, and when she continued he realized that she had understood his bemusement all the time, even to the inexplicable jokes she and Josh and Lena seemed to find against themselves at what they frankly admitted they could not understand about their faith as the Bible expressed it but which they accepted in all seriousness nevertheless: "If there is beauty in this world, it is of God. Surely if I believe that I should want to see of it what I could."

Before him there was nothing beautiful to be thought about or looked at; on the unyielding darkness of the late winter that would not bend to spring, while in the south the ice was softening, soon breaking, here it remained iron: no planes now for weeks probably; nothing to expect now from the south even if something erupted over there across the channel where the only light he could ever see from the porch was gleaming on the snow. Unmoving he stared at it; whatever besides drink ran on there he should blast — blindly committed to Josh's what is it after all any more than just stupid hanging on — and Sally: "To begin with force means you either make it or are broken; there is never a middle road, or a reconciliation; you either win or leave with a curse."

He stamped his feet and returned to the half-tempered warmth of the store with its smell of merchandise and faintly-fatty fur bins. He thrust the bolt behind him, walked through to the living quarters, hung up his coat and adjusted the heater. Following the spot of his torch through the kitchen and up the narrow stairs to the single bedroom under the eaves, he switched on the ceiling light and took off his clothes and folded them on the chair beside the bed. After the escape from the ice off Quebec he had decided personal mementos were clutter; a few toilet articles on a crate, the chair, the blanket covered bed: no one at Frozen Lake had ever seen this room so no one was ever likely to wonder at its anchorite austerity. From long habit on the trail he never slept in night-clothes; he sat on the bed-edge and stared down the naked length of his body. A slow, sardonic smile formed at his lip-corners: empty room, empty body, to be lived in as necessary and then left, no mark to betray who or what inhabited it, nothing personal, human, left behind; when left, left completely like the husk of an insect that has long contorted and at last thrown off the hampering for what instinct tells it will be perfection at last. But he had no instinct for perfection, no belief for metamorphosis. Only nothing: so he had told himself for so many godawful years. He shifted his eyes away from himself and adjusted the transept opening with his toe. Warm air loafed up. Then he leaned over, flicked the light and rolled under the blankets. He had timed it well, as well he might after his years of practice: the moment he pulled the blankets in tight he was unconscious and he had no concept how long he had been asleep when he was awake again. Hearing the banging below.

It went on and on, a dull pounding without let-up or rhythm while he pulled on his underwear and trousers and stumbled down the stairs, his mind awash in sleep that was swiped away by one look as he jerked open the door and thrust the other back in the very middle of a hammer that almost knocked whoever was outside off the small porch. But the figure recovered itself and staggered forward in his splash of light; he saw the convulsed face and he stuttered as he caught her into the room,

"Lucy! What's happened? Violet —?" The child was blinking in the strong light, her breath gasping in her throat, whether from running or crying he could not tell, perhaps both, and he lifted her to a chair at the table, bending so close that without conscious focus he saw the looped grey rims of sore-scabs on her scalp at the edge of the scarf tugged tight about her head. "Lucy," he said more quietly, "can you talk? Quick."

"Mr. — Mr. Ross, they got her — up the store —"

"Violet?" She nodded. "Who is it? What are they doing to her?" He dropped his hands to her shoulders as if to squeeze her breathing into control so that she could speak. "Now, take three deep breaths. Easy — yes — then talk —" and her eyes lost a little of their frantic brilliance as he held her quiet an instant, then she could say,

"The men — they got her come —"

"Which men — Alex?"

"Yes, Alex — and others — but only Alex, after her so long, come out at night to see him and tonight yes, and I followed, and then men come from the bush when they talked by the school —"

"Lucy, listen, which men?"

"Amos, Joe, William McKay — many —"

"Wagoss?"

"No — but after in the store he was —" which made sense but there was no time for such thought and he interrupted,

"Okay, they took Violet to the store — they were drunk yes, Alex too?"

"Yes, a little —"

"God, and Violet went with him — what's the matter with her —"

"He follow her, months —"

"Yes, yes —" he caught himself in irrelevancies and spun around, his mind clear of all save one need, "What do they do in —" though suddenly he knew he did not have to ask but Lucy was already saying what there was no need to

261

explain, ". . . women too and make them drunk and clumb up there and they," she did not even reach for the Ojibwa word, though ordinarily she would have lost herself in shame, as if what happened in that loft could only be described by an obscenity in the language the whites had brought here with their liquor and other perverting filth that even as it ruined the whites far from the outer restraints of their society so it thrust the Indian more deeply into morass than his own tribal imagination could ever have hammered him.

He said swiftly, buttoning his shirt, "Sure, sure. How long when they took her in —"

She stared at him an instant, then, "They catch her by the school, she waved, like she told me — to run to you — but —"

"They don't know you've come?"

"They don't see me — I stayed — away — and by the store Wagoss let the door open when they all came in and they drank a long time — I don' know —"

"Why the devil didn't you come right away?" he swore, jerking into socks and felt boots but she stared at him silent, and whatever fear she had for her sister was obviously tempered by a curiosity: anything else would have been impossible not to expect from this girl of twelve in any case, but which he swore at now under his breath as he reached for his parka, turning, "Well?"

"And I saw through the window Alex push to the ladder by the wall, made her go first, he behind her and reaching up under —" and she stopped then, scarlet, for this was obscenity only the most drunken or perverted Indian would ever commit in private, leave alone before others reeling and laughing as they watched, but before he could get out of that thought even to curse automatically, though his entire mind in one part of him at least was doing nothing but cursing now, the violent purple fringe to all his other squid-armed thoughts, she said, "And she got to the top and kicked him in the face and he fell down, off, and she got up and pulled the —" she hesitated, groping for a word —

"Lid — the loft-hole lid that fits —" he barked, but she was nodding,

"Yah, yah, the lid — and Alex climbed up, mad, swearing, he

couldn't move it and they all laughed and some fell — fell — over and Wagoss sitting on the counter and rolling on it laughing and I run to here."

He was at the cupboard spinning the loaded revolver chamber, "They hadn't hurt her — yet—"

"No, but —"

"I know. Are your father or grandfather — or Albert Crane — home?"

"They're at fur-camp — but William Crane, he was drunk too —"

"Sure, sure —" he hesitated, thinking frantically, his mind so convulsed now he could not seem to sort alternatives — just charge over — it would take her too long to go down this side for George and then back across — who — he reached for the door, "Listen, go to Mr. Bishop — you're rested — run as fast as you can, cut across the ice and tell him to come to Wagoss store, right away — as fast as you can." He threw her a glance. "Rest a little, but run as fast as you can." The girl nodded and he was already out the door and at the darkness he thought and wheeled back in, "Here," he flipped aside a cupboard curtain, "Take this flashlight, you can go faster," and he rolled it over the table to her hand and was out the door, reaching down his skis and poles and running in them across the familiar flat and shooting down to the channel while snapping the torch to its usual hooks on his parka, even as the door banged behind him and he knew Lucy had not waited.

He understood now he should have crashed them long ago. Bust them up; maybe he could have persuaded George and James Sturgeon and Albert Crane; not with everything going their way this stupid kind of rescue dash — ha more mop-up than rescue — he did not decipher the ugly overtones of that word or of what exactly he would do as he hit level, legs and arms driving and slipping on the bare ice streaks and broken snow, the iron in his right parka-pocket banging against his leg, his eyes intent on the lightpath for fissures, knowing himself faster on skis than running yet still too horribly slow as if laboring nowhere in the molasses-like darkness. As he schussed down the slope he had seen the yellow reflection on the far bank; now he jerked his head up occasionally and the blotch remained an indecipherable mark to work towards because he did not know whether it indicated she was still holding them out or whether they kept the light on all the time. He looked up again and could make out the store now from the lighted window in the roof-peak. He had no plan — what is there to plan except charge in and they attack and use the six bullets and pick the shots and madden them into attack and make damn sure of the first shot the impotent pimp! — he was at the snow covered wharf now and he shook off skis and poles and sprinted up the trodden path to the store, mind lost at his own abysmal stupidity of not thinking of such a simple solution before, in his violence now unconscious of his remembered and sometimes re-lived horror of what he had had to do during the war and that though it might have ordered the Frozen Lake chaos long ago in cold blood he could no more have planned or actually pulled a trigger on his fiercest enemy than on the woman he loved had he loved one, when he looked up as the lower store-windows popped bright-lit above the snowbanks and between the blur of shadows shifting through frosted panes light splayed yellow through the opening door. He stopped for immediately the immense figure of Bjornesen filled the space, head turning, cursing violently in English, "You drunken sonsabitches, you'll never get at her that way! I'll get a ladder for outside — get back you —" and he back-handed someone reeling into the store, "I don't need you to snoop through my shed" and came striding out of the perimeter of light as yells and laughter followed him.

Abe had sunk almost into the snow, his hand finding his torch to flick it out — a division of forces! — and when he saw the Icelander's light play on the lock of the warehouse he plowed silently from the path, wishing he had his skis if only to keep down his panting. He gained the corner of the warehouse, hearing a violent tumble of boxes and barrels inside, and then the end of a ladder emerged out of the door following a beam of light and he stepped close, hand raised as Bjornesen materialized, still cursing under his breath. Abe could just make out the shadow of his uncovered head with white hair bristling as they always did even when a cap or

hood had weighed them down, and he brought the gun-butt down with a crash at just the point he knew it must hit (he did not even have time to marvel how, after all the years, he still could hit the spot exactly despite the dark) and the trader sank in the trampled snow like a puppet with all strings slit, the darkness blotting up his fall as the torch fell under him. He seized an arm — damn it all to hell I have no excuse to shoot him now why didn't I let him get back! — he cursed all the time he was dragging the heavy weight back into the shed, flicking on his torch and trussing him with a length of rope coiled behind the door. He found a filthy handkerchief in the trader's pocket and began to stuff it in the mouth when he realized abruptly he was juggling false teeth — the best-kept secret in Frozen! — a vicious laughter welled in him: if the old devil stumbled out toothless among the Indians — god! — he pried out both plates and backhanded them out the door into the snow. The handkerchief; he jammed it loosely between the jaws, feeling the muscles already beginning to resist a little — good! — he leaped out, heaved the ladder aside and swung the door shut. The torch was still shining a small yellow circle squashed in the snow; he mashed it with his boot, running again, breathing heavily but alert as he had never been — now face them at last! — and he burst around the corner of the store. Amos Quequeish stood holding tight to the doorjamb, muttering something impossible to understand for the noise and shouts flaring through the open door. Abe had no time to marvel that Bjornesen would allow such carryings-on in his store every drinking night; he simply leaped to the porch, rammed his shoulder into Amos's yielding belly to hoist the drunken Indian rump-first into a snowdrift and jerked erect in the doorway. He yelled high above the tumult:
"HIYAA — Anishinaby!"
Silence like a pall fell in the smoky store as all wheeled to stare at him calling their name. But he said nothing more. He had seen all he needed in their crowded, staggered turning in the glint of their dull eyes, and he was between them in four huge strides, reeling them aside like reeds before canoe thrust, and was at the counter where Alex stood on the one section dragged under the loft-lid, the new shining axe with

which he had been chopping upwards still half-raised in his amazement. Abe said, quiet and sharp, "Get down," and the momentary astonishment faded as the face above him contorted,

"Like hell —" and the axe lashed down at his upturned face.

But his hands were already on the counter-corner and at the motion he jerked with all his strength, the counter bucked and Alex, hanging one instant in wild balance, crashed behind it, his head striking the last rung of the loft-ladder as he fell. Abe was behind the counter, had caught the axe away, and with a heave that gloried in the violent power of his shoulders slid the half-stunned youth over the planks to the jumble of men's and women's legs in the center of the store so that someone had to thrust out an arm to prevent him ending against the barrelheater.

For an instant there was no sound in the crowded room except Alex's stifled groan. Abe glanced over them swiftly, his heart violent in his chest, eyes searching out each man. The women did not matter; in any case they were the most degenerate of the band, soused at the first few drops of brew, but the slovenly men, despite their drinking and his startling appearance were too well drilled in the instantaneous reactions required of hunters not to understand what had happened and to be partially sobered by it; suddenly bellows outside focused at the door and Amos appeared, snow-covered from his wallow in the drift, face suffused with drink and rage. All turned to him as he roared, cursing in English and shifting without dropping a decibel to Ojibwa, "— Frobisher dog — tear him apart —" but Abe shouted,

"Amos! Amos!" and the long-ingrained deference held at least once more as the hubbub lowered momentarily.

Glaring at them hunched together in the store's center, some men tilted against the counters, women cowering down, a few at their very feet, Amos like a huge blotched gargoyle in the doorway, he knew with a wrench from their glances sliding aside that they were afraid. Even the pseudo-bravado of brew would never push them against a whiteman and though he had never thought of pushing them against him before, at the moment he knew like a vision exploding in him he had to hammer this thing through once and for all. He squeezed all his anger into scorn as he said in Ojibwa into their growing rustle of movement, "Women, cowardly women," and he was staring at the men only, largely at Amos and then at Alex sitting up hand to head, and he sensed the shifting glances, so near him in the tiny store, harden against his face, "Silly weak women," he went on, the scorn raw on his face and tone, "must get drunk, to chase stupid skirts, make them drunk before they spread legs for you. You, men? Hahahaha!" He laughed so hard that it appeared convulsively, violently funny even to himself for an instant and the laughter that bounced about the fetid room rose almost maniacally before he cut it off with a lunge of determination and wheeled to Alex, "You, big man from white school — big job with trader — needs all these — men —" his tone hung a moment on invective "— men to get him one little girl. Not much man last summer, eh, big man!"

He laughed again loud and deep, but his eyes intent to watch them. Alex was standing, face twisted in a paroxysm of humiliation and rage so that he could not even shout anything for a moment, then he cursed viciously. Abe yelled him down in English, "Shut up you filthy-mouthed brat! No one understands you anyway," and Alex turned to the others, shouting,

"Wagoss! Where's Wagoss?"

Abe roared, jubilant above the sudden noise, "Sure, get Wagoss, make you women, all women! Listen! Listen!" and his yell controlled them, "hear him in the shed," and in the held silence they all heard thudding on the heavy shed-door. "I tied him — he lies on the floor, banging heels — baby in a cradle-board — your great Wagoss — and —" he laughed again, out of himself almost, "with no teeth, like a baby, no teeth, banging — go, help him, great man-baby!" and as several rushed out he could have leaped for happiness knowing he needed only one thing to bring it off quickly, before anything else happened (what that else might be he did not even have time to think, though it squatted in the back of his teeming mind somewhere, a blackness which when recognized would drench his present resolution) and glaring about he recognized the final jolt needed as the head of William Crane thrust up from behind one counter section that had walled off a corner and emerging beside William's the head of Mary Sturgeon and he roared, all turning as he pointed,

"See William Crane, who had never even one little dream — drunken with skirts behind a counter! His brother runs his trapline, feeds his wife and family —" the stunned silence hesitated in the brink of derisive laughter, than which the Indians enjoyed nothing better, and sensing this as rage slowly spread over William's half-drink-stupid face he flashed at the woman whose head had vanished, "And Mary Sturgeon, no more need widow's allowance from the government, now, with great hunter to — provide — all you need — so much greater than —" and the rest was lost in the great cackle of laughter that burst from all, except Abe noted as he stared about, Alex and a few sagged beyond comprehension in drink. But he had to inflame them all, everyone in the shambles before him, and there was no time for anything but to bellow at them, "And William McKay, so made well at the hospital and bring back healthy lungs and something in his pants burning," he used an English obscenity for which they needed no translation, "from the city. And Amos, big belly and empty head and pockets, and —" he scoured them all, dredging up every gossip rind of which he could recall the faintest slur and inventing where he could not remember, prodding them to rage until there was no more laughter even from the by-now standing women, to greet his salvos. For an instant, watching their livid hatred as whatever little they had left of themselves was stripped to its smallest and meanest under the ultimate insult of his barely-acquired, stumbling Ojibwa, he was afraid he had baited them too quickly, but a bellow such as even his lungs could not produce thundered outside the door and Bjornesen charged in, his two freers at his heels, a length of rope still dangling from his arm fist-clenched in the air. Abe roared, "Look, look, the great Wagoss, baby, no teeth," and all stared at the Icelander. Abe yelled again, "I picked them out, like picking berries — and threw them —" and he reached behind him to a small heap of cans still intact on a shelf, and hurled one over their heads and through the top of the window beside the door. "That's all for Wagoss — needs women — drink milk, a baby —" but despite his rage and the Indians' amazed dawning of derision at his puckered face and the incredible insult, the trader was too quick for the trap and instead of leaping at Abe spluttered loud, "The axes — knives — he's alone, all together," and seized two men nearest him and pulled them forward with him. At the words Abe leaped to the counter and the black .38 glinted above them.

"See," he yelled, "the little gun, the gun the spirit of Kekekose brought last fall — you saw." They stared at him, the Indians at least immobile. "The first knife — the first axe — Wagoss is dead," the barrel was steady now, unwavering, not having to aim, eyes holding them all motionless, his marksmanship already legend with them. And suddenly the only sound in the building was someone's rasping breath and he realized that it was the old trader's. Nothing moved, not even the scant eyelashes of the women huddled on the floor now against one pushed-aside counter and staring up as a paralysed rabbit at a fisher. In English suddenly Abe screamed,

"Goddamn you all to stinkin' hell do you want him!" and he flicked the gun aside to the great earthen crock from which they drank and as the shot blasted in the room it splattered into a million shards against the corner wall and the liquor flamed black over the grimy logs and counter boards. He was staring at Amos then as the people stared at the ruin, a sound like sighing their mouths, and he saw the hatchet glint when the big Indian's arm sprang back and his finger was tightening on the trigger like a caress when a shout leaped at them through the open door.

Joshua Bishop stood in the doorway, his eyes immense in his narrow face pale as if that instant he had fallen out of the sky. With them all Abe stood as petrified, gun still circled on Bjornesen, finger still crooked, tense, and only when Josh moved forward did despair stir in him — great god that was the mistake — one more instant, just one, and it would have been complete and irrevocable but now knives and axes showed everywhere and it was too late for Josh was between him and the man he must have first.

He was almost sobbing under his breath as he twitched back and forth on the short counter to try and find the range, impossible in that tiny store, "Josh, Josh, for the love of God — stay out — why — stay out —" and then the missionary was in the half-circle below him and he had a clear shot again but he began to understand slowly with an abruptly bottomless despair that he had lost. For Josh was holding his arm wide before the people, murmuring against the tumult now rising under Bjornesen's persistent urging, Josh not even trying to be heard but merely standing, his slight figure with its outstretched arms and great staring eyes forcing himself upon their recognition until even the trader's insistence fell quiet for a moment without any of them having moved, though about the door axes swung high above heads, and Josh's voice could finally be heard,

"My friends, my friends, my people," the richness of warm Ojibwa caught them all and for an instant every sound and movement ceased. Josh said, "You want to kill each other now. Then you must kill me too."

Bjornesen barked in English, his toothless jaws clacking a little, "Bishop get out of here — it's none of your business — you teach kids and leave men to —" but above him came the Ojibwa of Amos, shouting,

"Get out of the way, he insulted us —" and then William McKay was shouting too,

"He's just your friend — you work together" and Josh silenced them with a barked,

"No!" not even twisting his head to respond to Bjornesen still talking English, "I am friend to everyone who will have me. Will you be my friend, Amos?" Josh moved forward a little, hands out, empty palms upward. "William? Joe? He," he shrugged at Abe on the counter above him, "is my friend, yes, we can talk together and have joy together of one another in our homes, on the hunting trail. But you do not come to be my friends? When I come to your houses your children and wives stay, you go away. Why? I would be your friend. Now."

Bjornesen's huge face under his upright hair bulged purple. He roared in Ojibwa, "Kill him too then! Kill him too!" and he lunged forward, arm and fist high, dragging one man with him and Josh just before him screamed at an unearthly pitch, whirling with his back towards all to face only Abe and leaping up on the counter in one fantastic movement so that the thrown knife sliced through the space where he had been into the wall behind the shelf even as Josh's open palm knocked up Abe's barrel and Abe found himself staring into unearthly eyes, his body hidden behind the other, his wrist held high to the ceiling, seeing Josh's lips form words impossible to hear as the second shot that would have dropped Bjornesen forever crashed unendingly harmlessly upward into the logs. "Abe, Abe, no, no, no." And when, after an eternity of facing those eyes, absolutely impotent to move and knowing only that on the instant the body sheltering his would be jerking with knives, Abe felt the rungs of the loft-ladder hard against his back and he comprehended at last that except for a groaning and scrabble on the floor all was silent. He tore his glance aside. Past the fringe of Josh's hair he saw the Indians then, two of them sprawled over Bjornesen flat on the floor with Joe Loon's arms tight around his legs but all, even Joe, face contorted with effort, staring at Alex standing just behind the stove, empty-handed, arm sinking.

Josh turned, feet moving carefully on the narrow counter; he looked at them. Slowly he broke open the revolver he now held in his hand, slid out the two spent and four still deadly shells, dropped them in his pocket and handed back the .38 to Abe without looking. Abe thrust it into his parka pocket, feeling suddenly as stifled, sensing his fingers slip on the gunbutt. He looked at Josh's hand. The one that had caught the gun aloft was bleeding but the missionary did not move it, as if it held no pain for him however it had been torn. He was nodding to the men still holding Bjornesen. They pulled back and the old man shook himself ponderously erect. He threw one glance, indecipherable under his bushy brows, at the counter, turned and jammed his way quickly out the door. When the crunch of steps on snow was gone Josh began speaking.

Once or twice in Kekekose's speech Abe had sensed, faintly, the power of oratory possible in Ojibwa. But he had not heard it as Josh used it now, the full deep roll of soft question and softer answer. What had become of the once-great people at Frozen Lake, of the Anishinabay? Beyond the memory of the oldest they had lived here, hunting, trapping, marrying, bringing home food for their wives and children, keeping them warm against the cold. And now they had been insulted, yes. But it was a proper insult, for how many of them now cared for their families and wives, trapped and hunted, kept the incest and moral laws of their people? How many of them lived only to have one more drink, to force one more appetite, to steal one more drunken fondle? Abe, tilted against the wall, could not but marvel at the way the missionary probed through all that he himself had known of their rottenness, more than he had imagined to hurl at them, but now spoken in a softness that pushed the shame into the people, not to outward violence to silence this fearless man standing before them and speaking as they themselves had almost forgotten in their tongue but seeking them out where they lived, where they felt, where in the recesses of themselves they still knew themselves human and alive and a part of a once-great people that could not just be squashed but must live on because this lacerating voice in its very accent and warmth bespoke trust and faith in them. Where in all this fear and drunkenness and agony after drink and undernourished families and sick children and wives was the good life, the pimadaziwin they had always, would always long for? Its blessing would never come to them, even as their own beliefs told, while all this evil conduct drove them from passion to hate to the very brink of murder, where no undrunken friend, no not the very school children were safe from abuse. And why? Because they had given themselves to the demon drink and they were slaves now, and they could not tear themselves away though sometimes they might cry for that. Oh, a few of them had done it just now, and stopped a killing or two or three, but they had drunk almost enough tonight and they would be sick for it tomorrow, and what would they do when the great thirst came back to them in a day, in two days?

They would again come here, they would again terrify children, and perhaps even worse. As had been done.

In following Josh Abe had almost forgotten the people; suddenly he saw them again, listening as they always did to a speaker, but deeply held now. The women sat — in their brightest clothes like a goddamn party! — swaying a little, some crying openly. The men stood about, eyes down, none leaving. Alex leaned over the counter, looking away from Josh, wiping his nose with his sleeve. Studying the people, his own passion sinking and theirs obviously overspent, Abe thought, Let him talk a bit longer and he'll have them all where he wants them: a little more and he's made it. But as he thought this Josh stopped, looking at them until one after another lifted the bleary, a few tear-marked, eyes. He said,

"It is time we went home. There is no head now between us for clear thought. Only remember: when we are the worst slaves (he used the strange word again, almost an archaic one which he had explained once to Abe as referring to a prisoner of war used long ago when the people fought the Sioux and took prisoners for torture, and though the Ojibwa had not fought wars like that for about a hundred years they clearly knew what the word meant) the Kitchi-manido wants us to be free. And he has sent us his son, Giin Jesus, to make us free completely. Do you want to hear of him?"

"Yes," said a voice at the door, and all turned. Kekekose stood there, Lucy beside him. The old man had thrown on some ragged clothes but his long grey-streaked hair hung uncovered over his shoulder. "Come to my house tomorrow. I will listen." He looked at them, one by one. "Go now."

Slowly, without glancing at each other, the people left, the women going off as a group in open sobbing. When even Amos had gone into the darkness Josh moved for the first time. He bent and with his uninjured hand jerked out the knife that had driven between the cans of milk into the logs of the wall. He dropped down from the counter, went over and laid it beside Alex's hand. The lad, staring rigid at the wall, did not touch it. Presently he straightened, placed his hands as if with tremendous precision on the corners of the counter and began to pull it back into place. Josh went to the other end and began pulling also.

There was a sound above. Jarred from himself, Abe remembered and he was up the ladder even as the axe-gashed trapdoor shifted, spiralling thin dust on him, and he helped heave it aside with one hand and jerked himself up, "Violet, Violet are you all —" and then he stopped for as he swung around, his feet still on the last ladder rungs, he saw in the feeble light of the one naked bulb in the peaked loft two figures and it was a long thought-vacant moment before he could decipher Violet and then Sally Howell.

"What the dev —" he stared at her uncomprehending. "Lucy —" but his mind contorted and Sally laughed unsteadily,

"No, I've only been here a few minutes — while things were — levelling out down there," she gestured behind her and he understood the cold air in the loft came from the gaping back window. "The ladder lay by the shed."

He could finally pull his eyes from her to the girl huddled beside her on the dirty-gritty planks. "Violet," he hoisted himself off the ladder and stepped forward under the yaw of the roof, "Are you all right?"

"Yes. Yes." Her eyes were enormous in the light's shadow, her face tear-streaked.

"They didn't hurt you — Alex —" he didn't know what to say; he could not admit it consciously even to himself but in one flash he wished they had hurt her in some fiendish fashion so he could slide down that ladder and thrash that insane brat within an inch of consciousness, and his tone must have betrayed him for Sally and quickly,

"Abe, there are bruises on her arms, but otherwise she's okay —"

"Sure," he said quickly, his emotion boiling because of them crouched there so pathetically, wishing, as he had not while down on the counter with gun cocked and ready to fire once or twice and hurl himself at them to smash the herd into insensibility or it him that he could only have acted and not be forced to control. "God and the devil!" he said under his breath, and then he comprehended the two women watching him, faces in shadow, and he put out his hand to Violet's arm. "Sure," he could say finally, "Kekekose is there with Lucy. She's a good girl. You go home now."

Violet crouched a moment in the dimness where he could not read her face. After a moment her voice: "Thank you, Mr. Ross, thank you," and in one swift movement she was down the ladder. Abe hunched around.

"Come on," he said, and then he felt Sally's hand on his sleeve. "Huh?" he had not heard her voice beginning.

She said again, "You wanted to kill him, didn't you." It was not even a question.

"Yes," he said, hunkered down and looked past the silhouette of her head towards the window gaping in the cold. "Yes. Like I haven't wanted much for long time. One shot. But I didn't want to shoot Alex — huh-uh" and she could not but have felt the muscles of his arm bulge in ridges under her fingers as he said, "Come on" again for he suddenly realized from a glint of reflection in the thin light that tears were streaming down her face and she was not putting up a hand to wipe them aside. Sitting, eyes unblinking, with tears running out of them. "Hey, what's the matter —" and suddenly she was sobbing against his shoulder and his mouth was on her hair, her body shuddering against him. He had no conception of what it was he felt.

She pulled back abruptly, her hands to her cheeks. "Abe, did Kekekose say in front of them he would listen?"

"Yes."

"Oh! I was so afraid I only wanted to hear it so terribly!"

"Does that mean Kekekose wants to —" he did not know how to label his thought.

"None of the men have ever said that, in public. It could be the start — it must be the start!" Her eyes shone as if a beacon had flamed up in her. "Abe, will you take me to Brink Island cabin on Friday?"

"What?" his exclamation rang in the bare loft.

"It's Good Friday then, and ten days without school. If Josh could begin now, a few men wanting to hear him, a few women hear Lena, oh, Abe, I have to go to the cabin and pray God that he will move here, at last!"

"But if something's beginning here, shouldn't you stay and help?" He could not comprehend her.

'But the greatest help I could ever give would be prayer, unbroken prayer. Our Lord said to his disciples that certain spirits are never moved except by prayer and fasting."

"All alone in that wilderness?"

"And all blessed quiet," she seemed to misunderstand him completely. "And I had sort of half-planned it. Josh was going to take me with the team, but now he couldn't. Abe," her voice, as he would never later when all was over, forget, spoke out of the darkness. He pushed up half-erect against the sloping roof.

"There's two days yet. We can talk about it. Com'mon you first."

Her eyes glinted momentarily as she looked as him, nodded and placed her hands on the high rung and swung down; he knew as she did so that she knew he had already decided not to do it. Then he was down the ladder too in the store where only Alex was still scraping things around, piling supplies on the shelves and for a moment he stood rooted. Revulsion he could not have imagined ranted through him as the lad, back turned, worked steadily piling cans. Then he felt Sally's hand tighten over his clenched and her voice, quiet as always, "Alex, the back window upstairs is open," and out of the corner of his eye he saw Alex's startled twist at the teacher's voice, then his head drop and his shoulders seem to sag, finally.

They said nothing the long walk to the Bishop cabin. The winter's unending overcast weighed on the night like a pall. When they reached the porch Sally took her arm from his and looked at him in the shadow of his small torch.

"Will you, Abe?"

"Yes," he said, sadly, for he understood that he would never be able to refuse her anything when she asked him in that way.

15

WITH a tremendous lurch winter suddenly threw aside its dull oppression and for two days flamed in sunlight. Friday before they travelled an hour the sun found them on the open channel of the river, glazing the snow in warmth. The trail was hard; three fur-camps lay down-river. Abe ran, the bristle of green pines and grey poplars on the shoreline with here and there the lee of a rock upthrust as scab on the snow edging the frame of his vision toward the sky's blue scoop around each bend, the team like some featureless line bobbing the lure of the bright red hood before him as he ran, as he could have rejoicing run forever.

The hood turned and she was shouting. He ran closer, then saw her pointing arm. Bending in his run, the color driven to her cheeks in the morning air, he shouted "Yeah! Right! Half-mile Rapids." He waved left, "Portage trail, about half-way." She shouted again and he simply guessed, ears covered and blood suddenly pounding in his head, "Mug-up. Down below," and she nodded smiling up to him, and to see that smile he would have run the twelve miles again.

The trail veered to shore; Sally lifted herself on her arms and for a moment they looked down the great curve of the ice-scrambled rapids falling out of sight between white-splashed pines gleaming bronze in the sunlight: as if the frost had seized the water lashing the rocks and petrified it with one clenching of its iron fist. She looked back at him, not speaking, her mouth and face shaped in wonder. He laughed, the black shadow of the trees swinging over them, and the dogs, answering to his halloo, scrabbled for foothold up the slope and raced around the bend and down the tilt so that he had to sprint to catch the sled-handles and nip a spill. He leaped to the runners when the sled steadied and, with the dogs flat out to stay ahead, they shot down between the trees, swaying wildly in short tight bends, Abe balancing lightly above Sally's head thrown back, mouth caught open in a soundless scream. "Left turn! Lean with me, left!" he shouted in her ear on a short level stretch where the momentum was just enough to swoosh them through a dip up another rock-ridge, hesitate on the brink of an even sharper drop, and she shouted back, "Ohh — it's too narrow!" and the dogs lunged into harness as he yelled at them and they were falling, running for their lives before the sled while the trees slid by like pickets and Abe leaned low as they neared the bottom where two tall spruce stood sentinel astride the last bend, seeing Sally bend with him, but it would not be quite enough as they flew, the dogs open mouthed and silent with no breath but for running, and the trail turned away from them and he eased his weight on one handle, sliding his feet off the runners to drag legs and body and with a lunge that reeled them almost out of themselves, the loaded sled lifting momentarily to one runner, they were around with the spruce branches whipping over them as they slid sideways to the softer side-snow that choked their speed and in a moment they were back on the straight trail, coasting easily down the last gentle incline to the level snow of the pool below the rapids. The wheel dog gave a little hop, the sled slid under him, and with the other dogs running slack, the wheel dog seated erect, tongue lolling, on the prong of the sled, Sally and Abe laughing aloud, they glided into the brilliant sunshine and across the pool to the base of the shore before their momentum was lost and Abe caught back the sled with a shout and they stopped, the dogs falling spent to the snow. "Mug-up time!"

"Woo — what a ride!"

He bent to help her out. "Beats Coney Island, eh?" he laughed.

"Have you been there too?"

"Sure. We could have met there? Hey, old man," and he brushed the wheel dog onto the snow, "off you get."

"Let him sit where he wants! He deserves it, doing most of the work on those bends."

"So he worked — he's had his ride." He shook his head gravely. "White women never are any good mushers — too soft. Dogs take advantage of them. Aha —" he had been scraping at the dry snow with the side of his boot and now he found the rock. "We can build the fire here. Won't melt out of sight." He went back to the sled and pulled out the camping sack. Sally stood in the sunlight, watching.

"How did you know a rock was there?"

"I should. Dived off it long enough, last summer."

"Oh."

"Yeah. Kekekose did it easier." He waved the hatchet, "Back in a shake." When he returned she was not in sight. He laid the fire, humming a little under his breath. When he leaned back to fumble in his pocket for matches through the blaze of the sun almost directly in his eyes the red glint of her jacket moved out on the ice near the final heap of rapids. He jerked erect shading his eyes, and then he sprang to the sled, caught the long coiled whip from the sled-handle and was sprinting over the ice, shouting, "Sally! Sally!" He saw her look back and he waved, still running, and then she was standing, waiting for him but not coming back, standing waiting until he ran up, his breath almost gasping in his throat. She was perhaps twenty feet away from the base of the iced rocks sprawling like a long glacier above her against the dead-blue sky. He stopped ten strides from her and beckoned. "Sally, please, come here," and then she came, her eyes squinting at him against the sunlight.

"What's the matter?"

He had almost caught his breath then, and he felt his knees shake but not from the dash. He put his free hand on her shoulder and turned with her, "Come on a bit further," and she walked with him, not speaking. Finally he said as they stopped in the middle, looking back at the crushed ice leading up between the trees, "Never go near rapids in winter." Though he did not look at her, he knew her face was reddening but he had no time to say it more politely; better this than to forget, ever.

She said presently, "But it must be two feet thick, look at that piece rammed up —" she pointed.

"Sure. Here it's probably three. But not over there. There it's running where you'll never see it till the snow-crust breaks under you." He said deliberately, "And somebody might by accident find what's left next summer in his fishnet."

She stared a moment, then turned quickly so that his hand fell away and began walking.

She said, not looking back, "You're crude."

"Just to help you not forget," he said, almost cheerfully, "That's all."

"It's beautiful — the water's the nicest thing about this country."

"Sure. Travel on it winter and summer, airplane, sled, kicker canoe. But mix it with the land — like that jumble," he gestured, "it's lethal. There's grave-houses at every portage on this river — some up higher here, but they're snowed over."

The dogs lay on the ice, ears cocked at them approaching, the wood scattered on the grey gash of rock. "All right, Mr. Know-it-all, I submit my ignorance. And you carried that all the way out there for my benefit so you can whip me now, in front of all your dogs!"

He was laughing by then, for though her face held rigid its expression, her voice betrayed her and he did not have to explain in what case of desperate necessity he might have needed the thirty-foot whip. "I only use it when the children won't learn — never when they do," and at that moment the wheel dog, all white save for a long black strip down the ridge of his face, barked sharply, eyes intent on the whip, and they were laughing together, the absolute stillness of the sun-shining white and green world echoing about them. "He knows," Abe tossed the coil around the sled-handle. "So let's get some tea before he turns lazy on us."

In a moment the wood was burning under the smoky pot

heaped with snow; he sat on an extra piece of wood, content with rest. He comprehended the air was beginning to warm; a squirrel sounded in the pines behind him and then a covey of snow-buntings swooped out of the trees, trilling squeeks of notes and fleeing in lilting waves of flight over the pool to the far shore. He watched them out of sight, then looked at Sally. She stood behind the sled on the wind-packed snow, humming, and as he watched she began to move in what he slowly understood was a sort of dance, shifting from foot to foot, swaying a little, her head bowing to face the snow and lifting again until the sunlight sought out its every feature, her eyes closed and body swaying gently to the tune she hummed thin and high. Lost in wonder he watched her, the warm air drifting around him in the white silence save for her little tune, and the dogs too shifting to her, prick-eared. The tune played tantalizingly along the edge of his recognition but glanced off, like the sheen of her face flashing momentarily in the sun. So he pushed thought aside, watching only and listening until she stopped.

He said after a long silence, she looking back to the notch of the portage, motionless, "You're strange."

She dropped her arms, mouth open a little in breathlessness. "Because I dance?"

"Yes, that."

"Dancing is beautiful — for everything. One of the hardest things to believe was when I became a Christian some people said I mustn't dance any more. It doesn't bother Lena or Josh, but — well, some can't help their prejudices." She grinned, slightly roguish, "You won't tell on me will you?"

"No," he said, "I wouldn't know who, anyway."

She turned abruptly toward him, "It's just a way to give room to happiness a little, dancing."

"And you're happy today?"

"Yes. Even you wanting to whip me can't stop it, see." They both laughed a little, but unselfconsciously.

"Why?"

"Because —" she blinked but her glance did not waver, "because the evil at Frozen is opened at last and Josh has talked twice with Kekekose and Joe Loon was there yesterday — and four women came to Lena late last night — but mostly because for a little while I can leave the mechanics of drilling children in language and arithmetic and simply pray for my friends."

"Mechanics?"

"Ugh, that's not the word! It sounds so much like 'machine' — and I don't want to do anything else but teach but sometimes you — you feel you're nothing but a drillmaster — over and over and over and you get stamped out of you almost other essentials, like prayer."

"And you have to go alone somewhere for that?" he spoke half-smilingly, having been how often over this terrain in the past two days and still not able to grasp her necessity.

"Yes. Sometimes."

He looked at her, face half-brilliant in the sun. He realized suddenly he had never seen before such serenity — can I trust myself to admit anticipation? — and he felt a jolt he would have disdained to identify as jealousy. Immensely happy, happy beyond any expression except perhaps dance — like anticipating a tyrst with some celestial lover — he shook his head, dropping his face away from her level glance. He said, avoiding, "What was that tune?"

"Don't you remember? The children sang it at Christmas."

"Oh I knew I'd heard it somewhere. Sing it."

She laughed, "It's too simple and undecorated for you," then sang, moving through the lilt of the carol:

> "A virgin unspotted the prophets foretold
> Should bring forth a Saviour which now we behold
> To be our redeemer from death, hell, and sin
> That Adam's transgression involved us in.
> Then let us be merry, put sorrow away,
> Our Saviour Christ Jesus was born on this day."

"What a song to sing on Good Friday," he said.

"But to be our redeemer Jesus had to die today. And to die, he had to be born. Our Lord was born to die."

The water was bubbling; he dropped tea bags into it before he said, "No one will ever touch your logic either." He watched the brown ebb away from the bags, buffeted by bubbles, widening itself like a tinted violence in the snow-pure water. She was silent — god that had sounded cynical — he said, trying to erase that edge but far more out of longing to probe her strangeness, her immovable serenity that lifted him from his oppressive self-consciousness as if it had never been, "You talk as if — he was — a someone you knew — or something."

He did not glance up from the darkening pot but he knew she was studying his face. "Yes. That's it, exactly, I do know him that way and that's the only way to talk about him. Easter follows Good Friday, and that was when Jesus Christ came alive again. He still is."

"Alive?"

"Yes. Otherwise what would be the point of Easter?"

"Sure, sure," he reached for the cups she had set on the rock skirting the fire, "that's what church people say. He lives. But who sees him, like other living people? Why doesn't he come around and show himself?" He spoke with nearly bared facetiousness; it was the shallow usual statement, and he was more disappointed at her than he had thought. But she grinned as she held out her cup,

"You wouldn't believe it anyway."

"What?"

"Jesus Christ coming across the ice over there and telling you he was the son of God. The Jews didn't, and they were really waiting; you're not even doing that."

"Probably not. No," he was staring into his teacup, "I wouldn't believe it if he came over the ice."

"So what would be the point of his doing it?"

"Well, maybe we'd understand if he did some things that proved him," he shrugged.

"Like what?"

"Oh, do something — god-like — a miracle maybe, to prove himself alive and beyond the human —"

"You mean like Kekekose handing your gun back out of a pool twelve miles away?" He stared at her; he had never thought of that before. Sitting on the very rock for which he had fought, time after time, coming up with chest bursting. Presently she went on, "Those outside kind of miracles don't work anymore. The old man's obviously got something but you'd never want to become a conjuror, would you? Mechanical miracles are too common — we push them aside by saying we haven't discovered the law yet that makes them work."

She had her cup to her lips; their eyes met and held. "Sure," he conceded, "sure. You're right. So there is no way for the divine — for Christ, if you say he's divine — to get through. So what difference does it make, if he's god or not, to me?"

"Couldn't he prove himself through people, work some miracles in them?"

He thought a moment, not daring quite to think where she seemed to be. "What do you mean, miracle in people?"

"In some person, transform him into a person that's never been before, giving goodness for hate, kindness for jealousy, happiness for —" she stopped at the expression on his face.

"Maybe just a quirk of personality; who'd believe it unless it happened to himself?" he grinned, unaware of what he had admitted because her face led him on. "And you talk like you have to go meet him, like going to some assignation or something —" he stumbled, his words already too far and her face flamed suddenly like a spring-rose bursting to the violent sun, but he dared not pause now, "to meet at a particular —"

At that moment the dogs leaped howling to their feet; they both started as if stung. Yelping from around the point answered, and suddenly Sally was laughing. She put down her cup to avoid spilling, and then Abe was laughing too as a dogteam emerged from around the corner of the point, a single man running behind it. They were still laughing when Abe recognized the lead dog and bent to Sally, "He doesn't have to prove anything. That's James Sturgeon, his trap-camp's out here." He scooped the pail full of snow, and placed it in the fire's final flame. Sally stood up, waving.

The big smile on James' sun-blackened face told them no long invitation was needed. When the tea was diluted, Abe explained, "I take Miss Howell to Brink Island cabin, get back — tonight."

The Indian glanced up, "She staying long?"

"Island? Oh, a few days — seven, eight." He looked to the loaded sled. "Trapping still good?"

James lifted his cup in morose gesture. "Beaver's okay, but it'll be a poor spring for muskrats; too cold, the ice is like rock."

"Warm today."

"Yeah, but not enough to do much. Two-three weeks anyway before the ice is soft enough for rats." Sally was already settled in the sled; Abe went to his dogs and the trapper stood up and smiled at her. "Thank you — tea," he said, using most of his English vocabulary.

"Abe, please tell him I didn't make it."

"What?" Abe laughed, "And let him believe I did woman's work when there's a woman around? Not much!" James was pouring the last of the tea into his mug, twisted the pot in the snow, leaving some of smoke-blackness behind, then handed it to Sally. Abe said to him, "Funny thing at Frozen; some men with Good News Man, talking out of black book."

James turned and stared. "What happened?"

"Plenty." Abe grinned humorlessly. "To everybody. They tell you at Frozen better. Bonjour." As his whip snapped the dogs sprang against their traces, the sled broke loose and they were running — funny all right for a trader to try and shoot homebrew out of a band with a .38! — when he looked back at the turn, James had already vanished up the portage trail.

It was twelve o'clock before they halted on the crest in the heavier snow of the last portage and looked down the long wide valley where the Frozen and Brink Rivers joined. Just before the juncture Brink Island thrust up through the ice, its snow level not much lower than the ridge where they stood as if a primeval core of something in the worn valley still defied the rivers' worry, its immense bristle of pine strangely taller than the mainland. The cabin could not be seen; had it been summer the roar of Frozen Falls would have been crashing on the right, its spume flashing rainbow above the trees. But now, as they looked, the dogs collapsed and panting, there was no sound about them in the overwhelming brightness;

only the pulse of their own breathing and now and then the cry of a bird in the warming air.

There was no rush down this incline. Braking the sled, Abe remembered the tussle with the canoe and packs the summer before: steep and long almost straight against the face of the high rock. Then they were on the ice safely again, the island looming a few hundred yards before them and to their right, the falls silent in their mass of rocks and ice blocks like gigantic crystalline teeth smashed between the flanking trees. Close now, the sled sliding over the glazed-iron snow, they could hear the trickle of water somewhere beneath the facade, then they were past and under the brow of the island. Abe strapped on snowshoes and beat an angled trail up; the cabin sat knee-deep in snow under the spruce.

In its cave-like darkness Sally pushed back her hood, looking about. "My, it must have snowed since we were here at Christmas! We had the snow packed down, all around. Now you can't even see the wood-pile."

Abe was scraping snow from the doorway. "Snowed even more here than at Frozen. And it's colder, you notice?"

There was no answer. When he had cleared the step he peered back in; she materialized out of the cabin's rear lean-to. "There's no point using that room — I'll close this and I don't even have to fight anybody for the upper bunk! And I can use the table for a desk by the window facing the falls, and —"

"Hey hold on!" He was frowning. "You're violating the first rule of any lady that's been hauled twenty rough miles by dogteam after a very early breakfast. Stop rearranging furniture! Get a pot of snow on a fire and feed the man that's run all the way. First things first, milady."

"Yes, lord and master." She attempted a bow. "I regret, sire; I must remove a layer of coats which at this moment prevent my proper obeseience."

He caught her tone and mood quite. "Good. There is to be kindling and wood behind the heater. Here are matches. I shall clear the wood-pile and bring in the required stuffs." He stopped suddenly. "By the way, I may presume you know how to start a wood-fire?"

She deigned no word. She had swept off her red hood while

he spoke, now bowed once and with a face set in disdain wheeled to the heater. Laughing, he watched her rattle its tin lid aside. "Very well, maid, you have your orders. But I shall skin and gut the rabbits myself, since I require them for lunch. I do want to make a relatively early start." He ducked fast and the chunk of kindling she threw rattled harmlessly against the doorboards. He poked his feet into the snowshoes and tramped down a path to the woodpile. A fat grey and white whiskey-jack quivered a spruce branch above him and stared at him curiously as he dug, whistling.

The thin clear membrane of banter held them throughout their chores; when they sat down to flour-fried rabbit she had disdainfully managed to perfection on the redhot surface of the heater they were in that state of suspension found between two persons only by accident, and that rarely, where all that beckons is enticing and every certain knowledge of the future sublimated in present delight. He said, "I won't have much chance to spoof you about cooking again if this tastes like it looks," but she refused to be nudged.

"I am certain," she said with heavy demureness, eyelids fluttering, "that any succulence you may find in this poor repast, most grave sir, was magically imparted to it by your expert shot that slew the poor beasts."

He laughed then completely, holding the entire shank and thigh of the rabbit before him, and he contorted his face so oddly behind his heavy beard that she could not maintain her role and their laughter rang together. He sank his teeth into the meat and she said, still laughing, "When you do that, Abe, you look like a friendly satyr."

"Rabbit, like chicken, needs just fingers and teeth." He held the bone between his two forefingers, hesitating, then said what ordinarily he could only have thought, "And a nice girl like you shouldn't know what a satyr is, leave alone what he looks like."

"That's the second time you've said something like that. Why?"

He chewed a mouthful. "Why what?"

"Why do you always say, 'a nice girl like you shouldn't—'"

"I don't say it *always*. You just said it's only the second time."

"But it's the sort of thing people never say twice unless they think it a lot."

"Oh." He put down the leg, almost stripped to the bone, and reached for the biscuits she had brought along. He was touched too near to rush into speech and he was still trying to verbalize something he felt when she continued,

"Are there certain things someone like me shouldn't do, or know, do you think?"

"Well, I guess maybe —" he stopped, feeling foolish now, as if he, not even an amateur, had been asked to coach a professional; but the tone of his wandered words assented and she accepted that.

"You're probably right. Maybe a Christian and a spinster getting older every day shouldn't admit knowing some things, leave alone doing some. But I can't help it: I knew about satyrs before I heard of Jesus Christ" — kneel down and thank your god for that! — "and even when I heard, by accident like turning the radio or something — I grew up very enlightened you know." She smiled a little, humorlessly, "Father taught Jamsie and me to believe only in the goodness of man — till the war began anyway — until in my freshman year at University I was doing a paper in elementary psychology on religion — I was a very industrious student — but Buddhism seemed more attractive than Christianity." She was silent a moment.

"Why?"

"Perhaps because in some theory they're quite similar and there weren't many so-called Buddhists around to disillusion me. Anyway, Jamsie's death made me look at religions' attitudes on war and historically Buddhists have always been the most peace-loving of people; they make pathetic soldiers. Christians — no need to mention their bloody wars. But — well —"

Abe said quickly, intent to keep her talking, "Then how come you became a Christian?"

She smiled fleetingly, as if the question remained a mystery to her also. "It wasn't very dramatic — outwardly — though it was exciting — too exciting sometimes — when I began to know more of what it could mean. No great death-bed repentance or vow; I don't even remember myself crying, then. There was another girl in the psych class doing the religion topic and we exchanged reference books and talked. I suppose I sounded very worldly-wise about the 'theory' of Christianity so she invited me to meet some Christians on campus — practicing ones, and I was quite willing. After all I was at Varsity to have new experiences! They talked about what the Bible said. I went a few times and one night after a meeting I read through all the gospels and the Acts of the Apostles at a sitting. And I can never explain what happened. Someone just looking at me the few hours it took wouldn't have seen a difference, I guess, but a sort of alarming thing was happening to me. Next day I talked to Beth, after psych, and told her somehow I couldn't shake the idea that Jesus Christ could mean more to me than anything I had ever known. It was still mostly a 'thing,' an 'idea.' Beth told me some parts of the Bible that might be helpful. She had a seminar to meet but when she left she said she would pray for me. I didn't really have much idea what it meant, and her saying it in the Arts Building corridor with profs and students bumping past sounded odd, but somehow I accepted it quite seriously, without knowing. I went to my room and read again — almost all of the gospels and some of the other places she had mentioned. And suddenly I knew I wanted to be a follower of Christ. And when I knew that I was so happy for some reason I couldn't even explain I sat and laughed for a long time. Maybe I even danced a little."

She was sitting, smiling, lost in the remembrance. Abe slowly put down his coffee-cup, reluctant to interrupt but levered within himself. "But how could you just — do that — decide such a thing for life, as apparently it was — without — you were a thinking person —"

"Yes," she said quickly, "yes, but I knew then as I still know and have always known even while being hammered — and I have been — lots — that Jesus is alive, living, in me, and that he's the only person in the world worth following."

"But — how can it start? You just think it up reading an old book?"

"No. It really hasn't anything to do with that kind of thinking because, for one thing, it isn't an idea that convinces — that's real to you. It's more like a small flame starting which you can't snub and that flame is Jesus Christ, in person. His realness isn't of your own doing or imagining. It's an act of grace, complete irrefutable grace from God catching fire in you, and it's real. That's what makes you so happy; you couldn't, you haven't done this. Your *do* is shucking aside your particular resources, everything you've built your life on, and praying, in a prayer you don't even recognize as that, 'God, fill my emptiness.' And he does, in his grace."

Abe studied the dregs in his coffee-cup. "It makes no sense."

"Does it have to? Love can't be explained reasonably. It's experience and conviction, not idea first of all."

He did not dare look at her, and so he was never sure of the expression on her face when she said it. After, he would want that one look and abuse himself for his flinching as from fire, but now he simply could not. After a long silence he said, lightly, "So, you became a Christian and ever since have done what was called for, huh?" He had not thought what she said had staggered him so much, for at her next words he realized that it obtusely stated the exact opposite to what they had begun.

"Not exactly!" She laughed aloud. "I still seem to be trying to learn what it means. That night I had a date — one of those terrifically important UT dances. I was so happy Mike asked what was up — he'd never seen me having so much fun. He was one of those emancipated fellows who decide when they get to Varsity they've grown out of weekly Sunday school and YP, at least while away from home, and drink very seriously and take crash courses at city dance studios — this I found out that night, though he was so suave I'd never have known if that evening hadn't pushed things — anyway, when I told him while we were dancing that I was so happy because Jesus Christ was alive and I had decided that very day to be his follower, he almost fell over. When I convinced him at last, he stopped even pretending to dance. It apparently was something I, if I was a Christian, couldn't do. So we left and sat in the dorm lounge and he told he was long over all that and tried to prove by arguments about the robbed tomb and folklore and Freud and Greek myth antecedents how foolish the whole thing was. He might have bothered me any other night, but not that one. I hardly heard him. I laughed too much anyway, he was so dreadfully serious to enlighten me. And he didn't like my laughing so he suggested we go for a walk; but all he did was wriggle his arm around me — he must have been looking for some erotic area he'd read about in one of his enlightened books, and it was all so perfectly ridiculous standing in the shadow of Massey Hall that I started to giggle and couldn't stop. He walked me back in a huff and I went upstairs to start reading the rest of the New Testament."

Abe was slowly wiping up the grease in his plate with the last half of biscuit. She said, her tone quite changed, "Abe, did you have a childhood — like that? You seem to know a lot about a certain kind of Christianity."

He swallowed before he could answer. "I dunno. I was blessed, as they used to say, with a Scotch Presbyterian home, the absolute-law-giving kind. It didn't take till — till university to squitch that out my ears. I dunno if you'd call that a 'certain kind of Christianity' or not." After a pause, he added, "It's long ago. The dirty thirties."

"But you still can't — honestly — forget it."

He pushed back his chair heavily and stood up, though she had hardly begun to eat. "Sure." He stared out the window over the crystal-sharp snow to the contorted ridge of the falls between flanks of winter-brown spruce. "I did forget, years at a time. And I've even decided quite a few times in my heavy-headed way that whatever it was it wasn't worth any more getting mad about it. But" — why did she say 'honestly' — "but Josh and Lena, and you, don't let me forget, some things."

If he had expected her to respond quickly with proofs he was disappointed. There was no sound whatever behind him. Finally he turned, eyes intent on his wristwatch. "You'll have to excuse me, not even waiting for you to finish. It's two-thirty and if I want to get back before dark —"

"Of course. And it's uphill for the dogs."

"Without much load. Just me."

She smiled, hesitating, as if not thinking of what he said. "Just a minute," and she went to her bag on the poles of the lower bunk. He was buttoning his parka when she turned.

"Would you take this New Testament? You might want to read something sometime, in it."

"I wouldn't want to take yours —" the book was paperbound, battered.

"Oh, I have another Bible here — two, in fact. I read various translations. Please."

"Okay." He went out, roused the dogs, unchained the leader and untangled their harness. They were rested now, eager for home and feeding; he had to brake the sled tightly as he looked back at her. She was standing on the little porch, her arms hugging her sweater tight to her against the sharp air, the cell-like cabin yawning behind her, and suddenly he went around to the head of the team, took the lead dog by the collar and pulled him back with him to the porch. "Just so they won't run off without me," he laughed a little. She was smiling at him; the sunlight sought out the edges of her lips and the fine almost imperceptible down above them. "Sally, you know I don't like you staying here alone — so long — I haven't any right to say it except as a —" he stopped foolishly.

She smiled, "Oh Abe, I'll be fine. I had to come and —"

"I know. And because you say so, I try to understand your reasons for this —" he could not voice what she had called it. "But till a week tomorrow is too long. At one stretch anyway. Couldn't I arrange for someone to come here, say Tuesday or Wednesday, just to check? Maybe George — he wouldn't bother you, just make sure —"

"Okay. Fine." Her smile was widening. "Send George. But it is a long way, and if the weather warms for rat-trapping —"

He flapped his mitten in her laughing face, "Don't you worry! I'll find somebody." He looked at her a moment. "Take care of yourself," he said and opened his hand; the dog sprang away. "Hey, you hounds!" he yelled, snaking the whip over them, and caught the sled-handle as it lurched by. Down on the ice, he could settle himself in the sled, the dogs running furiously. Skirting the broken ice of the falls he turned to look; just a line of snow-plumped roof among the giant spruce. So he had only the memory of her to take with him on the run home, the memory of her face and voice and tone of her understanding that pushed him back — god isn't there something else to hammer through but what I've always been able — back at last to his youth. . . .

Part Six

16

*F*ROM the beginning, it was an excuse I used. Legitimate perhaps — if anything ever in my life was legitimate that was — but still an excuse. And all the long years to hug that one decency in memory, forcing forgetting on all the rest of the sixteen, the seventeen years, every instant that even hinted at memory of him because he was no longer to exist and would not and did not; he was nothing, just a nothing that had never been. And against that which I understood now I had deluded myself into thinking was nothing all these years after, except for — legitimate enough but still only — an excuse I could never have said a word leave alone yelled back till fury boiled up in his face or slammed the door shut on him, and her blanched look, trudged the four miles through snow to Selkirk or even outfaced the night agent at the railroad to sit for three hours waiting for the train until at ten-thirty when the train was still four hours away from arriving he finally found a truck loading at the creamery and I thanked him, looking at nothing still, even when he told me, standing with his eyeshade pulled down on his bony forehead. The truck shivering in spasms on the gravel road: I would never sleep again or even fall into unconsciousness; simply, without effort, through all the days and nights of life, hate. The driver suddenly turned, his paunch hard against the wheel,

"Hey, ain't you Adam Ross's boy?"

Through the cracked window the white fields flat from the road ended in barn and farmhouse roof bumped small against the night sky and I said tightly, no, that I came from way north, not here, though I knew my very way of answering scored my lie as surely as my face. But I could lie with only a faint rattle of conscience despite his voice hammering remembrance into my ear "All liars shall have their part in the lake which burneth with fire and brimstone!": there was no brimstone falling, or boiling up. Only the bald stars shining and the dull truck-lights skimming the rutted road. He wouldn't sleep either tonight. For the first time — how many years — since I the oldest was born, he would not know where each one was. Young Adam would be alone in — his — half the upstairs, the girls in the other and he and mother in the downstairs bedroom. How many of them sleeping, though after midnight? The young ones, sure, even young Adam. He didn't have that much in him to cut sleep. But not mother, lying perhaps thinking of the five dollars she slipped me while I tied together a shirt and socks and the quarter she found to thrust into my pocket somewhere "for meals when the sandwiches are gone," kissing me quick at the door; wondering if she should tell before he asked for her five dollars. Maybe he had already and cursed her too with a Bible verse. She would not sleep. Nor he. "Yeah," the driver was cupping a match, light flaring at a bulgy cigarette "Yeah," small eyes turning in the half-reflection from the headlights, "I coulda swore I seen you with Adam Ross last month at the stock show. I loaded up that steer. You was there, staring. I coulda swore, by jesus. Eh?" So repeat the cold denial, even the faint nag of it gone for I remembered the driver then prod Curly up the chute, the reserve grand champion I'd fed hot barley all winter and groomed day after day till he shone tongue-licked: even a squint-eyed truck driver noticing me stare when he sold Curly just like he sold everything I grew or raised, selling and giving me a nickel to buy a chocolate bar. A nickel. I wished like a curse I had them all, all four others to burn a hole in my pocket for what had begun when I was ten and I cried for the last time that night after throwing the first nickel in the Red River, going away from him on Main Street and crying without a sound, just saying yes — lying at ten with the horror of brimstone seething in my head — when he asked whether I had liked the chocolate. And I could feel the final nickel — Curly's — bright and hard in my pocket, folded inside the bill she had saved for her trip from hand sewing bed-quilts the few late minutes of a day she might have and could still keep her eyes open after the day's work, we all working every day except the Lordsday when we all got into the buggy and drove to church and listened to him thunder what somehow during the labor of plow or hoe or pitchfork or axe or shovel the Lord had stomped into him that day; working to make the farm the best the country had seen though it had already been the best when grandfather died and let the weight of it and the family that had farmed it for three generations fall around his neck. But that neck never bent, an inch. Tall and erect whether glaring over the pulpit in the church down on the people, Lordsday after Lordsday or when, as he did every fall, he drove us to school — walk after — the first day of September and went around to each of our teachers, pulling me into the room September first and saying to Miss Milne as he had to every teacher I had ever had that if I stirred a bit of trouble just to let him know and it would be straightened out, that his family worked, at home and at school, and there never was any need for anyone but himself to discipline the children the Lord had seen fit to grant him. And Miss Milne, looking at him and shifting to me quickly — outside boys were throwing the softball across the diamond — saying in a voice I had never heard before or would ever have believed existed, so soft and clear, except perhaps a dream I sometimes had of mother when I was little, that she did not expect any problems. The desk-arm I was gripping in my hands squeeked then and he looked at me too. He said I should watch out and not ruin a good desk, laughing a little to her that I was just at the awkward stage where I didn't know my own strength and it had cost him too many pitchfork-handles already. And when we went I saw her great dark eyes for an instant as I turned. To leave that too. The driver was talking as the truck shuddered violently around a corner ". . . and anyway, s' nothin' to me how many guys take off." He laughed, his heavy stomach thumping against the wheel, whether from laughter or the heave of the truck it was impossible to tell. Down a short hill and the long frozen gleam of the Red River on the left and the road, black between snow banks, snaking ahead and the square-peaked tower of St. Andrew's on the crest right. "Ain't nothin' to me," the driver said again, "The agent just said you was Adam Ross's son wantin' to get to Winnipeg. Eh?" So the words I repeated then, as twice before, were suddenly true. No brimstone ever would scald me for this, for his voice intoning the curse out of his red-blotched face above the hunched massive shoulders had hacked me off completely, forever. I had not remembered that because I was screaming in his face as he thundered, screaming in the kitchen bright in late-winter-afternoon sunlight with mother burying her head in her hands and apron and sobbing to stop, that she would not go anyway even after twelve years or ever if this was what happened and that we must stop oh god we must stop. Her gnarled hands that for two winters had stitched a quilt, and Mrs. Robertson gave her five dollars because she said it was beyond anything you could get, even from Scotland. Then she ventured at last as in passing with all of us in the room that perhaps she could go see her brother again. For six days it lay there between us all, her faint suggestion, his invulnerable silence, and finally on the seventh he said just after he told me it was time for chores, though I was already pulling on my barn-jacket, that her brother had been in this last way for half a year now and there didn't seem to be much hurry about it and that he needed the five dollars to make complete payment on the prize broodsow MacLaren was selling. Mother just looked, dead-faced, like a man who has all his life fed a sawblade and who knows that one moment, sometime, he will forget and one instant after maybe years feel a twitch and looks down and see his fingers gone. I saw then, exact as a camera focusing, her look when she turned and held out her arms to catch me jump the last long step down to the porter's stool at the train, the smiling black-polished porter helping her down first as if she couldn't step down by herself, and walking down the long plank platform as the train hissed away, the strange valley of the town opening after it to the rounded hills beyond with us walking up over the river on the huge bridge, looking between the girders at the water foaming around the piers, and then along the wide road away from town, she carrying the cardboard suitcase and the parcel (the box of sandwiches was long-gone; she had said we would eat in a restaurant before the evening train back) and I holding tight to her skirt before she pointed out the huge buildings on the slope of the valley and I ran ahead a little, kicking stones in the spring sunshine, careful not to step into the road where an occasional car rumbled or, more often, wagons lumbered behind trotting horses. Then we were on smooth walks between grass clipped as a shorn sheep and inside the buildings and the tiredness of the long ride and walking was gone at all the ladies and men walking along immeasurably long halls in stark white dresses and pants and jackets. After a long wait where she talked with three or four people in white who stared mostly at me, and finally a man in a black suit coming from somewhere to stare at me too, we went into a room with no walls, only windows all around where you could see back down the valley to the town, the muddy bending line of the river and the long black streaks of the freightcars standing at the station with engines blasting white smoke into the blue sky. Suddenly a man was in the room, the door with its small square window clicking shut behind him. He was tall and thin in grey coveralls and white hair combed flat to his head but standing in a tuft at the very back. His face looked very familiar and I stared at him a long time while he and mother just stood looking at each other, not saying anything, until I understood that it was exactly her face even to the corner droop of thin lips, except for the white hair and the eyes which looked off in different directions, except for a few minutes when they shifted around together and were looking down at me. Then the lips pulled up a little. My mother's hand had been on my shoulder, hard, all the while and she looked down at me and said this was my uncle Andrew and didn't we have a little present for him? I jumped to the table where she had set the parcel and gave it to him. His hand touched mine an instant, warm and softer than any woman's, but strange, as if it did not feel mine or ever felt anything. He bent forward, placed the black hat he held in his other hand on the table, took the parcel in both hands and slowly untied the string. We had dug them up only the morning before, in the oak and poplar grove in the pasture, and the crocuses stood half-opened like purple jets in the packed soil of the coffeetin wrapped in red paper. He finally sat down, still not saying anything though he was smiling, and mother sat opposite him in a chair and talked of the woods in spring and of little Adam whom we had left with a neighbor and how we had a wonderful train ride on a train like one of those over there across the river, talking on and on like I had never heard her while my uncle sat looking at the crocuses in his hands, never answering a word. Then suddenly, with a jerk all over him he placed the plant before him on the little table and stood up, standing very straight, his hat in his hand, eyes somewhere beyond the window, and opened his mouth and sang in a thin voice,

> "Shall we gather at the river,
> Where bright angel feet have trod?"

For an instant the tune faltered though the expression on his face did not change

> "... the beautiful ... beautiful ... river ..."

then it caught again, and held,

> "Gather with the saints at the river
> That flows by the throne of God."

He stood motionless, hat tight against the grey coveralls over his chest. I looked at mother. Her head was down; then he moved and placed his hat on the couch and sat down directly on it, still looking away out of the window. After a moment he stood up, picked up the crushed hat, reshaped it carefully and sat again, smiling a little at mother who slowly lifted her head and smiled back. When we were on the train that evening, just as I was falling asleep, I remembered and asked her where Uncle Andrew had learned the nice song about river angels. She said in church. But I had never heard it, and she said that that song was not sung in a Presbyterian church. True. Angel feet were of very little interest in our church, that I knew even before I was quite five when the praise of God in 'Old Hundredth' sung in the heavy voices had already ground into me the massive weight of the grasping glory that was his due for no other reason than that he had made us and made us to want mostly what he most swiftly might damn us for while in front his face led the singing, the face hunched together now in mild surprise at my speaking after he had spoken and there was, according to all that had ever happened in our family, nothing further to be mentioned: "She hasn't seen him in twelve years! She earned the money!" So he did not bother to answer; just turned to go out and as he did something went over me like a spasm and in a moment we were shouting both, I almost as tall as he leaning over the kitchen table, the younger children cowering in terror at the door and he bellowing at last would I take back what I said and receive the beating I deserved and I long past caring, having hurled all to the wind the instant I ventured the first words: "She hasn't seen him in twelve years" and then he had snatched the Bible down from the shelf above the table and holding it before him like a high and mighty weapon, intoning, his voice so hard I could not batter mine against it, beyond myself though I was, "If ye will not hear, and if ye will not lay it to heart, saith Jehovah the God of hosts, then will I send the curse upon you, yea, I have cursed you already: Cursed be he that dishonoreth his father. Cursed. Cursed." And he lifted the book, high, his terrible face like a rock, and mother sobbing behind him, "Abe, Adam, Abe." The truck thudded, sluing violently sideways under the feeble lights of the city. The driver cursed under his breath as we rolled down the grade under the railroad tracks. The station was left. After a time he braked squealingly for a red light and I rammed back the door-handle. "Hey, it's just a red light. Drop you further downtown, I ain't —" and then he saw the worn quarter, "Na, I ain't taking —" and I left it on the seat and dropped to the cold street. When I looked back from the curb he was staring after me, though the light had changed. The city squeaked and groaned, deafening even after midnight; an empty street-car rattled along the tracks that had jogged the truck and I went back down the street to where the station would be. Only here and there was there a man on the long, ill-lit street, but one of them angled over and bumped into me though I stepped nearly into the street to avoid him.

"Hey, buddy, gotta nickel for a cuppa coffee? Be a good guy, huh?"

I stared at him a moment before I understood the man was drunk. I couldn't say anything, even had I known what could be said to such a request after his ceaseless intoning of where drunkards spent eternity. I turned away from him, my bundle under my arm, hand in my pocket, and when I got the bill unwrapped from the coin I turned to him but he had slouched on, mumbling. He was weaving slightly under the canopy of a darkened movie house, his arms visible through his one, tattered, shirt perhaps already frozen in the winter night. I ran after him and he spun around with a curse when I touched him, a curse that melted immediately when he understood the feel of the Curly-nickel in his hand. "Chriss buddy thas good, chriss —". And I left him under the movie canopy and hurried away.

Even catching the first train, it was well after noon before I got to Brandon. The second, and last, flower shop had what I needed and by three o'clock the nurse led me into the long corridor. Though I had tried to remember from what little I had seen twelve years before, when I was in the dark little cell of his room with light prying in from the sun outside the high square window, it was some time before I could comprehend him lying as if cast in the narrow bed. Only after an immeasurable time did his chest stir in breathing. His face was impossibly emaciated, even worse than mother's, but the resemblance between them was fiercer than ever. The nurse had remained outside. I touched the bed, feeling for a hand, touch remembered since childhood and understood suddenly he was wrapped tight in a long white cocoon of impossibly-white cloth. I opened the package then and placed it on the table that stood far from the bed; where, if his eyes ever opened, they would see the purple flame of the crocuses in the gray room. Presently I went out. Several years on the day in the middle of February I mailed a postcard to her blank except for signature; it was not until the draft and the February of squad-training that I could face the sure knowledge I had refused till then: he inevitably saw each card first and would never give her the slightest hint they had been sent; the one last act of love and decency paid to her now so long dead recognized at last as nothing but the final twitch of excuse to scream back at his voice still pounding in my ear, cursing and forever disowning me and forbidding me the right to step on his land, to scream back at him every year again, "You slave driver! You God damn stingy slave driver! Working us all to death to buy your God damn stinking soul into heaven!"

Part Seven

17

KEKEKOSE, standing beside Joshua Bishop at the table facing the circle of seated Indians: under the sudden unusual three-day rain the rim ice had turned soft enough for rat-trapping around the lake, not only the southern marshes, and as Abe looked about he understood that for the first time since the conjuring last fall nearly everyone of the band was at Frozen Lake; his mouth opening to speak, his wrinkled face lit by an incredible happiness, when the first dog across the river ice near the few cabins beyond Frobisher howled. The old man's intent sagged, the life-long knowledge of that sound too rooted to throw aside without hesitation. Then his face bunched into a broader smile as he looked at Josh and said, "My people and my friends —" but he got no farther. For all around, as if hunkered between the winter homes barely rained bare of snow, answering dogs suddenly rolled chorus. Like willows under wind the people shivered; Abe stared about with them, but strangely not a dog was to be seen. As if signaled from across the channel, every dog in the settlement. At the moment when Kekekose, standing on his doorstep with Josh by the table and its kitchen-pail of water because the sudden massive press of people wanting to see and hear whatever was going to happen despite the temporarily hanging drizzle pushed them outside, opened his mouth to speak.

Seeing the people and hearing the howls crescendo while

Josh looked about bemused, Abe thought of Sally at her dedication. He needed no jog of incident to think of her now; she was always recognized or unrecognized in his mind, her looks and her words, or sometimes merely her presence like a cloud in her premonition of a doom hanging over Frozen Lake which despite what he reported kept her on Brink Island when he had gone back on Tuesday. Three days: a life-time to remember knocking and no answer and opening, calling, and the lurch of his heart in the obviously empty room. The hours driving fast as the dogs could move down the hard river — the rain first caught me near Half-Mile Rapids coming back I should have made her — thinking of her at the window perhaps once or twice, in a stray thought, waiting for him to bob up over the rock-ledge of island; where could she be? There was nowhere to go: everything in order, the upper bunk neatly made; he wheeled in the doorway. The snag-toothed rasp of the falls, stuck upright between the pines and snow of the giant ridge, flashed to blindness in the sunlight. He stepped out, eye regaining sight around the clearing. Only a squirrel chattered — her boot-tracks sure — he strode along the path tight around the unwindowed corner of the cabin and turning, eyes intent, he walked into her.

From wherever she had been she was coming back. The top of her head had nudged his face before either knew the other was there and even as they gasped their arms were about each other. Her face lifted and they were kissing, barely a face-touch first, then hard, fierce as if all their lives they had searched relentlessly for no more than this one unspoken, violent contact. They broke apart and stared at each other, chests heaving, and in the same instant they said, "Sally, I —" "Abe, I —" and stopped. At arms-length they laughed in the spring sunlight.

Presently she said, "You say first."

As his hesitation held him her smile widened. He said, "Except in a rush, I can't. I've never said it before. Only wished."

She was silent. His gloved hands clenched on her shoulders. "Sally, I love you."

"Abe, I love you." And they were kissing again.

"I left the dogs below at the landing, to surprise you. But you surprised me."

"I was feeding the squirrels. Anne and I made friends with one at Christmas that couldn't get to sleep — and I heard the door scrape." They sat hand in hand in the doorstep. The great banks of snow under the spruce and across the straggle of clearing variflashed mosaic under the brash sun. "Was the river good to travel?"

"Better closer here — it's been really warm around Frozen and it's a little slushy there. Some of the people have brought in rats, from the south. It even rained a bit, yesterday."

"Will the lake break-up soon?"

"It'll take a few weeks of steady sunshine at least, George says."

"It hasn't rained here at all. It wasn't even very warm, yesterday. I thought you were going to send George."

Their eyes met and they laughed, helplessly. After a moment she said, "When did you start to love me?"

His hand tightened in hers. "I don't know. I don't think I even dared thinking it — it probably sat in my head without me daring to look at it, I think. And then I found you upstairs there with Violet and I — I don't know — it was something I had never found before. I couldn't avoid it in my thoughts and I had to think about my childhood somehow and — but when I came and knocked and went in and you weren't here, I" he was looking into her beautiful calm eyes. "Sally, I've been alone all — since a kid and I've sometimes felt empty and useless, but that minute when I came out of here and walked around the corner — I've never felt so like nothing, so completely with nothing before. And then there you were."

He looked away, holding her, her arms as strong around him. "I've lived a long time. I think I couldn't dare hope."

She ruffled his somberness: "You haven't lived so *dreadfully* long —"

"Huh? You wouldn't dare guess."

"I would too. You're not forty yet."

"I knew it! I turned that corner long ago — last summer. See," his fist under her chin, "I'm old."

"I wasn't a year out!" She was laughing. "You're right,

you're as old as the eternal hills! And sadly, I'm a tender sprite of thirty-three!"

"Sure and you're a sprite well enough," in the lift of his emotions, his arms empty all the years of his manhood feeling at last the resilience of love within their circle, he was in the accent and rhythm of Caledonia long forgotten in some child-crevice of himself. "And who would have thought at all to find you in this unending bush, Sally-o," her eyes held a rogue's gleam and his voice hardened.

"Sure and you're a mere child. According to our Frozen friends you should be grandmama, several times at the least."

"Abe! What's happened?"

"At Frozen? A little of everything except drumming. Ha — or trading for me. All the south people just go like sheep to — but Bjornesen tried a bash on the week-end and only about half the usual men and no women at all showed up. They're getting the traps ready; if the weather stays everybody'll be out for rats around the lake and then we should —"

"Josh and Lena, have they —"

"They're tired out, and look completely happy. The people on the marshes go out early and come back late afternoon with their rats. By then Josh is usually talking at Kekekose's, or at one of the other houses so —"

"Whose?"

"Oh, James Sturgeon or Joe Loon when he gets back — it doesn't matter where anyway; the door's open and the others sort of drift by and listen a little. But mostly it's at Kekekose' house — he's really excited." Abe mused, remembering, "On Sunday afternoon I went over and he had one of Josh's Cree Bibles — he reads the syllabics very well, Josh says — and a worn-out child's scribbler and whenever Josh said a verse he'd look through the Bible and make a mark beside it and stick in a strip of paper. When it got too dark to see his whole Bible was sticking full of strips of paper. On Sunday they jammed to the door too, with Matilda lying on the bed."

"How is she — different?" Sally's narrow face shone with happiness.

"No. The women are sometimes there, skinning rats and Lena talks to them. In that cabin — I don't know — I thought

I could take just about any smell, but skinning rats all day — she takes anything, and for all they can understand —"

But Sally had not heard the last fading to doubt. "And Violet? What's she doing?"

"I don't know, I was only over once" — you couldn't dream girlie what nerve I have to screw up to face the few in the store leave alone walk over and smile at them in front of their own houses as if no Tuesday night ever — "Sunday afternoon she was with some women, listening."

Sally sat rapt, looking down the clearing. Her voice was low: "I'm so happy. It will come; I know certainly it will come. It all seemed so — slow. As if nothing anyone did or had done made the least difference to them. Violet asked about everything last winter, every possible thing except Christianity. As if it didn't even exist. The Christmas songs were just — just songs. Like 'Pop Goes the Weasel'!" She laughed in a little burst. "And now she's listening! Maybe I could take her out with me this summer — maybe find a good school —"

"Didn't you and Josh say the thing was help them live here, not drag them off and try making whites —"

"Yes, yes, of course, for most, but they will need leaders too, who can help them understand the white world they can't avoid even if they try. And you know — Indian women are drudges; if Violet had a chance to develop her mind —"

"Ha! Like Alex, that sku —"

"No, not like Alex! That was wrong, just shipping him out without a friend or anyone — to that school — I don't know how they run it but a lot of impressionable young Indians all in one place and all trying to become like whites is a terrible way to try and educate them — he lost the beliefs of his people and found nothing to replace them."

"Sure sure, but you can't excuse —"

"Abe, I'm not excusing him!"

"It sounded a little —" he half-grinned at her.

"To try and understand isn't excusing. He did something terrible but he felt insulted beyond endurance and pulled this way and that — there's love in it too," she saw his incredulous stare, "yes, I think they love each other. That innocent child—"

"Sally," he could not keep the reflection of his thoughts out of his tone, "she's beautiful but hardly innocent. All last summer — I told you about that, and the night of the conjuring she practically propositioned me."

She looked at him in mild wonder. "What difference does that make? She doesn't have to have my standard of morals, or yours."

With his right hand Abe wiped melting snow from the instep of his rubber. How did he always end seemingly defending what he expected her to defend; she somehow accepting what he also knew but never could, somehow, accept. He said slowly, "Well, selling yourself isn't exactly right to Ojibwas either."

"Of course, but sleeping with someone in the hope he'll marry you is."

"But she'd been doing that all summer and if she felt anything for Alex — you say love —"

"Abe, I'm not excusing her — just trying to think what she thought. She was confused about Alex and maybe she thought you would —" Sally shrugged, eyes frank and sober on his, "maybe help her out. I don't know. That it was a silly way to try she found out soon enough."

He said nothing for a moment, avoiding her glance and the recrimination of his own thoughts. He laughed a little, "Okay Miss Know-it-all! And she stopped with Alex because of incest taboo. But why wasn't this out in fishcamp already?"

"I don't know, Mr. Know-so-little! Maybe Alex just ran her off her feet, just back from school. And he had to prove his superiority somehow, so he persuaded her, headstrong as she is. The social pressure really hit her only after her father sent her home — humiliated."

"So last week Alex was going to force her, break everything so he could have her, even if it took serial rape. How in all the world can you use the word 'love' there?"

"I think in his way he loves her. He probably thought that if all the band, drunken, had her, the taboos wouldn't matter.

What did he care whether it ripped the last shreds out of the band?"

He finally found his tongue, "My god Sally, what are you saying about love!"

She was staring across the clearing to the falls where the icechunks glittered, blunted by the sunlight. Her voice had a kind of unbearable sadness now. "I am saying that human love, the best we can find in us, if worn down far enough will show something terrible."

Hands on her shoulders he pulled her around to face him. "Sally, listen. I've killed men in war and I've drunk myself into oblivion and I've paid women and used them. But I have never, not in the most blind drunkenness, violated one. I thought of it — once I dreamed of it coming out of a drunk, but even in unconsciousness I know I never could because there is nothing more —" he shook his head as if to clear his sight. "I left home at seventeen and I have never been able to say to anyone before what I can say to you. 'Sally, I love you.'" His hands clenched like vises on her shoulders. "I could never imagine — never to the last tortured inch of my life — how —"

"Oh Abe, Abe," she was in his arms, tight. "My darling, of course you couldn't. I love you. I couldn't imagine it either." He had no consciousness, only that they were holding each other. Then she pulled back, "I am just saying what the Bible says. When weighed in the final — God's — balances our very best, or what we think it is, is little more than scum."

He looked away, heaviness like bile in him. "I can't stand such a god," he said.

"Me either." His eyes flicked to hers. "He would be unendurable without his grace."

"What is that, 'grace'?"

"It's easy enough to recognize when you meet it, but maybe impossible to define —"

"Then why keep using a word you can't explain?"

She was silent so long his coldness at what seemed to him her quibbles almost broke through to his consciousness, then "It's like the verb 'to be', I think. Basically indefinable but you can't build a vocabulary without it. In a Christian's vocabulary God's 'grace' is the verb 'to be'." She paused, looking closely at him. "That help?"

"No."

She rubbed her nose in his beard. "If I didn't know what I was trying to say I wouldn't know what I'd said, either." She pulled away, laughing a little. "Peripherally it means God's favor to man, who's done everything not to deserve that; and included in it is the power to make a man pleasing in God's sight, holy as he is. It is the most vital essence in the world."

"Even beyond our love?"

"Of course. Our love would be impossible without it."

They said nothing for some time. There was no question in him that he loved her but what she said was as inexplicable as it had ever been, perhaps more so because it seemed to him now that, more than ever, this very inexplicableness in her was what she really was, and what drew their love — how can you love what you don't know and can't understand? —

"Abe, look at the sun! It's past noon and you coming all the way this morning with nothing to eat!"

He smiled at her. "That's true. Now that you mention it," he drummed his stomach reflectively. "I brought a few things — I'll get it —"

"Right!" She kissed him like a feather-touch and before he could catch her she vanished, her laugh floating.

Working together demanded an almost interminable time to prepare lunch. Abe tried to nibble a bit of the beaver-tail he had brought, now frying in the pan, and she shooed him away so he caught her off her feet and danced her around the room, she almost crying with laughter and trying to pry his head up from where he was nuzzling her neck with his beard while shouting, when she had breath between gasps, that he was tickling her to death. He set her down gently before the heater where the soup was boiling over and swore on bended knee he would hack the beard off on the spot but that he had left all his shaving things at Frozen Lake and the axe was too dull and the scissors would only make it bristly, that is, worse when he kissed her. But she wheeled to him, the handle of the still-boiling soup-pot in her hand and told him if he dared cut it off she would throw him out of the cabin and the soup after him and never talk to him again, so there! When they finally sat down across from each other at the table to eat what was left of the soup and the fresh bannock and beaver, they could only look at each other and laugh more.

"I've never laughed so much in my life as since I met you," he said, eating.

"Some people, especially certain — well, anyway, some people think I'm giddy. Especially about things far too serious to be laughed at. But I can't help it, much. When I'm happy I laugh, that's all."

"That's one of the first things I liked about you. You laughed, even about things you're serious about."

"But you laugh easily too."

"With you. But I really haven't practiced much. We didn't laugh much when I was growing up. And not at all Sundays."

"Oh Abe," the happiness on her face clouded. "That's cruel."

"Yes," he said.

They ate silently for a moment, then she said, "You ran away from home?"

He grinned a little, studying a strip of browned beaver-meat. "In a kind of way, I guess. When I was old enough to have an excuse to finally tell him how I hated him."

"Why did you hate your father?"

"I haven't thought of him as — if you can wipe fatherhood out with a curse verbatim from the Bible, he did. Very well. I once looked all the references to 'curse' up — public library concordance and a Gideon Bible worked fine. He used the best. He knew his Bible!"

"Why — why did he curse you?"

At her stricken look he felt the old emotion quicken in him. But he could tell her now, straight, as he knew now it had always really been.

"It's an old story. He was a lay minister in the Presbyterian church and he had his god all figured out, a god of success and law and absolute election and absolute damnation. If you were a success on earth — made money — that proved you were the most highly elected of all to stand up with a ramrod back before the judgment throne and say, 'Here I am, your honor, with the wife and children which you entrusted me to break in fear and trembling before you. I have done so.' And then God would lean over and say, 'Well done, good and faithful slave driver. Take your rightful place beside me and help me judge them.' He never said that, but there came a time when I knew that made him move. And he was using us, mother, my brother, my two small sisters, me — everyone of us to prove to himself he was of the elect, redeemed from this hellish earth. So I told him, when I understood; when I got the nerve."

"And they were all in the Old Testament, weren't they?"
"What?"
"The curses you found."
"Oh, sure, sure, with a whole list in one book about what will happen if you make a molten image or lie with certain people or dishonor your father or mother — you know, he gave himself away there because he never mentioned mother at all — just said, 'Cursed be he who dishonors his father' — as if mother didn't count. She never did, to him."

She said slowly, "Have you —"
"Gone back? No, I was — effectively cursed. I don't know where any of them are. Or even if they're alive."
"Oh Abe." She looked down at her soup bowl and the tone of her voice twisted in him. "Your mother —"
"I sent her a card a few times, but he always went to the mail; she never got it. I heard in Winnipeg last summer she died just after the war."
"But surely you must have heard — sooner — from —"
"I moved a lot, but sometimes when I couldn't help it — but never that. And I stopped them, if I could, so maybe — maybe I could of heard sooner."
"You're as hard, as implacable as he."
His eyes wide to her, of whom he would never see enough, for a time she did not register visually. The gathering comprehension — is it horror? — on her face pushed him into himself and finally he could say what he might have known himself but what he could never, until now, have grasped — my god what have I ever thought of myself! — in total perspective dimension, "Yeah. You're right. No way around it.

318

He cursed me to be his son before I was born." Her beloved face with its foil of sand-tinted hair merged into focus. "I'm a middle-aged man and solid in my pattern. His curses never cut me free; they just shaped me." Like a fault in the strata of his thought the laughter they had shaped between them, in their little time together thrust up in him. "If I'd laughed as a kid, laughed ever, at myself, ever —" He saw her then as a woman in love and he slid back to his bedrock, no longer daring to think; deliberate in negation against her — damn him to hell eternally! — obvious pain. "Nothing like this would work with me. You'd wear yourself to nothing against me in half a year. It would never work."

"That's not what I meant —"

"I know, but it's clearer to me than you. You had the first insight, but I can think about those seventeen years now. And my own twenty-three or four. My mother was just a marionette opening her mouth to sing when he felt like twiddling his —"

"Abe! Stop it!"

The sunlight flashed at him as he turned his tableknife against the beam on the cloth. "I'm sorry."

"Don't you see that that's the difference," she said fiercely, "the difference that matters more than anything? That you know it, and he didn't? That he, as long as he needed it, which was probably all his life before perhaps God in mercy gave him a long sick-bed or something where he couldn't do anything for himself, that he had only his own goodness and rightness to hold him? But that's paganism, not Christianity."

"So?" he asked, but she did not catch his tone, continuing, "To follow Christ means to hope, *believe* always that his grace, not your own merit, will succeed despite what you think you are, despite your best. Certainly never because of it."

"So?" he said again, and her look questioned him. "I'm not even, as you say, a 'pagan.'"

"Thank God for that," she was smiling faintly. "So?"

"So you will marry me?"

Her glance did not flinch nor did she hesitate: "I can't say."

"What?"

"I can't say, Abe. I believe a marriage between someone who follows Christ and someone who doesn't isn't a marriage."

His look must have told her there was need to explain; he knew as precisely as if a diagram had been drawn that if they married there would be a core of themselves which would remain separate and untouchable to each. Who could call that marriage — ahh who? — numbed he could not keep the pain out of his voice, "You don't seem very concerned about it."

She reached across the small table for his hand. "I'm not. The primary motion of faith, like calisthenics in exercise, is that you trust God in what happens to you one day to the next. I came to Frozen Lake as a teacher; you came as a trader. We both did our jobs and in doing them we understand we love each other. That's plenty for now, to trust him for the rest."

Seeing the calmness of her trust that seemed to illumine her face as in a flame, such happiness for her welled in him that he forgot his own longing. He said, "These four days here, have they been good to you?"

Standing tense now behind the seated band of Frozen Lake Ojibwa, the dog howls rising to bedlam as Josh, after speaking quickly to Kekekose beside him, looked about with clearly growing apprehension and the Indians shifted and stared over their shoulders beyond the shacks and channel and into the bush, a thin child's whimper rising here and there as the howls dropped momentarily only to heave up more wildly, he remembered her happiness like a slash through him. It had been a happiness locked away from him, impossible to share. And though she had shown, and even said in so many words, that part of the joy of her aloneness at Brink Island was her sure knowledge that she loved him, this joy, this love, was inextricably tangled he could not see how with her love for the god in Jesus Christ she had left Frozen Lake to pray to and worship alone in silence; whom she, while she insisted she knew him as personally as any visible human, she yet had to search for, apart, seeking not in bush or imagination but somewhere in a mystery of reading the Bible to find him

— find a spirit? — while at the same time pray to him whose will she insisted she knew and whose acts she could not and did not want to change, that he heal the people at Frozen Lake and give Josh and Lena the wisdom to show them the way to himself. There was in this tangle no wraith of reason Abe could clutch to attempt anchor. And yet, as contradictory as everything else, now before him at the table and all around facing it was a tiny beginning of what she had longed for in her foreboding of doom in a happiness so confident of its certain coming that she had no more repressed than wanted to hide it. The tangle was impossible for Abe; he could listen to her explain how she had felt God speak to her — how do you feel speech? — watch the fire of her happiness burn brighter in her eyes, knowing that this was the core where they could never touch until somehow he shared with her this all-consuming, transfiguring faith. He understood with a kind of dread for himself that their love, whatever there was of it now — is it possible there be more? — was as nothing to what might be if they could somehow share this divinity, this terrifyingly perverse heavenly lover she now sought and who found her alone. The very pictures this jerked alive in his mind were too strangely violating to confront — like plunging into some great river of the divine now springing in burning through her — the contradictions of this all were too much; he could not endure his thoughts. And at that moment Joshua Bishop's white-bandaged hand — yeah and who had pulled the trigger — flickered before his eyes and the voice rang above howling bedlam,

"Inkatis-seyan! Inkatis-seyan!" He was using a word Abe had never heard him address to the Indians before: a word used by a man to refer to his household, the family for which he cared, "Inkatis-seyan, do not let howling dogs disturb you. That is only the last resort of evil. I will pray; pray with me, to the great God, who can." His voice, high and thin like all outdoor orators, carried clearly over the howling. He spoke his words so deliberately that even the crescendoes around them, when it seemed the very fiends danced in their heads, had to abate between them and when he lifted his hands in prayer they could hear his voice, calm and strong, everywhere over the damp clearing: "O great God, our Father, we bless your name, and the name of your son, our redeemer, Jesus Christ. Let it be known, today, that you, oh Lord, are God of heaven and earth, and we your children. Hear our prayer, as you have always heard when we cried to you believing." As Abe listened to the prayer that did not even request anything specific, he realized the clamour was dying; as Josh said the last word there was no sound whatever except wind sighing like a voice among the spruce beyond a near cabin. It was too awesome to believe. He swung his head, staring, and saw a great white dog lope into the grey underbrush, tongue lolling as after a hard run. That was all; no other dog was visible as there had not been since the fantastic assault began, and abruptly, seeing the people staring about he had a sense of Sally sitting at the table with her Bible open before her and looking out over the clearing and the ice-bound falls, south towards Frozen Lake. She sat that way sometimes for hours she said, sometimes reading, sometimes thinking, sometimes voicing prayers, but always trusting for a breakthrough. Perhaps this was what she meant with that, for Josh was saying ". . . and when God is working we can expect the Evil One will work too. It has been that way always. When Jesus Christ himself was on earth the powers of evil tested him, tried to ruin his work. But believing prayer, that breaks them. Always." He was smiling at them in their quiet. The very children had calmed and nestled against their mothers; the few older men who sat in front looked up expectantly. They wanted to listen, the almost-terror of the dogs howling now past and forgotten, and Kekekose could begin again:

"My people, for as long as most of you can remember, even as long as I can remember, almost, I have been a man who could speak with the spirits. When I was young I had a great dream, and I have had many since. I had them when I was weak from fasting, almost dead, and the spirits that come to me took pity on me and said they would help me. And in the conjuring tent they did. You have seen what they did. What was done in the conjuring tent was done by the spirits, not me. And what was done under the beat of the drum was done by them also, not me. I called to them and sometimes they came. And always we, all of us, like our fathers for generations before us, dreamed for pimadaziwin, the Good Life, here on earth, and always we hoped, expected that the spirits would give it to us.

"But you have seen, and I also, how evil and sickness and violence spread among us. And though the spirits — what they are, no man can say; I only know that sometimes we knew they were there — though the spirits sometimes helped, sometimes they also destroyed. And, most often, they were not to be found at all. And against the greatest evil of all to come to us here, they were no help. Rather it seems that when a man, or even a woman, falls into the storm of this, the greatest evil we have seen here, the soul is taken from him and the very spirits that rage and struggle in the conjuror's tent and sometimes stalk over the land to devour the people, the windigo, I mean, that this very — thing — rages inside the people and they destroy themselves and want only to destroy others, friends, brothers, the ones they love most, with them. And against this, whenever spirits came at long last and were benevolent, there was nothing to be done. Only wait until it destroyed us, all.

"In this helplessness, we saw two people who had lived with us for four seasons. They lived like us, and we were welcome in their house. Though they had the power whitemen always have, and soon the government itself gave them its power, they never used it except for good, in fairness to everyone. They did not speak against what we believed. When we wanted to listen, they would tell us of another way. And when we would not listen, which was usually, they spoke to who would, sometimes only the children. But far more than speaking, they did. Good things. Showing us how to build better houses, grow gardens, cut logs and saw them, and all the other things you know they have done. Soon there was a government school here all the year, where before we had only had a few classes in the summer. And the teacher, too, was like them: kind without concern for herself. When people live with us for four seasons and only wish to do good for others, no one can say, 'It means nothing.' So we called him the Good News Man because he talked about it sometimes, when we would listen, though we did not understand what the good news was. Only we knew that he was good."

No stirring in the crowd; they loved oratory, especially when it explained what they themselves had experienced. A softening of the overcast, almost a hint of sunlight in the warm water-heavy air, drew their motley sharply. It had rained heavily, almost without let-up except for this near-drizzle, at Frozen Lake since he met the rain driving in so hard at Half-mile Rapids on Tuesday — it's impossible that it's only three days! — he should have gone for her today; tomorrow it might pour worse. The wind was stiff and the piled clouds moved like blankets from the southwest. But he had promised her Saturday, not Friday, and the ice-surface on the channel here was now suddenly so rotten with the warmth and rain — the poor devils won't get any rats if this keeps up and neither will I to nudge that terrible balance — that it was as impossible to negotiate that with the team as the rain-sodden snow of the landtrail — god damn this rain where there hasn't been one in ten springs to choose this! — and if the ice moved over the first rapids he could at least get there by canoe and save her those six miles of trail-wallowing. But if he had ever faintly suspected that the spring would hit like this, suspected that if she stayed another day she would have to hike out with that sometimes hip-deep snow impossible in places even for snowshoes, he would have persuaded her that surely four, almost five days were enough and that perhaps a few 'practical' things at Frozen needed her doing. She had come into his arms, his smile inviting her, and kissed him, then pulled back: her look telling him without words she must remain for a little at 'practical prayer.' And where her self was involved with his, it was good, better, for now that they stay alone too. And this he understood, at the time; in a part of him he did not want her to be where he would have to go and see her if he but physically could; somehow she was somewhere ahead and he could not dream to ask her retreat: it was he must move down a path he could not . . . Kekekose was saying in Ojibwa:

". . . we must find a path, perhaps a new one, I told him, and he could make the way clear by breaking the evil that held us, by forcing the things that had to be forced, because he had the power, for the government listened to him. And understanding us and the evil and our helplessness so well and loving as he had shown now for years, he said nothing would be changed if people *had* to; if they must act differently to keep getting their rations, their allowances, or to keep out of jail, or get part of the logging paper. We had to *want* to change, not be forced to. For force always hardened some, and broke some, and the love of the great Manido was for all, even the most evil, and the great God could not wish that any be lost. So he would not force us; only did his work as always, and when the evening came he kept us from the killing by stepping among us to take the first blow. And even in drunkenness, who of us was not shamed? Who of us is not ready to listen" — where does he get the 'we' when he never drank nor raised his hand? — "and I most perhaps because I had talked to him before, alone, and knew what strange things were necessary. And when he now talks of the great God's love living among men, that the evil which comes to us from spirits and powers outside is not nearly as powerful as the evil that lives in us, which we *want* to do, when he told me this before you all, then I saw a light far away, as when you stumble long on a black trail and after you have already forgotten to hope but are walking only because you have no will even to stop, and then the light of a campfire flares up and you stumble on and find it is your brother who has been long looking for you. I believe now, not in spirits which used to come to me, but in Jesus Christ, the son of the great God, who lived on earth and who gives us power to leave evil and to love. Like the Good News Man."

Where had the old man found the strength to change, to accept what most of his life he had never heard? Was this the power that could break not only Bjornesen, as once they talked the first day of fur-trading, but all the evil at Frozen? He had hated the churchmen who manipulated the naive minds of the Eskimos into super-religious fanaticism, but here he could not find basis for that apprehension; rather only confusion. For if only one or two of them followed Josh, what difference would it make to the band? Or what good Frobisher? He shook his head angrily at that — but if it gives a couple the guts to stand up in front of everybody —

Another man was speaking: James Sturgeon. Stuttering a little more than usual in shyness at speaking of himself, but speaking doggedly, ". . . especially after my brother died" — no Indian had ever called that anything but a killing! — Abe twisted, looking about; Bjornesen was nowhere to be seen, but a group of younger men dawdled past, cap-peaks reverted in the Ojibwa sign of the hunt, either game or girls, throwing side-glances at the speaker but strangely keeping their laughter to themselves. Just beyond them he saw Violet and Lucy and Anne in a huddle of school-girls — oh for Sally there — faces intent on James ". . . my son told me what they talked about and I learned some of the verses and said them over on the trapline. I — sometimes — wanted to ask the Good News Man about some things I read, but I was — ashamed — to say something, even when he read out of the Book. So this week I was happy to hear him, before you all. And last day he talked about being changed, and I asked him. He said it happened different to different people but for him it had been seeing how he could do nothing good and yet he wanted to, and that he had stopped trying to do it himself and had asked the Giin Jesus to live in him, and then he felt happy as he had never felt before. When he talked like that, I was happy. For it happened to me like that too, but I did not know that that was what 'change' was till he told me. Then I knew it had happened to me."

In his wonder Abe thought nothing: simply stared with them all. Then Josh was speaking with an oratory that was almost conversational.

"The good news we have tried to live here and which you hear is this: that the great God is love and that he gave himself to die for the evil of men. This gospel, this good news you have not believed, though you have heard of the Christian god and some of you were even baptized as little children. Baptism is nothing if the person himself does not know what it means; so baptism to a child means nothing. What does mean something for us, now, is that we know that the great God made us, that he is not far beyond and uninterested in us but that he is near, that he loves everyone and wishes to prepare us for the perfect life both here but far more in the future, in heaven, in the Land of Souls, as you have heard in your own teaching. But you must be clear of one thing. You believe that the great God has no interest in you; only lesser spirits take pity on man. It was not the great God you worship, but lesser things, whatever they were, good or evil. And the greatest evil a person can do is not killing or stealing, bad as they are, but believing and worshipping things, even spirits, and not the one, great, God. So, as Kekekose said, we all, I at one time and you now, have fallen into helplessness. Perhaps you say: we do not know what to do; the ways of our people no longer seem to help us; wherever one looks someone is breaking them. We have nothing left to believe. Then, when we are helpless and do not know of ourselves what we should do, then the great God says to us these quiet warm words, spoken by his son Jesus: 'Come to me, everyone that is tired and bent over. I have comfort for you; I have rest.'

"And when we say in our hearts, 'Yes, Lord Jesus, I am sick of sin and pain. Come into my heart and clean me and give me rest from evil, he truly comes. For the great God is one God. He has made the earth and us all and he has at one time shown himself to men as Jesus Christ and he lives in every person who believes, who loves him."

It was either too hopelessly simple or too hopelessly profound to make sense; Abe could not decide which. In one way it sounded, wherever he had heard it, as it always had; in another it could not have sounded more different: as if one more step would provide the angle that shifted the puzzle into a gigantic pattern of meaning. Or maybe a thousand steps.

Josh's voice: ". . . publicly show their sadness for sin, and their belief, by the ceremony shown us in the Bible. Two have spoken; two will speak when I ask them the question. Our Lord long ago was baptized in a river, but here is ice. The biblical way is to believe, confess, and be baptised. So this water will do. Would all who wish to be baptised come forward."

Kekekose; James Sturgeon; there was a craning and a woman arose: Abe recognized the widow Sturgeon. Then through the cabin door Albert and William Crane came carrying their mother, paralysed in her frame hammock. There was no sound as they placed Matilda beside the table — William helping the drunken sot! — Josh was reading slowly from the Bible, holding his cap over it as the drizzle seemed abruptly to begin again out of the spongy sky:

". . . John saw Jesus coming towards him and said, 'Look! There is the Lamb of God who takes away the sin of the world! This is the man I meant when I said, 'A man comes after me who is always in front of me, for he existed before I was born!' John gave this testimony, 'I have seen' the Spirit come down like a dove from heaven and rest upon him . . . and I declare *publicly* before you all that He is the Son of God!'" Josh put down the book; Kekekose knelt, head high, facing the people. The sky was dark over them and Josh glanced up momentarily as he placed his bandaged hand on the old man's shoulder. "Kekekose. Do you believe with your whole heart that Jesus Christ is the Son of God and that he has forgiven your sins?"

"Yes!"

"Then I baptize you, in the name of the Father, the Son, and the Holy Spirit. Amen." The left hand lifted dripping from the bucket and turned over on the grey-streaked hair. Down the seamed forehead and cheeks the water mingled with the beads of rain already glistening there.

And the other three followed, their voices as loud and clear; even Matilda, inert on her blankets. Then Josh had prayed, hands over them, and one by one helped them to their feet. He was lifting his face to the silent band when from far away a high cry carried through the air. Someone was standing near the river, shouting, "The ice! The ice!" Twisting about, they all heard, as they had not caught up in what was happening before them: the groaning of the ice.

The wind, Abe suddenly realized, was blowing hard over the long southward arm of Frozen Lake; among the cabins here it was difficult to judge, but the tree-tops beyond leaned down — is the ice really that rotten the wind can force it open? — and the band scattered, baptism forgotten at the new spectacle, the children charging down the slope to the great mass of the river groaning like a giant beast but obviously, against the bent trees of the further shore, moving.

— how far will it move? — he stood motionless on the slope, the swift gathering of shapes below not registering — how far — George's red jacket moved past and he wheeled, shouting, "George!" The handyman stopped, lifting his head. "Is that ice going out? Is it that rotten?"

The other's puzzled shake of head trimmed the raindrops in shower from his cap-rim, "I dunno — I haven't seen this before here, so quick, and no rats even caught except in the south —"

"Will it go all the way to Brink?"

"The ice? Nah, it always piles down the first long rapids and rots."

He stared at the river; there was something in the writhing gelid movement he did not like moving downstream toward her though it might be only six miles. "Maybe I should go; there's still some daylight left to get —"

"To Brink Island? Not tonight, on that river, it'd be fine further down but —"

"What if it goes?"

"It wasn't warm there Tuesday, was it?"

"No, but with this rain — it may be raining there long and who knows —"

"Frozen ice never gets that far. And the island's high, never been touched." George looked at the channel, then up into the overcast. "It's probably raining there; maybe tomorrow we can take the canoe to the — a ways anyway, and hike in. But we aren't getting rats, that's sure. I better get the canoes higher."

He watched the handyman stride away; frustration churned acid in his stomach. And then he became aware of Bjornesen standing beside him, long face in the usual slighting grin. The trader said easily, "Quite a little show, that. Maybe Josh can cash in on four years."

Still watching ice, Abe said hard, "He's finished you anyway."

"Oh," the trader looked at him a moment and laughed loudly. It grated Abe like a raw nerve scraping.

"Good you found your teeth so you can laugh again."

When the Icelander spoke at last there was the barest edge of scoffing left in his voice: "Oh, I know you wouldn't hit harder than necessary." He snorted a little. "And don't tell me our little friend didn't mess up your plan that evening, and you just itching to pull it. Oh, you're a real Frobisher trouble shooter!" His big laugh boomed.

Abe felt something spurt in him and he wheeled, "Listen, Bjornesen, you've been around too long to make the mistake of thinking only you can be pushed far enough to —" he gagged then, the word formed on his lips.

"Go ahead. Say it." Bjornesen's voice was curiously flat, and through the haze of his own self-discovery Abe understood that for the first time in their sketchy acquaintance the older man was speaking without double meaning. But the deeper understanding was of himself: success was as essential to him as it had ever been to — to my father — He had not faced that before; until now when he had actually admitted to himself and Bjornesen what he had been willing to do to succeed; admitted it beyond the veiling delusion of all the other reasons he had always, so carefully, enumerated. The older man was staring back at him and for a moment there was no sound save the shouting of the children at the shore and somewhere Amos cursing, and the crashing of the ice.

"Sure, Sig," he said at last — but god almighty I can't just back down quit give up! — "I can't say it. Because we both know what I — wanted, and we both know if it had happened it would have been worse — it's bad enough as it is." He paused and an idea began shaping itself. "Look, he's doing his job and it makes our throat-cutting look less than cheap." The other's growing amazement helped him push on. "Here's a deal. Both Frobisher and Bjornesen Trading get out."

"What?" the trader's tone was incredulous, as his face. "You mean he'd trade —"

"You know him better than that. No. Sell out to the

Indians — let them try a co-op or something. George knows as much about supplies as I — he's been doing them all winter — and if we got Violet out of here Alex might be good for something —"

Sarcasm overrode Bjornesen's astonishment. "If I'm finished, why bargain?"

Abe stared past him, too uncertain to even find anger in himself that his clutching for a face-saver was so transparent; uncertain of everything. Finally lost. The words arranged themselves as he spoke. "Maybe I'm just sick of us bloodsucking these poor buggers dry for a few lousy bucks. Maybe that's why. Neither of us'd be here if they weren't worth skinning. Only him. He's here because they're human beings."

They looked at one another steadily for a moment, without emotion, then Abe walked by down the slope. It was raining harder. Most of the grown-ups were gone, either to the cabins or to straggle along the shore, hoping against forlorn hope to fish some stray traps away from the moving ice. A pack of boys came racing along the trail by the river, stopped, and then the leader charged up the slope towards him, the others squitching after.

"Mr. Ross! Mr. Ross!" It was Eli Crane swinging a muskrat in a trap, "I got it out myself. All myself. Mine." The crowd panted up, and Eli swung the drowned rat again.

"Where?"

"Around the point. I set there and got it just out when the ice moved."

"You got wet — say, you could of —"

"Nah — just my legs. He was there, all the time. I set it myself, last night. In the — iya wayte washush — how you say —"

"Rat push-up."

"Yah." He swung it around. "Trade for candy?" His dark face gleamed up in the circle of rain-glistening faces.

"Sure" — cats Frobisher may get one rat after all! — "bring it when it's stretched and dry."

With a whoop they were gone; for a bare instant he had almost laughed; then he was by the channel looking at the ice. George had pulled his canoe high on the bank, above the ice-chunks; they were large enough but he would have to sprint, pushing, leaning on the canoe — better move further down where it's a bit narrower — he straightened and stared into the rain scudding hard before the wind that jammed the ice up tight from the lake. An old verse bobbed into his memory:

> *O western wind, why wilt thou blow,*
> *The great rain down can rain?*
> *Christ, that my love were in my arms*
> *And I in my bed again.*

The boys had laughed at that more than once on a blustery night without leave in England. Or the night trenches in Holland. But now, as he lifted the canoe to his shoulders and heard the rain drum, he would more nearly have called it a prayer.

18

*I*F there was a God, it was his act.
In the old legal sense, the way an insurance policy would hold at arm's length a happening without human agency, an accident, somewhere in the abyss of no-precedent a beginning of dominos toppling that went on and on and on and done, and you looked back and could easily see how but for a razor-edge of chance nothing to think twice about would have happened. Just accident . . .

But with her it would be an act of God; there was no loophole of 'chance' to squirm through in her light. No; as deliberate and premeditated as any battleplan and even if you tried to twist and say the laws of nature are what they are, whose after all, she would insist, was the finger that set the process going: the hard winter that held on like a friend and the sudden ferocious day-and-night-long pouring of water just when unprecedented muggy warmth and wind heaved the ice to moving? He had to sit, apprehension shading with slow time to desperation, knowing Josh and Lena as desperate across the channel and the water falling from the sky like logs and the edge of river with ice grinding higher and higher and finally over the wharfs and rocks to the very base of the shoretrees till he wondered whether the universe had turned to water and they were all to strangle in it. Rain. All Friday night and Saturday and Saturday night and Sunday morning when the river was not yet unclogged enough to float and he told George he was going to at least try hiking to the Brink, he didn't give a damn what, the assistant staring at him from under his streaming hood as if he were a maniac. And he slogged over the rocks and muskeg for three miles, the trail indistinguishable with the once low trickles of stream between rock-ridges now like bulging rivers he had to wade already drenched above his hip waders until he reached the first main tributary of the Frozen, choked with ice gnawing its teeth under the rain that blinded him when he raised his head. So he pushed right through the brush where there wasn't even a trail, the tree-caught water falling on him unnoticed in the downpour, trying to get higher where the stream might narrow enough to cross and at last despairing of finding that he tried without the buoy of canoe to sprint over the broken cakes but the first one vanished as his boot struck it and he sank like a rock in his massive rubber clothes, though close enough in shore to gain his feet an instant and grab a branch after he butted his head up between the ice-cakes. He would not have reached Frozen Lake after that, the last of his strength being drained when he staggered back to the trail in a final deliberate clench of his mind to keep moving, had George not followed him and been standing, already hopeless, before the flood of the tributary and half-dragged, half carried him the three miles back to Frobisher. All afternoon and evening he sat wrapped in blankets, gulping whiskey to drive the cold out of him; on Monday morning he found himself holding the empty bottle and the record-player smashed against the wall; but he could stand straight and stare out the window at the still driving rain.

He was lying now on his bed upstairs. The sunlight beat in from the fresh blue sky. If he remained perfectly motionless, at the barest edge of the black tunnel through which he seemed to have been dragged, he could perhaps avoid the end; but only by remembering the beginning. The bed felt like rocks under him. He rolled aside from the brightness, hate arsenic in his gut. Sunshine. What the hell difference did it make now, sunshine and birds singing and the river probably wide and falling fast and a few days, who knew or cared how long, after the marks of it almost gone except here and there the gouged earth and a few ice-cakes melting among the spruce or high in the hanging debris. All so fast now and irrevocable and in a few days all erased, brushed away with one lazy swipe yet when you wanted time to move it hung on, a bloodsucking leech, unbudgable, and endless acres of rain falling in sheets for every minute the second hand tugged itself around the watch-face. Only rain for Saturday and Saturday night and Sunday and all night and unrelenting in the morning, though by then he could move again to go out and saw the channel cleared of the heaviest ice; even before he got his canoe down he heard Josh's coming and they met on the rock-edge above the submerged dock, staring at each other through the rain, not saying anything. James Sturgeon had come over with Josh, and he took George in the Frobisher canoe and they partly paddled, partly pushed by kicker through the thickening icepans six miles down the river until the pack at the first rapids stopped them completely. They maneuvered through to shore and tried to reach the portage trail, but an inundated swamp stopped them, already soaked despite their panchos and wading boots. He and George hacked through to the top of a ridge and stared at the great bulge of the river rammed tight with ice to where sight vanished in the rain. George flicked a glance at him from under his hood.

"Just rain — I dunno —" was all he said.

The wind, the by-now terrifying Master of the South Wind was flying again when they got back to the others and the canoes. The river was running against them in whitecaps. One man had to sit in the bow and try warding off the ice driving at them out of the wash of the waves. They hugged the shore for its poor shelter, but once where the wind blasted around a point Josh with his one unbandaged hand lost control of the kicker for a moment and an ice-cake crashed and sliced through the aluminum canoe. They would have surely drowned had not James in the bow, kneeling in pouring water, wrenched the canoe against shore and clung to a tree-limb until he and George arrived. So they lost most of the equipment in that canoe, though they pulled the cut shell above any possible reach of water and struggled back to Frozen in the other. And when finally they gained Frobisher there was nothing to be done but lie hacking, drying out again, listening to the storm on the roof.

The roar on the roof was gone; in the darkness he rapped his head with the heel of his hand: still the gentle patter, and for a moment he thought he was dreaming of boyhood and lying in the house-loft hearing the spring rain murmur through the night, and he made the usual wrench to blot out this betrayal of unconsciousness when he gasped he *was* awake and in a Frobisher bedroom. He looked at his watch; two forty-seven. He was up, dressed, and running through what was now merely shower over the squitchy ground to the warehouse and was again counting off the equipment he had mulled over so long as essential. By three thirty-five lightness showed a crack in the east; the rain would be ended by morning, probably. George came to the door at his knock, rubbing sleep from his eyes as his other arm pulled up the pancho and in a few moments more they were over the channel at the Bishop landing as the strip of morning and no rainclouds widened. Josh came out of the house to meet them, and behind him emerged the giant shape of Bjornesen. Before Josh could say a word the trader said, "We'll take my twenty footer." Something in his silence in the morning darkness stirred the old man to quick rawness: "Look Ross, you'll need a extra —"

He was cursing him; cursing as he knew later he had only been capable once before in his life, at the absolute unadulterated intransigent gall-burning stupidity, a convulsion tearing away his soul to its very roots "— and but for you you jesus h —"

"— Abe!" Josh's face an inch from him bored through to consciousness. "We need that big canoe, and his know-how!"

He jerked away, knowing it mercilessly true, his mind leaping away. "God who cares if the devil comes, let's move!"

Suddenly it was childishly simple: sit in the bow and watch the muddy water, stippled by the slowly decreasing rain, glide by. How could it only yesterday have been so difficult? The first long rapids, where the ice should have been, were so high in water they ran them with full canoes, not even looking at the shore-trail. And there was only a scattering of ice riding easy in the long wide passage below. He did not look back at George; there were other rapids and bays still. Ponderously the day brightened; when they got above Half-mile Rapids the sun behind the thin overcast almost poised on the horizon, the long shadow of its dawning reaching across the ice-free river almost to the tip of spruce at the portage. They had to negotiate debris and heavy logs to get to the eddy of the portage, now high above the usual landing. He dragged the canoe the last few yards and clambered part-way up the trail. When he came back, sliding, Bjornesen said, "One carry."

"Yeah!" he grunted. "Two men on that canoe, I'll take mine — and two motors?"

"Com'mon, I'll show you a carry! Get those motors side by side here!" Bjornesen lashed them together wrapped in raincoats and the deflated dinghy, set his tumpline over his head and they hung the motors, almost too awkwardly heavy for two to lift, in the line on his back. Josh with a pack and one gas can led up the trail and Bjornesen followed, stooped almost double, the two propellers spinning a little when they dragged, a huge bumpy shape like a mechanical beast plowing through the mire. The old man negotiated the steep descent better than he with only a pack and the fourteen-foot canoe on his shoulders. He did not trust himself to balance; he waited till Bjornesen reached the bottom, using every tuft and root for foothold in what during the rain must have been a water-chute, and then he schussed down the canoe in the mud, guiding from the rear, trying to keep the rocks scraping only along its thin steel spine. George and James waited, then carried down the other to join them at the foot in the sinking mud of flooding trail; after packing they paddled the rest of the trail opening to what had once been the broad turning eddy, the water now high over its flat rock. No more than half an hour and they were again on the open river.

Did he think as the motors roared down the turgid river? He didn't know; he kept his eyes on the next bend. Several shorter rapids could be run with paddles; on others they did not even waste time to unload: Josh took the larger motor to his shoulders and the smaller one was put in the canoe and, with a man on each end, they staggered around what were now roaring waterfalls, not feeling backstrain and exhaustion. The ice was gone; only stray pieces caught among the trees, and he did not even bother to think of what that meant as they moved inevitably nearer the high falls above the island, not quite daring, he realized now such an eternity later, the dullish daylight opening as they roared on without opposition so that there was nothing to do but evade the worst possible thought of what might have happened, hoping almost that something would happen that would require mind and action though not wanting that either because that would slow them down reaching what in some ways he did not dare to want to reach and yet which he could not bear not finding out. The larger canoe never more than fifty yards behind them, they approached the last bend before the falls a mile beyond, the waterline now not much higher than he tried to remember of last summer but he could not be sure because he had not looked so sharply here and setting his mind only on picking out the portage trail because then he would know exactly how high it was: if he could see the trail, for the ice could be in that last great channel before the falls. But as they approached the last wide turn and the western shore opposite pulled itself inevitably from behind the shoulder of the firred rock to the roar of their motors — if they had been silent they would have heard the falls surely — he knew that even if the ice was there, somehow piled high in some incredible arch based against the rocks through which the river broke, there was not enough space in that last mile to matter and thinking this he saw, staring from low in the canoe, that there was no ice at all in the last long stretch. Over the slate water he could just see where the vacant river vanished and in the grey unraining overcast the far ridges beyond the Brink Valley.

George had already begun the usual turn to cross the river right angles at the bend, but he twisted, yelling, "No — no — straight to the trail!" and the other cut the motor. "Yeah! Straight over — the current's not bad — step it up!" hand gesturing, his face must have been fierce for George without another look turned the throttle and they roared on, the other boat hesitating, then following as Bjornesen in the bow swung his arm up and back at James by the motor.

He could not stand it. He stepped to the seat, to tip-toe, and tried to catch a glimpse of the valley. The canoe slewed wildly and George yelled, one great bellow from a throat that never before had yelled at him, and he realized his stupidity. But in that erect instant he had found a memory — was it real or had he dreaded so much to see it that it had been drawn there by his apprehension — of a white sheen in the valley beyond. He could not be sure, he had told himself then, no, he could not be sure. Perhaps it was nothing but the dull light on the muddy river reflecting against the trees of the long slope he remembered so well in the haze of last summer and so achingly well seen from the ridge of the portage trail, the long sprawl of it white in the winter sun and the broad tuft of giant spruce on the island.

They were nearing the portage and he could see the water hardly higher on the trail than usual, but ice in a jumble heaped up among its lower gashed and broken spruce. He looked at the opening of the falls half a mile beyond, and it seemed that it yawned wider than he had known. The flotsam ran no faster against the ridge that partly protected the portage and against which the current turned back across the channel for its final run at the falls. He hunched around and shouted, "The falls — are they wider?" The motor cut back a little.

"What?"

He shouted again, and George answered, "Yah, the ice! Maybe stripped trees. On that near shoulder, jamming."

"Yeah!" The current was high enough, sluggish enough to try. "Stay against the shore?" Abe gestured to the loops of tiny bays that, in summer, were almost eddies in wake of the current's deeper run opposite, "Get to the rocks, of the ridge?"

George was looking at him, not understanding, staring at the wind-angry river. "I dunno. What's the good —"

"Save portage! If the left ridge's bare, save portage — just drop a canoe —"

But the other was already revving the motor, nodding, the following canoe bobbing in their lee and he shouted. "Along the edge here, to above the falls!" and turned ahead not bothering to look if they agreed. George hugged the shore just on the lip of the fastest water as they cut for the corner of the point; the motor strained and paddle in hand, he dug furiously to pull them around and out of the current into the next small bay the point of which still cut off view of the valley. Together they fought around that too, in much faster water now, and George aimed for the final rocks scraped and crushed bare to stumps by the ice; and he saw like a blow what he had feared to admit to him all along: the whole Brink Valley filled with ice. And high — so high he could not think of what it meant.

The rocks were straight ahead, the water running to their right with the mud-glazed smoothness of enormous strength. But George tread the edge of the current, having already picked the one possible anchor spot the instant they turned the point, nodding as he turned, mind blank, gesturing with the paddle. They were sliding by within an inch of the grey rocks the river had not yet chewed through in its plunge, the motor silent an instant and Abe scraping the paddle to jab into a long fissure and hold, body braced, stretching against the canoe, and then the stern banged tight against the rock also and George had caught a rock crack. Still half-holding onto the paddle, motor screaming in a full reverse, he clambered into the slimy rock-fold. He jammed the paddle rigid, tied the anchor rope and waited only until he saw George up and firm, the bow snaking out an instant as the canoe swung free before the Indian could tighten the rope, waved to the other canoe that had hung back on the last point, turned, and scrambled up the rocks littered with branches, slimy mud and twisted stumps. The incline seemed to rear back on itself, endless, the sweat bursting on his body, boots and fingers slipping and gashing unheeded as his momentum drained away and he just inched up and saw, hands and chin holding him, the long wide valley of the Brink mottled like leprosy piled high its length to the horizon. He really did not see that. All he saw were the giant spruce stuck like fingers out of the ice where Brink Island should have been.

He never knew how long he heard the shouting below him. He shifted his head a little. Three men in the canoe; George balancing on slippery rock, waving a rope. He could not comprehend how he had climbed up that slimed stretch; he could hardly heave up his body-length. He caught the thrown rope and looped it about the remainder of a stump that seemed solid. He heard them scrabbling up but all he could think of was the odd stifling of the falls, falling to no rocks now but bending at right angles like thick slate-colored cream into the level pool, the push and draw of which bobbed ice-chunks here and there, but most of them kept at bay in a tight perimeter of mud-gelid water. Then the men were up and he pulled to his feet also, feeling faintly his cut fingers. They stood in a huddle, looking.

"Heavenly Father —" it was Josh's voice breathing in his ear, thin shoulder pushed against his arm. Bjornesen said, "You couldn't see the cabin from here anyway. Too many trees. Maybe she's on the roof —" and his voice lifted, "Halloooooo!" Above the purr of the falls the sound seemed lost in the terrible valley. They listened. Abruptly he turned, forgetting the slime and would have fallen on the round rocks except for hands clutching him. Bjornesen muttered, "Watch it!" but he jerked away to scramble to the nearest stumps where George and James now stood. Even as the trader said, "Maybe if we all yelled," he had the revolver out and the two shots barked almost together into the air. Sharper, they seemed to carry, but again there was nothing. Josh said, "All the rain — she may be too weak — and if she had to get into a tree —" James was muttering to George in Ojibwa, pointing, and George said, "He says the water isn't — shouldn't be — over the roof, at least — it's not up to the bottom — see, the trees, there" "Yeah," Bjornesen said, "or she may be in one of them big spruce behind the cabin —"

"Can the talk and get me over there."

The first nineteen miles were child's play, the last one-third impossible. The ice beyond the suck of the falls at the base of the ridge was too thick for the canoe, too smashed and broken to support a man sprinting behind one. Working on the nearly perpendicular cliff, their feet braced against the few spruce hung there, they cut and trimmed saplings, laid them under the inflated dinghy and then he lay flat and tried to push himself with a canoe paddle over the ice that bobbed and squirmed under his weight. Before he had labored fifty feet the ice had slashed three compartments; the saplings were simply too sodden and thin to buoy him and the men on shore hauled him back by brute force with the line about his waist, the dinghy in tatters before, half-drenched, he could clutch their hands. They tried two huge dead logs lashed wide apart with a small platform on which to squat; though it rode well enough, it needed super-human effort to move even a few feet. The two canoes lashed together — but they would have been cut impossibly. It was almost eleven o'clock when they lay exhausted all upon the rock, just as far as ever from the island. He lay staring at it, shivering now and then.

"The current keeps the ice thinner here," Bjornesen was saying. "If we could get around to the right side of the island it's probably thicker — from that side the river —" "A long time to get through the bush — start way back," George gestured to the deep run of the current on the far side. The rocks there fell straight into the edge of the falls. "Yeah, but we'd at least have a chance maybe —" Josh, bandaging an axe-gash in James' leg, skillful even with his own bandaged right hand, said, "When Abe was out on the dinghy, it seemed to me he almost got to some thicker ice — at least from the top here it looked like it. Doesn't it come around the left there too, Sig?" He suddenly comprehended their talk and looked down to where he had almost floundered. The ice patterns kept grinding, shifting, imperceptibly. Perhaps. He said,

"Once you get out there all you'd need was something big and broad, like wide skis. Start with the two logs, the skis — could get over then."

Josh said slowly, "But there might be thinner areas — once you got out so far —"

"Something long, thin, flat —" and even as he said it he knew. "The canoe," he hunched to his feet.

"Canoe?" Bjornesen said.

"Cut in half, beat the sides flatter here," he gestured to the rock drying in the diffuse light of growing noon.

Josh said, "They'd still cut through and —" but he was not listening. He was standing erect and looking at the tuft of the island. It was so close with a little run he could perhaps jump it. Or wave his arms and like the grey bird gliding over them in a minute be lost among the spruce-tips. Just a great hand to reach down and drop him there where she — his foot slipped down the rock and he fell on hip and arm, jarring up through his shoulder and twisting his neck before his boot-edge caught. He pushed erect ponderously, conscious of a heavy ache now, when he understood it was Bjornesen's big hand that had flung out to give his foot anchor. He stared at the water bending over the rock-lip and said to no one in particular,

"What does that matter? Just sit till it dries up?"

They had hacked the air-compartments off the ends of the canoe and were trying to split the spine lengthwise when George said, "Listen." Bjornesen's axe stopped in midair. George's finger was pointing down the valley. "See there? Listen," and they all stared, every nerve on edge.

Then he saw it, a dot moving low against the overcast where the ice piled up it seemed to the very sky, "Helicopter! The Air Force helicopter!"

"Yes!" Josh gasped, "that's it! If we could only get it up here —"

Abe's mind leaped. "We'll get it here! We have to! How — a fire, set the ridge on fire —"

"It's too wet!" Bjornesen barked, "It won't burn —" and he spun around,

"Then how the devil —" but Bjornesen had not even stopped, "Just a coupla trees — clear around and soak 'em with gas and they'll go like a torch — there —" pointing above them to the higher stretch of the ridge. "Com'mon!"

While Josh watched the helicopter, which seemed to remain where it was, circling, they worked like fiends. In minutes they had two spruce isolated and gasoline soaked and when Bjornesen tossed the match to their base they exploded in flame that leaped up like a pillar through the needles past the very top. But the sodden trunks and branches damped it quickly into smoke standing straight and black above them in the breaking overcast. They soaked the smaller trees they had knocked down and threw them on the pile until the fire roared too furiously to approach behind an upflung arm. Josh was shouting from below, "Look — I think it's coming!" and they stood panting as they watched. The blue blot grew large and larger until they could see the glint of light on its glass nose. He said, "Keep that thing going!" and plunged down through the trees to stand momentarily beside Josh. He slid down the rope to the big canoe tugging in the current, seized one of the yellowish raincoats and in a moment was up again. As the helicopter trundled nearer, they waved it together. With an agony of deliberation the machine came whirring to them directly over the island and he dropped the coat, gesturing as if climbing. He did not even recognize Marsden's face staring down as the rope ladder dropped and he got his hands on the third rung, his foot on the first, Josh shouting, "Be careful," and he was swinging like a pendulum over the falls, climbing. Marsden's hand gripped his shoulder as his head came level with the door, already shouting,

"Get over the island — don't hover — over the island!"

Marsden shouted over the rotors, "Get up here! You can't —"

"Sally," he yelled, clutching the handgrips now, feet swinging, "she was on the island — turn this goddamn —" and he sensed Marsden's hand tighten on his shoulder, then his face jerk away above him and the order barking and the craft tilt and wheel. He gasped, holding the grips, the sharp crease of the officer's trouser-cuff rubbing his gashed fingers. "The cabin there — she was — resting there over — Easter holidays — when the rain come —" and Marsden did not say anything, hand still clenched on his shoulder. Then his voice above,

"Do you know if —" and he gasped,

Nothing. We just got here this morning and we couldn't get over — the ice —" They were both staring down at the blotchy patterns of it, splotches green as bile and off-white and Marsden said, the tips of the dark island spruce pulling nearer,

"It's jammed about five miles down the valley. Of all places to go —" and he said, for there was nothing to say except the innocent words that could forgive nothing, especially afterthought,

"It's the rain — it's never flooded that any Indian remembers — not the oldest."

They were over the trees. Marsden said, "We should swing the length of the island —" but in the circle of spruce he had found the cabin roof-peak above the water, the empty cabin roof-peak. He shook his head, shouting,

"You do that — drop me on the roof — now."

"Okay — but test it first, before you let go the ladder —" and Marsden turned back to the pilot an instant. His feet felt the roof-ridge. He could not tell if it moved under him or that he had lost all sense of solidity but he let go on the instant. He crouched, the helicopter thudding above him, staring around at the circle of trees. He could not recognize them with their lower branches in the ice-logged water lapping high on the eaves of the roof where he stood. The cabin stirred as in a breeze. There was nothing in the trees that he could see; nothing on the roof but the stubby tin crest of the stovepipe. He waved Marsden away. As the helicopter lifted he tore away the pipe, set like a cap on the ridge and not even a pipe falling away inside splashed. He hunched forward; except for the round glint on the water his head interrupted, it was black. He swallowed, and said as loudly as he could,

"Sally, it's me, Abe. Sally."

He listened, shutting out the helicopter and the rubbing of the trees in ice, listened as he had never listened before. And he heard nothing. He said it again, more loudly.

When the helicopter came beating back and Marsden clambered down, he was tearing up the roof. Strange, how tough it was to break it back, held only by a few nails in the round rafters. But then all was sodden. The cabin swayed under him, groaning the ice-chunks a little. Marsden said, "Can you see if — there's nothing in the trees —," and he jerked up a board that broke at the officer's feet. "Here."

Marsden handed him a torch and they knelt together. The water's foulness thrust at them. Methodically he swept the black water, back and forth over the floating boards and table-top and an empty bottle riding on caught air. There was only debris. He handed the light back and began taking off his jacket. Marsden said, "Abe, that water's deadly — there's no point you too — she may not even — look, I've radioed the base and they'll be breaking the jam with bombs in a coupla hours and this'll go down — there's no —" Tugging off his left boot, the draft of the helicopter above beating his shirt against him, he said,

"The cabin'd never hold." His right boot gave. "I'd never find her when it goes."

After a moment Marsden said, "Okay. You got a rope?"

"Huh?"

"A rope — you got a rope to —"

"Yeah, sure — in the jacket pocket —"

From the level of the water on the roof he knew it was not more than seven feet deep and he slid into it with the cabin methodically quartered in his mind. He could not have imagined it so cold. His eyes were useless but he spread his arms wide when his hands sensed the floor and thrust to the wall, then along to the corner, and back. For an instant when he blundered into the roundness he believed he had found it, but then he realized it was only the tin heater. He had to surface then, quickly, having lost his reserve when he touched, and Marsden supported him with the rope around his chest. The second time he found and left a wad of clothes and her rubber boots washed into a corner. When he got his head up he did not know whether he could finish. He was just aware of the light-beam lying beside him on the water, Marsden's shadow leaning down, holding him, "Abe, for god's sake it's no good, you can't —"

He gasped, "One — one more —," his lungs gained another gulp of air and he forced his head down and felt the rope drop him. He had no reserve left now, only desperation. His forearm thumped into the beam of the bunk, bent, broken, and he knew he should have tried that corner first. Up it he moved, and found the hanging blankets and then he sensed something tangled in them though his hands could no longer feel. He pushed forward, down reaching, and his arms were around her waist pliant in the gelid underwater and he tugged her to him at last in the blanket's snarl with his bent arms and useless hands crossing. He could just push up for his head to break water once, holding as he had never held, and he remembered only the rope jerk in his armpits.

He had been staring at the sunlight in his bedroom window he did not know how long. The window was open a little; outside a bird sang the same curt song over and over, furiously. He turned and the rope-burn stung across his chest and under his arms. Odd, he did not feel any of the other bruises he must have. Or even sick. He raised his hands to eye-level. The middle three fingers on the right were bandaged. He couldn't remember how Marsden pulled him out without caving in the roof. Maybe the helicopter; that would explain the burn. But he hadn't let go of that he was sure. Perfectly sure.

When he opened his eyes Josh was standing there. He blinked. "I didn't hear you."

"You were sleeping. When Lena left an hour ago she said you were sleeping perfectly." A cool hand touched his forehead. "Say, that's better. You feel better?"

"Okay. What day is it?"

"Thursday afternoon."

"Then I've been —" he thought ponderously. "It was Tuesday morning and noon," he stopped, eyes following the other reaching to the upended box beside the bed. "Is she buried?"

"Yes. In the Indian cemetery. Yesterday." A bottle chinked against glass and he sat up to drink, whoozy as Josh held his shoulder, but the glow of the whisky steadied him. "Her father telegraphed back we should do it here. He'll be here, perhaps tomorrow. We couldn't wait."

He was lying back, staring at the ceiling. "I should of thought of it right away — the corner bunk," he said.

"It had collapsed, hadn't it?"

"Yeah."

"From her clothes, she must have been sleeping when it spilled her. She liked that top bunk, at Christmas. Just like Anne didn't."

His mind had wandered and he said after a silence, "Was that you in here once when it was dark. Kneeling?"

"Were you conscious?"

"I guess; I seem to remember."

"I was praying for you."

"Well, it worked. I guess I made it."

Josh said gently against the edge in his tone, "I wasn't praying for that so much. You're too tough to die of exhaustion and fever."

"So?"

"Partly for your recovery of course, but mostly that you might see God's mercy in this — to us all — that most of all."

"Oh sure." And having thought about all of those days — how can they have been? — thought of a few things and forgotten or not noticed ever to remember so many others, he was conscious only that he held a dry shard of hate in residue not potent enough to glow heat in his tone. "Sure. If there is a God, he did it."

"That's true. God does all, directly or indirectly, permitting it. But for those who see it as his act, it draws them to him. We accept events from his hand, and trust his mercy."

"I don't know anything about 'mercy'." After a moment he added, "How you can say that, knowing her for what she was maybe better than I."

Josh's face was turned and he said nothing for a long time. Then, "What is there else in the world for a man to say? She was such a person, one of the best and purest. She believed, and we with her, she must go on a spiritual retreat: We saw some effects of it at the baptism. It will work on. That's God's mercy. And then a natural catastrophe — one in a century, maybe. If I could not say what I did, that I love God yet, above all, then — then I could only hate."

Abe looked at him.

"Belief that God is opens you to the worst of all temptations: to detest him in helplessness. But when all is done, we recognize his work of grace in us and we still believe that God in mercy is better to the worst than the best deserve. Surely those who love him best can best accept death. And when we have known one of the best, as we did in — her — we must be happy for that — and for her, now."

Her Bach tune drifted in him, the bass high and gliding down,

> *Thou shalt be with me today,*
> *in paradise, in paradise,*

the word moving in wave after wave, sinking and rising again, and each time higher, while the strong deep alto held the unshaken keel

> *In death I sleep, calm*

— there's no way to say it or think it without the imagery of love — "Sure," he murmured aloud, "her heavenly lover."

"What?"

"Nothing." He stared at the ceiling, that momentary feeling gone, feeling nothing. Then his reason caught on something and persisted, as with a purely academic question, "So why pour it on me, who couldn't care less, about him?"

"Who knows how close you have been all along, or are."

Presently Josh said, "Were you reading in her Bible last week? It was open on the box. Mind if I read a little?"

"Huh?" He saw the Bible in the other's hand. "If you want." Nothing. As if he had turned to a final sheet and found it quite blank, even unruled, where he had expected some ultimate blasphemy. After a moment he heard the missionary's voice and he remembered the words in their warmth, not categorical or asserted, but as if the writer too, whoever he had been, battered, had at last held to one thing:

> ". . . I consider that the sufferings of this present time are not worth comparing with the glory that is to be revealed to us. For the creation waits with eager longing for the revealing of the sons of God; for the creation was subjected to futility, not of its own will but by the will of him who subjected it in hope; because the creation itself will be set free from its bondage to decay and obtain the glorious liberty of the children of God. We know that the whole creation has been groaning in travail together

until now; and not only the creation, but we ourselves, who have the first fruits of the Spirit, groan inwardly as we wait for adoption as sons, the redemption of our bodies. For in this hope we were saved. Now hope that is seen is not hope. For who hopes for what he sees? But if we hope for what we do not see, we wait for it with patience."

"Yeah," he said finally. "Groan to redeem the body. That's almost what Hayes said."

"Hayes?"

"A guy I knew — years ago." The sunlight lay on his blanket, and suddenly he sat up and swung his legs over the side of the bed. His head spun, but settled. "There should be clothes, somewhere."

Josh had his hand on his shoulder. "Abe, you better not —"

"Just one more drink and I'll be okay." He was reaching for his boots where they should have been beside the bed.

"Lena's broth would be better. She sent it along just in case you could eat —"

"Good enough," he stood up. The room reeled, but finally steadied a little.

There were several Indians in the store; they stared at him, murmuring replies to his "Bonjour." George looked at him incredulously from behind the counter, then came around and handed him a yellow telegram envelope. He looked at it a minute, then back at the handyman, who gestured at the shelves, the silent people.

"It come on the plane yesterday. Here, just usual business."

"Yeah." He went out to the sunshine of the porch and leaned against the wall, tearing the envelope. "What day is it?"

"Thursday, the thirtieth," Josh said.

He thrust the paper in his pocket. "Horst Jeffers, my boss'll be in, probably this afternoon." He blinked at the dazzling sunlight glancing off the channel of the river. On the far dock someone — perhaps Alex — was rearranging gas barrels that shone black and white and dull-grey. "Take me around in your canoe."

Josh looked at him wordlessly. Then, "Com'mon."

He had not thought himself so wobbly — it's just down the slope and sit down the ground is ten feet away — the splayed ruin of his canoe flashed from the rocks beside the wharf. "How'd that get here?"

"The Air Force. Three other helicopters came in and took us all back. They blasted open the dam-up too."

The wharf thudded under their feet; Abe swallowed against the taste that burnt suddenly in his throat. "Sure. Always buzzin' around after the fact."

Josh steadied the bow of the canoe and he got in. "Last night Sig came over and was talking about —"

"He knows Frobisher's finished."

Josh answered something but he did not hear him; he was carefully coiling the tie-rope at his feet. In a moment the motor caught and they were out in the channel. He watched spray spurt from the bow. They turned wide at the point; an Indian paddling nearer the shore was passed as if standing still.

There were two canoes pulled up on the sand of the little cove below the bluff. Josh said, "I'll come back."

"Okay." He nudged the bow away, breathed deeply and started up the short steep path. The older graves under their tiny sapling-built cabins rimmed the bluff and he stopped there panting, bent double, elbows on knees. Some grave-houses were already lost behind the persistent poplar brush, but the fetishes and beaded jewelry that hung for years above the little hole in their eaves blinked between the bare stems. He followed the trodden trail past more huts, newer now and built of boards, beside the long plot covered with river sand to where he heard the tapping under the long spruce in the clearing. The group of children sitting silently looked at him; he recognized Eli; Lucy; Simon. They had driven peeled poplar stakes all around the mound and Kekekose looked up from where he bent, driving in a board cross. The old man nodded, then picked up the last of the stakes and tapped them in behind the cross. One Ojibwa word, the children rose and in a moment the sound of their going had gone. Abe squatted. On the cross-board was carved her name: Sarah D. Howell.

The date and her age — thirty-two and besides they got the "2" backwards — then it rose in him like a wave and his head tilted against the cool stakes, their sweet-sap smell mingling with that of the spaded earth and he was crying.

Crying in tides that crested and fell and rose again: all the years of dearth moving in him at last to balance again the ledger of his humanness, not of agony but of tears. Crying for the break of joy he had seen dawn in his life and which was now wiped away and driven into the careless earth; for the futility of it all; of even struggle; crying for his Sarah his beloved his oh so most dearly beloved. A consciousness struggled through and he felt a spurt of relief that he could not recall the water's abuse of her, that he would remember her eyes looking into his when they came around the cabin and she first said, "I love you," and then his weeping rose again in the quiet clearing.

The afternoon cooled. He understood that there was someone else there, squatting silently, head-bowed. He leaned back to get at his handkerchief; he saw then it was Violet at the foot of the grave who looked at him fleetingly through the palisade, her face too distorted by tears. After a moment she pushed forward a handful of pussy-willows and spread them over the piled earth.

"She's with the Lord Jesus," she said.

He was crying again. Silently now but with a tearing in him that was not for himself; though grounded in the decades of pride and self-dependence that had held him far from not only the memory of his family, even his mother and especially his father, and those who tried for goodness and failed, but also from anything beyond the human — the spiritual, the beyond-reach divine: it was beyond himself a crying for the vacancy of all lone dangling humans, all the millions suspended in voids by self-assurance, by righteousness, with nothing. There was no need in him now because at last he understood and tasted to his very grounds that he had no meaning; there was in him of himself simply nothing that could ever voice with this child, "She is with the Lord Jesus," and throwing away the husk of whatever the impossible metaphysics of it might be, believe it forever fact. That was what held him now: the having to say that, not as a need but as life's prerequisite to need; to be; and without it seeing beyond all the coming roads and rivers of his life only this vacant terror, waiting, into eternity. And in that long dry crying, did he hear a voice like an echo of all the passed roads and rivers of his life: "You have run and hidden far, and you are tired. Turn to me now, come now"? In his nothingness he could not know; only later: But he found within himself that he could voice at last: "I am a miserable sinner. By your grace have mercy, have mercy." And belief as a child being born in him by the laughter, the happiness of her faith that shone to a beckoning of great light beyond.

After a time he could look up. The girl was still there, and she met his glance. There was a cut on her cheek; in wiping her tears with the back of her hand she streaked red across her face. He said, "You have hurt yourself."

She gestured between the stakes to the sprigs of white, "I had to go far up the creek. They are not out here yet."

A breath of air stirred in the spruce above them; she rose and bent to gather the poplar bark scattered around. "The children peeled one, each. For the teacher." She was picking up the strips beside him, the tears running down her face.

"They will build a fine school this summer," he said. "For next fall they will find a teacher."

"Not quick one like her."

No, he thought, and momentarily it rose to choke him and he bent his face and beard against the bitter-sweet poles, not soon not ever one like her.

Violet had come back from the edge of the clearing, her hands empty, and stood looking at the cross. "Kekekose made a mistake," she said. "I want to be a teacher, like her."

"Don't you want to marry Alex?"

She did not say anything for so long he looked at her finally. "No," she said. "I want to go out, to high school, and — the other school and come back and teach."

"That would be good." He heard the distant waver of a plane and he got to his feet.

"Cessna," she said.

"Yes, that will be my boss coming." She looked at him swiftly. "I will be leaving here soon."

What she asked then was possible, he realized, only because they had sat weeping together. "Where will you go?"

Strangely, he did not hesitate. He would remember often, later, when he understood better, though still in sorrow, how these days had been. "To a city perhaps." The roar of the plane was almost over them and as they looked the orange shape of it topped the southern trees, banking. "Yes, to some city." He looked at the clods of earth, the cross, the pussywillows and the little stakes; he understood that this spot would never again be of absolute importance to him because all that she had been and promised to be was flickering, alive in him. Though it made the life he still had to live hardly less fearful. "Let's go," he said, and they were walking away, back to the bluff side by side, his steps slow and heavy in the sand of the waiting burial plots. They heard the plane roar die as it landed and he lifted his eyes.

In the notch of the trail he could see across Frozen Lake to the westerly sun. It was hidden now behind clouds tumbled like greyish toys neglected after play. Between two thunderheads the light drew a gold line, a straggle of lightning distorted and solidified and held in crumpled ribbon. As he rested, watching, the line slowly diffused into the cloud, widening imperceptibly but ever widening, soaking it in brilliance until whole turns and loops of thunderhead shone through with the incredible glory of the golden sun falling away behind the earth's turn.

He followed Violet down the path to where Josh sat, head bowed, in the waiting canoe.

FINIS